KELOWOW TO KANSAS

By

Martyn Benford

ISBN 978-1-915292-76-6

Printed in Great Britain by
Biddles Books Limited, King's Lynn, Norfolk

CONTENTS

ACKNOWLEDGEMENTS

I offer my thanks and appreciation to all who have helped me in some way to produce Kernow to Kansas. Firstly, Mac McCarthy who originally introduced me to Macdonald Tamryn, Debbie and Ashley of The Old Mill House, Little Petherick. Tim for his excellent artwork and Jacquie for her support. Once again I would like to thank Charlotte, Jane, and Dudley. Many thanks to Jay and everyone at the former Maltsters Arms at Little Petherick. Thank you too Ann Marie Driver of the RSA for providing the great Christian name 'Lourinda'! Thank you, Wikipedia. Last but not least, a big thank you to the Benford family for their continued encouragement and for allowing me to read the journals of George Benford. The recollections by George Benford and to a lesser degree, Joey Tamryn may have been embellished slightly regarding William Butler Hickok, Martha Jane Cannery and Jack Bridges and Billy the Kid.

BEFORE AND AFTER

We're not the first nor last
to pass along this way
Others have gone before us
or so I heard one day
Who were they,
these folks who had our name?
They're not us but our ancestors
Were they different,
were they the same?

We will not be the last
to pass along this way?
Others will surely follow us
on some much later day
Who will they be,
these folks who share our name
They will be our children
Will they be different
will they be the same?

KERNOW (CORNWALL)

Cornwall is recognised by Cornish and Celtic political groups as one of six Celtic nations, alongside Brittany, Ireland, the Isle of Man, Scotland and Wales. The Manx and Welsh Government also recognise Asturias and Galicia. Cornwall is represented as one of the Celtic nations at the Festival Interceltique de Lorient, an annual celebration of Celtic culture held in Brittany.

Henry Tamryn, a Cornishman and David Evans a Welshman, may have hailed from different countries and quite different tribes if you like but the two have something valuable in common, they had a seemingly unbreakable bond, they were both Celts!

Martyn Benford

PROLOGUE

Eighteen fifty five and in arguably the smallest village in Cornwall, Henry William Tamryn was born to a typical farming family at Innis Downs, Cornwall. Where once there was a small but budding community only a handful of typical Cornish cottages close to where vehicles now speed back and forth along the county's spine at seventy five miles an hour.

With six hungry mouths to feed, Henry's father grafted hard on his small holding with only the aid of his eldest son and eldest daughter, Patricia. Once reaching the age of twenty, Henry leaves the farm and travels to the United States in the hope of seeking his fortune. David Evans of Cardiff is of the same mind. Although these two almost come to blows at their first meeting, they will somehow forge a friendship until only one remains!

CHAPTER ONE

Beers, Baths and Beds!

With the last of his strength he throws himself forward and upwards, just managing to snatch at the hot steel handle, he pulls trailing legs up to the footplate of the freight car and claws himself inside to what he believes to be safety. He discovers some other free rider might have left the sliding Oak door partly open while maybe departing from the slow moving locomotive and its trailing carriages. Once inside, he congratulates himself on his agility. He knows he can soon rest aching feet. It had taken him some time and distance to get up to speed to catch the red hot handle on the side of the carriage door.

It is unfortunate the semi darkness of the car has prevented him from seeing a mound of hardening vomit until it is too late to be avoided. Well-worn boots spread the drying food and a forward impetus deposits him onto his backside. He curses loudly and is glad no one else would hear his series of profanities! He wasn't brought up to be polite unless in the company of a lady. He was taught to be pleasant and was taught to be tough as and when an occasion might warrant it. There was never room for softies in Innis Town, a 'town' in name only it is a small collection of Cornish stone cottages where every occupant knows the name of every other, so small it is easy to fall out with a neighbour, but it didn't happen too often.

1

He had seen more than his fair share of vomit in the six weeks aboard the ship. A four-masted clipper, the Cleopatra had rolled, lifted, plunged and swayed seemingly endlessly, as it carved a restless path through the forbidding, storm-laden northern Atlantic, having departed from Falmouth some five long weeks earlier. At least now he is dry, whereas every day aboard he was not. A heavy sea had been relentless!

A little bit more won't make much difference he decided. He found himself muttering, just above a whisper, while thinking how lucky it was the bag which had safely held his few possessions had not landed in the recently discarded food which was quickly resembling crusted porridge.

"A pity you didn't see that in time friend, hope you're going to clean yourself off, you'll stink to the high heavens in this heat. You best keep your own bloody stomach in order. You'll be getting off this train sharpish if you don't. Be warned mister."

He had initially thought myself to be the lone occupant of the carriage. The gruff voice made him realise his mistake. He thought it only right to introduce himself to his fellow traveller, whoever he might be.

"Bloody? It's bleddy! You don't have to worry on that bleddy score friend. Henry Tamryn here, to whom might I be conversing?" Henry had ignored the thinly veiled threat of physical violence from his fellow traveller. Henry doesn't scare easily.

"Well now Henry Tamryn, you might be speaking to the President of these damned United States, but you are not, you are conversing with David Evans also known as Davy or Taffy, which I don't often answer to. There are so many named Taffy in Wales and I don't want to be known as just another in future. Once of Cardiff, now of here wherever it might be, as if I'll care a damn once I get out anyway."

Henry found he had little or no problem understanding David's rich, Southern Welsh brogue. He had at first thought his would-be fellow traveller was an American. The words of the newcomer are easily understood. He had met and worked with many of his new-found companion's countrymen while occasionally working as a doorman in various alehouses around Charlestown and even as far away as Mevagissey. Henry easily recognised his travelling companion's Welsh accent.

"Make yourself comfortable as you can Henry, how far are you going man?" David Evans' words already begin to soften a little towards his fellow passenger now that he knows the two of them might have something in common, a shared interest possibly.

"As far as I can get, providing I can stand this terrible smell, it wasn't you, was it, David?" The Cornishman points towards the discarded food, as he asks his question.

"Now, do I look like a man that could produce such a miserably small pile of puke as that?"

Henry screws his eyes a little and squints through the semi dark of the carriage. What he sees is a surprise even to him. David is huge, barrel-chested, and bull-necked. Henry guesses his fellow traveller might be near twenty stones. Henry is just a modicum lighter.

Henry Tamryn is a big man himself, over six feet, and stockily built. He would not match up in height and heft of the magnificently muscled Welshman he can just see sitting with his back to the wooden carriage. Both men laugh at the given answer.

"No I wouldn't think so. Where are you travelling to, what is your own destination, David Evans?"

"Same place as you I'm guessing, Henry Tamryn, nowhere in particular at this moment, but I'll know when I get where I'm meant to be, providing the nosey little guard doesn't change his mind by checking in here again. Best he doesn't. He looked in once through there." David points towards the end of the carriage where in the wall could be seen a sliding wooden shutter. "The old bastard thought better of it when he caught the whiff. I had to throw the puking little foreigner

3

off when he started emptying his guts. A German I think, I guessed, I hardly cared awfully much. Don't know where he was from, couldn't understand the lingo; German was my bet. I should say, arrogant little swine, nasty he was, thought he was anyhow. So he wasn't best pleased when he hit the ground outside I'm betting. You still got some on the back of your jacket." David had pointed at visible spots of unrecognisable food.

Henry took off the garment, and by beating it against the wooden door, allowed the remnants of food to fall away. "Thanks David. What do you hope to be doing when you get to your destination if you don't mind telling?"

"Well my friend, I'll be doing a little bit of this and a little bit of that. I am a carpenter by trade, a good one. I can use these pretty well too." The Welshman bunches his fists, possibly a small threat to a man he has only just met. "I like to fight a little." Again he displays two huge, bunched fists. "I have never been beaten, at least fairly. Don't intend to be either. I earned my ticket money from following the Marquis of Queensbury. That's how I got across that bloody awful ocean."

Henry thinks about the things he is being told. Very quickly he likes what he hears and what he can see of his fellow traveller. He and the Welshman might even form a temporary partnership in what could be uncertain weeks or months to come. Henry folds his recently cleaned jacket into a thick pad so it will cushion him against the hard floor. He sits with his back to the Oak timbered wall of the carriage next to the big man, he stares at the still just partially opened door. The draught caused by the train's movement helps take away any remaining smell of food that is almost completely solid again now that it has been spread more thinly by the Cornishman's unfortunate entrance.

"Where did you sail from, Welshman?"

"Travelled from my hometown, Cardiff to Falmouth first, I saw you get on board the bloody boat my friend."

"You did? I didn't see you. It's bleddy!"

"And you, Henry, I believe I can guess by your bloody accent, boyyo?"

"I am a local, I am from Cornwall itself. We are both Celt's, David. It's still bleddy!"

The two men become quiet. In the silence, David Evans lowers his eyelids and attempts to sleep with one eye half open temporarily. Henry dozes nervously also. He does give some thought to what he might do when it is time to vacate the slow-moving oven. Henry has come to America in the hope of fashioning a future. He had come from a relatively small family. Being the eldest at twenty, he had left a younger brother and two sisters in the capable hands of the oldest sibling, Patricia. Patsy would help her mother to bring the younger ones up now. Henry had done his bit to help his mother and father from an early age, now it is Patsy's turn to nurture the younger members of the Tamryn family.

Henry had dreamed almost forever of getting away from Innis Town. Once enough money had been scratched together from a meagre wage, there was little but the family to hold him back. Henry's dream is beginning. He had heard tales of 'gold paved streets' a land of 'Milk and Honey.' Recently landed sailors frequenting the numerous Taverns of Charlestown and Truro would tell how a man could travel for days and not see a soul, unless it might be a Native, perhaps a hunting party of young, almost naked and painted drunken warriors.

Henry had heard also about some of the more warlike and bloodthirsty 'Redskins' that roam the country, ever ready to 'part your hair' or worse, it had been suggested. He had embarked on this adventure which had begun to form, piece by piece, in his middle teenage years. Now for him the pieces are beginning to slot together!

Both men had slept eventually as the train began to slow almost to walking pace.

"Wakey, wakey, boyyo." Henry humorously attempted to mimic his still dozing companion. "Time to get off I think, there's a stop coming up I believe and I don't want to be buying a ticket now we've come this far. What about you David, are you coming man or are you going on elsewhere?"

David wakens fully and jumps unsteadily to his feet. Both men look through the gap and out into the hazy afternoon sunlight that has almost been hidden by the part opened door.

"I'm with you Henry and it's just Davy if you would be so kind. I'm sure it's easier on the tongue, it is for me anyway though I rarely talk to myself." These two may had slept but both have thought the same about their travelling companion. Neither have friends here in the United States, neither know they are right now in the South of Kansas just North of an area known as the Texas Panhandle, a mass of land named in honour of a cooking pot for a fried meal, due to the shape of the most Northern part of the Lone Star State.

The two men leap out and forward at the same time. Followed by two rising dust clouds, they roll down and away from the hot tracks, both men instantly relieved to be out of what was fast becoming an unbearable oven. Quickly they get to their feet, brushing away gathered dust.

Henry suddenly realises he hasn't picked up the folded jacket and quickly begins to clamber back up the slope. The carriages are almost static now; he pulls himself back inside and snatches at the clothing and prepares to jump down once more.

Even now a short, balding, suspicious guard approaches. At the same time, David is inching his way silently back up the slope.

"Hey!" He shouts.

The uniformed man turns towards the yell. David's well directed fist connects with the guard's chin perfectly. The man crumples, with nothing more than a slow dispelling of air the only sound.

"Bloody hell, Davy! I believe you have killed him, man!"

David rubs at his knuckles. "No, it was a pulled punch, I only gave him a tap, he'll be alright soon enough. Let's get out of here, Henry Tamryn."

"Henry, or H will do fine, if it's all the same to you, Davy."

The two men stumble back down the slope and into the long swathe of brush that lines the course of the super-heated rails.

Henry carefully slides the jacket into the bag and tosses it over a shoulder. They struggle through the prickly trackside vegetation that leads to a lively but narrow creek and stride through the thigh high water to the opposite side. The two recent strangers approach the few dilapidated buildings that signal the beginning of the tiniest of a straggling township. A village by any other name and one that might be even smaller than where Henry had spent most of his life. It's hardly any bigger than Innis Town Henry decides for himself.

Following the uneven wagon wheel rutted track, they come abreast the first of the buildings, the lower timber framework supporting its tent shaped canvas top. A badly shaped sign hangs lopsided over the doorway. The message 'Beer, Baths and Beds' one large 'B' crookedly initialling the three crookedly daubed words. Their wetted trouser legs are already drying as they walk forward.

The two men move closer, and without speaking they pass through the shaky, poorly built doorway. Heavy, dusty boots clump towards a plank-topped bar. A skinny, smoking barman looks up with a minimum of interest at their sudden arrival.

"What do ya want, boys?"

"Firstly, some manners would not go amiss, boy!" Henry puts heavy emphasis on the last word and there is no hint of friendliness in his demand.

"You want manners, go to Boston or anyplace else. You want trouble, I'll give it to ya, right here and now and no mistake. Manners don't go well around here, mister."

David moves swiftly in front of Henry. "Well now, there is a mistake of your own here, a big mistake mister, trouble is my preferred occupation, are you ready to go to work with me, boyyo?"

The foul tempered barman has simply been stupid enough not to realise the newcomers are together. He looks David and Henry up and down, deciding just maybe these two men are not a pair to antagonise or tangle with physically. Quickly and perhaps sensibly, he attempts to change his attitude.

"Beer?"

"Two, please!" Again Henry puts emphasis on his reply. "Two hot baths and two clean beds!" Henry flips the three Dollar coins on to the planks. The scrawny barman snatches at the cash. Henry adds a final order. "Two meals!"

"What makes ya' think we got any food?"

"I can smell something burning, feller."

The bartender growls the food order over his shoulder at some unseen person behind a long filthy rag that doubles as a curtain.

Pouring two beers and throwing the small collection of coins into a box behind where he stood, he scowls at the strangers and ignores them until a tan-skinned woman with lank hair appears with two plates of scalding, black stew, a crust of bread nestled on both plates.

Henry and David take the offered food, pick up the beers and walk across to a vacant table. The two remain silent until both plates have been completely emptied.

"So Henry, what are your plans?" David's tone has softened since his first harsh words to Henry in the searing heat of the rail carriage. Conversation comes easily to the pair now.

"Easy Davy, get rich, and bleddy quick. This is America unless I got on the wrong boat."

"If you did, I did. Sounds good, mind if I stick around awhile, see what you get up to, keep you out of trouble and suchlike?"

"Was hoping you'd say that, Davy. Stay as long as you like, but you best hold on tight, I'm in a mighty big hurry right now. You may well need to get me out of trouble here and there."

David nods his agreement and approval. Standing up, the Welshman returns to the bar and takes enough coins from his pocket for two more beers. He returns to the small table with the two misty-sided glasses. "I would expect you to do the same. I don't hold with exchanging chit chat with ignorant scum like our host. This'll have to do for now Henry, I'm almost broke, just have enough coins for sleeping tomorrow."

"Don't fret yet my friend, I have all we might need, for a day or two anyway."

Henry still has most of the little savings he had brought when leaving his home county, he is happy to spare some for his new acquaintance. "We better think of some way to re-fill our pockets whenever we can, David."

More customers enter the saloon as the two men continue to talk quietly. Some of the newcomers lounge idly over their beers and the food-stained planks as others take up the sparse seating. Chatter fills the air between loud bouts of raucous laughter.

"I have an idea, Davy!" Henry stands and walks across to the bar before David can venture a reply.

"You got some pasteboards?" Henry asks with no inference of friendliness. The barman reaches below the planks and produces a badly worn deck of cards. Henry snatches them up and returns to the table.

"Let's play Poker, Davy."

"Don't know how H, I was brought up strict Methody. There was no gambling for us. We drank our ale to a song mostly!"

"Good answer matey! Trust me and put any money you have left on the table, I'll do the same. Just try and look as if you know what you're doing, at least for now, we'll see what happens. I will let you beat me for a while. Nothing attracts men and their money more than poker and the ladies, though right now the ladies are in short supply it seems."

Henry and David manage to get through a half dozen hands with little trouble. The pair play alone but for each other for almost an hour. Henry allows David to acquire almost all the coins that had recently come from his own pocket. Pretty soon the game begins attracting interest from one or two of the idling bystanders.

Soon there are three players, then another and later another. With these five at the table, David follows the suggestion Henry had made earlier while they were playing together. 'I'll let you win some hands. When we get some interest I'll take the lot off you and you pull out and leave me to it. Don't worry, you will get yours back and some.'

Henry's plan has worked perfectly; he soon has all of their pooled money in front of him. Within another hour he had doubled it. Some players leave the table, others sit in. By early evening Henry is holding almost two hundred and fifty dollars. His prediction had materialised perfectly, as he was certain it would.

There are only three at the table now, and soon just two. Henry does not bet either heavily or lightly as the last player loses his remaining three dollars to him. Matters suddenly take a turn for the worst. The remaining player becomes sour and disagreeable at losing his stake that amounted to everything he owned.

"You're cheating, you lousy son of a bitch, I want my dollars back, you cheating bastard. See how lucky you are with this, mister!" The hard-case drops a hand to the heavy pistol pouched at his side; he pulls it from the leather sheath and squeezes the trigger all in one quick movement.

Luckily for Henry, David's arms have already encircled the man's waist, even as the bullet is beginning its journey through the barrel. Soft but lethal lead tears a path through the canvas ceiling and soars into the night sky. David has not yet finished with the bad loser. He sends the man in a shorter but similar direction to the leaden projectile. Not travelling quite the same distance, the sour loser instantly collapses in a heap of broken wood and glass, partly caused by his hard landing on the next closest table.

Straightening with a growl, David waits for the right moment; an arm comes back and powers forward, skin and gristle mingle below the man's already watering eyes as David uses more force than he had when dealing with the much smaller train guard.

The hard-case falls back. He tries to lift himself as pain sears through the nerves and into his brain. The brain, needing respite, quickly allows the man the temporary luxury of unconsciousness.

David looks at Henry. A wink accompanies a wide satisfied smile.

The scrawny bartender is already pointing a loaded shotgun across the bar. "You boys have got some damage to pay for."

"Says who?"

"Says this!" The barman lifts the shotgun slightly higher until the ends of the barrels are pointing directly towards the Welshman.

David starts towards the gun and just for a second his body hides Henry from view. At the same time Henry takes his chance by ducking down to snatch at the recently fallen six-shooter involuntarily discarded by the unconscious man. He pulls back the hammer as he straightens.

"Now I say you're wrong feller, that thing might talk loud but my bet is this'll talk a damn sight quicker! Are you and I ready to let them converse or are you just going to stand there and shiver?"

The confused bartender is now a little uncertain as to the meaning of some of the words Henry is using but he is positive of their heavy threat and allows the 'Greener'* double-barrelled shotgun to drop down onto the stained planks.

* W.W. Greener is a sporting shotgun and rifle manufacturer from England. The company produced its first firearm in 1829 and is still in business, with a fifth generation Greener serving on its board of directors.

"You ain't heard the last of this feller, someone has to pay for the damage you bastards have done. I'll be out of pocket for this." The bartender continues to whine.

Henry scoops up all of the cash from the table top. "Well now, that's a bleddy shame. I'll tell you what my friend, I have a remedy for your problem. How about I put this pile into your grubby little hands, in exchange for this whole bleddy shebang?" Henry spreads his arms wide, indicating he would exchange the cash for the tented saloon. "Let's be honest, you don't seem to be cut out for this line of work, do you? What do you say David, half each?"

"I'd say, we could just burn the dump right down. Let's see what the little weasel has to say about it."

David turned to the bartender. "Well, you choose mister?"

"It's yours! Give me the dollars!"

Henry throws most of the cash into a loose pile on the bar top. "Take it and get your arse out of our saloon." Henry pauses as he adds "Don't show your face here again. If you do, David here, or I, will rearrange it. We might make some improvements possibly!"

The scrawny man scowls as he eagerly scoops up the money and shovels it into his pocket. Taking off the filthy cotton apron he throws it at David. David brushes the rag aside and steps menacingly towards the newly redundant bar owner. Suddenly losing his nerve, the man turns away with a growl.

"Well my friend, that solves a problem or two for us I reckon."

"What's that, H?"

"Now we won't have to pay for our beds, man!"

The bloodied face of the fallen man looks upwards at his victors. "Think we ought to show him to the door, Davy. If you wouldn't mind, I'll clear up the mess he made while you show him the way out!"

David turns obligingly; one hand grabs at the man's collar, the other at the back of his trousers. The Welshman easily holds the man horizontally as he kicks the door open and proceeds towards the creek where he tips the groggy cowboy into the swift flow.

On re-entering the saloon, David lays down the law. "That's the way of it from here on in boyyos, any trouble in here and that's the way it will come to an end. If you're behaving, you can come here as often as you like. Any little bit of trouble will get you more than you might like or want."

A dark skinned woman decides now is the time to see what has been happening in the saloon she had shared with her now recently departed partner. She had heard the sounds of fighting and at her reappearance, she questions Henry.

"Where is Jack, the miserable bastard son of a bitch?"

"Do you mean the unfriendly fellow that was here behind the bar, madam?"

"That's the one, where is he, what have you done with him, is he dead? I sure hope so!"

"Not dead, retired to pastures new I believe. We made him an agreeable offer for the place and he skedaddled with his pockets full of cash. Are you telling us he was your husband, madam?"

"Was, sort of, ain't now, though you two boys ought to know that half this place belongs to me, what do ya say to that as if I might care?"

David looks toward Henry. The Cornishman speaks quietly "Madam, how would you favour owning just one third, the same as my friend and I?"

"Sounds real fair to me. Seeing as how you got rid of that stinking bastard, I'll agree. Just one thing mind, we weren't legally married or nothing like that, it just seemed that way! Another thing, if we three are to run this place proper like, we should get us a cook who can."

"Oh don't worry madam, I was about to suggest the very same thing. I'm Henry, you can call me H if you prefer, Tamryn, late of Cornwall, England, this is David, Davy Evans, late of some terrible place God must have forgotten all about, called Wales." Henry smiles at David as he speaks. He wants the Welshman to know his comments are not of a serious nature but a small show of innocent banter.

"I am Renee! Now then, iffen you boys get any ideas about courtin' me, don't, unless I invite you, got that? Business is business, so be warned damn ya!"

Both men look at the lank haired, greasy faced woman with her clothes hanging in tatters, her broken and mis-matching shoes tied with lengths of dirty twine. She could have been fifty, she might be thirty, possibly younger.

The ragbag woman rubs her grimy calloused palms on the rags. Both Henry and David display their good manners to shake hands with and smile willingly at her.

"It seems to me we should drink a toast to our new partnership!" Henry steps around and behind the bar; taking three glasses he pours three beers and hands a glass to each of his new partners before reaching for his own.

"What about me? Don't I get one?"

"Oh, this is Joey, this is my boy. Get back to bed boy!"

The lad had heard the commotion and had nervously ventured into the saloon from behind a piece of torn curtaining. Clutching at Renee and a little afraid he is still half hidden behind her.

Without thinking, Henry pours just a half glass of beer, informing the boy it would be foolish to expect another as he passes the glass. The boy steps forward and a little reluctantly accepts the glass of cloudy liquid.

David moves behind the bar as he notices a customer waiting to be served. The annoying coin tapping ceases as he speaks.

"What'll it be friend?" The customer retreats with the requested beer. David looks down at Joey. "How about clearing up the rest of this mess son, would you mind?"

With the woman's sudden appearance, Henry had thought to clean up and wash down the small pool of blood left by the badly beaten loser. He would not need to worry now as the boy, eager to please, soon disappears and quickly returns with water and cloth. Already Joey likes this big Welshman who has asked if he would mind. He thought about the man Jack, knowing he would have kicked his backside and told him to 'clear up, or else.' Joey worked away until there was no trace of the bloody mess. His task complete, he stores away the tools and quickly returns to the Welshman's side, eager to please once more if called upon.

"Anything else you want me to do, Mister David?"

"It's just Davy to you my young friend and I would say it must be about your bedtime, isn't that right boyyo?"

Joey looks at Renee; she nods approvingly at David's suggestion. "I'll come back there and see ya goodnight in a while, Joey." She shows a smile at her twelve-year old son as he leaves. It is a convincing smile that belies her recent existence. Joey cannot remember the last time he saw his mother smile, at least since Jack had taken complete control over their lives.

Joey empties his glass. "Goodnight Ma, goodnight Davy, goodnight, H!" The boy is suddenly more cheerful now than he could ever remember being during his short life and although he would rather have stayed up longer with his mother and the two men who had treated him so well, he went to bed without argument.

"Seems to me we have to get this here place looking something more like it Davy, Renee. For one thing we need some more seating. Another thing, I don't want any cheating at cards in here, it causes trouble."

David looked at Henry. "You got your nerve H, no cheating at cards, huh, damned English hypocrite!"

"Cornish, I'm bleddy Cornish!"

"Anything you say, Celt!"

"I didn't cheat, it's not my fault if you're the worst Welsh poker player ever to come to Kansas! I take it we're in Kansas, would that be right, Renee?"

Renee looks from one man to the other; still not knowing completely what had happened earlier she is unable to comment, but feels certain that some shenanigans might have occurred in her absence. She isn't particularly upset; the rat has gone, something good has come from the unseen ruckus, she is quite certain of that.

"You're in Kansas, both of ya. Fact is that you boys are gonna have to share the space behind the curtain on account that son of a bitch Jack never had no rooms to rent. He put that sign up out there just to get people inside here to spend their wages. I'm glad the lying bastard has gone!" She points to the grubby torn curtain at the far end of the room. "Joey and me share. So can you pair, behind there!"

"Renee, we've shared worse, haven't we, Davy?"

David, like Henry, thought back to the rail coach and the foul smell of the ejected food. "Aye, we have friend and partner. What time do we close this place up, Renee?"

"Used to close when Jack and his friends fell down mostly Davy, I reckon things might be a little different now."

She believes her life and the life of her son might be about to make a sharp and welcome upturn. At least she hopes it to be the case.

"Let's say One O'clock tonight, shall we? Give these fellers here a chance to get to know you two some, what do ya say?"

Nodding their agreement, both Henry and David are happy at the woman's suggestion; they don't mind at all now there is the promise of a bed after their work is done. The ship and the carriage ride did not allow for such. There was little sleep for either man during the passage and the rail car journey. Their baths would wait until tomorrow.

Henry makes the suggestion the remaining customers should each be given a free drink 'for the evening's inconvenience.' Those present are in complete agreement and they show their appreciation until the appointed hour.

Renee watches the two strangers as they work, pleased for herself and the now sleeping boy she had slaved twelve years for to keep fed and clothed. She could see a chink of light now. Once the rat had turned up and wormed his way into her life things had gone quickly downhill for her and Joey, until now!

'He had regularly bullied and beaten us both' she had told them. Now Renee thinks to herself, there might be a God after all. She would wait and see, hoping that a good feeling just might return for them both.

She has no inkling these two men had known each other for just a handful of hours. For now she would put what little faith she had left in their hands. It can't be any worse, she thought.

At One O'clock the bar had emptied, no customer had dared to ask for more, every man had departed without complaint or argument.

David's beating of the bad loser had had its effect, as well as the sudden banishment of the surly saloon keeper.

Henry respectfully allowed Renee to count and record the cash while he attempted to lock the recently damaged door before turning down the lamps until just one illuminated the rough bar area.

David washed down the planks while making a silent promise to get them replaced with a permanent Cherrywood bar, one he might see his reflection in.

"Now I'm about ready for that comfortable bed you promised, Renee."

"Me too." echoed David.

"Now I never said it was comfortable and it ain't but it's clean and dry! I'll see you fellers tomorrow morning and I'll rustle you both up some breakfast, it'll be the first and only time I do. After you bathe mind, you both smell. Goodnight to you both. And....thank you!"

She watches as the two go behind the filthy curtain, before joining Joey behind theirs. Renee pulls the blanket closer to her chin and as she waits for sleep to come, she promises herself an early morning bath.

"I surely hope she keeps her promise, Davy!"

"The bath or the food? Anyway I'm with you Henry, she sure don't cook too special!"

"Aye to that!"

Thinking back to their early evening meal, both men chuckle quietly at this last comment, before well-earned sleep eventually arrives for them both.

Two men, a woman and a young boy sleep soundly in the sudden silence that has lowered itself onto the half built village.

Not far away, a drunken bully is much less content with his lot. Jack is particularly unhappy now he has no regular income!

CHAPTER TWO

A Buryin'

Renee intends to keep the promise she had made to herself when it was so late into the previous night; before daylight she climbed quietly from the bed so as not to wake the still sleeping boy. It is a short while before dawn as she begins boiling pans of water on the stove. As she waits for the pots to boil she cleans purposefully places she hadn't cleaned in such a long while.

Renee is impatient to bathe. With all the water she can heat in the little time she has, she soon lay soaking, thinking and not a little confused at what has occurred in such a short time. She is unable to remember when she last felt as free as she does right now. Like the cleaning, it has been a while since she had even bothered to bathe properly! It is as if the foreign strangers have lifted a great weight from her shoulders, the rat is gone now, she hopes never to see him again. Renee prays she might safely start to think of herself as a real woman again. There might be some purpose in life for herself and even more for her boy Joey, who she dotes on and only lives for.

David Evans and Henry Tamryn had in such a short time given her new purpose. Renee towels herself down before searching her meagre belongings for something resembling a dress. She quietly rummages around in the sparsely furnished room she shares with the boy. She ties her freshly washed hair into something other than the ragged pile it had seemed to have always been.

She remembers to put on more water for the two men, assuming they are still sleeping behind the curtain. She begins her next task which is the preparation of the promised breakfast. She prepares ham and eggs in a skillet, to be followed by pancakes and hot coffee. Renee knows her limitations in the culinary arts. With almost excessive concentration on her part, she produces a meal for the two who have burst into her and Joey's life so fortunately.

She ponders over her efforts, hoping she has missed nothing in her preparation of the breakfasts. Satisfied she has done her best, she decides everything is ready. She will wait for the pair to rise and bathe in the partially refreshed and steaming water. Now she sits alone day dreaming of how her life might now become but somehow still doubts her recent luck will hold. Renee knows she had been sinking close to the depraved depths of the now missing bully; there had been little to choose between them even though she considers herself to be better. Renee fills another pan, the last.

She doesn't hear anything other than the bubbling of the now heating water. There is complete silence behind the curtain just a few feet away. Renee almost can't wait for them to rise to give her confirmation last night had not been a dream.

She is about to laugh aloud in relief that she is free of Jack as she feels two rough, bony, and sweat encrusted hands slide silently, threateningly around her recently scrubbed throat. She can smell the rancid breath of her assailant. Renee knows who the hands belong to as they tighten, grasping her throat; she begins to choke. Even under the circumstances she notices the sounds behind the hanging rag are still silent. She believes they are silent because she is about to die.

"Where's the rest of the money you filthy whore?"

Now the stricken woman feels the unmistakable coldness of steel below her chin. Renee could still here the bubbling and the heavy breathing from her attacker. Joey has dressed and left in search of milk from the store along the main street. She is fully aware her nemesis has returned and won't give a second thought to ending her life here in the kitchen. Whatever she might do or say, she is about leave her son an orphan. She had been so certain she was going to live a new life. The boy could be alone with no hope of a decent future, which even at this moment is being snatched away as suddenly as it had appeared.

Renee's own dreams are suddenly evaporating like the water in the nearby boiling pan. She can only think of the boy as she strains against the sudden violence. The rat hisses again.

"Give it to me you filthy bitch!" Her assailant freezes instantly at some sudden interruption. A knife handle sticks out of the earthen floor as he drops it in shock. The redundant barman had not known the two men had stayed.

"I'll give you something right now and you can be damned to hell!" Completely naked, Henry Tamryn stood half out of the torn curtain he and David had been sleeping behind, the heavy Colt pistol is already lined high at the rat's head, the hammer is pulled back and without any further thought, Henry simply let it fall onto the waiting forty-four calibre cartridge. A fountain of brain matter showers outwards as blood spatters down Renee's fresh clothes. The rat falls breathlessly. With nothing to hold her up now, Renee topples downward instantly.

The naked man shouts needlessly "David, Davy!"

David Evans is already inside the room, the shot has brought him at a dead run.

"We have some more removals my friend."

"Jesus Henry, you don't like a man to sleep, do you! Renee! Oh Jesus man, is she dead?"

"I hope not, mind you, when she comes around we might wish we were; look at the mess he made of that lovely dress.

As for sleeping, I reckon this bloke will be doing plenty of that!" Henry points quite needlessly at the still warm corpse.

"The mess he made? You blew his brains all over the bloody place, man!"

"They had to go some bleddy where and there is little of them unsurprisingly. I had no time, if I hadn't shot when I did, he would have cut her throat most likely. It is not my fault old chap, it was his own. It's bleddy for Christ's sake, how many times man!"

"Fair enough, he asked for it."

Henry steps away and slides behind the curtain after he realises he is still naked. He returns partially dressed and picking up a jug of water that has not been heated yet, he gently pours some of the contents over Renee's forehead.

At that moment, Joey walks through the shaky door. Ignoring the two men, he dashes forward to his mother's side. "Ma, ma!" The frightened boy is quickly relieved as he hears her stifled groan.

"Are you shot, Ma? Wake up ma, please!" Joey heard the shot as he walked back with the milk, fearing the worst.

As if in answer to the boy's plea, Renee opens her eyes. "Is this heaven?"

"Not likely, more like hell I'd say!" replied David. "You alright girl? Get your ma some coffee, no, Brandy, Joey get some Brandy, be quick lad." The boy scuttles off obediently, he returns quickly with a tall glass of the suggested liquid.

Renee shakily begins to sit up. "What happened? Look at my dress." The shock and sudden violence has brought on a temporary bout of memory loss.

"Don't worry Renee, it's over, the rat has died of poison, lead poisoning. One less rodent to worry about in this town. You can get yourself another dress, two if you like, isn't that right, Davy?"

"Certainly, H!"

Renee finds herself suddenly embarrassed at the sight of Henry who is only partially dressed. She quickly looks away.

Henry had awoken just in time to hear Jack's demands but had not had time to find clothes. Knowing there was immediate danger he had disregarded his nudity and with little thought, snatched up the Colt.

Joey wantonly kicked out hard at the now stiffening corpse as he sought his mother's arms again. "Bastard!"

Fully recovered from her shock, Renee uses some of the hot water she had boiled for the two men to wash away the spattered remains of her recent common law husband.

Wide awake now and bathed, David and Henry begin their work at cleaning away what is left. The two men had taken the corpse to the undertaker's lean-to workshop not far down the street from the saloon. The squat man would deal with the disposal and the 'bill would be forthcoming.' Henry agreed to pay the costs, deciding four dollars being a small price to pay to dispose of the remains of the bartender. The undertaker had promised his best efforts; Henry and David had told him there was no necessity to do so.

Law is so far absent in the fledgling, Southern Kansas settlement. David and Henry are not in the least worried at the death of Jack. They would hold up their hands and plead guilty if and when there might be a need.

The three adults, aided by Joey, used the morning for the purpose of temporarily improving the facilities of the saloon. Little time had been used to ponder the early morning shooting. David had previously confessed to being a 'dab hand' at carpentry. 'How do you think I got these?' David's shirt strained tightly over his flexed biceps.

Renee soon got over the shock of the shooting. She could not even think of one small reason to mourn the man's passing. Managing to eventually find some more 'half decent' clothes she set off in search of a replacement cook. 'If we are to do this, we will do it right' she had stated defiantly while pulling the door shut behind her.

Her search is almost instantly successful. The new cook is even smaller than she and even her son but at least cleaner and a little smarter than the now departed Jack. An aged Chinaman is soon in his element. Already he is setting up the kitchen for better things. He brought a large black cat along with him. The oriental would be unaware the only resident rodent had already departed. All the cat has to do is eat and sleep and there will be no rats to chase!

By noon on the same day the saloon is open and ready for a day's business. Good hot food is at the disposal of customers. No sign of the recent shooting remains now.

Henry took up a position behind the noticeably cleaner plank bar. David had gone off in search of 'good timber' for early make-shift improvements. Joey followed the Welshman everywhere as if a shadow.

Renee stood in the centre of the room. She could not, even now, comprehend her swiftly changing world. She feels as if it is out of control at this moment, a climbing spiral after the depths of despair of the early morning when she thought the promised changes in her life had already outworn their welcome and were about to vanish. All had gone downward at such a comparable speed since Jack's arrival, now suddenly it is in reverse as she tries to steady the spinning thoughts.

She looks above. "We have to get rid of this damn filthy canvas, Henry." The huge tarpaulin is stained with tobacco smoke.

"Don't you worry your head Renee, Davy has everything in hand. Let's get this place open and making some money, for all of us. Then we can make all the improvements you want or need."

"Amen to that Henry, oh why didn't you boys get here earlier?"

Henry understood Renee's plea. He ignores the question as he shoves open the rickety front doors whilst making a gentle joke. "Why, did something happen we don't know about?"

Sunlight streamed in, almost as if it had been requested, The bar room now took on a brightened, cheerful atmosphere even though it is only a short time ago Henry had needed to kill a man inside the room behind the curtain. Renee almost felt the sun was shining just for her and Joey. Jack's malevolent presence has departed with the intruding but welcome brightness, as at last she rewards herself a smile. She soaks up the newly supplied warmth.

Henry had donned a half clean cotton apron; Renee had washed and scrubbed it as best as she could that morning before she had lain in the tub, imagining what might be to come. The Cornishman had told her he would be proud to wear it. 'Just don't you be thinking to ask me to wear a necktie' he had commented, half-jokingly, half seriously.

David returned. "The lumber will be here in a week, H. Give me two, and we'll have ourselves a decent roof over our heads, in fact we'll soon have rooms up there too boyyo, how will that suit you?"

"Sounds good Davy, you're the man, I'll do whatever you need me to though I am not a carpenter."

"You sell the beer. Who the buggary is that?" David points at the tiny Oriental as he suddenly trots into view from the cooking area.

"The constable, he wants a word with you about bleddy pest control."

"Me! What did I bleddy do?"

"I'm yanking your leg Davy, he's here to be our new cook. I am so glad you finally learned to curse properly, my friend."

"Perhaps you might want to earn us some wages funny man. You go to Hell."

"There's no point, it's full thanks to me."

The first customer of the day appears almost reluctantly at the open door. The dishevelled man leans just inside the broken door.

"Can I come in? I won't do nuthin' wrong" the young man states nervously.

News has travelled fast around the tiny settlement; the happenings of the previous night and the early morning shooting had already become common knowledge about the hamlet.

"Come in boyyo, Henry there will pour you the first of the day, make yourself comfortable." The barfly is still a little reluctant to approach. David shoots another look at the early patron's hungover features. "On second thoughts, perhaps it isn't the first mister." The scruffy barfly perches nervously on a hastily repaired stool.

Renee had washed almost every trace of the blood out of the stained dress she now hung to dry. David thought she looked a different woman in her second outfit of the day. 'There's pretty' he had said.

Renee had shot a playful glare at the Welshman. "I told you, no courtin' but thank you anyway, Davy." Renee smiled a little hesitantly alongside the friendly rebuke she had aimed towards the Welshman.

David sits in front of the plank top, as he begins to explain his plans for the upstairs extension in detail to Renee and Henry. "I can do all the work myself, we'll save unnecessary expense, young Joey can be my runner. By the way, I managed to talk the undertaker into renting part of the back room from us, he'll be working from here at the end of the week. It'll save me having to carry all your bleddy corpses to him, Henry."

"We hardly have a proper back room, do we?"

"Don't worry yourself Renee, you will have by the time I'm finished."

"We might need to hire some help for the work upstairs, there must be some out of work ranch hands hereabouts."

"Not a chance, no need Henry, I can cope with most of the work. I'll call you for the heavy lifting."

"Whatever you say. I told you, just call me 'H' you're wearing out my bleddy name, Davy."

"It's all good with me. Is that Aitch or Haitch, Cornishman?"

"Whatever you can manage, Welshman."

"So be it, H!"

"Fool!"

Business increased slowly during the first day of the new, already flourishing partnership. 'H' and David assumed curiosity to be the most part of the cause. Word of the eviction and eventual slaying had spread amongst the small, local population. Most of their lunchtime customers would state loudly they were in favour of the replacement proprietors as they departed with full bellies, all wishing the three good luck as they went out of the door.

'Tungsaw' the wizened little Chinese chef, was an instant success. At times Renee was waiting for diners to finish their meals so she could wash plates to be used again. The little cook more than once had to send Joey to the general store for more ingredients. No one even wondered how he had appeared at a time when he was needed.

"If this business keeps up, we'll have to think about turning this place into a proper eating house, Renee. Methinks we can do a good trade." Henry had already thought about the possibilities.

"Yes, that will surely be an advantage, Henry, I mean H! There is no other eating house in town as yet. Think we might need to get another waitress though." On this first day, it seemed to the two they had served meals to almost all of the inhabitants of the settlement, though no one quite knew how many that might be.

"There's to be a meeting here tonight H, some of the local folk want to start themselves a council and find someone to be their Town Marshal, a policeman. I heard talk at the general store and suggested they use this place as we have the biggest room in town as far as I know."

"Good, that's good Davy, we'll take more good money tonight. Do you know Davy, I might put myself up for the Mayor's job, what do you think?"

"Couldn't do any harm H, splendid idea, Boyyo. You do what you think is best. You'll get my vote providing you stop shooting everybody. There'll hardly be anyone left to put their hands up. What about you, Renee?"

"Oh, I don't think I could be Mayor."

Henry explained to Renee, a Mayor would usually be a male. 'One day perhaps' he had added thoughtfully.

"I'll vote for you, Mr Tamryn." Joey's voice came from the kitchen where he was helping wash used dishes.

"Well that's that then, Joey's made my mind up for me. I'll stand for Mayor if I get the chance. Seems to me it was a good thing I shot the rat this morning."

"Why's that, boyyo?'

"Why, because as you mentioned, the Mayor can't be seen to go around shooting all the townspeople."

"That won't do at all, no Sir. Besides, most of them seem to be customers!" David replied.

"I reckon you're right. I will be more careful who I shoot from now on." Henry felt no regret at shooting the previous owner of the premises, it was him or Renee and he knows whatever happens now, he made the right choice.

The afternoon went quickly by, the need for meals slowly diminishing. As the day's food trade quietened down, David took some time roughly drawing his plans for the improvements and enlargement of the saloon. Renee and Joey made a visit to the dress shop. Joey had pleaded with his mother to be allowed to stay with David, but she had been adamant he must go with her.

Meanwhile, Henry scribbled some notes in readiness for the evening meeting.

Tungsaw worked hard completing the cleaning and organising the kitchen so that it would be better for working. Happy with the results of his efforts, he prepared ingredients for the possible busy supper trade. The always alert feline watched over the Chinaman with a careful and approving eye, all the while hoping for something tasty to fall to the freshly swept floor. Sometimes morsels were dropped purposefully by his caring owner.

At the appointed hour townspeople began moving in for the meeting. Most of the seating is quickly taken up. David allows the plank bar top to be used for extra seating by some. 'Mind you keep your feet over that side, boyyo.' When it seemed all the adult population was present, the owner of the general store and hardware supplies establishment made the decision to conduct and chair the evening's discussions.

Jasper Hawke had high hopes of the Mayoralty and to take charge now would put him in the forefront. He brought the gathering to attention.

"Well now, we all know why we are here, we need a Mayor, a policeman and a jail. Firstly, I think we should decide on our first Town Marshal, is that agreed? A show of hands, please."

The audience all nod and show their support of the motion.

Four men are nominated; David, the lunchtime drunk and Henry had raised their hands to show their interest in the post. Hawke put his own name forward.

Henry decided he would not stand against the others though he had stated that David would make an excellent Town Marshal. A vote was asked for and the count was taken. David, to the drunk's surprise, is elected the so far unnamed settlement's first policeman.

"I suppose I'll have to make you a badge of office" stated the also newly arrived in town, Blacksmith. "When you have voted in the town council, I'll be asking for the expenses." The blacksmith is almost the same size and heft as David. Henry is of a similar build, only shorter and stockier.

It was agreed the law making and statutes would be decided upon once the Marshal could discuss them with the soon to be elected mayor and other council members who had hastily been chosen.

Next, the question of the jail is raised. Jasper Hawke had been wise enough to have a cellar built under his general store. He suggests the use of the room until a proper jail could be erected. This was also voted upon and agreed by all those who were interested enough to put their hands in the air.

There was some understandable reluctance to this suggestion, mostly from the drunk and hardly anyone else.

Now was the turn of the Mayoralty. There are just three nominations: Henry, the drunk and Jasper Hawke. Hawke easily won, the drunk looked surprised and Henry, although disappointed, congratulated the victor. Henry made a vow he would try again at the next mayoral election whenever it should occur.

The drunk shoves a hand in the air to get the attention of the audience. Everyone turns to him as he shouts "Can I be the jailer?" He slurred his question and as there is no other applicants, the vote is unanimous. Once more, he shows his surprise.

"Ladies and gentlemen, there is one more item of business. As Mayor, I believe I should bring to the attention of you all that as yet, our town has no name. We are most remiss!"

The audience look to each other, some gasp followed by animated conversation and numerous suggestions were shouted forward.

"It seems to me that we should hold another meeting, say this time next week, collect all of the suggestions and take it to a vote. In favour, raise your hands. Against? Good, until next week then, meeting over."

Tungsaw appears from the kitchen. "We vote Mayor now?"

"No, you go backee kitchen, you missee vote." Henry laughs off his own disappointment with his light-hearted and inoffensive dismissal of the Oriental. Tungsaw does as Henry had suggested, muttering to himself as he walks away, in a language only he could understand.

"Never mind Henry, there's plenty to be getting on with here, without worrying about anything else right now."

"Yes Renee, you're absolutely right. In any case, methinks Jasper will fit the bill. By God, I forgot, Davy, you are to be our Marshal, congratulations old chap. Now have you given thought to where you might have your police station?"

"Well boyyo, seems to me that sharing with the undertaker would be best all round, don't you think?"

"Oh yes Davy, capital idea, just perfect, in fact. If we could get the jail built out there, we might even get the contract for supplying any prisoner's meals, as well as the jailer's" Henry adds while looking across at the beaming and recently employed drunk.

"You don't miss a trick Henry Tamryn, but I agree" said Renee. "We should get all the business we can. You never know when someone else might open a saloon here if and when this place begins to grow as it surely will now it's to be organised. If David can build another storey up there, he can put another one above that. Then we'll have proper letting rooms too. A regular hotel, what do you say to that?"

"I say you're a woman after my own heart. What do you think Davy, can it be done?"

"It can be done Henry, don't you worry about that. When I put the first floor up, we'll leave it nice and easy for the next. Soon as we have the necessary timber, it will be done. There's one other little building job I have to be doing soon, at Jasper's request."

"What's that, David?"

"Schoolhouse. The mayor had a quiet word in my ear about it at the end of the meeting. I said I'd do what I could. I told him it would have to wait until the new roof was on here first."

"You ain't expecting me to go to this school." Joey had heard part of this latest conversation and as it would concern him, he is bristling and ready to fight tooth and nail against his taking in education. "I won't do it, never, you hear me? Ma!"

"Quiet Joey, the school isn't even built yet and you already don't want to go. Get yourself behind there with Davy, find yourself something useful to be doing."

"Sure Ma!" Joey would not need to be told twice to be with the affable Welshman.

"Davy, are you going to buy a six-gun, with a holster?"

"What for Joey, do you think I might need one?"

"I heard Wild Bill Hickok carries two big Navy Colts. He's the Marshal in Hays City, carries a big Bowie Knife too, I heard."

"This Mr Hickok must need them. I don't think I will be needing a gun, we will have to wait and see, Joey."

"God help us all. If Davy takes to carrying a gun, I'm leaving to join the bleddy convicts in Australia." Henry chided his Welsh friend.

"Seems to me that would be best all round, Henry! The place is so full of cut throats and murderers, I heard, you'll mostly feel right at home amongst them!"

Nobody had noticed the disappearance of Renee. She had gone behind her curtain to try another dress on; she had no mirror, she did not need one. The feel of the fabric had the desired effect for her. She is unable to remember if she had ever had such a thing as a new dress before. She thought not. Again, she set her hair and returned to the bar room.

"My oh my, where's Renee, you must be an impostor. Davy, arrest this person for impersonating a lady, throw her in your jail."

"How will I do that, we don't have one yet!"

Renee couldn't help herself as she laughed out loud at Henry's and David's jocular statements. She likes the attention these two men show her. This morning it could all have been very different. Joey might now be alone if Henry had not awoken when he had.

One week later, Renee had another dress. She had the new shoes she had promised herself. A waitress, Maria, had been employed for a few hours a week and David is about to embark on the building of the first floor. Monday morning begins with a deep blue sky and bright sun streams into the hole left by the removal of the heavily patched and grimy canvas that had been the only cover so far from the Kansan elements. David had planned everything with precision; he had prepared the timber sections like pieces in a jigsaw, ready to fit into each other as soon as they were hauled above.

The now mostly sober drunk offers his help. Joey, Henry and even Jasper Hawke have volunteered to lend a hand. The sections are heavy and they have to be slowly winched up the side of the original building. All of the men and the boy work tirelessly throughout the day.

Later in the afternoon, no one notices the darkening sky until it is too late. Lightning forks spear down suddenly, thunder crashes, in minutes a torrential downpour begins.

Tungsaw yells up at the soaking wet workmen. "Kitchen, kitchen, you flood my bloody kitchen, fools. You get roof on pretty quick Davy; no roof, you get bloody soup!" The excited little Chinaman waves his small, almost fleshless fists at the group above him and at the sky and at inquisitive and amused passers-by who have stopped amid the deluge to see what is occurring.

Henry glances across at the now dripping Davy. "Wish I had that pistol up here with me, Davy. Joey, pass me that gun."

"That wouldn't be very clever Henry, shooting a Chinaman in front of the Marshal, now would it?"

Joey pushes his dripping hair back from his eyes. "You wouldn't shoot the cook Henry, would you? We'd have to go back to ma's cooking for one thing."

"I hadn't thought of that Joey, well done my boy. I'll stop his wages instead."

"Can't do that, H."

"Why the devil not, Davy?"

"We don't pay him yet. He just gets his meals and a roof over his head."

At this statement, it is all Henry and the others could do to cling onto the wetted edge of the building. The workmen laugh so loudly, the Chinaman resumes shouting and waving again. David joins in. Joey too could not help himself from joining in with the laughter.

Renee looks up through the yawning gap. "Look at my dress!" she pleads, not realising the fresh but cold rainwater had slicked it to her now chilled body. Renee had been so anxious to get the new dress, she had not yet bought any undergarments to match.

Customers, hiding uselessly under their broad-brimmed hats, gaped wide-eyed at Renee as she swears swift vengeance on the work party.

"By Jesus boy don't look, it's not for your eyes" Henry warned with a wink, whilst doing exactly what he told the boy not to do.

Soon all are laughing at Renee's present predicament. The woman soon joins in, she doesn't even care, nothing could spoil this day for her. Early this morning she had thought she would never see another. A drop of rain could not dampen her newly gained freedom and happiness!

Before turning in, Henry took up his journal. He had promised his sister he would write every day so that in the future she might know what he had done since leaving Innis Town. He had forgotten until now. There is a lot to put down, so much has happened in a short time. He had kept up the diary as much as possible while aboard the Cleopatra, he had some catching up to do. Henry can hear David snoring. His friend had worked so hard since their arrival in Kansas. Henry began to write, but sleep came to him before a second sentence was completed.

CHAPTER THREE
Hickok

At the Welshman's insistence, Renee pushed open the new door. David has worked swiftly and professionally. This is her room. She can hardly remember having her own quarters before. She does recall her young son Joey had never once had a room of his own.

David and Henry had made the decision to provide Renee with her own quarters first as her need was greater. She gazed around the still bare room. Her eyes well up, it is all she can do to stop the tears from cascading down her already flushed cheeks. She can hardly believe her eyes. She has been aware of what was happening above but had never dared look until invited inside.

Not even in her own early teens had she had a room she might call her own. It seemed to her that she had moved from one shanty to another, sleeping wherever there was cover and at times, there was no cover to be had. She had been thrown out by strict parents after telling them she was carrying Joey, Renee became homeless. She could begin to think differently today. It is one vast improvement to her life. If only the two friends had arrived before, she thought to herself, as she had done many times over the days and the nights since they had walked in.

Renee thought back to when Jack had found her and the boy. He was good to her in the beginning but it did not last. They had set up the canvas saloon and had done little to improve it since those early days. Jack had no intention of even trying to make any changes. Now Renee remembers him with nothing but hate and loathing. Before too long Jack had realised that Renee could improve his pocket-book in more ways than one. He had cajoled and bullied her into sharing her favours for money and for his own use. Renee hardly ever saw any of the cash as Jack gambled it away mostly. Yes, he had won occasionally but she had never had a share of any of it.

Renee had been trapped as she had her child to think of. She soon gave up any thoughts of getting away from the misery of slaving for the man who is now lying dead in a wooden box, which right now stands horizontally on the boardwalk outside the undertakers shop, the timber lid leaning to the side.

There had been more than one time Renee thought she might be better off sleeping out on the Plains with just a blanket, or beneath some broken wagon-bed somewhere. If it had not been for Joey, she most likely would have taken an even easier, more final way out of her misery. She had thought of this way out many, many times. She could not have left Joey an orphan. Renee just did what she had to, thinking there would never be anything better for her and her young son. Even the boy will now be able to sleep soundly. No filthy curtain, just a plain, varnished wooden floor for now but a door will soon be attached to the frame. David had promised him. He could hardly wait. Soon, he will have his own door to open and to close as and when he felt like it. David had promised Joey's room will be next to be completed. For now, Henry and the carpenter would continue as before, the need is greater for the mother and her son.

David had not made the doors, they had been ordered and purchased from Jasper's store. Everything else had been nailed, screwed or glued together almost single-handedly by the hard-working Welshman. The whole first floor is the result of his handy work. Henry and Joey helped when help was needed, but it was all down to David's knowledge and expertise. It has not all been plain sailing, there had been small, inconsequential mishaps along the way though improvements had come thick and fast and constantly, in a very short time.

Renee remembers her first morning of freedom; the sudden storm, the ranting chef, the boggle-eyed customers, Henry and David staring down at her slickness. Laughter had come come quickly, she had even laughed at herself, nothing mattered then and now, other than what she has. David had promised rooms and to her; a beautiful room had been delivered.

Like Joey, Renee would have to sleep with her blankets on the floor tonight but she knows it is better than under a wagon-bed. There had been no time yet to put decent beds in the rooms. Joey is already under his covers and hoping to replenish the energy he had used up today. Renee isn't able to retire yet, there is an evening's work to be done in the saloon; her saloon, hers, David's and Henry's saloon. Now not just a drinking establishment but also a home.

If some stranger had told Renee two weeks ago how things would be now, she would have laughed in their faces and cried simultaneously. In the pigsty Renee had shared with Jack, she had almost forgotten the sound of real laughter apart from the loud, drunken sounds that had filled her evenings and sometimes her nights. It had been these sounds that had made her contemplate ending it all. Now real laughter did not come with difficulty for her.

Every day there is some wild antic from one or the other of these two men that had appeared in her life so suddenly and violently. Perhaps because they knew how it had been for her, they did it purposely. The sounds inside the building are so different for her now. The days of two cowboys arguing about who would be with her for a night are long gone. Most importantly to her, she is holding her head high and fast rediscovering her self-respect.

Her outfits are finished off with the new shoes that hurt her blistered feet. It didn't matter to her, pain is nothing new to Renee. It is a different kind of pain anyway. She could take the shoes off if she wanted to but she resisted. Shutting the door again, she walked down the stairs with something other than painful feet. Renee now had pride in her appearance for the first time in a long while. She can hold her head high because of the strangers.

David stood behind the bar, the silver badge gleaming its serious peace-keeping message: Town Marshal. A town by any other name. So far the settlement has no official name, one is to be decided at the next meeting of the inhabitants who call it home.

Henry is already busy doing his best to encourage some card playing. Henry is a card player, not a tin-horn gambler or a professional cardsharp. He will just show interest, get a game going and leave the players to it. While they are playing, they are drinking, while they are drinking the business is profiting, not hugely, but increasing all the same. There was no more cheating!

'Tungsaw' is doing his utmost in the kitchen. Even now, halfway through the evening, suppers are still being eaten. Other customers that don't require a full meal could help themselves from the makeshift free food counter at the far end of the bar. Cutaway strips of meat and crispy potatoes are on hand as a snack to those in need.

Joey is asleep and Renee is having this evening off from any physical work; she is playing the role of the hostess, talking to customers, making them feel comfortable, making them stay just a little longer than they might have originally planned. Renee takes to her task like a duck takes to water, she is thriving in her new and respectable role.

Jasper Hawke has even brought Mrs Hawke tonight; he is treating her to a first taste of Chinese food, a meal that has been specially prepared for her and Jasper by the busy

Tungsaw. Renee can see their plates are almost empty, hardly a scrap remains for the kitchen cat.

She remembered the morning when the old canvas came off to be replaced by a temporary one until the permanent timber one is complete. The poor man who had sat at the same table as Jasper now, had his plate filled with the cascading rainwater. 'Wishy Washy Chop Suey' he had called it as he cursed the wholly innocent chef. Renee smiles at the memory as she walks over to Jasper and Mrs Hawke's table, wishing them a good evening before moving on.

Henry approaches her after leaving David to tend the bar. "Renee, come and sit down, there's something I have to say to you, something you and I need to talk about." The pair move to a small side table and Henry pulls back a chair for her. She sits, waiting as the Cornishman settles himself next to her.

"Renee, I speak for both myself and Davy, we want you to know just how much we should be grateful to you. You could rightfully have refused when we suggested our partnership. Davy and I wouldn't have taken this place from you, we would have moved on. We hadn't intended to stay here, we had no plans at all, we had only arrived in your country a day or two beforehand. We will take our leave even now if it is what you want."

"Henry, stop!"

"No, let me finish Renee, Davy and I owe you a debt of gratitude. Way I see it is this, we'd like you to see a lawyer and get a legal contract drawn up. Davy a third, myself a third, you and young Joey, one third, everything all legal as it should be. What do you say?"

"Yes, we should get a contract and one third each is perfect. No more talk of moving on." Renee's tone was one of stoic finality. Henry looked over at David, he smiled at his friend. The Welshman nods back knowing an agreement has been reached to benefit them all.

"If that's your final offer, we'll take it." Henry stated jokingly. "You drive a hard bargain, young lady!" Henry reaches across and takes Renee's hand, he turns it over and gently kisses the back.

"Henry Tamryn, are you trying to court me? What did I say to you!"

"Certainly not, I wouldn't dare." Henry had not forgotten her early warning. He is hoping she might soon forget.

Renee might have been secretly disappointed. She knew she and Henry were of a similar age, though she is a year or two older than him, it did not worry him and it did not worry her unduly. It is obvious Henry doesn't see it as a problem. She could not be totally sure what he thought of her, she had knowingly and almost instantly realised she had the tiny beginnings of feelings for this man who even now, is treating her like a lady despite everything that had gone on before. She would keep those feelings to one side for the time being. There's no rush now she knows he's going nowhere.

'You'll keep, Henry Tamryn.' Renee mouthed only to herself as the evening turned into late night. At one-thirty, David is able to convince the last of the revellers that they would be better off in their own homes. The three partners, with the barfly's help, roll up their sleeves in order to get the saloon in readiness for the following day. Glasses are washed and shined, floors swept, cash counted and balanced close enough.

The drunk who had appeared that first day and the man who is now the jailer but so far has no inmates to concern him, had also been taken on as a cleaner in the building. The young man could hardly believe his luck, going from no job to two jobs within a matter of days. He managed to convince David, who had taken on the task of hiring and firing for the saloon, though it is a job which is hardly needed. He had promised he would drink very little while working. He had so far kept his word. With all the late evening chores completed the three partners sat themselves at a table, ready to begin their late night winding down period. A time for just talking about the day and maybe discussing more plans for the future of the business. They had formed a habit of sharing a drink together at this time, it giving each the chance to make any suggestions as to improving the running of and improving the profits of the business. The premises could not be called smart right now though it is improving in every respect as each day passes. Renee is first to make a suggestion as the three sit quietly after the day's work is complete. Her idea had been welcomed and quickly accepted. She had put it to the two men that perhaps they should separate the eating area from the drinking area, 'just in a small way.' The little Oriental had so far been a great success. His culinary skills have easily surpassed their expectations and perhaps it is time to allow the diners their own space. David had allowed that alterations could be easily carried out; it would not be too difficult to erect a partition wall and he could provide a separate entrance for the diners. The kitchen too would not be a problem to renovate. 'We'll block up one door and cut another through' he had suggested.

Henry had asked if this extra work would affect David's duties as Town Marshal. The Welshman had given a negative reply. 'See now Henry, I can't even arrest the drunk now, he's always bloody sober!'

"Bleddy, it's bleddy sober, for god's sake, man!"

"What?"

"Never mind, I'll learn you if it kills me."

David looked across at the barfly. "Go and get yourself a beer now boyyo, works done." The man did as he is ordered without argument. He has made an enormous effort to improve his demeanour and it has not gone unnoticed by the three who even now are watching him and waiting for him to stop looking for something more to clean.

"Methinks it's time we started giving that fellow some wages Renee, perhaps you will arrange something?"

"How strangely you speak, Henry Tamryn! You're right Henry, I'll deal with it. I'd say a dollar a day; that with his meals and a dry bed should be a good start." Renee knows that a dollar a day is a high reward when including the extras such as meals. She hoped that it would encourage even more loyalty from the barfly.

Both men agree to the suggestion by a nod of the head. The swamper overhears the conversation, he is quietly elated with the sudden improvements to his employment. Henry had ignored the half question from Renee regarding his dialect.

"Something occurs to me. When David is busy with his official duties, we might need another to help tend the bar. What do you say, Davy? Think you might make a silk purse out of a sow's ear?"

"I don't see any reason why not, H." David looks over at the now resting swamper. "Just what is your name, me boyyo?"

The resting swamper shows a reluctance to answer the Welshman's question. "You all have to promise you won't laugh if I tell you?"

"We won't laugh." Renee looks to her partners for their solemn compliance.

"Gladstone." The barfly's voice is hardly audible at this admittance.

"Gladstone!" He stated it again when told to speak up. David and Henry look at Renee for her reaction.

Renee is trying hard not to smile. Unfortunately for Gladstone, she is unable to contain herself. Henry and David too are soon consumed with laughter. Gladstone soon saw the funny side, as he in turn joined in their laughter. He looked at David and Henry. "I don't see how you two can laugh at me, H! Huh. What kind of name is that?" The laughter between the four is restarted and Gladstone now feels he has been fully accepted as an integral part of the budding business. He has also acquired a third job without realising it.

"I have an Aunt called Gladys." states the Welshman with a hint of a guilty smile.

The following morning sees Gladstone looking very different. He is sporting a dark woollen jacket, dark pants and a narrow piece of black cloth as a necktie. His thick, shiny hair has been slicked down and shines cleanly with a parting through the centre.

Today is the day for Davy to keep a promise, he would begin to train him. The ex-barfly and former scruff is determined to look the part and make the most of his opportunities.

The little Chinaman appears suddenly in the room and after shuffling towards the newly spruce swamper he stretches up onto tiptoes and sniffs at the pristine parting. "You son of bitch, you steal lard from kitchen, you put lard on bleddy hair!" The Chinaman produces a wicked looking slicing knife. "You come with me to kitchen, I slice you up and fry you in own fat, you son of a bitch!"

"Whoa now Tungsaw, leave him be, there's a good fellow, it wouldn't do any harm for you to smarten up. Come on Davy, let's get the lard, see if we can improve our little friend here, can't do any worse. It's good to hear he is cursing in a proper way."

"You leave Tungsaw alone, you come in kitchen you get big trouble bosses. I warn you." The Oriental resembles a swash-buckling pirate as he walks away swishing the glinting blade in mock drama, a grin stretching his taut skin even more.

"Now then boyyos, let's be getting Gladstone here turned into a barman while we are all still in one piece. He certainly looks the part I must say."

David opens the doors to the premises for the day's business. Steadily but surely he will allow Gladstone to take over from him. Gladstone has never been given any respon-sibilities such as he is being given now. He is determined not to let himself or his new employers down. David would not have to direct the bar operation this evening, Gladstone has learned willingly and quickly! He had, unknowingly to his mentor, watched the Welshman as he had propped up the other side of the bar. He had seen everything he had done and even Jack before him. He performed his new duties in exactly the same way, not without a little more panache.

The Welshman is satisfied with what he has seen so far. He could now concentrate on the further improvements that have been suggested without the worry of tending customers at the bar. The remainder of the roof will go on a lot quicker now. David will be able to spend more time in drawing up further plans. He had hoped his next job of joinery would be the erection of the schoolhouse; he would need to put those plans to one side for a while longer. David had informed Jasper Hawke of the difficulty. The Mayor accepted his promise to start the building 'within the month.' The fact there are less than a dozen school age children in the still so far unnamed hamlet makes the decision that much easier. The figure does not yet include Joey but it will do eventually, whether he likes it or not. It had so far been decided by all but the youngster.

The evening that follows is the one set aside for the naming of the tiny Southern Kansas town that lies less than a handful of miles from the Texas Panhandle and its border with the Lone Star State.

The bar room fills to capacity in very quick time. Jasper calls the meeting to order, asking all those that had suggestions to put them forward. Almost everyone wants to shout his or her selection first. Jasper needed to bring the meeting to order once more. It is agreed that paper and pencil would be passed around, each nominee would put down their choice then everyone present would be able to decide their choice and the vote would begin and eventually counted to find a winner.

From the twenty or thirty plus suggestions some, but not many, were the same. Jasper is able to whittle the choice down to just five and then only three.

A show of hands would next be employed to decide the winning title. Jasper would call out the name in third place, followed by the choice with the second highest amount of votes. Last will be the winner and will be decided upon without argument, everyone present had agreed. Just as the new mayor is about to speak, the partly repaired door from the street seemed to blow itself open or at least it had looked that way to the assembled and surprised congregation.

Every person present is distracted at the sound of a latecomer opening the door. They all turn as one and the space is filled. It is as if a giant is suddenly filling the void. The man stands easily more than six feet, broad shoulders covered with long, wavy, dark brown hair, tapering down almost to the matching butt forward Navy colts that ride high on his hips. The identical pistols are each adorned with a single pearl in the centre of the handles as they cover the screw heads that keep the polished wooden handles of the weapons safely in place.

Joey breaks the silence first, he somehow knows who this man is instantly. "Wild Bill, Jesus Christ, its Wild Bill Hickok!*" Joey's head swings from one side to the other as he makes his already redundant pronouncement. Hickok moves stealthily into the otherwise silent room, he steps slowly towards the bar. A hand drops into the pants pocket pulling out a silver dollar, the Deputy United States Marshal flips the coin up onto the planks.

* *James Butler Hickok (May 27, 1837 – August 2, 1876), better known as "Wild Bill" Hickok, was a folk hero of the American Old West known for his life on the frontier as a soldier, scout, lawman, gambler, showman, and actor, and for his involvement in many famous gunfights. Hickok earned a great deal of notoriety in his own time, much of it bolstered by the many outlandish and often fabricated tales he told about himself. Some contemporaneous reports of his exploits are known to be fictitious, but they remain the basis of much of his fame and reputation. Hickok was born and raised on a farm in northern Illinois at a time when lawlessness and vigilante activity was rampant because of the influence of the «Banditti of the Prairie». Drawn to this ruffian lifestyle, he headed west at age 18 as a fugitive from justice, working as a stagecoach driver and later as a lawman in the frontier territories of Kansas and Nebraska. He fought and spied for the Union Army during the American Civil War and gained publicity after the war as a scout, marksman, actor, and professional gambler. He was involved in several notable shootouts during the course of his life. In 1876, Hickok was shot and killed from behind while playing poker in a saloon in Deadwood, Dakota Territory (present-day South Dakota) by Jack McCall an unsuccessful gambler. The hand of cards which he supposedly held at the time of his death has become known as the dead man's hand: two pairs; black aces and eights.*

"Beer feller, when you're ready!"

"I'm s s s sorry Mr Hickok sir, the bar's closed while the voting gets done." Gladstone is nervous and almost shaking as he stutters his reply to the renowned Lawman's request.

"Well, in that case I'll wait." An audible sigh of relief travels around the whole of the room. There is hardly a person present that hasn't heard of Wild Bill Hickok. The same number would know of his awesome gun fighting reputation.

The tall man from Troy Grove, Illinois, turned, leaning his elbows on the bar, suggesting he would indeed wait patiently for the completion of the town's meeting.

"Ladies and Gentlemen, I have a suggestion." Jasper's voice quieted the now animated crowd. "We have in our midst, I'm sure he doesn't mind my saying, Mister James Butler Hickok." Jasper glances towards the tall, bedecked lounging man. He accepts the slight nod as permission to continue with what he is about to say.

"Now it seems to me, and you can vote democratically on it of course, that we should add another name to our shortlist. I personally would nominate 'Hickok' to be the name of this fine young town of ours, what do you say to that my friends? A great American, with a great American name."

Jasper is unable to count all the hands that instantly rise. Instead he simply announces, 'motion carried.' A solid roar of approval fills the room. Hickok waves an arm in acceptance whilst nodding and smiling and turning back to the bar for the now waiting glass of beer Gladstone is pouring in haste.

"One last thing good people of Hickok, the bars open, let's raise a glass to our town, to 'Hickok'!" The mayor had caught the mood of the congregation and made the announcement, as if it was needed.

The newly named Hickok's first public celebration would last well into the night and into the first light of a new day. Gladstone was a stalwart, aided now by David, Henry and Renee. Even Joey was kept busy collecting glasses, almost until he dropped asleep on his feet.

Tungsaw, under orders from the three partners, had kept the free food counter well stocked for as long as he could, until even he began to feel the need for liquid refreshment for himself. The little man had never been a drinker, but being the honorary Chinaman in 'Hickok' it seemed everyone wanted to see him drunk. Their wish is soon granted. Last seen before unconsciously hitting the floor, he had been attempting to play a violin that belonged to another of the revellers. Although falling on the instrument, it is luckily undamaged, as too the cook apparently. Any damage will almost certainly become apparent later in the morning when the diminutive Oriental becomes fully conscious.

Wild Bill Hickok had stayed and participated in the evening's celebrations. He had told Henry how honoured he was to have the town named after him and that he would visit as often as his travels and duties as a United States Deputy Marshal would allow. That promise would in the future be remembered, and a fateful one for the citizens of Hickok.

Joey had stood shamelessly in Hickok's vast shadow anytime he had caught up with his glass collecting, marvelling at the huge cultured dark brown set of whiskers and more than occasionally, eyeing the enormous, decorated handles of the Navy Colt's and huge Bowie knife. But soon Joey's eyes had begun to close while he was still in an upright position. Renee had seen his predicament and had, with the visiting Marshal's help, put the boy inside his blanket. Hickok had picked up and carried the already sleeping boy with no amount of effort required. Wild Bill had returned to the bar room and chatted amiably with David about law matters, with Henry about business matters and with Renee about anything she cared to mention. He had been the perfect gentleman but had quietly intimated that he would like to see her at some time in the future 'if it is possible, ma'am.'

Renee replied. "You'll be made welcome here Bill, any time, but don't come a courting as I have my heart set on another." Wild Bill easily accepted Renee's announcement and with good

47

grace. He added with a hint of mischief that he would shoot the favoured Beau, if he gave her any grief. Renee had told him that she would shoot him herself if such a thing occurred. Renee also told the Marshal that he could stay over for what was left of the night and the invitation was gladly accepted.

"I have to be movin' on come morning, got to go see an old friend, seems he might have a job for me."

"Marshalling?" David asks.

"No, acting, I'm to be in a damned sideshow! Colonel Cody, that's Buffalo Bill you know, wants me to join his travellin' show. I'm gonna think about it, though it seems to me that it ain't my kind of thing. All that fancy dressin' up and trick shootin' tame Indians and suchlike."

Henry had a hard time hiding the smile that attempted to seep from his lips. He hadn't been in America long, but from lounging cowboys he had heard snippets of tales of the legendary trick shooting and horse riding of this Lawman sitting opposite him, wearing a gaudy fringed buckskin coat, a wide gun-belt wrapped around the outside, the long trained whiskers and the flowing locks reaching almost past his pistols. It seemed to Henry, acting would be right up the Marshal's alley. Henry did not presume to voice his opinions. Although he had shown himself to be capable with a pistol, he was not about to tease and test Wild Bill Hickok about his colourful dress sense and exaggerated flamboyance.

Joey had awoken early the following morning, wide eyed awake, even after the long day and night that had preceded this morning. As soon as his eyes had opened, the memories flooded back. He took the newly completed stairs three at a time, bursting into the bar room with shouts of 'Where is he? Where is he? Is he gone already?'

He had not, Wild Bill is sitting and talking with Henry and David. He smiles at the other two men and summons the deepest voice he could muster. "Over here, son." Hickok had growled at the youngster.

"You're still here, he's still here!" Joey spoke to anyone who could hear him though everyone present already knew! Joey leant on the great man's shoulder as the long locks flowed down.

Renee appears from the cooking area. 'Tungsaw says to tell you breakfast is off. He's feeling head sore, serve him right. I'll make you something Bill, what would you like?"

"Just coffee for me girl, plenty of it, thanks, strong please, lady."

Henry and David had previously warned Wild Bill of Renee's unpredictable and limited cooking skills. Heeding the warning, the lawman had managed the refusal carefully and without giving offence. Renee had instructed an irate Tungsaw she would cook the lawman's breakfast She completed her task of making fresh coffee and joined the others, listening to the talk, occasionally asking questions of her own.

"I heard you're a friend to Calamity Jane*, Bill, is that right? What's she like?"

"Let me put it this way girl, Martha Jane's the one should be called Wild, and even that ain't nearly enough, I wouldn't say it in front of her mind, Calam' can be a mite feisty to put it mildly."

The group chattered for some while. Soon Gladstone appeared "Good morning, Mr Hickok, sir."

"A good morning to you Gladstone, bar open yet?"

"Oh no Mr Hickok, I was hoping you wouldn't ask me that."

"Don't you go frettin' none Gladstone, I always allow a bartender two refusals. Though it makes bartending a bit like Poker, don't you think?"

Gladstone ignored the comment. "Then what?"

* *Martha Jane Cannery (May 1, 1852 – August 1, 1903), better known as Calamity Jane, was an American frontierswoman. In addition to many exploits she was known for being an acquaintance of Wild Bill Hickok. Late in her life, she appeared in Buffalo Bill's Wild West show and at the 1901 Pan-American Exposition.*

"Then this!" The left hand Navy Colt appears as if by some magical means in the Deputy Marshal's hand. Joey's breath whooshes in and out again at the almost unseen hand movement. Henry, David and Renee too, marvel at the lightning fast draw as Hickok follows up the manoeuvre by spinning the pistol around his finger so fast it can hardly even be seen.

Gladstone is equally impressed. "That was real good, sir."

"It's what I call my early morning draw. Slow!" Hickok looked at the bewildered Gladstone. "Good to know ya' feller, you're one of the best." Wild Bill looked around the table and stood up. "Well folks, gotta go. I will be back first chance I get. I'm thanking ya'll for your generous hospitality. Adios!"

CHAPTER FOUR

Boys will be Men!

The evening visit of Hickok had been fortuitous in many ways. Not only had the lawman willingly given his name – though he did not seem to have a choice, his mind was very much made up for him - to the fledgling town, he had helped in a small way to give the inhabitants an even stronger sense of belonging to their community. The gathering in the saloon was only the second real occasion the villagers had all come together for a common interest and they could now build with hope from the set foundations that have slowly but surely begun to exist. The door had opened that evening as if fate had taken a hand in the fashioning of the little trackside settlement's future. It was a day that would stick inexorably in many memories.

It seemed as if Wild Bill Hickok had arrived in time to give a seal of approval. For now Hickok the man had departed. Hickok the town has arrived. Certainly the visit could not have been better timed.

With Gladstone willing and now able to keep the beer tap flowing, David is free to commence the work on the dividing wall for the restaurant, as well as other improvements, Joey again at his side. His conversation is littered incessantly with 'Wild Bill' this, 'Buffalo Bill' that. "Did you see the draw? I never seen anything like it, Davy."

"I can honestly say the same, Joey."

"I wonder why they call her Calamity Jane, Davy?"

"I've no idea Joey, but I guess the clue could be in her name."

David listens patiently to the boy's continued verbal meanderings. He did not know the answers to all or even half of the boy's questions, having only been a citizen of the United States for a matter of just a month. Though the boy is still some months short of becoming a teenager, David is surprised at the way he wants to be involved with all things leading to improvement regarding the town. David is also aware Joey is an eager work hand, proving his worth and pulling his still meagre weight with the fairly simple construction work. The fledgling town will need people like Joey to take it further forward one day. Joey's mother, Renee, has plans to secure their own future of what is becoming an eating house as well as a saloon; she wants tablecloths and a proper waitress to see to their customer's temporary needs.

The sparing but highly energetic musical entertainment on the night of the town naming had put forward another idea. Although the quality of sound and the musical abilities were not great, it was wholesome. Renee is certain she can to do something better for their customers, though right now, she did not know how it could be achieved. 'It would suit the ambience' Henry had opined. Although Renee did not understand what her partner meant, she had given a smiling approval to his short statement.

David had shown Renee his plans for the eating area. She was pleased with the way it might work. The original idea had been to just put in the divider. He further suggested small booths, giving diners just enough privacy, along one wall. 'It won't take a lot of effort' he promised. Henry too had given his blessing when he had been shown the well-drawn plan for the improvements.

"You do know what we have to do when we finish here, Joey!" The Welshman felt like teasing his young workmate a little bit.

"Yeah, I have to help you build the schoolhouse. Even worse, you all will make me go there every day when it's finished. I'd rather be taken prisoner by the Kiowa, it couldn't be worse." David admitted his ignorance of Native American tribes in general. Joey proceeded to 'educate' the Welshman as they worked. He had told that although the Kiowa were predominately wanderers of the Northern Texas Plains and a large part of the huge tract of land that made up the 'Indian Nations' a large area which would eventually become Oklahoma Territory, they were apt to venture further North from their Texan homelands into Kansas spasmodically. He added that to be in their vicinity in any of those places could be disastrous. 'You'd end up with a worse parting than Gladstone!' Joey had added, with a teasing smile.

"I'll do my best to keep my distance Joey, you can count on it!"

"Best you do Davy, best you do!" The boy spoke with some learned authority having overheard tales from passing cowboys and salesmen.

While David and Joey worked feverishly away on the restaurant improvements, Henry and Renee were attempting to put together plans for turning the so far unnamed saloon into a real Hotel. They knew their partner was capable of eventually bringing the plan to fruition, they also knew he would need the provision of extra help to achieve the required result. Once the restaurant and schoolhouse work was completed, they would hire someone from the town to provide further labour if and when required.

Henry, with David's expertise, had been able to compile an order for the required timber and glass and all the other items needed to complete the proposed work. He had taken the order to Jasper. As well as being the newly elected mayor, the owner of the hardware store had satisfied Henry that he would give it his earliest attention. Jasper Hawke is the only timber stockist for many miles and his own business is thriving so much more since the two men had arrived in town. They have been highly instrumental in the increases and Jasper will give them small but regular discounts now due to the extra trade he had received.

Henry, David and Renee had discussed suitable names for the establishment, but neither had so far come up with an agreeable title. The partners had also discussed Joey's endeavours and agreed the boy should ease off a little. 'The youngster should be enjoying himself at his age' Renee had said. Joey was informed. Rather reluctantly the boy had agreed that it 'might be fun to do other things, sometimes.' Joey decided this evening to venture away from 'home.'

It is not quite dusk as he kicks a rock along the centre of the uneven street that is Hickok's only real thoroughfare, all the time his mind still on the man who had willingly given his name to the settlement.

Joey pretends he is Wild Bill, all the time drawing and 'banging' as fast as he could, as he walked along the wide street. In his dream world, he does not see a buggy coming closer. Luckily for him the driver is alert and he swerves the vehicle around the wandering and wondering boy as his curses reverberate back to him.

The driver pulls the horses to a rump-grinding halt outside the door of the Way station owned by the blacksmith that had first given the initial inspiration to the building of the now ever growing community. The driver again curses up the street at Joey. Joey completely ignores the overweight, tobacco chewing man's curses. Bravely, the boy throws a curse or two back at him.

Something else soon caught Joey's attention. He turns towards the two passengers in time to avoid a stream of black-stained spit the driver has fired so cleverly and purposely at him but easily misses the boy due to his agility.

Stepping down from the open carriage's bench seat comes a slight woman, in her early to middle forties, Joey guesses. She is followed by a youth, Joey thinks is around the same age as he, perhaps a year or so older but not by much. Joey retraces his steps a short distance until he can see easier. The lad's face is awkward looking, he thought, even ugly. Joey ambles closer. The gawky boy notices Joey's part innocent interest.

"Who're you looking at, kid?"

"What's it to ya?" Joey answers with an unusual sharpness. "You looking for a fight, I'll give ya your needin's. Just say the word!" The other kid's mother has already disappeared from the street, having stepped into the Way station to freshen up and take whatever food might be on offer before she and the boy would embark on the next section of their journey to Silver City, New Mexico.

The ugly adolescent attempts to blow out his scrawny chest and walks towards Joey. "Get to it kid. I'll shut your damn mouth for ya!"

With small, clenched fists on both sides the boys meet. Instead of the expected punches each grabs a handful of the others clothing; they fall, tumbling and rolling, one on top, then the other and so on, all the time spitting manly curses at each other. Fighting continues for many minutes with little sign of a winner.

With the mother inside the station 'powdering her nose' the driver engages in filling his already large stomach and so there is no one to stop the battle, that is until Mrs Hawke spots the melee. She steps forward determined to bring the street fight to a halt.

"You boys! Stop that now, stop that at once, do you hear me? Joey, is that you? Well I never!" Mrs Hawke stretches out a hand to pull Joey away from his opponent. The stage boy stops and glares at the well-meaning woman holding Joey's and his opponents shoulders tightly in an attempt to keep them apart.

"Get your 'ands off, you old bag" the boy yells at her with a broken, but distinct voice that has it's accent possibly from the Irish quarter of New York slums situated in lower Manhattan.

It is unfortunate for the boy traveller, just as he is about to turn towards his new antagonist, Joey has clenched a perfect fist; he swings it at the other with all his might and the knuckles meet with the boys teeth perfectly. Joey yells with pain as the teeth cut into his knuckles. The stage boy instantly falls backwards with the impact of the punch.

Joey hides his damaged hand under an armpit, hoping the throbbing would soon disappear. The stage boy gets to his feet. Mrs Hawke holds an arm with each of her hands and shakes the boys until their struggling ceases, though not immediately did they give up on their manly curses.

"Now then, what's all this about, why are you fighting with this boy? What's your name, lad?" she asked of the elder protagonist with some authority.

The boy fingered his newly crooked teeth. Blood showed on his fingers. "Mind your own business you old bitch!" The recently shifted teeth making the boy look even more repulsive than he had previously.

Mrs Hawke shook the lad again. Once more she asked his name. "Henry, Henry McCarty, you satisfied now old woman?"

The boy, Billy*, glared at Joey again. He sneered, "Next time I see you, I'll kill ya. Best you remember me boy cos one of these days, I'll be famous, I'll make you famous too when you're fucking dead!"

---

* Billy the Kid (born Henry McCarty; September 17 or November 23, 1859 – July 14, 1881) McCarty was orphaned at the age of 15. His first arrest was for stealing food, at the age of 16, in late 1875. Ten days later, he robbed a Chinese laundry and was again arrested, but escaped shortly afterwards. He fled from New Mexico Territory into neighbouring Arizona Territory, making him both an outlaw and a federal fugitive. In 1877, McCarty began to refer to himself as 'William H. Bonney' Two different versions of a wanted poster date September 23, 1875, refer to him as "Wm. Wright also known as Billy the Kid!' Sheriff Pat Garrett shot Henry McCarty, popularly known as Billy the Kid, to death at Pete Maxwell's Ranch near Fort Sumner, New Mexico. Garrett, who had been tracking the Kid for three months after the gunslinger had escaped from prison only days before his scheduled execution at Lincoln, New Mexico, got a tip that Billy was holed up with friends. While Billy was gone, Garrett waited in the dark in his bedroom. When Billy entered the room, Garrett shot and kicked him.

The gangly youth pulled away from Mrs Hawke. Rubbing gingerly at his swelling lips, he slunk off toward the station to search for the absent parent and seek some attention.

On deciding to leave the notorious Five Points area of Lower Manhattan, the mother had decided the fifteen-year-old Henry McCarty needed to grow up in a place with streets less violent than those of the place of his birth. She will have her work cut out!

Silver City, New Mexico might improve the kid's demeanour, she had decided. She could never have known that place would be the venue for the first of her teenage son's killings — that he would kill again in Arizona Territory even before his nineteenth birthday. She wouldn't know either the boy would himself eventually be the victim of death in cold blood, a victim of assassination by one-time friend and lawman, Pat Garrett.

Joey decided he'd seen enough of the outside for one day. Making his way back to the saloon he went in search of the still toiling David. Finding the Welshman hard at work Joey took up where he had left off, running and fetching, though the usual look of easy going cheerfulness was now absent.

David could see something was troubling Joey. "What's the matter, lad?" he asked after some silent minutes had passed.

The boy is at first quite reluctant to explain why his clothes are dishevelled and grubby. Neither did he realise his face had been marked in the short but lively bout in the street.

"You have been fighting, boy."

Joey mumbles a reply that David hardly understands but he is certain his assumption is correct. It wasn't the first time Joey had engaged in a street fight. Though it come as a surprise to him that it had occurred, he had not been physically hurt, apart from the grazed knuckles. The fight had upset him. He had made the decision to become involved without much thought to any consequences that might occur, self-preservation being a pre-requisite of his era.

"Yes sir, Davy, I been fighting, I didn't start it, some boy who came into town on a buckboard, he bad mouthed me and then Mrs Hawke. We got to scrapping. I shifted his teeth for him some. Henry McCarty won't forget me in a hurry. Mrs Hawke stopped the fight. The kid had had enough anyway, I reckon. Said he'd kill me next time we meet."

David ruffled Joey's hair as he passed on some well-intentioned advice to the youngster. "We all say things we don't mean when we get riled, Joey. You should forget all about it. McCarty eh?"

"Sure Davy, guess you're right. I never was one for fighting mind."

David and Joey could never know if McCarty would hold a grudge for the beating the facial alterations he received. Knowing for himself that he was no oil painting, he now knows his features have been permanently altered by Joey's determination and his small but well directed fist. Possibly even now, while sitting next to his mother in the stage bound for Silver City, he might begin to plan revenge, maybe swear an oath to return to return to Hickok some day and carry out the spoken threat.

Henry McCarty would be described, perhaps wrongly, as a simpleton by some. A loyal friend to few but by most, a psychopathic killer. A killer with a very long memory, a killer of anyone unfortunate enough to cross him.

Renee brought supper for the two, they didn't need to be told twice to take a break. Renee didn't notice the difference in her son's appearance, she would assume incorrectly that the lifting and carrying of materials caused the boy's untidy state. Renee had suggested as the hour was getting late the two should call a halt soon. The saloon is filling. 'Customers would not want to be bothered by 'banging and crashing' she told them. David promised he and Joey would continue for just another hour with their task. 'Then we'll call it a day.'

Henry is already coaxing the gambling fraternity into their now nightly rituals. Gladstone is at his post behind the bar. Renee takes her recently acquired smile from one table to another, satisfied that this would be another busy evening for the saloon. She still cannot get over what happened just a handful of weeks ago, how Henry and David had arrived and changed her life around completely.

Henry called across to Renee to come and sit with him at a vacant table. She excused herself from her latest conversation and walked towards her partner's table. Henry pulled out a chair for her.

"Seems to me there is something you haven't told me, Renee. Now, maybe I'm speaking out of turn here, you can say so whenever you want. Some of the ranch hands have been telling me about the side lines the rat had going here." Henry did know what she had had to endure previously and wanted to broach the subject once and for all.

Renee looked at Henry with instant guilt in her eyes. She knew what side line Henry was suggesting. It was a secret that she hoped would stay hidden from him but was certain it would come out some time. She sipped at her beer, staying silent until Henry had finished his quiet speech.

"I didn't have any choice Henry, what could I do? We were like prisoners to that bastard. I thought about doing away with myself. If it hadn't been for my Joey, I would have done it too. Joey needed me, Jack knew that. I had to go along with him, there was nothing much else I could do!"

"Renee wait, I'm not pointing an accusing finger, you have the wrong end of the stick here." Renee gave Henry a quizzical look. "I've been around girl, I know what these fellers need. It was hardly any different in Redruth and Bodmin, back where I come from. I'm sorry if my bringing the subject up has upset you, it was not my intention. There won't be any more of that while I'm here mind and I'm going nowhere."

Renee smiled weakly at the suddenly embarrassed Cornishman, realising that he was worried he might have spoken out of turn towards her. She quickly put his mind to rest. She accepted and brushed off his apology and the two talked of other, less delicate subjects. Henry would never again raise the subject of Jack's use of Renee as a prostitute after that night.

Joey had retired to his bed early, he was still unhappy about the fight with the McCarty kid, it bothered him. Although Joey had never been one to look for trouble previously, he had been involved in similar scraps before. This one was unprovoked and had happened so quickly he hadn't had time to think about it. Thinking a good night's sleep would help, he told his mother that he would see her in the morning. After washing himself with the refreshingly cold water poured from the jug in his room, Joey is soon beneath his blanket. The sound of raucous drinkers and his still throbbing knuckles did nothing to stop the boy from quickly falling asleep, the fight forgotten for a few hours.

David, having completed his day's work, had also washed. He put on a change of clothes and had left the saloon. He had taken it on himself to use a late hour of each evening to walk the main street of Hickok, checking locks in shop doorways and looking down darkened alleyways, more importantly to see late strollers got home safely. Turning out of the saloon, David walked to the very edge of town. Stopping, he looked out across the huge grasslands. Nothing stirred here, no sounds returned from the grassy emerald sea. David turned and crossed to the opposite side of the dusty uneven road and walked to the end of the plank sidewalk that is still not complete in places. The Marshal is pleased the town is quiet, it seems to him that anyone that might be still about would probably be in the saloon that he now shared with Renee and Henry, not forgetting the sleeping Joey.

The Town Marshal walked slowly back. He could hear the shouts of revellers. Entering the saloon he could see everything is running smoothly. Gladstone is in command behind the bar, Henry is engaged in conversation with Renee and he is quite certain Joey is now asleep. Everything is as it should be, David thought to himself as he approached the table his friends are sitting and relaxing at.

"Sit yourself down Davy, I'll get you a beer." Henry crossed to the bar and informed Gladstone of his order, waiting patiently while the ex-barfly poured the requested drink.

Henry returned to the table. "Gladstone has just given us an idea. He thinks we need a piano, it'd be a quick and simple way of getting some musical entertainment in here, don't you think? Maybe not simple but useful to the business."

Both Renee and David think this to be a worthwhile plan. "Best way if you ask me, is if Davy and I go fetch an instrument from Independence or Fort Dodge or maybe Hays City. If we take a flatbed, we should be able to bring one back. Take a week at least, maybe longer to get there and back. Obviously it'll take us longer to get back than it will to go. Well?"

"It works well for me, Henry."

"Me too, well done, Gladstone." Renee shouted her appreciation across to the beaming barman.

The three carried on their discussion of acquiring the musical instrument, certain that the acquisition would benefit the saloon's customers and of course the takings. "Gladstone, Joey and me can easily hold this place down while you are away. I think you two ought to go at the end of the week, the sooner the better. Don't forget you have to make a start on that schoolhouse soon, Davy." Renee had thought it all out.

"I have been thinking about that, Renee. Did you know that you can buy a whole schoolhouse? They can be found in some catalogues. I was thinking that maybe we could make a donation towards the purchase, perhaps Jasper, Jakey the new blacksmith, any of the businesses in town could put a little towards the cost. The mail order people will ship it out here, we have the railroad at our doorstep. All we'd have to do is put the sections together once they arrive here. It will be easier for everyone, no doubt about it."

"I'll speak to Jasper. No better still Davy, you talk to him, see how the land lies. What do you say, Renee?"

"I say talk to Jasper, Davy."

"I will, first thing. Time for me to help Gladstone with this bunch." David could see by the condition of most of the remaining customers it is nearing closing time.

"One more me boyyos, then it's time to find your home and beds." David passed behind the planks to help the barman to serve up the last rounds of drinks of the night. Apart from the occasional small disagreement, the saloon's clientele are mostly trouble free. Often noisy but not really troublesome. David's task of sending them on their way is one of ease.

Renee sits quietly thinking about the piano. Suddenly, another thought crosses her mind. "What about The Plainsman?"

Henry placed the small pile of notes next to the stacks of silver coins that were the evidence of another night's brisk business. He looked with some admiration at the woman who had made the sudden statement. "It has a fine ring to it Renee, 'The Plainsman' gets my vote."

Henry guessed correctly Renee is suggesting a name for their now flourishing enterprise. He liked the sound of it. Henry knew too that Wild Bill Hickok has been what is commonly known as a Plainsman, having worked as a Buffalo hunter and food provider for the railroad construction gangs. Also well known as an Indian fighter and lawman and an army scout. Henry knew there were others, the already famed Buffalo Bill Cody held the same honorary title. "We'll ask Davy when he's done, yes it has a ring to it, I like it." Henry emptied his glass, returning to the bar for replacements for himself, Renee and David, now that the last of the local drinkers had departed.

Only the four were left in the saloon. Gladstone, after having one solitary beer, was soon disappearing to his own quarters. The partners could complete their discussion in complete privacy now.

"Renee has something to put to you, Davy. She has come up with a useful name for this place, I think you'll agree!"

"Well now, let's be hearing from you Renee, what's it to be my girl?"

Renee couldn't wait to impart the information to the impatient Welshman. "The Plainsman'. What do you think, Davy? Well?" She waited impatiently for the Welshman's reply. It was soon in coming.

"What do I think! Well I think it's a capital idea, I like it, perfect. I couldn't have thought of anything better, I'm all for it."

That night, the three partners drank their first toast to the birth of The Plainsman.

It was also agreed between them that David and Henry would leave for Independence 'the day after tomorrow.' If that bustling metropolis could not furnish the required instrument, the two would redirect to Fort Dodge or Hays City in the hope they would find what they required there. If not, they would search elsewhere until they found the required piece.

The scruffy black cat which belonged to Tungsaw leapt silently onto the table, stretching out, licking and cleaning the street dust from its coat and all the while purring intensely. Tungsaw's pet feline's vocal contentment seeming to signal its own acceptance of the late night christening of his adopted home.

CHAPTER FIVE
Musical Chairs

enry clucks and whistles shrilly to get the horses into their forward movement. The two impatient mares, raring to go, tug hard and the flatbed pulls away easily from Jakey's corral. Davy sits beside the driver. The two have already agreed to interchange during their journey. Various people in the town had offered directions and the two travellers did not think they would need to worry about being lost in their quest to reach the city of Independence, Missouri, though many miles separate the two from their destination.

The rig had been hired from the genial Jakey, the blacksmith, who had charged them the minimum hire fee once he knew the reason for their quest. The rig is showing its age but it should be sturdy enough and would suit the purpose it has been rented for. Henry and Jakey had agreed the price of three dollars a week for the rental of the buck-board, a small price to pay. The journey could take at least a week and a half they were advised by Gladstone. He had told the partners ten days should be ample time for the whole journey providing they did not dally in the saloons of Dodge City. He had given further detailed directions for them to meet with 'The Old Santa Fe Trail.' 'After that, just follow your noses if they happen to be pointing North' the now regularly sober man had advised his bosses.

It would be a forty-mile ride from Hickok to join up with the already ancient highway, which since the Civil War, had witnessed the movement north from Texas of the masses of Longhorn cattle that would pass before the decade is out and will continue once the population had been culled to a manageable number for whatever ranches and ranchers are able to continue with their pre-war trades.

The two would just about cover the required distance on the first day, thought Henry hopefully. 'Look out for the Comanche' they had been warned as they pulled away from Hickok's broad and so far still unnamed main street.

The ancient wheel-rutted trail had been opened for use in eighteen twenty-one as a trading route between the United States and Mexico, which then extended much further north towards the rail-heads of Kansas. The whole route from the East to Santa Fe had originally covered eight hundred miles. Extensions were eventually made to take travellers even further; one branch leading on to San Diego and Los Angeles in California, another that bore the name 'Gila River Trail' leads through to New Mexico and on to Arizona. Both routes would also become sodden with traffic during the early gold rush years. The ancient wheel ruts would forever remain as a permanent testament to the 'Westward' procession of covered wagons and the pioneers who manned them. Many gravesites of travellers who were not strong enough to complete their journey can be seen to litter the trail side.

The two friends had made an early start. They'd risen before dawn and were travelling briskly within an hour. Renee had packed food for the two that should last for at least half of their journey. Davy had taken the precaution of bringing the various weapons he and Henry had acquired since their arrival in Kansas.

'Might do a little hunting along the trail if we get us the chance' he had told Renee. Davy had been handed an almost new, Sharpe's hunting rifle from the mayor's hardware store. The weapon possessed a range varying around a quarter mile distant, allowing for windage. One direct head shot on a Buffalo at that distance would bring it down instantly. A fully grown male Buffalo can weigh between fifteen hundred and eighteen hundred pounds.

Mayor Hawke had agreed to carry out David's duties as Town Marshall while the Welshman is away. The pair headed north, a direction which would take them close to old Fort Dodge. There they would be on to the old Trail and be moving easterly towards the village of Council Grove, where the massively wide main street will regularly echo to the sound of hundreds, even thousands of jostling Longhorn cattle, and onward to Independence.

The friends would attempt to purchase the piano at Independence. The bustling township was recognised as the starting point for thousands of settlers that had joined wagon trains in readiness for the long and arduous trek west to California, dreaming of riches from the Goldfields. At various times, Henry and Davy met and passed stragglers from these trains. They waved and called greetings, as did the already weary looking migrants, fatigued mostly but cheerful. Some were going in the opposite direction after failing in their personal quests for distant riches.

Most of these people joined a train for the benefit of safety, others because they knew they could not complete the journey without expert and professional help. Hardly any of them would realise the hardships that might befall them. Many were lucky, unfortunately not all.*

Along the Santa Fe Trail, The Gila River and other lesser known routes, attacks from the Kiowa, Comanche and other of the plains tribes pose a danger. Accidental firearm discharges another. Plain old-fashioned shootings or knifings, natural

* *The Donner Party (sometimes called the Donner–Reed Party) was a group of American pioneers who migrated to California in a wagon train from the Midwest. Delayed by a multitude of mishaps, they spent the winter of 1846–1847 snowbound in the Sierra Nevada mountain range. Some of the migrants resorted to cannibalism to survive, eating the bodies of those who had already succumbed to starvation along the route. The 'Donner Pass' lies within Tahoe National Forest, and the Donner Memorial State Park is nearby.*

causes even death in childbirth and disease. Starvation too might hang like a hungry vulture over the shoulders of the moving masses. Although Henry and David had made the journey West in somewhat easier circumstances, they could hardly guess what life was like for these people who might travel as far as two thousand miles in this way.

David had taken the reins from Henry now. They didn't halt until Fort Dodge was reached in the middle of the first afternoon. Here at the fort the two bought biscuits and replenished their water supply, without actually entering the confines of the quickly expanding town that had grown around the old fort, the adjacent trading post being the provider of their extra supplies.

The ride had been dusty and dry. Where the trail was over soft ground, the wheels of so many wagons had ground the earth to dust, which was at times unbearable. They had taken on fresh liquid wherever they found it available.

Where the road went over harder terrain, their wheels would slip into ruts formed by the hundreds of previous wagons that had passed along their intended route. In late afternoon the two men stopped. They agreed to make a night camp. Once they had a small but adequate fire burning there was bacon to cook, coffee to prepare. The two men drank several cups each before spreading blankets over the back of the flatbed. Conversation had been intermittent between them while on the road. They took the opportunity now, talking long into the night.

David had brought up the subject of boxing again. He hoped there might be opportunities when he could take up where he had left off in the back streets of Cardiff. He had beaten all comers in his native town and had gained much respect and a reputation as a heavyweight. Henry had promised that once they returned to Hickok and had completed the urgent tasks they had in hand 'we could get to organising a bout or two perhaps.'

The next morning the two arose early and once again skirting Fort Dodge, they would re-join the Old Santa Fe trail in the north easterly direction they required, which would put them on a direct route to Independence. It could take them two, three or four more days to reach this destination. Henry and David knew there was a possibility they might have to return and search the Fort for the required instrument if one couldn't be found in Independence. They had all the time they needed to achieve their goal and had agreed to make the longer journey first, hoping they would not need to detour to the old fort.

At the now newly named Plainsman, Renee is keeping everything running smoothly. The first evening without the help of her partners was completed without mishap. Business had been steady. Joey had taken over the role of waiter and had Trojan-like, given Maria, the newly employed waitress, his support. This allowed Renee to help behind the rough planks when needed. Tungsaw, knowing that it was a difficult time for his employer, created none of his theatrical tantrums, putting all of his efforts into providing good food for passing cowboys, Drummers* and townsfolk alike.

Maria, of Mexican origin, had been interviewed and employed the day before the two men had left for Independence. The girl worked hard. She had her own small quarters in a Hickok side street shanty. Renee had heard rumours she had previously followed a calling of a different, more earthy nature when she wasn't on duty at the saloon she had worked at before arriving in Hickok. She made a mental note to talk to her about this at some quiet time, in what she hoped would not seem a too hypocritical way. Renee knew of course, she should be careful in her friendly warning. Maria, like most of her ilk, was dark haired and pretty and only in

* Traveling drummers, salesmen or peddlers provided goods and services for folks living on farms in rural or frontier areas that didn't have easy access to town. salesmen packed their wagons with everything ranging from scissors, pots and pans to medicine, books and clothing and various other useful necessities.

her very early twenties, Renee thought. She might be a useful acquisition to her forthcoming restaurant plans; customers took to Maria. With the large amount of tips she got for her table service and the small, but adequate wage she was given by Renee, Maria fared rather well financially. She was thoughtful enough to share some of her tips with Joey each evening just a few cents each night that Joey carefully hid away. The boy, for obvious reasons, isn't quite as popular as Maria. Renee had noticed how Maria managed to leave every evening with one man or another. She was certain the girl would still be carrying on her trade. Renee isn't unhappy with the arrangement as long as the girl did not try to improve her 'business' by touting while on duty inside the saloon. This was something she would not approve of!

The third evening of Henry and David's absence would see the relative peace of the saloon shattered. After a long and arduous day in and out of the saddle, Richie Stark sat down to eat. Already he had consumed a large amount of beer and now he is determined to fill any vacant space left with hot food. Employed locally as a ranch hand, the day had been a tough one for Richie; chasing and roping rope-shy young cows in readiness for their branding was demanding work and just keeping one's body away from their rock hard hooves was a job in itself. Richie had been kicked many times by four hoofed animals of all kinds, and sizes. He was in a fractious mood and in a hurry to fill his already oversized belly and afterwards, wash the food down with even more measures of beer, chased by whiskey. His mood might change once he had placated his stomach. It was unfortunate the feline inhabitant of the saloon would have the nerve to want to share, perhaps even to snatch away Richie's supper completely.

Joey had delivered the steaming plateful. Richie is looking at it with relish. He reached to pull the Bowie knife from its sheaf attached to his belt at the rear. It is Richie's habit to use his own cutlery especially when a steak is on the plate, or a grilled pork chop as is the case this time.

The black moggy saw this move as an invitation to help the cowhand clear the plate. The cat was on the table in the blinking of an eye, claws protruding. It caught the hot meat at the first attempt. 'Cooking Fat' saw nothing wrong with his actions and more than once he had got away with the same manoeuvre in the kitchen.

Richie turned as the piece of pork was disappearing quickly over the side of the table. That same table was soon lifting skyward with the remainder of its contents before it returned to the floor again where it suddenly became firewood. Although David had repaired most of the furniture in the establishment, he hadn't, in reinforcing the tables, allowed for vertical take offs and landings, such as this one had been subjected to. The table disintegrated with its impact, the remainder of Richie's supper now decorating the broken slithers.

Richie is on his feet fast. The Bowie knife in hand, he is determined to retrieve the chop with the possibility of taking away one of the nine lives remaining for the cat in the process. Starch shot forward when seeing the cat disappear under a corner table. The now irate cowboy had not allowed for the downward moving objects; his feet caught in the raining 'firewood' and food remnants and his impetus sends him sprawling into a corner table.

Tungsaw had been cooking supper for Broadbent almost every night recently and had become familiar with the foreman. Each night when he arrived, the cook would call out the same greeting 'Ah Soul!' The other hands had been informed and Broadbent had a first name he really wasn't happy with. Few others would copy the cook and would only refer to the term amongst themselves. Soul Broadbent had never quite realised the implications of Tungsaw's now regular greeting, due to the Oriental accent.

Richie's head collided with Broadbent's backside and the two could be forgiven for almost becoming one. Another table became firewood, a second meal becomes mobile.

Broadbent swears, Richie swears, Joey laughs. Renee stares and Gladstone, who has watched the whole incident, keeps his face as straight as he possibly can under the circumstances and continues to pour beer to other waiting customers. The rest of the bar's occupants are unable to conceal their raucous laughter and it fills the already coloured air.

"Arsehole!" Richie states with a peculiar innocence.

Without warning, Broadbent, in suddenly realising the implication of the acquired addition to his Christian name, pulls back his right arm from the shoulder. Powering forward, the knuckles connect with Richie's nose. The noisy impact of bone on cartilage is sickening, though not sickening enough to stop other diners from continuing their meals. "There ain't no need to call me that, boy!"

Soul Broadbent looked down at the now unconscious, supine Richie. He turns back to the remains of the table with the hope of continuing to eat but another problem appears for Broadbent; his meal is still mobile. He watches as it slides in a downward direction. Broadbent sees the cat snatch the pork chop again and pulling his six-shooter, begins firing at the table, at the wall and lastly at the cat. Soul Broadbent is well known to be erratic when employing a weapon.

The animal is too quick for Broadbent. The shooting had now caught the full attention of Tungsaw. He looks around the curtained doorway of the kitchen and seeing the ranch foreman trying to kill his only real friend, incensed the little chef. The little Oriental is grabbing a cleaver and is instantly homing in on the shootist with the weapon held high.

"You shoot cat, I chop off hand and feed to cat. You won't be able to wipe arsehole!"

Soul Broadbent admitted to himself that the only chop he was interested in was of the porcine variety. He holstered his weapon on seeing the now highly excited and threatening Tungsaw, his threats making him nervous.

"Okay, okay, don't overdo it feller, I was jest tryin' to rescue my damn supper."

Renee thought now to be a good time to intervene. She glares around the highly animated room, the look serves its purpose and the laughter subsides as quickly as it had started.

"Now Soul, find another chair and Tungsaw will get you another chop. Somebody had better take Richie outside, there's a trough out there. He needs dipping!"

Richie isn't yet ready to regain consciousness.

Renee didn't want any more fighting and there was no telling what kind of mood the obese cowboy would be in when he did regain his full faculties and realises the recent damage to his face.

Two other ranch hands pick one end of Richie each and although they struggle to carry the big cowboy outside, they manage and taking Renee's advice, drop their load straight into the trough. They are both strong, but with Richie's extra weight they would take the first opportunity to relieve themselves of their burden. Neither man would foresee the eventual complications arising from their simple and largely innocent actions.

Cold water quickly helps Richie come around and he is understandably not happy. The two cowhands had re-entered the bar without looking back on him. On his revival, the fat and still hungry cowboy began to struggle to get himself out of the horse trough. It seemed it was not going to happen; Richie's hands had been caught behind his back when being dropped in the water, his ample waist had jammed him in the tough wooden container. Richie found himself to be almost completely immovable. He could move his hands, but that was of no use, as he couldn't move his submerged forearms. Richie is hurting, his nose is splattered and throbbing with pain. The water might have helped to dull the throbbing. His problem is that the liquid is only covering Richie's legs, shoulders and immense belly, there is no way of getting some of it onto his face. "Son of a bitch!" Richie yelled at anyone who might be able to hear him. "Get me outta here!" No one came. He thought about the pistol and realised it was useless now to get any attention as he can't reach that either.

Soul Broadbent sat at another table and for the second time he began his supper. The other hands continued their drinking now the excitement had ceased. Renee, Maria and Joey cleaned up the discarded meal as best they could. "What we don't get done tonight, we'll do tomorrow" Renee suggested as the cause of the fracas returned to see if he'd missed any of the now disjointed meal. Tungsaw, having completed his cooking duties, is in the process of cleaning up the kitchen. The chef looked at the now satisfied moggy. "You cooking fat, you cause big trouble for that arsehole." The moggy seemed to look at its benefactor with complete understanding. Tungsaw continued with his duties, a wry smile creasing the old man's face as he talked to his little friend.

The ever present noise of the bar still hides the shouts of the sodden man; he has managed to move slightly, but the movement only allowed further settlement into the trough. Richie Starch is helpless.

The streets are mostly empty as usual at this time of the evening. Nobody could have realised the cowboy's predicament, not even he. Richie tries to relax in the hope it would allow him to squirm out of his dilemma. Everything Richie did seemed to sink him further down into the water. The stricken cowboy notices the first flashes of lightning, he looks towards the end of the street. He counts the seconds between the flashes and the steadily creeping thunder. 'Twenty!' Another flash 'eighteen' 'fifteen and ten.'

Richie, being stuck in his position, entertains himself in this way for a minute or two. The storm is building momentum, lightning becomes almost instantaneous with the thunder and vice versa. Richie loses count, now he can no longer keep up.

A portcullis of vivid electricity descends on Hickok. The thunder brings Richie another problem - a headache. He is desperate to get out of this 'damn coffin.' He decides it is time to start shouting to his friends inside again but still nobody comes to help him. Not one could hear the yells of the stuck man over the sky born cannonade. Richie Stark is becoming hoarse. He stops again, thinking to himself 'if it rains, I'll be able to float up and out of this damn tree.' Richie becomes quiet at the thought, praying patiently for the welcome rain. He has no choice but to wait for nature to allow his release.

Inside, Broadbent is engaged in letting Maria know he still has some money in his pocket, making it obvious to her that he is happy to negotiate how to part with more of it.

Maria isn't impressed, she doesn't much like the stocky foreman at all. Luckily for her, Renee has asked the waitress to stay behind for a while that night. 'We'll have a drink and a yarn if you have the time' she suggested.

The ranch hands begin leaving. The two who had taken out Richie were at their liquid limit and they stumbled past the trough without giving him a second thought. However, Soul Broadbent does look in at Richie.

"Iffen you behave yourself good, I'll send someone out here to get you outta there in the morning" he slurred. Broadbent walks to where his horse is tethered and climbs aboard just as heavy spots of rain start to pepper Richie. His curses towards the ranch foreman are soon lost in the sound of the cascading liquid and the crashing heaven sent crescendo the spots had now become.

"You son of a bitch, I'll be outta here before morning!" Richie stated at the retreating man. "I'll shoot your goddam eyes out, you wait and see iffen I don't, arsehole!"

Broadbent did not hear the threat as the thunder and lightning were now almost one. The drops getting bigger, harder!

Won't be long now, Richie thought almost cheerfully, although he is stiffening with the coldness of the rising water. The rain suddenly becomes a torrent, the street is already flooding. It's hard to differentiate the street from the creek. Soon water is pouring into the trough from another source. David, when putting on the new roof had allowed some guttering to take away any liquid, and save the excess in the trough. The guttering had a down spout that emptied straight into the trough. Richie waits nervously now for his redemption.

Renee pours Maria and herself a beer. They take their glasses to one of the surviving tables and sit down. Gladstone continues to tidy the bar area. When his task is complete, he shouts a goodnight to the two women and disappears into the back of the building to await well-earned sleep.

Renee and Maria send him on his way with teasing blown kisses.

Joey had come over to the table and kissed his mother goodnight. He too had gone in more or less the same direction as Gladstone.

Renee explains some of future her plans to Maria. The girl listens carefully to the admissions, nodding occasionally.

The thunder continues to crash as if it is above the very building now and pounding on the newly completed roof. Renee walked towards the bar and having poured two more beers, she walked back to sit with Maria once more.

As the rain beats down heavier, the two have trouble to keep their conversation going. At times they have to wait until the thunder clap passes before asking or answering a question. The disjointed conversation went on until the rain and the thunder began to fade into the distance, taking the storm towards Northern Texas.

Maria decides it is time for her to return home. Renee walks to the door with the waitress and she locks it as the girl walks on her way.

Instant screams bring Renee back to the door. She carries the last remaining lighted lantern with her. Renee unlocks and quickly pulls open the door, she knew it was Maria that had screamed her name and worries she may have been accosted.

She peers outside. "Whatever's the matter, Maria? Are you hurt? What's happened?"

"Not me, Miss Renee, it's poor Starchy Stark, he's a stiffy now. I think he might have drowned, looks like. He came floating up as I walked past the trough."

"Oh my god, poor man."

Some days later, Henry and David pull the wagon into its destination. It seems that half of the population of Independence is on the street at their arrival. After stabling the horses and paying the stable hand, the two walk out onto the main street. It is late, they will find a room and sleep off the rigours of their gruelling journey.

After searching for more than an hour and finding no available rooms, the two journeymen return to the livery stable and secure a deal which will allow them to spread their blankets on the flatbed which is now inside the large building. Eventually the town quietens and the two are able to get well deserved unbroken sleep.

The pair again wake early. After washing in cold water supplied by the livery hand, they go in search of a hot breakfast. The two friends soon find what they are looking for. While they are eating they ask the waitress questions as to where they might find the special piece of furniture they require. She is unable to help at first, but tells them she would speak with the owner of the eating house.

The girl keeps her word and within minutes she has the information required. She gives rough directions to the hardware establishment that should have the required instrument in its stock room. Henry and David thank the helpful waitress and show their appreciation by leaving her a generous tip at the table before departing.

The main street has begun to come alive now. The friends make their way slowly along the sidewalk; they are in no immediate hurry now their stomachs are full of good fresh pancakes and decent coffee. Aches and pains have retreated since their long rest. They cross two of Independence's side streets and cover more of the sidewalk before reaching the named store. Luck is with the friends as they approach the double doors, the proprietor is at this very moment unlocking his premises for business. Henry and David wait for the owner to complete his task before entering fully.

"What can I do for you folks?" The suited man asks.

"We're here to find ourselves a piano." David answers. "Can you help?"

"Got just the one friend, it won't come cheap mind, it is a quality instrument."

"Well perhaps we might talk about the price when we see what you have." Henry intervened.

The store owner beckons the two men into a rear section of the shop and points to the piece the owner had begun to discuss.

Henry looks at David. "I'd say that will do us just fine. What do you think, Davy? Is it all tuned up, mister?" He asks the second question of the piano's owner.

David nods as the salesman confirms the piano is indeed all tuned up 'like new, sir' had come the honest reply.

Henry lifted the heavy lid and ran his inexperienced fingers along the creamy hued ivory keys.

"How much, friend?'

"Can't let it go for less than three hundred dollars, sir."

"Then we can't have it, can we Davy!" Henry purposefully avoids the salesman's eyes as he speaks.

"It's a great shame but we have to go home empty handed, unless we can find us one in Kansas City."

David had quickly caught on to Henry's line. "We came all this way too, it's a big disappointment, Henry. I've never been to Kansas City."

"Neither of us have, Davy. Biggest place I ever went was Plymouth and I never will return there!"

"Maybe I can take a little off the price."

"We can only pay two forty, that's our limit, it's all we have."

"Then you have yourselves a piano friends only don't you be letting on to others that I have a soft heart."

"Consider it part of the deal, we won't say a word." Henry took out the exact amount from an inside pocket and handed it over. "May we collect our item later in the day?' He asks gleefully but hidden to view how pleased he is while accepting the written receipt.

"Certainly! You have the means to carry her away?"

"Yes boyyo, don't you be worrying about that, we'll get it out of here easily enough. Why 'her?"

"Simple my friend, pianos are noisy and cantankerous individuals. They must be female!"

"Yes they are, I guess you're right at that." The three share the laughter as well as the joke aimed at womanhood in general. A safe enough comment as there are none within hearing distance.

The salesman promises there would be other available help to lift the piano onto their wagon, when the two return.

Henry and David thank the man and leave the shop in a cheerful mood after getting the discount.

They and Renee had agreed before their departure that they could spend three hundred dollars on the required article. They had come out of the shop with the spare sixty dollars. The deal had been done with both sides apparently satisfied and happy at the outcome.

All that is left now is to get the piano back to Hickok. David and Henry spend the intervening time exploring the town, which in mid-morning, was now a hive of activity. Wagons are being loaded and unloaded at every turn, men constantly shout and yell orders everywhere.

Henry and David can see an actual wagon train is in preparation for a noisy departure. More wagons are joining the line even as they stand watching. The wagons so full of furniture items and personal possessions, it seems the contents might spill out at the first bump in the road.

"Might be an idea to follow these people when they leave, Davy. We might be lucky enough to pick up a few things along the road." Henry half-jokingly suggests to his friend.

"You have an eye for a bargain Henry, I'll say that for you."

"There's no better bargain than something that's free my friend."

The two men walk on for a time until Henry suddenly stops. "Over there Davy, it's Mister Hickok."

CHAPTER SIX
Santa Fe Trails and Trials

Renee unlocked the front doors to the saloon just as Mayor Hawke arrives to find out the details of the previous evening's tragedy. Renee explains what had happened, how Richie's friends, in an attempt to cool his temper, had dumped him in the water trough. She told Jasper that she was certain there had been no real malice on the part of the cowhands, they had just not considered the possibilities nor the possibility a man could drown in a horse trough.

"It was just real bad luck for Richie, an accident, Jasper. Those two probably don't even remember what they did. To be fair to them boys, we all have to take some of the blame, myself included."

Jasper Hawke listened to Renee's explanation of what had occurred and decided the cowboys had no real case to answer. He decided he would make a visit to the Ranch and explain to the owner and employer of the three cowboy's how Richie's accidental death had come about. Hawke did think he would already have heard. A grapevine can extend to any lengths in such a place.

Hawke suggests to Renee he should go to the ranch and explain how Richie came to his watery demise but she told him there would be no point as Soul Broadbent, being the foreman, had seen everything, he would report to the ranch owner. She told him the undertaker had been made aware and there would be need of his services. He had promised she would not need to worry, that he would deal with the removal and proper disposal of Richie's sodden body later today. Hawke left happy in this knowledge.

She made herself coffee. Sitting at one of the bar tables she wondered what David and Henry might be doing. She hoped they were having a better time of things than she is right now. Her thoughts return to the hapless Richie. The cowboy had mostly been a pain but no more so than many others. She couldn't help thinking that drowning in a horse trough was a most miserable way to die especially when your friends have dunked you in the first place. She thought about what she had said to Jasper, about sharing the blame. Even David, though he is away, had made the guttering so that it would drain away to the trough. Nobody in this world would think that a simple overflow system would kill anyone. Renee poured more coffee. She is done with talking to herself now, she decides.

When she had breakfasted, she and Joey would need to get the bar in readiness for the day's business.

"When will David and Henry get back, Ma?" Joey had appeared and is anxious to know when his friend might return.

"Don't know Joey, I reckon they might not have made Independence just yet. Don't forget, they might have to go further if there isn't a piano to be had at Independence."

Joey could not have known he will soon be the topic of conversation many miles away at the time he and Renee were discussing the safe return of the two men.

The pair are about to begin the process of loading the plain black piano onto the wagon. Added help had been promised and was on hand to assist the lifting of the weighty instrument. Henry suggested some ropes and pulleys would make the job easier. David had declined, knowing there was going to be extra hands if needed, he convinced Henry they could manage. The two stopped for a moment to roll a smoke before they made a start.

As the two friends loiter, a stranger appears and studies the grounded instrument for a moment. She lifts the lid and instantly begins to play a melody in the middle of the street. As David and Henry listen, more bystanders appear and wonder what is occurring. The tousle-haired woman continues. The two friends stare and try to tell her age. Neither can make up their minds and forget about the challenge to listen to the melodic sounds. She stops after a few minutes and to her surprise, the gathering applaud and ask for more. It is a peculiar moment but the woman is oblivious as she plays the notes of a gentle waltz all the time encouraged by her expanding audience. She drifts along in her loneliness as some clap slowly in time with her tune. Henry and David are as mesmerised as the make shift audience have become.

"Have you ever seen or heard such a thing in Cardiff, David?"

"H, I have never heard of or seen such a thing anywhere, such a beautiful moment in time. I doubt we will ever again witness anything like it."

"I believe you are correct my friend, such an enchanting moment. If only she lived in Hickok. We surely could do with a lady such as she to play for our customers, what do you think my friend, is it worth asking the maid?"

"Maybe H, but not until she has finished playing, man. We will wait!"

"Sure we will."

The two continue to stand mesmerised as still others stop their work to listen. Her audience continues to grow until suddenly, as if a lightning bolt has cracked above their heads, the moment is gone! On the sidewalk just a few yards away from the friends, she stands scowling, the Bullwhip grasped in her hand still shivering from the recent use. She is dressed in greasy buckskin clothes, her hair lank, a snarl across her face. The whole scene is for a moment silent.

"Who the hell are you?" she questions the player who stands like a statue and stares at the interloper who she thinks may be attempting to antagonise her.

"Who wants to know?"

"You don't question me lady and you don't scare me none, so best you trim your sails and button your mouth, lessen you need me to do it for ya, I'll happily oblige ya!"

"You can try, I would much rather you didn't, Miss. I wouldn't like to cause you pain and my mother told me not to speak to strangers but I feel I should just this once. Are we done?"

"Not in a hell's chance we're done!" To prove a point, she cracks the Bullwhip above the head of the musician once more. She makes a second attempt and somewhat impossibly the tail is stopped by a slender hand which had just played a piano so gently and perfectly. The woman who was attempting to step down from the sidewalk is stunned, she had never seen anyone do such a thing. She is caught off guard as the pianist moves forward and delivers a toe-kick to the throat of the newcomer while still gripping the whip's tail. The antagonistic woman lets the handle of her weapon fall and drops to her knees, agony spreading across her face as she attempts not to wretch. Her choking ceases, a look of embarrassment succeeds her earlier confident guise. Martha Jane Cannery is beaten and she is fully aware of the fact as is the triumphant musician.

She is sprawled in the street dust, knowing she has been bested by the pianist and will never forget it. The Stage Driver and Bull-Whacker knows she will live with the embarrassment. What she doesn't know is how her victor will deal with it. The musician reaches down and grasps her hand and helps her stand. Calamity Jane is struggling with all that has happened. For a split second she thinks about pulling her pistol and ending this in her normal way. She decides not to, she isn't sure why. She has suddenly become gracious in defeat.

"What are y'all staring at? Get about your damn business and don't mind mine!" The stunned crowd do as they are told, murmuring in their own retreat.

Puzzled, Calamity looks at the piano player; "So, who the hell are you?" She asked the girl who has now let go of the whip tail.

"I am Lourinda, Miss, Mrs?"

"It's Miss, it ain't for long and it ain't forever. I'm gonna marry Bill Hickok when he asks me. Martha Jane Cannery, Calamity Jane to some but not all. What did you say your name was?"

"I am Lourinda."

"Is that all you got, nothing else? There must be more!"

"It is, I have not needed more, Martha. You are not hurt?"

"Only my pride youngster, don't you worry, I've had worse, I've been kicked by mules. I ain't never been kicked your way before mind. What was that you did? You need to teach me how to do it Lourinda, it could sure be mighty useful."

"It is Sav 'ate, Calamity! I am happy you are not hurt."

"Let's get this piano aboard, Davy."

David is still thinking about what he had just witnessed. Being a fighter himself, he would like to know more and he stares across the road at Lourinda. She is looking back at the Welshman, there is something, a hint of a shared smile.

Although Henry and David have been acquainted for some weeks now, Henry had never until this moment realised the enormous strength and physique that the Welshman possessed as he and the extra four cowhands had taken their grip, David his own.

It seemed to the Cornishman they are only steering the instrument; David Evans alone is lifting it upwards from the sidewalk. Henry stares at his friend, he can see the veins expanding almost to bursting point in his neck. He could see the cotton shirtsleeves becoming so taut he thought the material would tear open. He could feel the piano become lighter on his own arms. Henry thought his friend now had the whole weight of the instrument. The two helpers let go of their corners and climb onto the wagon bed ready to guide the furniture. Henry stares on. David must lower the piano slightly, he does so without any crashing of the large knuckle-like feet onto the rough plank bed which dipped a little with the extra burden. The two helpers shrug and after helping to secure the piano with some ropes, readily accept their dollar each reward. They thank Henry who has backed onto the sidewalk as they walk away, each marvelling with disbelief at the recent feat of raw strength.

Henry is unable to contain himself and is ready to voice his wonderment. Before he is able, another man speaks for him.

"Hell of a lift that Davy, I don't mind tellin ya'." Wild Bill Hickok had watched the loading of the piano from just across the street. He has now joined the heavily breathing pair. The recent helpers had gone and taken the promised reward into the nearest saloon where they will brag constantly about what they had just seen.

David took two or three seconds to regulate his breath; he wipes the sweat streams from his forehead. "Thanks Bill, first time I ever lifted one of these, it wasn't so bad and I had help from the other fellers."

Wild Bill shook hands with both men. "Good to see ya' both again, sorry I ain't been around your neck of the woods as much as I'd like, how is that little woman?"

Henry allowed David more time to cool himself. "She's well Bill, at least she was when we left. We saw you from across the street yesterday, you were looking busy, didn't like to disturb you."

"I saw ya' both too. Fact is, once I knew ya was in town, I was hoping to ask ya' a favour."

David is able to continue the conversation now. "What's the favour, Bill?"

"I got something for the boy, Joey, a little present is all, hoped you fellers wouldn't mind taking it back with ya."

"Can't see a problem there Bill, what is it you got for the kid?"

Wild Bill lifted the rifle up for the pair to see. "It ain't new, but it's a good first gun for the boy, little huntin' rifle for him, do ya'll mind?"

"No sir, Joey will be tickled I'm sure."

David knows very little of weapons, Henry even less. Neither would know the piece of light artillery shares the name, the 'Henry' a brainchild of B. Tyler Henry, an early employee of Smith and Wesson. Eventually, Tyler Henry would work with Oliver Winchester, owner of the New Haven Arms Company. Winchester held all his own patents; Tyler Henry was forced to work with the Volcanic Carbine, an early lever action rifle. Henry used the format of the Volcanic rifle to produce the 'Henry' rifle. The rifle would accept a 44/100 cartridge, it would project the pointed lead bullet at slightly faster than the speed of sound. The rifle in Wild Bill's hand is one of the first three hundred to be produced, it had an iron frame and a twenty-four inch barrel, it could fire sixteen times before the need for reloading.

"The boy can do a whole lotta huntin,' tell him I said hello, tell him I'll get down his way again one of these days and we'll both get out after some game."

"We'll tell him, be sure of that. Joey sure will be tickled with this, you can bet on it. Come on now Davy, we have some miles to cover yet today."

Henry shook Hickok's hand, David too accepted the extended palm. All three men promised they would meet up again 'soon' and the tall lawman went on his way towards Martha Jane who has now fully recovered from her recent shock. Soon after the conversation was ended and they had parted, the two friends were up on the bench seat behind the horses and on their way from town. Again they would need to spend nights out on the silent prairie.

The meeting with Wild Bill hadn't caused them any extra delay, the early afternoon departure was the original plan.

The rented flatbed followed some few hundred yards behind the wagon train that had been in preparation at the time of their arrival in Independence. David had again taken the first stint with the reins. Carefully following the wagon train and just staying a little farther apart from the last wagon than it was from its own predecessor.

Henry dozes while waiting for his turn at the reins. David surveys the flat, lush, rolling green countryside as he perches on the hard wooden bench. He wonders about the wagon-train's destination. He thinks of the girl he saw in Independence.

Although he nor David had not had to travel in that way, he knew of some of the perils those people would be up against. He knew that many of the Plains Indians were apt to take liberties with travellers, even those that had professional guides. The elements are a constant menace to the moving masses, sickness caused by lack of nutritious food another danger.

Henry jogs the two horses along at a steady rate. When two hours had passed, the friends changed roles, as they had continuously done on the outward journey. Once Henry had driven for his two hours dusk began to settle upon the range. He can easily see the rear of the wagon train, he could see also the long crocodile of wagons is pulling off to the side of the main trail. The wagon train is stopping for their night camp he rightly assumed. Lanterns begin to twinkle on their suspended hooks at the sides of the wagons. Henry wakes the Welshman before suggesting they follow suit and stick close to the column of the huge Conestoga wagons for the night.

Henry also makes the suggestion they might 'make a visit' with the travellers later. David is agreeable with this idea, and says so. The two men took time to set up their own small camp. A fire is set and the short flames quickly throw out some surrounding heat, at least enough to boil water for 'well-earned' coffee.

David and Henry chatted for an hour and a half. Complete darkness is broken only by the light of their own small fire and the distant circle of lanterns. They can see the flickering and decide to make a move towards the source. Stowing their coffee makings under the box seat, they pick up and ride the creaking flatbed a short distance to the train, where they are at once greeted and welcomed by the heavy-set wagon master, who allows they will have company for the remainder of the evening if they so wished.

The sight of a piano tied to the flatbed may have had more than a little to do with the easily given and accepted invitation. The man who introduces himself as 'Fe' Tylden waits for the inevitable inquiry into the strange first name which coincides with the historic road.

David asks and Tylden gives his stock answer. "Simple feller, I been up and back along this trail more than any other man alive or now mostly dead, once a year at least I reckon, sometimes twice. I'm just glad that no one ever called me Santa, tell you that for nothing!"

David and Henry respond to the friendly humour as they introduce themselves. It is difficult for both men not to comment on the 'Ho Ho's' Tylden emits along with his answer. They are unsure as to the validity, they are careful not to offend the middle-aged wagon master. The fact both his hands rest above the large brass gun belt buckle also suppress any chiding.

Sixteen wagons are set in a rough oval formation; the flatbed being the smallest on display is given enough space to come between two of the huge Prairie Schooners - the accepted range name form for the famous Conestoga wagon.

Henry and David embarrassingly admit neither could play the newly purchased instrument, when asked. Tylden told the pair he was certain there would be someone amongst his own party that could 'pick out a campfire favourite or two.' "Not me though." Again, Tylden once more emits his booming laugh as he walks away in search of the required musician. As he strolls into the distance, the burly wagon master gives a surveying look around the night camp, satisfied each driver has followed his orders regarding the wagon formation which resembles a large rowing boat in shape.

David and Henry look at each other with false sternness. David leans towards and whispers to Henry under his breath. "This bloke is out of his tree if you ask me." Henry looked unbelievingly at his friend as he spoke through the thinnest of mouths.

"With bells on, Davy."

Henry prided himself on his use of self-control at such times. In giving the Welshman the stated answer he had stretched the holding capacity of his bladder to the point of no return. The faintest of urinal trickles had sent him scuttling behind the nearest Conestoga. Even while Henry was relieving his internal water pressure, Fe, just a handful of yards away, had stopped and turned at the two friend's guffaws and inquired of David as to the sudden departure of his 'partner.'

"Henry needed a piss, Fe."

"Me too, I'll be back." The wagon boss walks away just as Henry, still laughing, returns.

"Quieten down Henry, I wouldn't like to be accused of making fun of Tylden. He might have a sense of humour, he might not, it isn't easy to tell." The two find it difficult not to snigger as the wagon boss returns. David looks up at the man whose hands rest easily on the Rosewood handles of the two worn looking Colt Peacemakers. David and Henry keep nervous eyes on Fe Tylden.

"Well I'll get to seein' iffen I can't find someone to play that thing for us. I'll tell the folks to get themselves over thisaway too. I'd say they all will be glad of a little entertainment on their first night out here, there'll be little or no more of it as time goes on. See you boys in a while."

Henry and David are able to keep control as Fe Tylden walks away. Neither the Cornishman nor the Welshman can see Tylden's wickedly smiling face as he again departs temporarily.

"I'm not listening Henry, you can't make me. That guy looked as though he was ready to shoot me while you were off pissing yourself."

Henry looked down at the dampened fly of his trousers. "I think I was pissing myself before I went, Davy."

"No more Henry, promise!"

"I'll be silent all night, Davy."

"Enough Cornishman!"

"Found a nice young lady, says she'll play for the camp." Fe had returned to where Henry and David were now sitting.

"Rest of the folks are gonna come over thisaway a mite. Reckon we can bank that fire up some." Fe points a thumb over his shoulder at the nearest pile of embers. "You pair mind throwing some wood on it, you'll need some of them logs over yonder." He points at a stock of stumpy logs to one side of the closest wagon.

"See ya' later boys." Fe walked away to make sure he'd passed the invitation to every one of his charges.

In the wagon masters absence, Henry and David did as Tylden had asked. The fire bursts back into flaming action and lights the immediate area. "He's taking the piss Davy, I'm sure of it."

"Well he didn't take yours! I'll get up and sort out the piano, give this girl some room to play." David left Henry playing around with the fire. Soon members of the train start to approach, bringing blankets, sleepy babies and even jugs of beer to pass around. Tylden had made it plain that there was to be no liquor on the train, but that he isn't against the drinking of beer. But even this allowance had been accompanied with 'I won't put up with drunkenness from anyone, that being my one and only golden rule.' Tylden went on to explain that occasionally trains such as his had become seriously disrupted by drunkenness; he would not think twice to use the threat of expulsion from the train.

The girl appears and the friends recognise the player immediately. They had last seen her in the middle of the Independence street. David's eyes widen as she approaches.

She plays melodies mostly known only to herself in the beginning. She plays as well as she had earlier. As the social evening stretches on, some of the listeners ask for their own favourite songs. The young girl obliges as and when she knows the accompaniment required for the requests.

A lanky Dutch youth with a violin did his best to accompany her when he was able. Other instruments came and went; a Harmonica, a guitar being the best of them.

Some people sang; David sang, his voice showed the usual good quality expected from a man of Wales. Henry commented on how well his friend sang. He also informed David he thought the girl had an eye for him. Henry had noticed that she had allowed her eyes to flit towards his friend on more than one occasion. He'd mentioned with a twinkle in his own eye how well the girl played considering she must have 'awful eyesight.' David had taken these friendly jibes with his usual easy going acceptance. Though he found he was pleased the girl had shown an interest.

"She might be blind, but she has good taste, no doubt about that." As he uttered the words to Henry the girl was to take a well-earned rest. The Harmonica player sitting at the fire took a turn at playing for the tired group. A lonely sound from the tiny instrument echoed hauntingly around the campsite and it might help put more of the children to sleep.

David got to his feet. Henry watches with interest as his friend sidles towards the girl. It is the first time since the two had met that he had shown such an obvious interest in a member of the opposite sex, he had been far too busy with his wood-working tasks. Henry is impatient to know the outcome of the intended meeting. He would have a while longer to wait.

David did not return to the spot he had occupied with Henry, instead he stayed close to the girl for the rest of the evening's entertainment. Even when she climbed back onto the flatbed to play the last of her repertoire, he followed closely behind.

Henry smiled to himself as he watched the huge Welshman and the tall but dainty pianist. He wondered how David could contemplate any thought of any kind of friendship with the girl, when he didn't even know where she was going. He also hated the thought David might want to follow her.

After almost another hour's play, Fe Tylden announces the evening would shortly have to come to an end. He informs the remaining listeners, many with their already sleeping young children had already retreated to beds under canvas, and beds under wagons.

Fe makes another announcement "Seven O' clock is our starting time tomorrow, no stragglers please!"

The small crowd show their appreciation to all the entertainers, warm applause echoed around the oval of wagons. The would-be settlers had all drifted away, leaving just Henry and the wagon train captain.

Fe Tylden took a small flask from a pocket in his vest, after sipping a little for himself he offered the flask to his company. Henry sipped a similarly small amount and passes back the flask with a question.

"Thought you didn't allow liquor on the train, Fe?"

"Well just because I said it, don't mean I meant it. Anyways, I never said I weren't no liar! I remember a time when I was just a young kid and I was first took on as a ranch hand. First night out, after I'd done my shift of herding, I was sitting at a fire just like this one, two old timers with me showin' me the ropes and such you know. Well these old cowhands was all bragging and such, you know how it is." Henry nods in silence. "Anyways, the older of these two fellers - I was just sixteen myself at the time - he told us about the time he had a rogue steer causing no end of trouble in the herd. Reckoned he jumped down off his cutting pony, took a hold of that Longhorn and wrestled that steer right to the ground. Held it down and bit it's nose 'til it had had enough of being ornery. Can you believe that?"

Before Henry could answer, Fe continued. "The second guy, well his story went thisaway: he told how he came across a rattler nearly twelve feet long, as he told it, the critter surprised him while he was taking a squat. He grabbed at that snake, bit the head off it and sucked out all the poison while he was still squattin'!"

"That's a tall story, Fe! Tell me one which might be true!"

"Well feller, I surely hate to disappoint you, but I was just a youngster then and don't have no more tales to recall."

"Did you not tell them two a tale then, Fe?"

"Naw not really, I just sat quietly stirring the fire with my hand!"

Henry rolled his body into the blankets he had spread under the wagon. He thought about Tylden's storytelling and couldn't help but laugh at the tales once more. He waits for sleep to come, nobody else witnessed the broad smile that remained. He is already asleep when David returns to do the same.

The encampment sprang into instant action just after six O'clock the next morning. There were no sore heads, beer had been shared and drunk evenly amongst the adults, but not in too great a quantity. The prairie glowed with an eerie silver light as dawn crept across the gently rolling greenness of the Kansas Plains. Henry and David climbed from beneath the timber base of the wagon. The two men had agreed between themselves to stay with and follow the train for as long as was possible, before they would have to leave the Santa Fe Trail and travel due south.

As Tylden had predicted, the seven O'clock starting time was achieved. There was lots of noise, shouting came from every wagon it seemed. Henry and David are again the back markers. Fe Tylden had agreed they could stay with the train for as long as they needed, he thanked the pair again for their allowing the use of the piano the previous evening.

93

Henry flipped the reins and once again clucked at the two horses, more for the want of something to do while he waited patiently for information from his friend as to the outcome of the dalliance with the girl.

The horses trot along at a steady gait, they need little encouragement to hit their straps. David is aware of Henry's need, but makes the impatient Cornishman wait.

Henry made various references to the subject of the girl but without any result. Half an hour had passed when he could wait 'no more.' "By Jesus Davy, let's be having it, you can't be keeping it all to your bleddy self man."

David smiles at his companion and makes him wait a few minutes longer. "There's little to tell. Lourinda is a wonderment, I could be smitten if I knew what it meant!"

"Lourinda, is it? She has a good name, Welshman!"

"She's a London girl, a cockney treasure. A rare part of her majesty's Crown Jewels, I believe!"

"Seems to me that smitten might be understating your condition, my friend!"

"Might be, Cornishman."

"So how is this love affair to blossom?"

"How do you mean, boyyo?"

"When will you see her again?"

"Later, when she brings her effects back here.' David looked at the puzzled face of the man holding the reins. Henry's reply is long in coming, he is digesting the Welshman's statement.

"You mean she's, Lourinda is coming back to Hickok, with us?"

"Do you mind?"

"Not at all. What about her family, the people she's travelling with?"

"They're not family, she came to them to Nanny for their children. Things haven't gone quite the way they had been planned. Lourinda has taken a dislike to the husband, she didn't go into detail, but they didn't hit it off for some reason.

She was going to leave the train first chance she got in any case."

"Fair enough Davy, I have no complaints, why should I! This Lourinda may be just what you need. It could be the family she works for would be a little put out. I hope you're not making a rod for your own back."

"Everything will be good, you'll see."

Almost as if by magic, the girl appears alongside the slow moving flatbed.

Two bulging valises lay testimony to a hasty exit, items of clothing had not been fully installed inside. David could see the girl had dried tears on her cheeks. The parting from her employers had not been kind to her, he could tell. The Cornishman slows the horses to allow David to jump down and take her bags; he throws them up next to the piano. David extends his arms to stretch around the girl's waist, lifting her as easily as if she were a feathered pillow. With her feet firmly settled he climbs back on board, offering Lourinda the seat next to Henry.

"I'll sit at the back here until we make a changeover, Henry."

"Good morning, Lourinda." Henry offered his hand to the girl and they shake. Lourinda smiles a little awkwardly. "Welcome aboard, maid!"

She is certain the two men must have had conversation concerning her joining them. She did not know how much David had told his friend and she did not know what his attitude would be. She very soon decided she need not have worried as Henry showed no concern and welcomed her so easily.

David had the previous evening informed the girl as to his and Henry's first meeting, how they had become solid friends in such a short while and how Renee and they were partners in a now budding enterprise.

She considered her position and made a promise to accept whatever outcome may occur. Henry could sense the girl's awkwardness and made further attempts to put her at ease. "David tells me you are coming to stay Lourinda, I must say you will be much better to look at in the mornings than he is."

"Thank you, Henry."

It is time for the changeover; David would drive the wagon now until the time comes to cut off from the Santa Fe Trail. Now that it is late morning, Henry is hoping he might get to shut his eyes for an hour, at least until they stop to eat some of the food they had purchased before leaving Independence. He settles back and as when travelling in the pukey carriage, Henry folded a jacket and used it for a pillow. Raised voices bring him awake an hour later.

A distinct Englishman's voice is challenging David. "Get down here and let's have at it. You'll not take that girl from us, we have paid for her passage from England and she will fulfil her contract."

Lourinda is suddenly scared as she watches from the shared box seat. She looks anxiously at David She looks back at the anger fuelled face of the man who is telling the truth about having paid her passage. She sees the innocent face of the wife and decides not to engage in the conversation.

"Henry! How much of those fifty dollars have we left?"

Henry recalled the purchases of food he had made for the return journey and of course the cost of the piano. "Around forty dollars." He hadn't forgotten the little gambling interlude that had occurred with the storekeeper. Henry thought the storekeeper would be unable to forget their encounter. He fished in a pocket, pulling the wad out carefully before handing three of the ten dollar notes across.

"Now then boyyo, you have two choices; you can take it and get out of our way or I'll do as you ask and come down there and as you suggest, 'have at it.' Only, if we have at it and you don't beat me, you don't get to keep the paper money. If you do beat me, I'll double it somehow." David gets to his feet as he speaks.

The Englishman looks David up and down; he had seen the Welshman from a distance at the social last night. In the dark, he hadn't realised just what a formidable opponent he might prove to be. He decided on the easy way out of his predicament.

"Give me the damn dollars, the bitch wouldn't be worth the trouble." The Englishman is still trying to show some bluster, he knows his performance is unconvincing. He snatches at the small bundle of notes. Turning away he directs his wife to follow.

Fe Tylden appears as the couple move away. "You folks alright back here?"

"Fe, glad to see you, we'll be pulling away again in a short while, like to thank you again for having us around." Henry reaches down and takes the offered palm. David also shakes hands with Tylden. Fe Tylden tweaks the front of his battered Stetson towards Lourinda and wishes her luck. She smiles back at the wagon master.

"Can I ask you a question, Mr Tylden?" The now relieved girl asked.

"Sure, go ahead Lourinda." Tylden again has his hands clasped above the large brass belt buckle.

"Have you ever thought about growing a beard?"

"I have not Miss, I sure will think about it. Whatever made you ask?"

"No particular reason, Mister Tylden!"

CHAPTER SEVEN

It's the Circus!

The return journey to Hickok for David, Henry and the now more relaxed Lourinda is mostly uneventful. Much of the time is spent in learning of the girl's background. Both men are interested to find out more about her, which part of London she had come from and why she had decided to leave her home and family and come so far. Neither Henry nor David had ever been to England's capital, their knowledge of it is relatively poor. They were keen to learn more about the place. Lourinda tried to answer all their questions; she also asked some of her own in return for the purpose of knowing more about her two travelling companions and those who await them back home in Hickok.

When Hickok is eventually reached there is little one didn't know about the other. David and Henry had divulged information that each had previously not known about the other. Neither of the three ever brought up the subject of the girl's former employer, her trials were kept silent. Whatever happened was her business alone. If she had wanted to share it with her companions, she would have done so.

Renee is unable to hide her delight when Joey winged his way through the door with the news of their return. At once she is outside with Joey next to her. She looks up at the now quite dusty, black instrument. "You got one." Renee walked admiringly around the other side of the wagon. "She's a beauty."

"She certainly is Renee, though I think you'll make the poor girl blush. I think we should give Lourinda a chance to get accustomed to her new surroundings." David is teasing his business partner, he's also teasing Lourinda and she knows it. Renee attempts to downplay her early excitement at the return of the two.

With David's words, Renee had realised there is a third traveller. She looks at Lourinda and nods. Lourinda smiles back and waits for the Welshman to help her down from the box seat, which he does with gentle ease. "Lourinda can play this thing Renee, she plays very well" said Henry, as he too stepped down from the wooden seat.

"Let's not stand here yakking, come inside Lourinda. I'll get Tungsaw to cook up a meal for y'all. These fellers can get that thing down without our help." The instrument will make a big difference for the Plainsman, it will allow the 'hotel' a little more class, she thought. She also knew the two men and the girl must be tired after their long trek but the piano does need to be brought inside before dark.

Renee instantly likes the look of the newcomer, but will reserve judgement until she knows more about the light haired girl. There would be time enough, Renee thought to herself as she led Lourinda inside. Renee bade the girl to sit. 'I'll go and find Tungsaw, she promised.' Renee left Lourinda alone to take in her new surroundings. Cooking Fat strolls towards her, he stops and rubs his head and side against her leg. It seemed to Lourinda the cat might be giving a seal of approval to her arrival, she hoped it will be the case.

The door crashes open as David and Henry wheel the instrument inside and over the rough board floor, promising to repair the door frame which has received some small damage during the transition of the piece of furniture. David had repaired the frame previously and more than once, he will now need to do so again.

Cooking Fat had immediately scampered out of range and into the kitchen at the site and sounds of the moving monstrosity as it was being wheeled into place in one corner of the saloon. David had not had to lift the instrument down on his own, two town loafers and Henry had helped lift the it down from the wagon bed making the task much easier for all as it rolled along on its wheeled supports. Henry had flicked the two a half dollar each, they are already at the bar and prepared to spend their reward as quickly as it was received.

Lourinda watches her host as Renee gives instructions as to where she wants the musical piece to stand. She changes her mind at least four times before being totally satisfied, still she scratches her head in imagined doubt. David and Henry stay patient with her for all this time, but are eventually relieved when she has come to a final decision which was the first place it had been put. Once the furniture moving is completed, the two tired men are able to eat and relax. They wait to hear of all the local news from Renee. They are both saddened to hear of Richie Stark's demise though they were unable to hear the complete tale without half smiling at the misfortune the ranch hand had suffered on his last day on earth.

Renee informs David and Henry how the council had agreed to accept donations towards the purchase of a school building; a building that had been agreed for the time being, would double for religious services on a Sunday and school classes for a dozen or more children during the week. Although there are no more than a dozen school age children in Hickok, some will already be employed on farms or in shops by their parents.

Jasper Hawke has attained a recent Colman Bridges catalogue; the price of the building would be reasonably low all things considered and the newly formed council has agreed one thousand, two hundred and fifty dollars did not seem out of reach. Of course, the prefabricated building would easily suit twin purposes, perhaps even more. It made sense to which all had concurred upon.

The Colman Bridges Lumber concern contained advertisements for prefabricated timber houses, churches, schools and could even supply a railway station house. The company also promised delivery by boat, locomotive or wagon. David is pleased; not having to build the schoolhouse himself would allow him more time for the remaining restaurant projects. Joey would now have no cause to criticise the Welshman's treachery as he will not now actually have to help build his own chamber of torture.

David, Henry and Lourinda eat the food that has been specially prepared by Tungsaw; beer is poured liberally to help the food to go down and to rinse the trail dust away. The whole of the next hour is used in describing the journey to and from Independence.

Henry tells Renee and Joey how they had come to meet with Fe Tylden, Lourinda and how she had seen fit to accompany them back to Hickok. He didn't try to explain to anyone why she had left the English family she had been travelling with as he knew very little of the facts and it wouldn't be his place to do so. Renee tells Lourinda unnecessarily she is welcome to stay as long as she needs or wants. The girl is relieved and in turn overjoyed with the reception she had received from even more, much nicer strangers than she had so far done. She has been asked to stay at the Plainsman and would earn her keep by playing, singing and participating in any necessary chores.

Renee had explained that the accommodation is still sparse but homely then went on to explain some of the plans for further improvements, so the girl will be aware it is not a fly-by-night offer.

While the two women talk, Henry decides it is a good time to give Joey the gift from Wild Bill. Joey had come immediately at the Cornishman's call. David holds the rifle, while Henry recounts the meeting with the Plainsman. "So Joey, we brought you back a present from Marshal Hickok."

"What is it, Henry?" Joey is puzzled. He could see Henry has nothing to give him, his hands are empty. The boy looked at the smiling David, seeing the rifle, but not connecting it with the forthcoming promise of a gift. It cannot be the rifle, surely not "You tell me Davy, what is it I got?"

The Welshman looks across at his friend. Henry nods, David reaches across and lays the weapon down in front of the youth who seems to have grown a little over the past two weeks while they were away searching for the required instrument.

Joey's mind begins its work as he looks down the barrel to see if it could be out of line. "The rifle, he gave me the rifle. Never! It must be broke inside or something, it must be!"

"He sure did Joey, she's all yours. I don't believe the Marshal would give you a broken rifle. Mister Hickok says he'll come along and do some hunting with you when he has time enough, I'm sure it isn't damaged in any way." Joey picks up the gun and hefts it; he puts it to his shoulder and sights down the straight barrel imagining a white tailed deer in his sights.

"Careful there Joey, best put it away in your room until you need it." Davy warned the lad even though it is not loaded and he will have to wait for tuition on how and when he can use it. The boy disappears to his room still clutching the gift, hardly believing how lucky he is.

Never once was the fight between Lourinda and Calamity mentioned. Neither Henry nor David thought it important enough to discuss, especially while in the girl's company, though they had been mightily impressed in her performance with the belligerent bullwhacker.

Henry searched around and found what he wanted in cleaning materials, with which to spruce up the dusty but obviously well-kept weapon. He took them in and handed them to Joey, who for most of that evening, will be staring at the weapon on the so far temporary bed where he picked it up and laid it down again a dozen times. Now he could perform the cleaning operation he had seen Jack do on occasion.

The three partners and Lourinda finished their meals while Gladstone had tended the bar. Renee took Lourinda to the small room she will share with Joey tonight. Renee had rightly guessed that the younger woman would feel the need to freshen herself up and make a change of clothes. David and Henry are of a similar mind. The three partners will not assist in the running of the bar this evening. 'Gladstone will manage' they had all agreed.

The Bartender would make sure drinks flowed for the clientele. Maria the waitress and Tungsaw, kept the early diners happy with hot food. Food trade is steady. As always, it peters out as the evening goes on and customers are only interested in liquid sustenance. David promised Lourinda he would show her around the small but fast growing town, once she had finished her food and was fully rested from the journey. The English girl had shown her eagerness at the suggestion.

Later the pair got up to do the rounds of the little town. He and Lourinda crossed the wide street and stepped onto the rough planking of the sidewalk. Although still not complete, more work had been done to the sidewalk while the Welshman was away. Lourinda put her arm easily through David's as they walk. The Welshman smiles contentedly to himself. The hour is late now as he checks certain doors as they stroll; it had become his habit to make sure doors and windows that opened out on to the main street were safely locked. Before the couple had reached the farthest end of the boardwalk they were met by Jasper and Mrs Hawke. They stop to talk to the elder pair.

David introduces Lourinda to the Mayor and his wife. Jasper was about to tell him about the intended purchase of the school building. He was stopped in mid flow and informed that Renee had already told him of the change of plan. David admitted to himself life would be made much easier without the worry. 'There's a lot of other things I can be doing,' he said.

Mrs Hawke made conversation with Lourinda until the time came for each couple to continue their mid-evening walk. After reaching the end of the slightly uneven boardwalk, the couple crossed back over and slowly strolled back to the saloon, occasionally stopping to look at some new house or shop that may have begun trading while David and Henry had been absent. Everything is moving fast in Hickok he thought to himself.

David turns and waves at Jakey, as the blacksmith is shutting down his business for the night. He'd been working late, re-shooing the two horses that had pulled the flatbed to Independence and back on the return journey. "Good to see you got back safe, Davy." The blacksmith shouted in return.

Lourinda is still holding the Welshman's arm as the two re-enter the saloon. The girl soon excuses herself from the party at the table. Telling her new friends that she is tired from the journey, she retires to the room she is to share with Joey for the one night and until provisions were made for her privacy. Renee had told Lourinda that they would arrange something better for the next day as she had not been expected.

Less than an hour had passed when Renee too informed her company that she was 'for bed.' Joey had gone earlier. Just David and Henry now sat at the table. Henry is again keen to ask his friend more about the cockney girl. Henry knows little so far.

"I expect to marry her" he said in answer to Henry's questions. "If she will have me."

"Good for you, have you asked her yet?"

"Not as yet, but I will and if she agrees, then we'll be marrying in that new church when it arrives. That reminds me, this town doesn't have a minister."

"Soon will have, so I hear. Renee tells me Jasper has advertised for one to come here, we'll need a teacher too."

"Ah well now boyyo, that problem is easily solved, Jasper should speak to Lourinda. She has some teaching experience, a small amount at least."

"So you are to marry a schoolteacher, Davy! I wish you all the luck my friend and I wish her more." The Cornishman winked playfully. Henry knows he can get away with teasing his partner. They may have only met a handful of weeks ago but to both men, it already feels much longer. Henry and David talk until closing time and a little after. Once the day's cash is balanced, the doors are locked and the saloon is in complete darkness.

Early the following morning, Jasper Hawke knocked loudly at the door of the Plainsman. Refreshed, Henry had risen early the morning after their return.

Henry had been keeping a journal. He had used this quiet time to bring it completely up to date. There is plenty to put on the pages since their journey to fetch the instrument. Opening the door he invited the mayor to join him for coffee. The two men sat up to the bar. They discuss the purchase of the schoolhouse, knowing the town can afford it now many of the more prominent amongst the population have pledged a share each; there would be enough to cover the whole expense.

Jasper asks Henry if he and David might help with the clearing and levelling of a suitable plot. "Jakey has promised to do all he can, I'm sure others will help. There are a lot of new folks coming in every day now. I believe we have a doctor coming soon. That will be a big step up for this town. I must speak to the council, it's only right that we allow him a good central plot to build on. A doctor needs to be accessible."

"I'd say it's the least we could do. The bigger this town gets, the more he'll be needed, it's only natural. Have you heard any more from the railroad? Are we going to have a regular station, Jasper?"

"Not so far, though I think it's only a matter of time, Henry."

Henry thought back to the day he and David had arrived in the village. The day he and the Welshman had ridden in the foul smelling rail carriage, how they had ridden ticketless and how they had jumped from the slow moving carriage and walked the quarter mile or so into the little group of half-timber, half canvas dwellings that sided the wheel rutted street just a few yards from the creek.

Henry thought about his most fortunate meeting with David and how the big Welshman and he were now inseparable friends. Henry knew there was nothing in the world he wouldn't do for the man from Cardiff; he was as certain as he could be in the knowledge David is of the same mind. Henry hoped his friend would find happiness with the girl Lourinda.

As the two talked they became aware of excited and animated voices from outside the saloon. Jasper stood and walked to the door.

"Well Henry, get yourself over here, see what's come to town. I see a giant ten feet tall, I believe that's an elephant, yes I'm sure, I saw a picture of one once, huge beasts." Henry did as he was told and stared. Both men walked out onto the sidewalk to watch the colourful and noisy procession that is still filling the street.

The sidewalk is quickly becoming full of sightseers. Henry pokes his head back into the saloon and shouts for Joey to get out of his bed. "Come out here and see this boy. Quick now lad, before it's too late, hurry boy."

Joey appears beside them, still wearing a long night-shirt and rubbing hard at his sleep crusted eyes, almost expecting the action would make the unbelievable scene disappear. It did not. Joey ran out into the road to get a closer view, he watched with fascination as the stilted man doffed the dusty, silky top hat in his direction.

Henry thought about admonishing the boy for running out. Guessing correctly Joey might never have seen a circus parade he thought to leave him to enjoy the spectacle. The Elephant proudly trumpeted its own arrival, making bystanders hop backwards away from the edge of the sidewalk. A flatbed, similar to the one Henry and David had ridden the day before, passed by them, a steel cage housed a handful of tiny acrobatic monkeys.

Jasper gasps unbelievingly at the huge muscular female sporting an even longer moustache than even he could manage to cultivate. A large, bosomed lady supported what looked to all to be the tiniest human being any of the watching throng had ever seen. Two hairy, minute arms are wrapped around her thick bull neck.

Henry turned his head to look further back along the prancing line; he is astonished to see the strange little head with two short stubby protuberances, the head seeming to float almost by itself, high above everything else. "By Jesus Jasper, what is it?" Henry thought the animal could possibly see into the unfinished first floor rooms of the Plainsman.

"Good morning Henry, Jasper, that's a giraffe my friend." David, having been woken by the commotion, had come to see what all the fuss was about. He had once seen a circus parade like this in Cardiff's Tiger Bay. He never forgotten the name of the world's tallest animal and watched fascinated as it stretched down to drink from the fast flowing water of the creek. Just a few yards back, three elephants are also drinking from the flow.

Renee and Lourinda now joined the group in front of the saloon. They too marvel at the sights parading before them. David, seeing the young English girl sidle towards him, lifts a brawny arm and drops it around her shoulder; she reciprocates, stretching her right arm about his waist. The parade continues for almost a quarter of an hour. The 'big' lady and the 'tall' man handed out printed flyers to the goggle-eyed bystanders. The legend tells 'a show' would be held outside town the following evening. Two shows, a matinee and an evening event.

The parade is completed with the passing of another cage bearing flatbed; the occupant is recognisable to all, an enormous African lion roars its way down the wide street. The crowd shrink back again. All the time the parade is passing, night-gowned watchers cheer and shriek, ooh and aarh, marvelling at the sight of a man juggling flaming torches as the lion continues to roar.

"That was something Joey, wasn't it!"

"I never seen nothing like that Henry, I'm going to follow them." Joey is gone before anyone could stop him. The group outside the saloon all laugh at the sight of the animated Joey chasing after the parade in the billowing night-shirt. The boy had realised and he didn't care.

"He'll be back, soon enough" Joey's mother stated as the four return to the inside of the saloon. They breakfast and sit drinking coffee accompanied by excited chatter.

As Renee had predicted, Joey was back inside the building within ten minutes. The boy ignores the general laughter, going straight into his room. In just a short while he is departing through the door again, now fully clothed.

Henry sat thinking about David's statement of the previous night. He could see why his friend is so enamoured with the English girl. The Cornishman remembers Lourinda had looked a touch strained when she played the piano on the back of the wagon that night. He saw a softening in her features since they had brought her away from the wagon train. He thought she seemed much more relaxed, easy to smile, a smile that lights her face. Henry is used to hearing an English accent, David too. Both for the same reason as their respective towns hosted many sailors from London, Liverpool and Portsmouth amongst many more.

Renee, who had lived all her life in the United States' mid-west was unused to the chirpy cockney speech. "Do all London folk speak the way you do, Lourinda?" She questioned the girl innocently.

Lourinda told her it is not the case. "Only those that are born within the sound of the Bow Bells, Renee." Lourinda went on to explain that the ancient church of St Mary Le Bow, in London's East End, houses the most famous church bells in England, in the United Kingdom. Lourinda did not know that her present church was not the original. An earlier church had stood on the same spot for many years previously.

The fate of that first church was sealed by London's great fire of sixteen sixty-six. Sir Christopher Wren would replace the church almost two hundred years before Lourinda was born. Lourinda did not know that the bells were originally sounded to signal a curfew for the city, that any within earshot to hear their ring should be inside their houses. Therefore only the hearers would be true Londoners.

Joey returned after nearly two hours at the circus site. His talk was of nothing else during the whole day. He pleads with his mother to be allowed to see the show. Renee agrees that he could go tomorrow. David suggests they should all go. "Let's close the saloon for the night, the whole town will probably be in that big tent anyway. We can reopen after the show is finished."

Joey had described the erecting of the 'big top,' he told them how he had looked through a small tear in the canvas and watched as the circus folk fitted together the wooden seating and rehearsed their acts.

"What do you think, Henry?" Renee asked.

"I think David is right, let's all go to the circus, tomorrow. Today we have work to do."

All that day Joey thought of nothing else. He promised faithfully to do any job he was asked to do and he kept the promise. Even while he lay under the blankets the same night Joey found it difficult not to think about the forthcoming treat. Treats have been few and far between for the boy in his short life. Even the rifle is temporarily forgotten. Sleep is hard to come by for the boy that night.

All the talk in the saloon is of the circus. As David had stated, it seemed the entire population of the town would be attending the performance. The little Chinese chef had even asked he be allowed to join the party. David teased 'he ought to know what a circus is like. Just like the way you run your damned kitchen.' He had added mischievously.

Tungsaw instantly switched to his Oriental tongue. David is certain the little man is being wickedly uncomplimentary towards him, all the same, he laughed. The more the Welshman laughed, the more the Oriental seemed to curse him. Tungsaw gave up first, retiring to the very room the Welshman had jokingly criticised but Tungsaw would of course be going to the circus with the others.

Once the laughter had died down, Henry had made the suggestion to put up a sign. "We'd better tell people we'll be closed. What about you Gladstone, are you coming to the circus with us?"

Gladstone had been listening to his employer's plans to see the show. He had silently hoped he might be invited to join the group. Gladstone is more than capable now of running the bar operation, he did so alone for the rest of the evening. He is another to look back and see how his own life has changed since he got a responsible job. In truth, Gladstone only drank because he had nothing to be respected for. It has all changed for the young man now with a real job.

David left the others, it was time for his regular tour of the town. Renee sat with Lourinda, she wanted to know even more about the city of the girl's birth.

Henry moved about the room making conversation with the card playing regulars, eventually settling down to play. The Town Marshal returned and joined Renee and Lourinda. The rest of the evening is quiet and uneventful. At One O'clock, towels are put over the bar, the streets become quiet.

All the occupants apart from David and Lourinda had departed. The two sat talking with only the light from one lantern. He was pleased he had the opportunity to talk alone with Lourinda. Already he is certain this is the woman he wants to be with. He prays Lourinda is of a similar mind. He is careful not to push too hard too soon, but is determined to use every available opportunity to make his feelings known, if only on a gentle scale. In his earlier conversation with Henry he had stated audibly his intentions to marry Lourinda, the words echoed through his head even now. David felt his skin must have been glowing like hot coals in a hearth since his admission.

The young Welshman could not have known that his recently gained happiness might soon be shattered. Even as he and Lourinda are talking, a lone man with thoughts of malice on his mind is surreptitiously leading a horse out of Fe Tylden's night camp.

CHAPTER EIGHT

A Tear for a Souvenir

avid and Lourinda with their arms tightly linked stroll towards the 'big top.' Gladstone, Tungsaw, Henry, Renee and Maria follow a short distance behind the two. Joey is in the front and itching to get to the tent flap first. Henry had kept his promise, the saloon will be closed for the night. It is soon obvious the decision is the right one. Every citizen of Hickok seemed to be making his or her way to the enormous, grubby, grey tent that had seen many better days.

Behind the group from the saloon, Jasper Hawke and Mrs Hawke walk with friends. The husband and wife did not notice that they too were followed. A shadowy figure dogs their path, the figure hugging a Winchester Carbine under his coat, close to his chest; the weapon half hidden by a man's woollen jacket, the collar turned up over his unshaven chin. A hat pulled down low over his forehead almost hides his dark saturnine eyes.

The large group walk towards the opening in the canvas where Renee purchases tickets for every member of the Plainsman party. Joey rushing straight to the front row of benches, quickly settles himself and leaning on his elbows is already oblivious to everyone else. Impatiently he waits for the entertainment to begin.

Families are still finding their seats as the Carnival begins. The red jacketed man with dazzling white pants and a tall, black shiny hat and almost knee-high boots enters the arena. He is cracking and flicking the tip of the long bull whip at every step, wanting to draw attention to the two trapeze artists high above everyone. The man and woman had already begun their swinging manoeuvres without the audience even noticing; separately each was already somersaulting while holding the wires that suspend them. Once their impetus had been built, they swung closer to each other and all the time somersaulting in unison without losing grip of the ropes it seemed.

The already enthralled audience roar their appreciation as the girl lets go of her wires, they gasp as she flies forwards to stretch for her partner's ankles. The two connect without interruption. Backwards and forwards they swing together now. The first girl's perch still swings in time with the other. She lets go the ankles, her hands stretch backwards and snatch at the moving swing behind her. She is safely back on her own. Again the crowd shows how much they are enthralled by the entertainment by standing, clapping and roaring their enthusiasm.

Joey is completely mesmerised by what he is witnessing, clapping as loudly as anyone and for longer than most. Before the trapeze artists are finished, two gaudily decorated horses come trotting into the arena. The same acrobats now prepare to entertain their audience from the horse's backs, performing somersaults and back-flips and toppling sideways to ride almost beneath the horse's bellies they gain more appreciation from the audience, the applause continues on until their act is finally over.

The giraffe is led into the vast circle. The tall, blotched animal is not required to perform even if it could; it is used to herald the introduction of a family of three elephants. Each is attached to the other by their trunks and gripping the tails of the one in front.

Joey watches as the dark skinned man approaches the three and leads them into the centre of the arena; with a series of commands all three are made to sit on hind legs.

Joey is unable to decide which animal to watch. "What did you call that high one, Davy?" Joey points to the tallest of the attractions.

"It's a giraffe Joey, they come from Africa, lad."

"What's that feller got that towel on his head for? Is he hurt?"

Henry looks to David to answer the boy. "Well?"

"He's an Indian gentleman Joey, a Sikh most likely, from India."

"He's sick?"

"No lad, a Sikh, it's his religion. All Sikhs wear them I believe."

"Okay, I understand, I think. I never saw an Indian with a towel like that and I've seen Indians before!" Joey is confused as Native American Indians do wear towels, a 'Breech-Clout' around their waists, between their legs and back to their waists.

"He's not a native of your country, Joey." Joey ceases his questioning and turns back in time to see and hear the caged lion that has been brought into the centre of the arena.

Everyone watches as the big cat is fed raw buffalo meat; they listen nervously as it roars its approval of the meal while bearing its huge teeth, it's jaws touching the bars.

David turns his eyes back to the entertainment too, occasionally stealing a glance sideways at Lourinda who sits three seats away from the Welshman, Renee and Maria separating them. Renee knows of the glances but says nothing. She, like the others, is more interested in the ongoing performances. Henry, Gladstone and Tungsaw sit at the other side of her. Nobody wants to miss a thing.

The party continues to enjoy the show until the ringmaster, now accompanied by two clowns and their silly antics, attempt to steal the whip from its owner! The circus owner brings the evening's entertainment to a close. The group wait their turn to leave the tent. Henry leads the line as they file out into the cool, late night air, all still animated at what they had witnessed.

David allows the others to pass him, he is the last to exit. The bullet sears into the thick bicep just above his left elbow. The Welshman hears the report of the rifle a fraction of a second later. He watches stunned as Lourinda groans and shudders. Thinking she had been surprised by the loud report, the big Welshman comes to a sudden halt so as not to collide with the girl. Maria begins to scream.

Something is wrong. David can see the back of Lourinda's dress is swiftly changing colour. He stares, hardly able to comprehend what has just happened. He looks at his arm, thinking the blood must all be his own. He looks back at Lourinda as she crumples seemingly in slow motion. It seems to David he must be in a dream, he wants to wake up and make it go away.

This isn't happening. People don't die like this in the street. David is sure his love is dying, his thoughts are all in confusion, his feet feel like clay. The big man stretches both arms towards the stricken woman. The bullet which had passed through her has continued its trajectory, burrowing through the flesh of his forearm; he feels no pain as he arrests her fall. The distraught Welshman sinks to his knees with her, gently allowing Lourinda's stricken form to stretch out in front of him, her head resting on his knee, as he feels the stickiness of her lifeblood spread across his trouser front, still oblivious to any personal pain.

Henry drops to one knee beside his friend. No sound comes from his mouth, his eyes speak for him. He stares in horror and disbelief at the sight of the murderous scene in the street. It seemed to Henry the girl had already died there and then. Unchecked tears course down his cheeks, already dripping from his lips to the ground, mingling with the fresh, warm blood. Henry and David have been friends for a matter of just a short time but the Cornishman has brotherly feelings for David a man could only have for a sibling. Henry looks about him, hoping no other members of the party have been injured or worse.

"Oh god, I believe she is gone Davy, there's nothing to do my friend!"

David gives no thought to his own injury. He raises his arms, pleadingly looking into Henry's face. "Why, why, who?" Henry remains silent, unable to answer his friend's agonising pleas, though he does have an inkling who the attacker could be.

Carefully, Joey puts his hand on the Welshman's uninjured shoulder and with a childlike innocence, he asks "Davy, are you alright?" Joey didn't know what else to say. The boy had seen much violence in his short life though never as close as now and only once fatally, just a month or so ago, apart from when Jack had whipped him, which he had done many times and just for the sake of it. Joey has no idea who might have fired the bullet but it could have been him there on the ground, it could have been his mother the bullet found, Henry, Maria, any of the party. Renee herself had half fainted; even now she is lying in the dust where the girl's blood is soaking in.

Tungsaw snatches the youth away from the tormented Welshman. "Henry, I will take the boy home. Gladstone, you stay here, you help Henry, whatever he needs. I take boy home." The Oriental is taking charge of the situation surprising both Renee and Gladstone, who is also in shock at the sudden tragedy. Tungsaw grasps Joey's free hand. Though the chef's wizened face is wet, there is no rain. The little man seems to have become a big man now somehow, he had spoken sharply to all and with authority. Every member of the party is taken by surprise by the change in the small Oriental. Renee has never heard him speak so calmly and authoritatively before. Tungsaw almost always talks so fast, no one can understand him even if he is speaking his broken English. No one at the saloon ever heard Tungsaw speak in such a slow and dominant way. At this moment, the 'big' Chinaman is not to be messed with!

The others returned to the saloon after leaving David. The Welshman had pushed Henry and Gladstone aside as easy as pushing away a new born Colt. Lourinda has only spent just one night sleeping in what should be her new home. It will be only her second night in the Plainsman; she will sleep there again tonight, possibly never to awake again.

Henry had not known what else to say to his friend. He shrugged uselessly into the sudden silence.

David, after slowly getting to his unsteady feet, stooped down again to touch her and she is cold, but he does detect some breath. He takes off his jacket and covers her to her neck as he stoops to lift and carry her to the saloon where he will lay her on his own bed.

Henry stepped across to where Renee is comforting the bemused Joey. He asks Renee if she had seen anything of what had happened. Both Renee and Joey told him the same thing, that they had seen nothing at all of the shooting. Neither knew from which direction the shot had come from. They both tell him they knew nothing of what had happened until they heard the rifle's report which would have come a fraction of a second after the bullet had struck. Henry confirmed he had not seen anything of a shooter. David stayed with Lourinda through the night, ignoring his own physical pain. Luckily the bullet had passed through the muscle in his underarm, missing any bone.

Gladstone had no inclination to approach the bar, he stands back inside the door, shaking his head as a negative reply to the question asked of the others before allowing his chin to rest almost at the top of his chest. The barman must feel for David in the same way as do all the others, everyone who had been in the circus party and neighbours passing by. Tungsaw would speak next.

"I see bleddy rifleman and I know when and where I will see him again. I will see him again! I will kill rifleman, remember I tell you this! You have Tungsaw's promise." The old man suddenly no longer seemed old and no longer spoke in the clipped American accent of before; he had reverted to his normal way of speech with just one difference, no one is in any doubt of what Tungsaw claimed he would do.

Henry looked at Tungsaw, who had always given him the impression of someone who had been caught in a huge rainstorm and then been shrunken by a roasting, Kansas sun. He could see something different now in the tiny Oriental. He certainly believed Tungsaw is indeed capable of killing the rifleman, not if but when he finds him. Henry shivers at the small man's sudden transformation. He did wonder how the Oriental could be so certain of his statement. Chances are he will find out.

"I'll be leaving first thing!" David had directed his words at no one, but each person present looked towards him. They see a different David Evans now. His expression appears to form a waxen mask, almost unnatural, fearsome, and empty of any emotion, other than a controlled hatred and anger. Henry believed he'd never seen a face so full of anger. The Cornishman looked at his friend for several seconds before assuming control.

"We'll be leaving! First thing! Renee, Gladstone, Joey you both know what needs doing here. Maria, Renee will need extra help from you. Gladstone, you have to see Jasper and tell him what has happened, I did not see him after we left the circus tent. Joey, your mother needs all the help you can give her. You have my trust boy, I know you won't be breaking it. Now it's time for you to find your bed, plenty for you to do tomorrow lad."

"I won't, don't you worry." Joey straightened, making himself stand a little taller. He didn't resent being called boy by the big man. By the time of their return he will have proved himself capable. He is proud to be given some responsibility and he takes Henry's last order without argument.

Gladstone promises Henry the same commitment. Henry nods his gratitude. Tungsaw listens quietly to these short but business like conversations before he too speaks again with the same committed voice of before.

"I will be ready when you are ready, Henry."

David and Henry look at the 'big' Chinaman with surprise. Each could see a look of fierce agitation in the finely creased features.

Renee disappears from the room. Returning with a blanket, she lays it gently across the little Cockney girl's sad frame. "So be it! You look after these men Tungsaw, I have a feeling they might need you with them." Renee too had seen the strange transformation of the enigmatic Oriental. She gave a shudder at the thought of these three formidable men embarking on their vengeful quest. The involuntary movements had been caused by thoughts of what might happen to their prey when they found it.

Early morning, while it is still dark, saw David seated some distance from the plank-topped bar. The blanket-swathed body still lay where he had gently placed it. David steps inside the bedroom and touches her chilled face as Renee enters to attempt to re-dress her.

Henry buckled the gun belt about his waist. He felt unusually comfortable with the side arm. Guns had not figured heavily so far in his life, but since the shooting of Jack who's rig it had been, he had secretly practised with the weapon. He felt he could draw and shoot the pistol with reasonable accuracy and speed. Shooting a pistol with competence has to be attributed to natural ability above anything. Henry thought he could at least put the six-shooter to better use than its previous owner, he had already done so once.

Tungsaw strode back into the bar, the tiny amount of still very black hair at the back of his head has been teased into a ponytail and knotted. His attire seems almost feminine-like; a white jerkin, pulled together by a tightly pulled, thick black belt, hung over white baggy trousers, a wicked looking long blade hung from one hip, a huge Colt's' Dragoon pistol at the other, it's long barrel reaching almost to the Oriental's knee. David stared at the almost unrecognisable man. Henry too is mesmerised by his appearance. Neither man speaks.

The three sip at steaming black coffee. Henry has already made an early journey to the livery stable, finding Tungsaw had beaten him to the purchase of three horses, three saddles and three riding rigs. The Oriental had paid for the transportation from his own pocket. Tungsaw had no intention of seeking reimbursement for his purchases.

Wait, Tungsaw exclaimed. "I have one thing to do, you all wait here, no move until I return." He went back inside the Plainsman, into the room where the girl lay in silence. He inspects the wound and rubs the palm of his hand in a circular motion over the bloody crust a half dozen times before covering her again. No one witnessed his peculiar action. He returned to re-join Henry and David. Tungsaw did not mention the gentle sigh that emanated from the girl as he walked away.

As the sky begins to lighten, Renee watches as the three friends ride out of Hickok. She wonders when she might witness their return. She is in little doubt they will come back safely.

Davy did not wear his gleaming badge of office now. A town Marshal's jurisdiction ends at the perimeter of the town he is employed to watch over. Neither one of the three members of the party has any official status at this time. They did have what they believed to be the freedom and the right to find and

* *The Colt Model 1848 Percussion Army Revolver is a .44 calibre revolver designed by Samuel Colt for the U.S. Army's Regiment of Mounted Rifles. The revolver was also issued to the Army's 'Dragoon' Regiments. This revolver was designed as a solution to numerous problems encountered with the Colt Walker pistol, its predecessor. The Dragoon Colt also went under the popular nickname the 'thumb buster' by owners of the weapon due to its heft and power.*

bring to justice, Lourinda's attacker. Tungsaw had given the impression retribution will come.

Henry had suggested they travel to Dodge City, Dodge being the Ford county seat. Hickok is situated just inside the Ford county line. His idea would be to ask for a temporary deputy sheriff's commission for each man. If they could acquire this status, they would be able to work more freely and more importantly, legally. David had agreed, Tungsaw had given an affirmative nod. Firstly they would follow the route they had recently taken to seek out the piano.

The Santa Fe Trail would also lead them to the trail driver's capital, Dodge City. Little is said between the three men as they cover the early miles. Tungsaw had hardly spoken to either of his companions as they forged onwards. A nod or shake of the head had been his only responses to any questions or suggestions. He had already been agreeable to the plan of first heading for the famous cattle town.

As the three venture onto the already ancient cattle trail, Henry voiced for the first time he thought their quarry would most likely be found with, or close to the wagon train commanded by Fe Tylden. David had been thinking the same thing.

"It has to be that smart talking English bastard. We have to find that train, Henry!"

"Do we have to find the train? I doubt that he'll still be with it Davy, I'm not so sure he would return to it."

"You are right, Tamryn." Tungsaw spoke now for the first time at length since the three had departed the Plainsman. He has found a habit of calling his two companions by their surnames. Not through any sense of reverence, it is easier for him to pronounce their second names than their first. "He will not be with them, but to speak to wagon boss first would be right thing to do" he added with authority. "I have other thoughts."

Tungsaw becomes quiet again after his short statements, allowing David and Henry to ponder their meaning. Neither man questioned the Oriental. The way he had spoken earlier suggested there would be little point. The three turned in a Westerly nature where they would reach the heavily travelled trail. This would take them in a different direction now to which they had taken on the journey to Independence. The three men rode at a steady pace towards Dodge. Tungsaw is leading the party now.

Joey yells and runs, screaming and shouting to his mother. He falls once, picks himself up and promptly runs straight into the midriff of Gladstone. He is trembling as he tries to speak to the barman and shout to his mother all in one voice. "Jesus, Gladstone!" the boy stuttered. "She's come back, she must be a ghost. Lourinda, I heard her, the blanket moved, the one ma put over her, it moved, I swear. Ma, ma!" Joey continued to shout for his absent parent.

"Calm yourself, Joey" Gladstone tells him. "Sometimes bodies make noises, even when they might no longer be alive. I heard all sorts, they even sit up sometimes, sit right up and belch, other things too. You should not have gone in there."

Joey, still trembling, looked at Gladstone, wondering what to believe. He couldn't imagine that a dead person might still move around, not unless there was some supernatural cause. Gladstone knew that he should go and see what was causing the boy's consternation. He was in no hurry, though he was sure his explanations to the boy were correct. He reluctantly led Joey to the back area of the saloon and to the back room. The blanket is still in place and he could tell Lourinda's body is still beneath it. "There now Joey, what did I tell you?"

"I heard it Gladstone, I thought she was going to jump right off them planks and go looking for the bastard that killed her!" As Joey's imagination begins to run wild, the shock leads him to exaggeration.

Renee appears from the street. She had seen fit to visit the blacksmith and ask him to make repairs to the shattered door now that David is unavailable. He would attend to it that afternoon. The door had been left where it had fallen. It is best to be repaired while the killer is still free.

"Gladstone, go find Mrs Hawke now. I believe the mayor is interviewing a doctor this very minute. Move boy, for pity's sake, go now, run Joey!"

Once again the saloon is filled with the noise of crunching wood. The doctor is already issuing strict orders. "Clear the way there please, let me see the patient."

Jasper and Mrs Hawke have followed the physician into the Plainsman. Renee, Joey and Gladstone stand to one side with the mayor and his wife. They watch from a decent distance as the doctor peels away the girl's upper clothing. Renee, realising that Lourinda should need some privacy even now, gave instructions to Gladstone and Joey. Hawke departs to wait outside on the porch. Renee had rasped the order. Deciding Lourinda is now in god's hands and those of the doctor, all but Renee had left. Their staying hadn't been through any thoughts of voyeurism, they had stayed only out of concern for the girl's welfare.

The doctor would spend many minutes probing and poking. Scratching at his lightly whiskered chin, eventually he made his pronouncement.

"Bullet may have missed her heart, no material entered." Ryder looks to Renee. "I'm sorry, there's nothing more I can do for this girl. The bullet has exited, so little chance of blood poisoning I hope. It's down to her and her maker now. Her breathing is shallow but regular. No promises!"

Renee looked at the doctor. "How can it be? We all thought the poor girl was dead. Poor Joey has had such a fright. We all have."

"Shock is a strange thing. A gunshot wound will always cause massive shock to a body and almost always it will lead to death. The longer she sleeps the better chance of her pulling through, Renee, she has a chance, a small chance!"

Renee listened to the medical man's explanation. She didn't completely understand all she was being told, but she was certain the doctor believed what he said to be true. Renee decides that with Maria's arrival to work, each would sit with her for two hour stints so she is never alone. The doctor will return to check on her every four hours. The saloon will stay closed.

Renee realised she had a problem and she did not know how it could be solved. She wondered how she would be able to get word to David. It might be best to wait until they come back. She isn't even sure where they might be. In any case, Lourinda may not survive. 'Fifty, fifty' the Doc' had grimly suggested.

Fate has once again played a part in the daily life of the newly named Plainsman. Gladstone stands behind his counter and decides to clean as there is nothing much else for him to do.

The sound of crunching of wood tells the barman someone has entered. "Good morning, Mr Hickok." The bartender is in sombre mood, after the previous evening's shock. Today he did not look with awe at the tall flamboyant lawman, instead he spoke as if welcoming an old friend. He poured the requested beer even though the Plainsman is closed. Gladstone then related the story of what had happened the evening before as well as what had had occurred this morning. Listening quietly, once the barman's story was done, Wild Bill asked if Renee might be available. He told her of his intention to catch up with the search party. Hickok is angry and it showed in the way he spoke. Having eaten breakfast, Wild Bill Hickok left town soon after.

CHAPTER NINE
Fire in the Night

Renee had given Wild Bill all the information she thought would be useful in his quest to find the search party, she had guessed rightly the three men had first intended to visit Dodge City and the incumbent County Sheriff, Jack Bridges. Her hope now would be that finding the wagon train would lead the men to the capture of Lourinda's would-be murderer. Wild Bill had agreed the probability. He promised Renee he would search for and inform the travelling companions of the recent happenings since they had taken their departure from the Plainsman.

Having departed promptly, Hickok followed the same rutted road that bore testimony to the passing of hundreds of thousands – possibly even millions - of four footed, Longhorn beast. The Santa Fe trail had been one of the main routes for Longhorn cattle being taken to the Northern markets for slaughter. During the 'sons and brothers' civil war the animals had been allowed to mate and roam freely across Texas and beyond; they had multiplied to the extent of more than thirty million beasts and became the main reason why the former Confederate States could get back on their feet at the end of the four-year conflict. The scars on the trail are still deep and may be there forever, Hickok thought.

The United States Deputy Marshal continued on towards Dodge. From there he would seek information as to the wagon train's direction and destination. The celebrated 'Plainsman' began his search at least eight hours behind the three, it is time for both to break for food and rest. After thanking Jack Bridges and taking a meal with him he had left soon after, the horse which had carried the lawman to Hickok being suitably rested. The tall, white and feisty Morgan stallion, now also well fed and watered is restless and ready to go.

Hickok stops for a smoke. He guesses he should be less than six hours behind the group. Wild Bill, armed with his superior knowledge of the range, is certain he would catch up with them easily. He had gathered further information on the wagon train's departure and direction from Jack Bridges, Wild Bill again takes up the trail of Henry, David and the lethally-armed, Tungsaw. He is quite certain he would find the three man-hunters before dark. The sun is beginning to set when the trailing lawman spies tall curling wisps of smoke rising from what he is certain is a clearing in a small wood. Leaving the trail for just a short distance, the campfire set by the very men he had been tracking comes into view. Wild Bill dismounted and walked the last twenty or so yards and into the growing light of the fire, calling out before stepping forward again. It is accepted rangeland etiquette to announce oneself to any campfire before approaching too close. A refusal could mean moving on or dodging a warning bullet from whoever had set the campfire. Many western travellers, ignorant of this fact could bare testimony to it afterwards; others might not be able to. Eighteen seventy-five is a poor time to be ignorant of accepted, unwritten rangeland rules.

Hickok's shout of 'hello the fire' is enough to inform the resting men friendly company is approaching. An invitation to 'come sit' went out. Wild Bill took his right hand away from the Ivory grip of his Navy Colt and relaxed as he walked forward into the fire's widening glow. Tungsaw had somehow already known the identity of the newcomer before even seeing him. He had imparted the information to his companions; they are suitably surprised at the truth of the statement when the tall man stepped forward towards the glowing light. Each man stood up from his haunches to shake the offered hand. Immediately questions flow freely from each before Hickok is able to explain his reasons for being in their company.

"I have some news for you boys." Wild Bill hunches down on his knees to deliver his message, his face stern and determined.

David feels he should speak first and does so. "Well boyyo, I doubt it is good!"

"I'm right sorry my friend, she hasn't made it, not yet anyways. The lady was still with us when you left and when I left. She might have lost too much blood to survive, David. The doctor gives her only a half chance to survive. At least it is better than no chance, my friend."

David stared into the fire, a tear finds its way down his cheek. If his companions saw it, there was no comment. The evening around the campfire would prove to be of little cheer. Very few words are exchanged and for three, sleep came early, for one, it hardly came at all. What sleep did come to David was spasmodic as he talked audibly to himself throughout. Daylight saw no change to the Welshman's sombre mood, though he does attempt to be his usual self, mostly unsuccessfully. The friends make allowances for his demeanour. Hickok, Henry and Tungsaw must take their words out and look at them before they are spoken aloud. They tread softly in the various short but necessary conversations held between them on the second morning of their search. David becomes silent whilst wondering how on earth he could not have known of Lourinda's predicament when carrying her flimsy, blood-slicked body to the saloon. He remembered how he had laid her down on the plank top of the bar. He remembered how he had wanted to take the revolver Henry now carried at his side and fire it at himself.

"Jesus, that would have been unfortunate!" David said aloud unintentionally. His three companions look across at the sound. David is annoyed with himself for making his thoughts audible. He colours up and attempts to put on a brave face but offers no apology; none was sought. The remainder of the group say nothing at all, there is nothing to say. They accept he does not need an excuse nor need to give an explanation for any more sudden outbursts that will no doubt follow.

"I will kill bleddy Englishman!" Tungsaw fingers the hilt of the long, glinting blade still sheathed at his side as he informs the riders of his intentions toward the murderer. All eyes are on the Chinese chef who doesn't look at all embarrassed by his statement. Henry, Wild Bill and even David are in no doubt Tungsaw would do what he believes to be justified if and when the opportunity arises for him.

"No need to get riled up yet, you bloodthirsty heathen" Henry states.

"David might want revenge, the law must decide his fate, Tungsaw. In any case, it seems to me you might be in more danger yourself, by the state of that damned pig-sticker* you're carrying!" Henry points at the long blade at the Chinaman's side, the point of which reaches below his knee, a heavy pistol rides on the Chinaman's opposite hip. Tungsaw makes no reply to Henry's chiding, though a sour look is directed at the smiling speaker.

"The son of a bitch will get what's coming to him, most everyone does" interjected Wild Bill.

Wild Bill Hickok would never have the chance to recall his own words the day would-be bad man Jack McCall fired a bullet through the back of his skull on August 2nd eighteen seventy-six. Wild Bill was by then half blind at just thirty-nine years of age, he had become shy of notoriety. Quietly playing Poker in Deadwood's Number Ten saloon, he would be murdered just so McCall could boast he alone had done the deed. The Plainsman was holding five playing cards at the

* _Pig-Sticker: Most early musket bayonets were of this type. Beginning in the early 19th century, knife and / or sword bayonet._

128

time, a sequence that would forever be famous as the 'dead man's hand' one pair of aces, one pair of eights and a queen. McCall would be hanged for his crime on March 1st eighteen seventy-seven. In the days before the sentence was carried out, he gave several accounts as to why he had performed the deed, all or none might have been the truth. McCall changed his story many times while behind bars. Newspapers of the day eventually grew bored with the saga. When asked in his testimony why he shot Hickok from behind, his answer had been simple, 'I didn't want to commit suicide.' McCall might have been a murderer but he was not a fool. Even with poor eyesight, Hickok had previously proved that he could shoot with unerring aim at a man's words. The Plainsman would one day accidentally shoot and kill his own deputy when the unthinking man had approached him from behind and addressed him suddenly. It was reported at the time Hickok was mortified by what he had inflicted on his friend. The accidental shooting in part would lead to Hickok's retirement from public office as a peace officer.

They decided to camp early. It had been a long trek that afternoon. 'The horses would need to rest' Hickok had put forward.

"Bill's right, we should all rest." As David's first words since his earlier strange outburst died away a voice suddenly came through the darkness.

"Hello the fire! Fe Tylden here, okay to come in to your camp?"

"Show yourself and keep your hands high for now mister." Henry is learning fast.

Fe Tylden immediately did as he was commanded. Only a fool would do anything differently.

"There now, would you believe it? Christmas Eve and we're sitting out here in the middle of nowhere. Come in Fe. Henry Tamryn here, David Evans too, some other fellers with us, one other anyway. Hard to speak of the little heathen fellow. Best beware of Tungsaw, Fe, he's armed to the teeth and riled up."

Fe Tylden walked into the light, his reins in his hand. "Mind if I tie up here for the night, Henry? Don't shoot me, Tungsaw!"

"To be sure Fe, make yourself comfortable man. You know David, this is Tungsaw, he's our cook at the saloon, I told you about him. Watch you don't pick a fight with him Fe, he's in a mean mood! He'd likely club you to death with his damn revolver than shoot you, or slice you for frying with his pig-sticker, as soon as look at you. He darn well scares me anyway! Now this man is Wild Bill Hickok, I reckon you might have heard the name" Henry pointed at the long-haired lawman. Tylden shook hands with the whole company and soon settled down at the fire with them.

"As Henry puts it, I heard of you Bill, there ain't many that haven't I reckon. I'm right pleased to make your acquaintance, Marshal Hickok."

"Well now Fe, I heard of you too. Likewise, wagon master, I believe."

"For my sins, Bill! Yeah well, if you don't mind my saying, I wouldn't take too much notice of these three foreigners. Now let me see what I can find in my canteen." Tylden stood straight again, walking to the tethered horse, he unhooked the hide-covered water bottle. Tipping it towards his lips as he returned, the wagon train boss took a deep gulp. He lowered it and offered it to David, not even knowing why these friends are out on the Kansas Plains.

"No offence Fe, I'm in need of something stronger than water, in any case we have plenty."

Fe Tylden offers the bottle without remark to Henry. Henry quickly takes the offered item and sips his own mouthful. In turn he passes it on to Hickok. The lawman takes a greedy mouthful, wipes the excess away from his chin after lowering the canteen and stretches his arm out to hand the bottle to Tungsaw. The little man takes his turn and passes it back to Tylden. "You sure you don't want some of this, David?"

"He Welshman, Tylden, heathen son of bitch, he maybe think water taste like bleddy Whisky." Tungsaw smiled wickedly at his own teasing of the downhearted Welshman. Tylden catches the implication and winks slyly at the Oriental whose features don't change in the slightest.

David gives way, thinking the wagon boss might indeed be offended by his refusal to share. He also thinks it might help his dry throat right now. The Welshman accepts the bottle, wiping the top on a sleeve end before drinking and in doing so, catches the distinct smell of the spirit. "You miserable bastards!" David swears at his fellow travellers. He even half smiles at the way he has fooled himself and takes an extra swig into the bargain. He passes it back to Henry, who drinks again. The interlude has lightened the Welshman's mood to something akin to his normal cheerful facade though inside he would no doubt still be thinking of the girl. He questions Tylden, who again is lifting the container to his lips. There is little of the spirit left now.

"Now then Fe, I seem to recall you weren't one for having hard liquor around that wagon train of yours?"

"Not with the train, am I? Anyway, let's just call it the Christmas spirit, shall we?" By saying, Tylden was allowing the four to know he had heard the remark as he had approached the fire. He laughed so they wouldn't feel awkward, they laughed along with him. All four lounge around the fire, all the while relaxing and becoming more comfortable and slowly but surely, just a little more drunk, until the leather container is completely empty. Stories are swapped between the men, some true and some that sounded distinctly doubtful. As the evening went along, Fe Tylden took some time to explain to his friends how it was his way to encourage the Christmas jokes, therefore confirming to David and Henry what they had already suspected on the first evening they had met. Again Tungsaw would fall by the wayside and is soon asleep. David wanted to know more from Wild Bill about any small improvement of Lourinda's predicament. He then asks what had brought him to the fledgeling village. It seems by talking, David is temporarily able to put the episode to the back of his mind.

Hickok answers "Well Davy, I had been trailing a renegade Indian, one that had left a government reservation in Oklahoma Territory without permission. This man had covered his tracks too well. I never did find the buck so I wished the renegade good luck and turned back. Realising I wasn't far from the saloon you boys now have, I thought to keep my promise of visiting again. I walked into your saloon amidst the furore. I met up with the Doc,' he told me how things are panning out."

"So we got ourselves a doctor in Hickok?" Henry asked.

"Looks that way Henry, the quack knows his stuff it seems. It was lucky he was there at the time. The way Renee tells it, the doc' had replied to an advertisement. He and the mayor were in the middle of their interview when the shout came for him to attend to the lady."

Fe Tylden's eyes lit up at this news of the shooting. "Turns out we had a similar mission Henry, I'd like to get my hands on the bastard too. The son of a bitch caused me no end of trouble; left a little pregnant lady with the train and skedaddled, left his own wife to fend for herself almost. Now I'm stuck with a baby. I just took me a trip to Dodge, had to get the little youngster some doodads to wear. That's how I turned up here, left my Segundo˙ in charge of the train. They'll expect me back in the morning."

"You see Tylden, what goes round, comes round."

"What are you getting at, Henry?"

"You been left holding the baby at Christmas, man. At least you got the little one some presents."

"Jesus Henry, you do crack me up some."

Henry and David glanced at each other. Conversation ceased for a minute or two as the they latched onto Fe Tylden's

* *Segundo, a second in command.*

statement, Hickok too saw the amusement and was consumed with mirth almost as much as the two big friends. Tylden waited, and waited. The dawn came, the penny dropped, four men laughed – most likely due to the alcohol that had been recently consumed - so loudly they woke the sleeping Chinaman. With no knowledge of the recent conversation, he stared around the campfire and followed suit. Now five men laugh in unison, one doesn't know why, it didn't matter. It was a sign and the group looked for their bedrolls. Before the stroke of midnight, David was the only man present still awake. He sat idly poking and prodding at the dying campfire, still hardly believing what had happened and fearing what might still happen. The thoughts of revenge on her attacker is back in his mind. There is only one way he might disperse them. David slept fitfully.

At dawn five men awoke with headaches. David, not having drunk as much of the liquor as his companions, did not suffer in quite the same way. Tungsaw again looked to be the worst off and he became the main target for the teasing from the remainder of the group. The five pooled and shared their breakfasts. Tungsaw cooked biscuits in the still hot embers of last night's fire. He somehow manages to make the best pancakes any of the men had ever eaten, using a small piece of tarp, he poured and stirred a mixture into a shallow skillet. The smell keeps all interested until distribution time. They share strips of roasted bacon and thick, black coffee before the time comes to pack up their gear and return to the trail. Three are going to the same destination, two have a different reason to be on the move.

It is a little after nine o'clock when Hickok separates from the others. He promises to return to Hickok the first chance he has. Tylden also makes the same promise to visit the Plainsman when he gets the opportunity. "I'll be seeing you boys, first time that big star shows up in the east." All five men laugh once more at this final show of humour from the wagon boss; again Tungsaw is ignorant, it doesn't matter as he laughs along with his friends rather than at them. Even a non heathen can have a sense of humour it seemed to everyone.

When the time had come for Wild Bill to part, all five had become firm friends, they had shaken hands and wished each other 'good luck and a happy Christmas,' "I hope she makes it, Davy!"

"Thanks, Bill."

Headaches almost forgotten now or at least diminished in ferocity, David, Henry, Fe and Tungsaw ride the last couple of miles slowly and with little conversation. David is in no great hurry but he still has murder on his mind. They won't even know if the Englishman has returned to the wagon train. On arrival at the large group of wagons they discover he has not been seen at all.

"We should get back, Davy, nothing we can do here my friend."

"I know Henry, the sooner the better for me."

The three were soon back on the trail towards home. Henry can't help thinking how in such a short time so much can happen. Just a few months ago he didn't even know David, Tungsaw and Hickok or Fe Tylden. Now following such a sad and awful loss, coincidence has manufactured an unlikely but powerful friendship. Born out of despair can come camaraderie and a loyalty from complete strangers towards each other. It makes Henry realise he and David still have a lot to learn about America and Americans.

Unknowingly, the three had made the return journey much quicker than the outward trek. Horses are led to the trough that poor Richie had died in before being tied to a hitching rail David himself had erected outside the saloon. The premises are in darkness as they dismount, not a soul is to be seen on the street. The men are weary from the long ride.

"Evans!"

David, Henry and Tungsaw spin around at the shout. The faintest glow of a wall-mounted oil lamp throws a glint onto the long barrelled weapon held by the shouting shadow. David knows instinctively who this shouter is. Henry knows too as he fumbles for the six-gun, realising at that very moment he has come up short as a serious gunfighter, instinct and awareness must go hand in hand with self-preservation to a top drawer shootist such as Wild Bill Hickok. Henry is not up to it this time.

"I'm going to kill you now, Evans!" The shouter could see the Welshman's bulk with the aid of the faint glow. David thinks the girl Lourinda might no longer be alive and it may be she isn't. Having failed in the assassination attempt by killing the girl and not her suitor, this man has decided to take his own frustration out on a man he doesn't know but hates anyway. He is going to shoot David, there is nothing the Welshman or the Cornishman can do about it.

The little Oriental has other ideas and eyes the situation with calm, with coolness and with sharp-eyed calculation. Quietly, almost silently, he slides the sword from its scabbard, surreptitiously pulling the blade back until it is almost completely behind him but perfectly horizontal, the blink of an eye would have the glinting steel moving forwards almost of its own volition, though the chef has first propelled it. The missile stays true to its course for as much as a dozen feet distant, before protruding from the ambusher's back and pinning him to a wall behind. The bullet from the rifle safely enters the surface of the dusty main street. The impetus of the blade has driven the attacker into the flaming torch hanging there, his now redundant clothes igniting as the flame becomes hungry and prepares to devour the stricken man. The only Englishman on that lonely street is dead before his body begins to distribute its lifeblood into the dust. David and Henry stare in disbelief at the Oriental. The small man had somehow kept his promise.

"Shish kebab!" The chef now has the opportunity to get his own back on his startled companions, He has manufactured a joke of his own they did not understand and maybe never would. The little man is still laughing as if a devil is in him, as David and Henry seek a container to hold water.

Renee wrenches open the partly repaired door. On hearing the outside commotion, she had decided to investigate. Her eyes take in the scene. Holding her own lamp high, she sees Henry, David and Tungsaw in the extra light she herself is supplying. She sees the flames enveloping the stilled corpse. The Englishmen is already deceased. Renee stands motionless and aghast at the sight before her. She is eventually able to speak as David and Henry are dousing the corpse with water taken from the trough poor Richie Stark had drowned in.

"Mother of god, what happened, Henry, David?"

"Calm yourself Renee, the excitement is over." Henry steps onto the sidewalk and standing next to his business partner, he explains what had just happened. He tells her how they had been dismounting, how the attacker had surprised them and how Tungsaw had brought the proceedings to a sudden gory finality.

Renee thinks about the offered information. "That poor man, how awful, it's a terrible way to die, Henry!"

"Rare enough but the little man knew what he was doing, Renee."

"How can you say that?"

"That's easy, he's a chef, more or less." They watch as the diminutive Oriental walks nonchalantly across to the body that has now slipped fully downwards onto the sidewalk. Putting one foot onto the still smouldering but unmoving chest, he reaches down to the hilt of the blade and tugs it neatly from its socket. For a moment he looks at the red stained 'spear' before nodding and pronouncing to the bystanders. "This one about done. Coffin maker take away now, Henry."

They all missed the Chinaman's second joke. David has just one thing on his mind as he enters the building and is already searching for Lourinda. He finds her and sleeps the night beside her waxen body, asking himself why he ever came to such a horrible place! David does not have the answer, he does know this isn't the time to give up. He has loved and perhaps lost almost in an instant. He dozes in a chair beside her and listens to her shallow but surprisingly constant breathing. David has hope as much as the girl Lourinda, needs luck. An invisible clock ticks like her gentle heartbeat. All thoughts of the Englishman now drift away due to the accomplished prediction of a 'big' Oriental.

CHAPTER TEN
Building regulations!

David gave little thought to the dead Englishman. He had walked inside and gone into the bedroom where Lourinda lay and stayed loyally and silently at her side for the remainder of the night. Sleep for the Welshman was at best intermittent, almost every hour he would turn his tired eyes to the silent, motionless figure lying there. Davy thought she opened her eyes more than once during the night. It is only imagination he thought in the half light of early morning. Renee came into the room at eight, moving quietly, stepping carefully, not wanting to disturb the peace and calm that seemed to permeate the room. Knowing the importance for David to sleep, she had silently left, unaware he had hardly done so.

Very soon David would creep out of and away from the bedroom. He went to the room which he would normally share with Henry. The Cornishman had already dressed and left. David lay down on the bed and is soon sleeping as peacefully as his injured arm will allow. The Doc' had cleaned and dressed the small hole where the bullet had entered and had done the same for the larger exit wound. 'It'll heal soon enough, Davy. You were damned lucky, you'll be fine' he'd informed the Welshman before his departure. David had stayed silent at the doctor's comments. He didn't feel lucky right then, he didn't feel anything but complete sadness which he thought might forever linger. Doc' Ryder hardly mentioned

Lourinda's present condition as he worked, not wanting to get the Welshman's hopes up while there is still a chance she might not recover.

While David sleeps on, Henry lounges in the company of Jasper Hawke. He is aware that once again the mayor should be informed of the latest sudden death in the town. Explaining all the events of the previous day in detail, Henry knows it is important to put Tungsaw's case strongly. He wants to make certain the mayor would be in no doubt as to how and why the Oriental had ended the ambusher's life so viciously and efficiently and promptly. Jasper nodded regularly as the information is imparted. When all the facts had been disclosed, Henry and Jasper Hawke agreed there was no other choice for the little man, he may even have saved more lives with the decision he took without consultation, there having been no time for discussion, little time to think. They had agreed that although Tungsaw had most likely not been the intended victim, his action should be excused; the life of the Town Marshal and possibly others had been in mortal danger and Tungsaw intended the one necessary death should save the lives of at least two others who were present. It just remained now for the two men to ponder over the Oriental's quick thinking and unequalled fighting agility. They discussed the Chinaman's possible age and came to no conclusion.

David does not show his face for the remainder of the daylight hours. When he eventually awakens from a long deep sleep, he returns to Renee's room and continues his timeless vigil at Lourinda's side.

It is early evening when Joey appears. David had not heard the door open. The boy is quiet, careful. "Davy" he whispers, just audibly in case he is actually asleep.

David looks at the boy, at once realising he might have neglected him since the shooting and his return. "Joey boyyo, it's good to see you, my friend. Is there something you want from me?"

"No Davy, I was wondering, are you going to do your rounds tonight?"

David is taken aback for a moment. He rubs at the still sore and throbbing arm, which injury he had received at the hands of the now deceased and interred Englishman, whose remains had already been put in the ground in the farthest corner of the little cemetery by Jakey. Joey's words rang bells for the Welshman. "Best I do Joey, Jasper will be looking for a new Marshal else. I'll soon be out of a job if I don't boy, thank you for reminding me, lad."

Normality did slowly return to the Plainsman during the following days. Lourinda improved slowly and more importantly, she steadily grew stronger. Seven days might see the cockney girl almost return to her cheeky best and out of bed, helping Renee and Maria by carrying out light duties only. She and David were able to spend a great deal of time in each other's company, though David is careful not to neglect his duties as the town's only peace officer, now Jakey had returned to his forge. Although there is little other crime of note in Hickok, the Welshman took his duties seriously enough to suggest to Jasper Hawke that there should be a regular deputy. The mayor had agreed without argument and asked David to give some thought as to who he thought could be able enough to fill the role. The Marshal knew of only two candidates; Henry would have been first choice, but David knew the Plainsman needed him more. He would speak to Jakey the Blacksmith at the first opportunity to see if he could spend some more time in the position.

During the evening of Lourinda's seventh day of slow but sure recuperation, she decides she is able to put her talents to use at the so far unused piano. She realises too that she should be earning her keep. Playing for the Plainsman's customers would be a good start in that direction, she thought. Lourinda had been carrying out her 'light duties' but in her mind, these small jobs were hardly enough to compensate.

The music proved agreeable to all of the evening's customers. Lourinda promised her new employers that she would continue with the entertainment now she is over the worst. There is no late night get together for the partners, the arrival of the schoolhouse has been promised for the following day. David states he would need an early night now his own wound has healed sufficiently. He knew that Jakey had set aside time to assist, it would give him the ideal opportunity to discuss the possibilities.

The gradually expanding town has moved slowly but surely in the direction of the area of the Atchison and Topeka railroad track, the same stretch of iron that had brought David and Henry to the fledgling town. Just before six-thirty, a slow gradual procession of villagers made their way towards the reserved area. David had arrived first, Henry, Joey, Gladstone and Jakey soon followed. Jasper Hawke came with Doc' Ryder. The doctor had already accepted the permanent position offered by Jasper and he had repaid the mayor's confidence in no small way; the complete recovery of Lourinda, not forgetting David, had been an early testament to his medical skills.

Newly installed Doc Ryder had seen the delivery of the schoolhouse as an opportunity to meet other members of the settlement. He had decided that to roll up his sleeves and get his healing hands dirty would help him to be more quickly accepted into the community, a necessity for Doctor and patients alike. David watched as Jasper and Doc Ryder approached. He had not personally spoken to the physician since the shooting. The chance to thank him properly would come that morning.

"To be honest David, I never thought for one moment she would pull through. She should not have and I don't know why. It is very strange as she had lost so much blood, almost half I would say, it's a mystery to me."

"Well she has Doctor and it can only be thanks to you."

Almost as if by request, a locomotive could be heard approaching the town with no actual station building as yet. A long 'whoooooh' from the steam whistle made the announcement. A small group of excited children had formed and helped make up the reception party. They waited eagerly for the stopping of the engine. Atchison and Topeka had agreed that as the rail was in such close proximity to the town, the building materials for the school house could be unloaded there. It would make sense.

The whole of that morning was needed for the unloading of the pre-formed sections. At the completion of the task, Henry offered beer to the genial rail crew; gratefully they drank. At noon the train pulled away once again. The school building was not the only thing that hadn't continued the journey; a range dressed man had stepped down from the train, an overfull carpet bag along with a Western saddle had been left in the shade of a tree and after discarding the wide, well cared for gun-belt and it's lethal contents, the man had rolled up his sleeves in readiness to offer his help. None of the tireless workers had thought to question the newcomer, strangers were adding to the population of Hickok every other day now. The heavy sections of timber had been their main interest. Now that the sections were adjacent to the recently levelled plot on which they were to be erected, the new man stood out in the crowd. It was obvious to all that there was something a little different about the most recent arrival. David had taken the opportunity to speak to Doc Ryder and now as the two stood together idly chatting, he spied the man dressed similarly to the local cowhands and ranch workers that came to the Plainsman. David excused himself from Doc Ryder and walked towards the cowboy.

"Like to thank you for your efforts, friend!"

Now resting beneath the tree that had shaded the gun-belt and its contents, the man looked up at the speaker. "No thanks needed friend, always willing to do god's work."

David's eyebrows raise up involuntarily. "Sorry, friend?" he apologised questioningly. A man of the cloth who looked more like a gunfighter smiled at the bemused Town marshal.

"I'm here to teach friend, I aim to use this beautiful new building of yours to bring the teachings of the good book to your neighbours. Jefferson Davies*, no relation!" The strangely garbed minister held a hand out to David. The two shook their acceptance. David did not know that a Jefferson Davis had been the Southern State's choice of President when the country had split into two when fathers, brothers and cousins had fought each other for the rights of the slave owners on one side and the rights of the Negro on the other.

"Good to meet you, Mister Jefferson" David offered.

"Not Mister, name's Jefferson, Jeff will suffice and yours?"

"David, Davy Evans, town Marshal at your service, preacher."

This time it was the stranger's eyebrows that lifted higher. "You'd better be Davy, I'll have to whup ya', iffen you ain't." The cowboy laughed and David followed up nervously.

David hadn't noticed until the joking threat, just how big a man Jefferson is. He stands as tall as the Welshman and may have weighed a little more he thought. "You and me could put on a shindig one of these days, Jefferson!" Since David's arrival in Kansas, no opportunity to box had presented itself. The Welshman could see from the Ministers heft and size that he would make a formidable opponent. Jefferson had made it obvious that he knew something of fist fighting.

"Maybe we will Davy, who knows?"

"Henry, Jasper, come and meet our new minister." David beckoned to his two friends. The introductions are speedily

* *Jefferson Finis Davis (June 3, 1808 – December 6, 1889) was an American politician who served as the president of the Confederate States from 1861 to 1865. As a member of the Democratic Party, he represented Mississippi in the United States Senate and the House of Representatives before the American Civil War. He previously served as the United States Secretary of War from 1853 to 1865.*

143

concluded. Each man knows the erection of the schoolhouse is of paramount importance now. David knows he must seize the moment and utilise the available help while it is available. He forms the volunteers into two groups: one group for the general fetching and carrying, the other smaller one for the more intricate joinery work.

The men worked through the whole afternoon and into the late evening. Even as darkness was closing in, the schoolhouse was still taking its shape. Lanterns were spread around the site to allow for the continuation of work. Men came and went and came back again. The wives of Hickok kept their husbands and sons supplied with food; picnics were brought out, chilled beer came from the Plainsman. No strong liquor was to be consumed, none was. Children ran backwards and forwards, sometimes helping, other times just being children. David had warned them not to be playing too close to the work site. 'Doc Ryder hasn't time for patients today' he told them sternly.

The Doctor, sleeves rolled up, had wanted to be included in the work party. The newest Hickokian too, kept busy helping to carry the pre-formed sections. Jefferson stayed the course until only he, David and Jakey were left toiling. It had been a day for everyone to play his or her part, the townspeople had done just that. They knew the building would not be complete by the time they stopped tonight, but one more good dry day would see the roof struts in place and another would see them covered. Davy, Jakey and Jefferson climbed down the makeshift ladders, picking up and stowing away tools. Jefferson pulled the gun-belt about his waist using two leather ties to steady the holsters against the outside of his thighs. David and Jakey waited. The three walked back towards the centre of town, as Hickok is now fast becoming in every way. The lanterns were left to burn themselves out. The tired men congratulated themselves on a good day's hard work. Their entrance to the saloon is greeted by those who had given up earlier.

It seemed to David the population of the whole town are once again assembled in the saloon. Tables are stockpiled with food and bottles, full of various liquids. Renee, Maria and Lourinda had laboured almost as hard as the school builders. Tungsaw, who hadn't come to the site with everyone else, had prepared and cooked most of the feast that now awaited the throng. Lourinda sat at the piano and played cheerful party melodies. Cooking Fat, as the black moggy is now regularly being called by all, sits atop the lightly vibrating instrument. Gladstone dispenses the liquid refreshments, nibbling at the banquet as he works to keep the beer flowing. Singing and dancing became the order of the evening. The violin owner is once again present and with Lourinda at the piano, the music is of a far better quality than the last time it was played. Tungsaw did not this time try to improve his fiddle playing, though later that night he was guilty of an attempt to take Lourinda's place at the ivory decorated keyboard. Having been informed of the Oriental's penchant for musical instruments especially after consuming the fiery yellow liquid, Lourinda, to everyone's relief, was able to repel the intended take-over without giving offence.

The evening was a great success, everybody who was present had said so. Jefferson insisted on a small prayer before the mostly impromptu celebration broke up. The revellers are respectfully silent for the duration of the short offering.

David and Jakey took up their tools early the next morning. Again, others came and went, putting in small but useful efforts when their businesses or household chores allowed. Even Tungsaw had deserted his kitchen to help out on the second day. Renee, who's cooking had improved with helpful patient and unusual tuition from the little Chinaman, had volunteered with Lourinda, to provide what was needed to feed the workers. One by one, the roof joists were secured together and covered. Windows that had been made to measure were fitted into their openings, the large doorframe is put into place.

Having left the Plainsman early again that day, David had been unaware that Lourinda had been unwell. Renee had heard the girl retching. Taking into account the time of day, Renee had quickly come to the conclusion that she is probably carrying a child. Renee thought there was no point to beating about the bush with her, she heard the girl crying and knew that her conclusion must be correct. Quietly sitting with her at the side of the bed, she waited for the girl to compose herself and allowed her to open the conversation. "I didn't mean for it to happen Renee, he forced me. He told me that I wouldn't have a job. I never thought this would happen. I hadn't done that before, it was horrible. He was horrible, he was vile towards me!"

Renee listened to Lourinda's story. She didn't interrupt and waited for her to finish her sad tale. Renee thought back to her own predicament; Jack had treated her somewhat similarly before the arrival of Henry Tamryn and David Evans. Joey's real father had been killed in the early days of the Civil War. Renee was left alone with the young boy. Jack had first befriended mother and son and then trapped them. Renee would have to wait many years to escape from her prison. She knew how Lourinda must have been feeling at the time. She knew the girl would need good, loyal friends about her, now more than ever. Renee vowed she would take care of her for as long as she was needed. She thought about David and wondered how the Welshman would take the news. "It's best we keep this to ourselves for now Lourinda, I won't say anything. As for the Englishman, he can't hurt you now."

"Davy will hate me, I know it."

"Don't judge him hastily girl, you have friends all around you." Renee again thought back. She had had no one, no one to help, no one to confide in. She remembered the times when she had thought to bring a permanent end to her own misery, Joey had been the sole reason she had not. Renee knew that Lourinda would need all her support during the coming months. She told the sniffing girl how it was going to be.

Lourinda's face reflected her inner joy at the sound of Renee's words. Spying Henry's approach, Renee quickly brought the conversation to a halt. She looked at the 'big' Cornishman and spoke quickly in order to allay any suspicions.

Renee and Henry talked about the new man in town and the impending completion of the building that was rising in front of them.

"Don't you think he's a little strange to be a minister, Henry?" Renee asks as they talk. Henry looks across at the gaudily dressed Jefferson with the fine pistols in their holsters and tied around each thigh to allow for the quick withdrawal when called for. He tended to agree, there is something strange about him, but Henry like Renee, is unable to put a finger on the reason they felt as they did. They both knew that so far they had taken an easy liking to the man. Joey joined the party now as they quietly watched, the current conversation is dropped.

"It reminds me of that day we put the new roof on the saloon Ma, you remember?"

"Like it was yesterday Joey, I don't need remindin' thank you!"

Renee coloured a little as she recalled the day her new dress had been soaked in the deluge. She knew that Joey wasn't referring to that particular moment in the episode, but she blushed at the thought of it. Henry smiled, no comment came from his gentlemanly lips, as he too had not forgotten the soaking. He remembered too how the rain had accentuated the outline of Renee's body. That snippet of the past had embedded itself in his memory. Henry is anxious and impatient for Renee to make changes to her early statement about the possibility of courtship, though he had made himself a promise not to broach the subject until she might do so. Renee reflected too on that day that Henry had seen fit to spoil another dress, the day Jack's blood and brain matter had despoiled the garment which she refused to wash, but burned. Renee, in her mind's eye, was picturing the naked Cornishman, naked apart from a portion of grubby curtaining. In the same way, she would hold on jealously to the scene that her mind occasionally conjured up for her. Never for a moment had she thought about the danger of the bullet embedding itself in her flesh, although she had felt the displacement of air as the leaden projectile had sped past her face. She shivered a little as she thought of the consequences of Henry's sudden appearance and quick thinking actions. Everything could have been so different but for the Cornishman.

David broke the extended silence caused by Henry's vivid imagination and Renee's pictorial recall. His words weren't directed at either of the daydreamers, but their spell-breaking ability had the right effect. "Now then Joey, I'm shorthanded, could do with some extra help. Sooner we get finished, sooner you can be schooling."

"You have a way with words Davy, though not a suitable choice methinks to get the youngster on your side" Henry joked and they all laughed.

"Joey, get yourself busy, you too Henry," Renee stamped her own authority on the trio of procrastinators.

The conversation was light hearted but had the desired effect for Renee and Henry. They were snapped out of their reminiscing by David's stated request. Henry took Joey's arm and the two crossed to the building site. "Come on then my boy, let's see what we can be doing, don't bleddy dawdle lad."

Renee made her way to the kitchen where she was confronted with an agitated Tungsaw. Lourinda and Maria had both tried unsuccessfully to calm the excited chef. Pleased to see the return of Renee, they left her to try and extract the reason for Tungsaw's not unusual histrionics.

Unbeknown to Renee and Tungsaw, Joey was already in the process of easing the Chinaman's pain. The agile youth had swiftly cleared the slopes formed by the schoolhouse roof and was shining up the little incomplete bell tower. Cooking Fat had not been seen since late the previous night, since the first day party to celebrate the arrival of the building, which Joey was now scaling with a youthful ease. The big black cat had made the decision that the top of the piano was an ideal sleeping place. When not dozing there, he could be found looking for scraps in the kitchen. Tungsaw is worried because the cat is not in either place.

Joey carried at Henry's suggestion, a small burlap sack tucked into his belt.

"That thing might not want to be rescued Joey, cats are funny like that" Henry had mentioned. Joey reached the belltower with little fuss. He grabbed at and secured Cooking Fat and started his descent. Renee and Tungsaw had been informed of the rescue and were crossing the street towards the building as Joey jumped from the porch, sack in hand. He put down the wriggling noisy sack and pulled at the opening. Cooking Fat strolled out nonchalantly at his master's approach. The beast gave a short hiss of annoyance and was soon moving fleet footed away from the swearing, chasing, Oriental. Renee watched as the pair passed her.

"Well then Joey, I didn't think you had it in you my boy, I'm right bleddy proud."

"What do you mean, Henry?"

"For a while there, you were top of the school, youngster."

Renee laughed at her scowling son. "That ain't bleddy funny, ma!"

"What did you say, Joey?"

"I said 'that ain't bleddy' funny, ma!"

"What does bleddy mean, may I ask?"

"I ain't sure ma, Henry says it all the bleddy time."

"And so do you now it seems."

"It's a mild cuss word, Renee. It's a part of our language in Cornwall, everyone uses it now and then."

"If you're going to swear Henry, then do it properly. Stop teaching my boy such things."

"I haven't schooled him, he learned all by himself."

"If he hadn't heard you, he wouldn't be saying it, mister darn Cornishman."

"I suppose you could be right, Renee."

"Of course I'm right mister, now go wash your bleddy mouth out with soap and don't let me hear it again." Renee's anger isn't real, she is just enjoying the moment and strengthening her wish to get closer to the Cornishman. Henry is oblivious and doesn't realise as yet what is occurring. A time will come when he will thank the day he did use the word and Renee and Joey will do the same.

Renee had not realised straightaway she herself had now made use of the word. Joey and Henry could hardly stop laughing at her, which made her even more angry. It was a little joke she had brought upon herself. She won't be allowed to forget it, Henry and the boy would make sure of it.

Renee had used the moment to good effect and damned the consequences!

One other moment that had occurred not so long ago would also strengthen their relationship. Renee will keep it to herself for now. Not so far in the future will come the time when she can't hide the fact the two had become one for a short time. She walked away smiling and thinking she had not contrived this situation, Joey and Henry had unknowingly brought it about. It had all been fortuitous and she had used it to her advantage.

CHAPTER ELEVEN
Finger of God

There was just one last thing to do to the exterior of the school building to bring it to completion, there is still plenty more to do inside. The bell needs to be hoisted into place in the squat tower above the roof. The sound would welcome children to school, and ring them out at the end of the day's lessons. It would call the townspeople to worship, it would be sounded for funerals and weddings and it would be sounded for sudden emergencies and even for occasional council meetings. Fire, Indian attack or tornado would be cause for its warning knell.

David, Jakey, Henry and Jefferson were nominated to tug the bell up and into the tower. Due to the awkwardness of the task, it took the four burly heavyweights almost two hours to complete the task. When it was done Mrs Hawke was nominated for the honour of pulling on the rope first. She did it amongst the cheers of everyone present. Instead of holding a service inside the new building, the Reverend Jefferson held the inaugural meeting outside. Prayers were said and hymns were sung with gusto. The piano was brought across from the Plainsman and Lourinda did her best to give accompaniment to the rousing singing. When all was done, everyone returned home happy.

Jasper Hawke appears at the Plainsman early that following morning. He has good news for all and was eager to share it as soon as he can. "We have it Henry, we have it.

The railroad has agreed to give us our own station, here in our town. We'll be on the map now, there's no stopping us! What do you say, Henry?"

"Well Jasper I'm pleased, but things will change you know. More businesses will arrive, each of our own businesses will have more competition." Henry is pleased with the news but he realises the possible consequences that success can bring. They would all have to accept the changes. He wanted Hickok to grow, even with the rail stop it wouldn't happen overnight, change is always slow in happening, Henry thought. It was on the way though and the Plainsman would have to be prepared for the day someone else will open a better boarding house, restaurant or saloon. He is glad that Renee had not had a change of mind about the restaurant. Someone new would open another and even two could appear he thought 'and good luck to them' they will keep us on our toes. We could build a reputation on good food, quality French wines even and good cold beer, which should stand the Plainsman in good stead if and when competition arrives.

That night Tungsaw died. Gladstone had gone to his room when he hadn't appeared in the kitchen. Doc Ryder had been called immediately but there was nothing to be done, the old chef was already cold. No one knew how old he was, but David and Henry knew what a good and loyal friend he had been in the short time they had been acquainted. They were all going to miss the little man's comical antics, Gladstone more than most. After he had found Tungsaw's cold body he had wept openly as he told Renee of what he had discovered. Although Renee had taken the news with sadness, she is already making plans for the little man's funeral. Tungsaw had been a good friend to her, to everyone, he was unpredictable, feisty and a very good cook. He could never have called himself a chef but he never turned out second rate food, every dish had to be just right. As for the early morning after Lourinda had been shot? No one would know he had been the last to see her before he, David and Henry had gone in search of the Englishman.

Nobody had seen the little man go to the room where she lay and what he did. No one will ever know now. Tungsaw has taken his strange action to his grave. As for his killing of the Englishman, it was something he never talked about again after the act. He had done what needed to be done!

Jasper suggested that they give over a section of the tiny cemetery to Tungsaw. He told Renee that almost all Western cemeteries had separate areas for Jewish people, why should it be any different for Chinese People? Renee wasn't convinced, thinking that the little man would be lonely on his own. Jasper argued that with only the most unfortunate Richie and the less deserving Englishman, as well as Jack the rat, that Tungsaw would be better on his own. Renee thought about this and in the end had to agree. She certainly didn't want Tungsaw resting anywhere near to Jack. 'No one deserves to have to lie next to the bastard. I know I shouldn't speak ill of the dead, but he deserves no less.' Renee apologised to Jefferson for her choice of words. Jefferson knew nothing of the rat's history, but decided Renee must have good reason to remember the man the way she did. Renee went to the small workshop at the back of the Plainsman. In this case, the undertaker was told to spare no expense. She wanted only the best for their ancient, little friend. The man promised he would take care of him 'as if he were royalty.' David easily carried Tungsaw's little body to the undertakers at the back of the Plainsman. Renee went with him to give her instructions.

"Ma, he's in there again."

"Who's in where again?" Joey had jolted his mother from her solemn mood.

"Cooking Fat, he's back in the bleddy tower, I saw him climbing up the roof before."

Renee thought about what Joey was telling her. She thought the cat might have somehow sensed its master was about to depart. Why else would the beast have gone up there yesterday and why has he gone back up today? He must have known!

Renee had a more pressing problem than that of the faithful black cat. She would have to get Maria and Lourinda together and organise the cooking for the Plainsman. Now that she had given her preliminary instructions to the undertaker, she would direct her attention to the kitchen. Unknown to her, the solution was already approaching and it came in the form of Jefferson Davis.

"Morning Renee! I believe you need my services."

"Well, we need to fix a date for Tungsaw's burying."

"No, that ain't it." Jefferson drawled.

"What then?"

"Way I see it, you'll be needin' someone to cook for the Plainsman and I'm here." Jefferson explained that he is as near qualified as anyone else she could think of. "I cooked for the brave sons of the South, I need a job too, ministering don't pay worth a d..." Jefferson broke off before using the mild but popular expletive.

"God moves in mysterious ways alright. The job's yours Jeff, as long as you want it, as far as I'm concerned. You can start when you like. You will have a lot to live up to mind, so think on."

"I surely will, where's the kitchen at?" Jefferson already knew the answer to the question and straightaway disappeared in the required direction. Renee walked outside and almost bumped into the ladder that stood there. She looked up to find the big Welshman at the top. She also saw a large bellied man standing back in the middle of the road watching her business partner with interest, while he attempted to nail a newly made sign above the doors:

'THE PLAINSMAN'

David had found some excess timber, it had been packing for the bell during its transportation; with a small amount of trimming and smoothing, he had been able to fashion the new and welcoming sign. Renee felt a welling of pride as she read the message. She looked across at the man in the road, she had the feeling that she perhaps should know the stranger, but was certain she didn't. The man, realising the woman's predicament, spoke first.

"Morning Ma'am, names Fe Tylden, you must be Renee, I reckon!"

David overheard the introduction and smiled as he turned; the ladder shifted and he fell almost on top of but only adjacent to the wagon boss. "How are ya' doin' Davy? You needn't have gone to all that trouble just for me, a simple hello would have done."

"You old bastard, you nearly got me killed there, do you have to sneak up on folks that way?" Although unconsciously rubbing at the bullet scar, David's arm has healed completely now.

Renee ignored the friendly banter and held a hand out to Fe Tylden. "Glad to meet you Fe, heard some about you, bad mostly I have to say."

"I sure ain't too surprised about that ma'am, them two fellers of yours could win a liars contest blindfold, I reckon."

"Hold hard there wagon man, don't you go telling any of your damn untruths about us. No one would believe you anyways thinking on it." David got to his feet and shook hands with his friend. "You bring that water bottle with you, Fe?"

"Why, sure I did, that old Chinese about?"

"You could say so, though he won't be drinking any more of your special water."

"He give it up?"

"Sort of, gave up everything, died last night it seems, poor old guy, he'll be missed around here boyyo. There isn't and won't be another like Tungsaw."

"I'm right sorry to hear that, only came into town to get me some of them pancakes for breakfast. That little yeller feller could sure whistle them up some!"

"Couldn't he just! We should be able to find something for you Fe, got ourselves a new chef, not five minutes ago."

"We did, Renee?" asked David, "I never knew that, nobody tells me any damn thing around here dammit. Get inside Fe, you're making the town look untidy."

"You can go to hell on a damn handcart, Welshman!"

"Davy, this is Jefferson, he's in the kitchen now, says he can cook with the best, the way he tells it."

"I'll be happy if he can jest cook on his own, Renee. Anyways we don't need more than one and there ain't room for two in there."

Renee led Fe Tylden into the saloon. David had told her that as soon as he had finished hanging the sign he would find Henry and tell him of their visitor. When asked, Jefferson had promised pancakes for the wagon boss. Few minutes would pass before he was already eating the favoured rangeland delicacy, a plateful of the fresh smelling items. Jefferson had also brought out a small dish of maple syrup. Tylden thanked the newly installed cook. David kept his promise and on finding Henry had brought him back to the saloon. The two men exchanged warm greetings. Henry waited for Tylden to finish his breakfast coffee before questioning him as to his reasons for being in Hickok. After washing down the pancakes with the hot coffee, Fe Tylden quickly came to the point. Addressing the three partners as one, he outlined a plan that had interesting promise. "I would like to bring the wagon trains down through here regular, there's good grazing just outside of town, you're a good distance from our starting point and I hear that Atchison and Topeka are making plans for a permanent rail stop right here."

Since the day Henry and David first arrived, the trains have hardly stopped for more than just a moment or two, but more recently, townspeople have been travelling away for various reasons of their own. The little station house is becoming well used. Now the rail company have decided to make Hickok an official stop.

"News travels fast, we only found out yesterday." The news had arrived with the stage. The driver had sought out Jasper and had delivered the letter marked confidential from A&T RR. "Seems we'd better get Jasper in here, he'll have to have the say on your suggestion Fe, he's our mayor." Renee shouted in no particular direction, for Joey.

The boy promptly appeared and she gave him the instruction to find Jasper. Joey is soon through the door and already searching for Mayor Hawke. David, Fe and Renee made conversation while they waited for the arrival of the other men. Fe told the partners that he would stay for Tungsaw's funeral before leaving and reporting his findings back to his sponsors. He explained that although he is in sole charge of the wagon trains he leads, the sponsors have the responsibility of forming and up to a point, equipping them. He explained too that the train he had been leading when the men had first met had completed its trek and those people that had travelled with it were now forming a good sized settlement somewhere in South Western Wyoming. In answer to David's enquiry as to what had happened to the young lady with the baby, Fe was hesitant to give an answer. Davy didn't push the questioning, knowing that Fe must have his reasons for not divulging the answer. Fe Tylden asked after the health of the girl, Lourinda. Renee answered that she is much improved and that she would be around the place somewhere.

Joey reappeared with Mayor Hawke. Fe Tylden told the mayor of the intended plans, going into more detail than previously. Hawke had arrived and listened intently to the wagon boss before giving his personal appraisal of the scheme. He informs Tylden there are members of a council to satisfy and he would talk to them at the first opportunity. Fe Tylden is happy to comply with the mayor's decision.

Henry suddenly realised. "Fe did not know what happened on our return from chasing the Englishman. Fe, did you hear about the other death we had here? I doubt you did, you being on the wagon train. The Englishman came back to finish the job, he didn't quite make it. Well, he made a try but the Chinaman fired him, literally."

"He sacked the bastard?"

"Nope, he fired him, he ran him through him with that damned Pig Sticker, then he fired him. He caught fire when he fell against the night lamp and if he weren't already dead, he surely burned to death."

"Not like the Chinaman I knew, he never burned anything."

The remainder of the day and the evening passed with the friends reminiscing about their previous meetings, with and without the favoured Tungsaw. Although Renee was aware of most of the amusing antics, she still laughed with the others as they were recounted and the tales once more embellished. She, like her company, would never easily forget the unpredictable Oriental.

The next morning was set aside for more solemn business. Jefferson had made the arrangements for Tungsaw's funeral. The piano was again borrowed and this time, taken inside the new schoolhouse. The little building was almost full to its capacity, temporary seating had been put in place to allow for the large turnout. Ranch hands put aside their duties to cattle and helped move the piano, Soul Broadbent arrived with the two cowboys that had dunked the unfortunate Richie in the trough, others from their spread sat with them. Stetsons and other headgear lay wedged between knees. The Plainsman was closed and Jasper had shut down the general store for that morning. Jefferson nodded to Lourinda as she played a slow rendition of the rangeland favourite 'All things bright and Beautiful.' Not everyone knew all the words but the song was sung, nonetheless.

Nobody even noticed Wild Bill step quietly into the back of the room, where he stood, hat in hand, for the entire service. All eyes were directed to the front, where Jefferson stood next to the smart coffin that Renee had insisted on providing. At the end of the service, David, Henry, Jasper and Soul carried the coffin out through the doorway and as gently as they could, laid it down on the back of the same flatbed that had recently carried the piano. Neither of the willing couriers would realise they were going against the opinions of certain groups in the 'West' that Chinese should be treated even at best, as second class citizens.

A walking procession followed the slow moving wagon to the plot which is situated to one side of and at the end of the town's main street and across the creek. It is a full ten minutes before the wooden box is lifted down again. Jefferson spoke solemnly as the coffin is gently lowered into the freshly dug grave. It had been noticed that Tungsaw had very little possessions of his own, the sharply honed sword and scabbard being the most favoured. A sad faced Gladstone knelt, almost delicately, as he lowered the weapon and it's well-fitting sheaf into the grave, placing them on the lid before it became covered with the rich, dark Kansas soil.

Sentinel like, Cooking Fat stared out across the town's expanse. From his vantage point he would certainly be able to watch the proceedings in the cemetery from his position. Cooking Fat stayed where he was for the whole of the day. He has adopted the little tower as his home it seemed. Occasionally coming down to chase a prairie mouse when hungry or to be chased by some boisterous dog, at times he would visit the Plainsman for some cooked nutrition, gladly given. Always he would return to the tower afterwards. Joey didn't ever climb up the sloping roof again.

The Tornado barged at Hickok late that same night. Even as the service at the cemetery was coming to an end, towering clouds were already thickening and darkening. In the far distance, thunderheads could be seen forming ominously. The majority of the inhabitants of Hickok would never have seen or even heard of a Tornado before, there had been many newcomers to the area. Occasionally, little dust devils spun and danced up or down the wide street, these being the nearest most would have seen of the death dealing storms too often apt to appear in Kansas, Oklahoma, sometimes in Texas and even though unusually, some of the more Northerly United States. The heat rose all that afternoon, the long prairie grass no longer swaying, it's rhythm broken. It seemed any little whiff of a breeze was absent, allowing the bubbling pressure of the atmosphere to become still. The wind did come, ebbing and flowing rather like waves on an ocean; the regulation six small ones would gradually pull more water back for the highest seventh. The hot Kansas breezes seemed to be saving themselves for the big wave. Now and then, the heated, gusty wind would return, only to hide away again. Lightning storms began to fork and flicker spasmodically, coming close to town then moving off, another seemingly taking its place coming from some different direction. No rain fell from the purpled sky until after dark. The wetting seemingly signalling an icy bombardment of hailstones. Even the heavy showers were not consistent, they too gave the impression of retreat after violent counter attacks.

There was no celebratory mood in the Plainsman the evening of Tungsaw's funeral. The Plainsman, later than usual, is open for business, though the mood is subdued, almost as if those present are expectant of some approaching disaster befalling them. Everyone could feel the tension rising. Small groups formed around the large room, voices seemed to be unconsciously lower in volume. Renee did her duty in moving from one group to another, adding comments to one or another conversation. Joey shadowed Wild Bill as he sat unusually relaxed with Fe Tylden and Henry. David talked quietly to Lourinda, huddled almost as if in some secret conversation. Gladstone half smiled as Maria skipped back and forth with glasses and emptied plates.

Lightning regularly seared into the Plainsman from all angles now it seemed. The sound of breaking glass in the kitchen is lost in the thunder that sounded like the tearing off of the new roof. Lourinda yells her defiance and swears uncharacteristically at the heavenly cannon fire. Another short lull led to many of the customers making hasty, homebound retreats. Some knew what might be in store for them, those that didn't still talked nervously, but expectantly.

Renee spoke to the remainder from the middle of the room, she was certain now of her facts. Although Hickok in its early days as a settlement had not been visited by the most powerful force above the earth's surface, Tornadoes had skirted the town before with one coming so close, ranch houses and barns had totally vanished, cattle too sometimes.

Renee remembered the amusing story that Soul had often related when they had found the ranches' bunkhouse backhouse half a mile from where it had been originally erected. Soul had sworn they had found Billy the ranch cook still in it and still reading an ancient copy of Harper's Magazine. The truth had been that the cook was still in the tiny three by three, but was unconscious, magazine still in his hand. Inside the magazine were hidden erotic photographs. From the day of the discovery, Billy had had to put up with his new and unwanted, but well earned, sobriquet of Backhouse Billy. Renee had laughed so much then and sometimes afterwards, whenever she thought about Soul's quietly explained description of the young cook's favourite pastime. She'd often thought about the hole in the ground that was there for no reason.

"It seems to me gents, that we might be in the wrong place, there's a twister coming I reckon and we'd all be best off in the schoolhouse. You can all make up your own minds, that's where I'm headed." Agreement is unanimous, each man and woman lifted their glasses and prepared to leave the saloon. "Now just wait a minute, I wouldn't think Reverend Jefferson would be wanting liquor in his church."

Jefferson instantly interrupted Renee's impromptu speech. "Well now Renee, let's look at it thisaway, if we are all gonna catch hold of this twister's tail, I'd rather have a beer in my one empty hand."

"You're the boss, Jeff."

"Well no ma'am I surely ain't, but I got his ear, you could say."

Hail clattered on the windows of the building once again. More lightning instantaneously, followed by deafening thunder now, this last seemingly giving the gathering the impetus to leave for what might be the safer haven. David, Henry, Joey, Gladstone, Wild Bill and Fe each agreed to spread the word as far as they could before themselves retreating into the schoolhouse. Renee had told all to be careful, especially Joey. She didn't want him to go, but thinking he would resent her stopping him, she agreed reluctantly that he could. "Five minutes Joey, then you get in that schoolhouse." Jasper had made his way to the new building, it was he who was sounding the alarm by means of the bell rope. When the five minutes had passed, Joey was almost blown into the dreaded building. Even in an emergency, it had seemed that he had not wanted to be associated with the shelter and the safety offered. The other men came in followed by a crocodile of animated and nervous townspeople.

The wind become an endless roar as the Tornado closes on the town. The dark purple sky is almost constantly illuminated now, the rattle of hail and storm debris sounding like an applauding crowd at the end of a concert in a theatre. David stared around the building he almost single-handedly put up, he heard the creeks and groans as the Tornado edged inexorably closer. The townspeople had gained the inside of the schoolhouse and attempted to converse with each other, most giving up as their voices were drowned in the waves of violence which were battering the wooden shelter. Frightened, they stared at each other as the thunderous fusillade continued, each one wondering and worrying what was happening to their homes, their stock and indeed their very lives. The roar reached its crescendo. To all it seemed God was hurling their very sins at them. Jefferson standing at one end of the building knelt, he closed his hands together and prayed for his newly gathered flock, some joined him on their knees, others prayed where they stood and suddenly, as if a switch had been thrown, silence descended on the building.

David and Lourinda had been in deep secretive conversation for some time. Lourinda had somehow whispered her secret to the big Welshman; he had listened without judgement to the girl's tortured recalling of her time with the Englishman and his young family. When Lourinda had finished her story, he spoke aloud.

"Can you marry us, Jefferson?" Lourinda had brought up the subject with perfect timing!

Although showing surprise at the sudden request, Jefferson quickly answered. "Sure Davy, have you got a date in mind?"

"Tonight's good for us as right now, this is a church." David looked at the girl holding his hand, she nodded smiling. She looked at Jefferson.

"Don't see why not, we'll most likely all be blown away to pieces soon enough. Let's get to it." Jefferson waved the pair forward. "You'll need witnesses."

David looked around them at the few who had not left the safety of the schoolhouse. "Got us some I would say."

"You sure have my friend." Jefferson asked for more room and started the impromptu ceremony. At each sentence the wind seemed to increase again, as if trying to blot out the words and the solemn promises. Jefferson raised his voice as the Tornado started once again to throw pieces of Hickok at the building. He instructed David to kiss the bride, the groom didn't hear the words. Jefferson ushered the two together and they understood. The Welshman learned then what the minister had been saying. Fe Tylden came forward and congratulated the pair first, others followed. It is like a scene from some silent play, mouths opening but nothing being heard, all conversation drowned out due to the storm. It didn't matter, as Jefferson's work was done.

CHAPTER TWELVE
The Aftermath

A s the first light of dawn raced across the moisture-freshened green Kansas Plains towards Hickok, they emerged, slowly. At first glance the scene is one of desolation. Although the battered walls of the schoolhouse are mostly undamaged, it seems from the haphazard piles of wreckage at the base, the storm had been hurling its might at the temporary sanctuary. Debris is strewn the length of the street, homeless chickens run loose, freed from their splintered pens by the storm. David's sign dangles loosely from one solitary nail. Renee looks up, relieved to see the new roof is still in place, it had been her biggest worry. She could see by the wreckage that others had been less lucky. Joey shouted "Ma look, its Cooking Fat, he's still up there. He must have been up there all the while through the storm."

Renee looked up. She could see the black feline pacing the tiny parapet of the unfinished bell tower. Although she was pleased the cat is safe, there are more important things to contend with. Neighbours would be needing help. Hickok had been lucky, the twister had danced a crazy path around and behind most of the main buildings. There is some damage along the town's main street, but of a sort that can easily be put right in time.

It seems to Renee the Tornado's power had been sent to strengthen the community, not to weaken it. The Tempest has brought the town together, no one is seriously injured, no one had died as far as she knows. The midnight wedding of David and Lourinda had given an impression of laughter in the face of adversity.

As Renee opened the unlocked doors of the Plainsman, she thought about Lourinda and David wondering if the girl had told the Welshman about the baby she is carrying. The child of a would-be murderer who will at least have a decent father now. Another Englishwoman is somewhere out on the plains waiting for and wondering where her husband is. She is sure Lourinda would have done the right thing and told David.

Renee is correct, during their quiet conversation the previous night Lourinda had told David everything. The big Welshman had taken her words in his stride. Although seething at the result of the girl's awful experiences, he had listened in silence. The recounting had only stiffened his resolve. The storm had presented him with the opportunity he had wanted; Lourinda's child would need a father, Tungsaw's actions had made life safe for the English girl. David would not forget the small but significant part the 'old' Chinaman had played in the prolonging of his own life!

That morning and the afternoon that followed would be taken up with beginning the clearance of the scattered debris. The townsmen formed themselves into work parties, systematically they worked with the neighbours that had become worse hit. When day became night they stopped. The next morning would also be used for reparation. By the end of that second day almost everything was as it should be. Fe Tylden and Wild Bill Hickok had played their part, each man had rolled up sleeves and dispensed with gun-belts as they worked for the good of the town.

David re-hung the sign and repaired breakages to the drainage system that had unwittingly contributed to the accidental death of Ritchie Stark and at exactly the same spot Tungsaw had carried out his gruesome but necessary work.

Lourinda took it upon herself to make a start at organising the schoolhouse in readiness for the education of the town's children. Now that she had no need to worry about the bullying Englishman, she threw herself into the task. Her condition isn't readily apparent at this point but David consistently reminded her to 'be careful' mostly when they were alone together. At each warning, Lourinda would laugh off his concerns. She bought chalk writers to go with the little black painted slates that Davy had fashioned for the dozen or so children who might attend. They weren't really slate, but David had black painted the boards three times so they might write easily on them. Latrines were built at the back of the school, one for girls and one for boys. Each shed held a row of four wooden seats, there was no privacy between each latrine.

Once the school building and it's outhouses had been completed, Henry had helped the Welshman bring round the timber that was once the bar top. The stout timber had been kept for the use of the children as desk tops.

On the third day following the storm, both Wild Bill and Fe Tylden had departed. Again both men made promise of further visits; Fe had promised he would be giving his sponsors a good report regarding the wagon trains. They had remembered to thank all for the 'hospitality and entertainment,' Soon everything was almost back to normal in the town. The Plainsman and the schoolhouse more and more become a hive of activity. Jasper's hardware and general store too is in greater demand.

Seven days after the storm, Atchison Topeka and Santa Fe came to town in the form of a surveying party. A gang of labourers accompanied the surveyors and work was soon put under way for the erection of the necessary buildings. A small, tented camp grew outside Hickok. In the beginning, the labourers kept themselves to themselves. Maria and others of her profession would make many visits to the canvas colony. The eager men treated the girls well by all accounts. The weekly train now became twice weekly. A platform is being constructed and the trains are able to stop and take on water piped from the creek. The platform will be lengthened later. Building materials, hardware supplies fresh foodstuffs and rolls of cloth were unloaded. Animals in the shape of chickens, goats, even the first oxen came to town courtesy of the Atchison and Topeka Railroad.

Two new saloons opened, Jasper along with business acquaintances from his past started Hickock's first bank. Jakey the Blacksmith turned his shop into a full scale livery business, Jasper, having more than enough on his plate, had offered the blacksmith his small stock at an agreeable price and Jakey had eagerly accepted. A full-time bathhouse and barber shop opened its doors. The blacksmith will keep extra equine stock so Fe can change tired horses for the stages.

Renee had long ago ceased the service that had been started when she still had Jack to contend with. The service had only been provided to encourage the promotion of prostitution. Jack's pockets had been the main benefactors from the lucrative trade. Now Renee is accepted and is becoming a respected member of the population. She in no way misses the occupation she had followed before Henry and David had arrived at the makeshift saloon. She would not let herself forget those days, though she would never deride Maria and her friends for following in her own unsteady footsteps. Towns, villages such as Hickok all had their brothels and suchlike. Jack was different, he bullied the ladies into what he wanted them to do, they got little for their services other than a roof over their heads and occasional meals.

Lourinda had with David's help, hung homemade bunting at the school porch; paper lanterns decorated the doorway, a feeling of achievement hung about the completed building. Cooking Fat strode about the bell tower, an air of ownership in his gentle steps, only descending for meals provided by the Plainsman and others. The 'caretaker' cat still visited the Plainsman occasionally, knowing he would always receive the regulation food. Joey had reported more than once seeing the beast coming from the graveyard, where his little friend, his owner, is now laying at rest.

Henry now has a comprehensively written record of the saloon's accounts, he would spend hours poring over them. When business matters were complete, he would update his journal. The partners still held their late night after business conferences, new suggestions as to how to improve the turnover were still sought and accepted, providing the ideas were viable. The undertaker's lean-to being damaged by the Tornado, was re-sited, though happily enough as business wasn't thriving like the others of Hickok. Jakey and David now had a cell in which to keep belligerent drinkers, though there were few. Jasper's cellar was now needed to house the extra stocks he was obliged to keep and so the council had sanctioned the building of an office and cell for the town's three lawmen to operate from.

Gladstone, showing now that he is a more than capable member of the community, had been accepted as second deputy; though his duties were minimal and mostly part-time, he proudly wore his badge of office whenever he had an official duty and whenever temptation might get the better of him, he just worked where he was wanted and needed. Gladstone always took his turn at doing the rounds late at night and when not on duty at the Plainsman's bar.

The recently commissioned Gladstone still missed the little Chinaman as much as any. The barman still wore lard in his hair.

Small side streets have begun to stretch away from the main thoroughfare; tiny cottages were erected in a day and rough-hewn shanties sprung up that sometime in the future would be improved. Town plots were being sought and bought from the council at encouraging rates. Some of the builders received annuities from the federal government; parcels of promised land being their reward for risking life and limb in the brothers and cousins war of the eighteen-sixties. Just a few of these veterans did have missing limbs. None in Hickok followed the trend of begging, unlike those in bigger towns and cities. Each had seen fit to try some enterprise allowing them to support themselves and any small families they might have. One of these unfortunates even took a job at Jakey's stables, handling horses with only one hand isn't that difficult if you know what you're doing!

Jefferson had for some time now left off the gunbelt, with its death delivering contents, his time now almost completely taken up with the church and aiding Lourinda with the education of the children. Joey had, with fierce reluctance, followed Renee's directive, picked up the schoolbooks and joined the small but eager class. Joey had surprised all by taking to the work with no small amount of endeavour. In a short space of time he had learnt to read and was soon improving his scripts. Jefferson and David had been instrumental in the boy's changing outlook towards education. Although his torrid past wasn't left far behind, he began to see himself in a different light, a more than useful member of the population. Renee watched the boy's improvements with pride and despite her own limitations in education, she too did whatever she might to help his fast growing accumulation of knowledge.

The school although still thinly attended, is at least up and running. The railroad buildings are rising, slowly but surely. David had watched whenever time had allowed. He'd not helped or interfered, the regular rail workers had plenty of experience to cope with any problems that might arise in the construction of the buildings, though the Marshal had watched in the interests of improving his own knowledge. Occasionally Cooking Fat would wander over to the site and cast an eye over the happenings there. The cat was careful not to feel the toe-end of a boot of one of the Gandy Dancers*, as the railroad workers were popularly called at the time. Cooking fat would look around but still return to his rooftop sanctuary.

---

* *Gandy Dancers There are various theories about the derivation of the term, but most refer to the dancing" movements of the workers using a specially manufactured 5-foot (1.5 m) lining bar, which came to be called a gandy, as a lever to keep the tracks in alignment as they were laid.*

The Gandy Dancers liked to amuse themselves playing baseball when the working day came to an end. At weekends too, they could often be seen on a patch of ground that was big enough and level enough to represent a makeshift Diamond. One night in the Plainsman, a gauntlet was thrown down. The men from the A & T wanted some opposition. Henry not being one to miss out on a sporting challenge agreed a team could be raised. "We'll give you a match boys, you name the day and we'll be ready for you." Henry told the challengers. July 4th Independence Day, is chosen, it being just two weeks away and the workers knowing the holiday weekend would see the station finished and their work in Hickok complete. The favoured day for celebrations and outings in the United States was agreed upon. Though most but not all of the Gandy workers were of European origin, no one could find any reason not to use the date that celebrated the separation of Great Britain and the American colonists more than ninety years earlier.

The next morning saw the arrival of a heavily laden 'Prairie Schooner.' Jasper Hawke stepped off the sidewalk and introduced himself as Mayor to the trail weary driver of the huge rig. "Good morning friend, you seem to have your work cut out with that wagon of yours. Are you passing through, or stopping awhile, friend?"

The driver stepped down from the hard wooden seat. Hitching the reins to a rail he answered the question. "Was hoping to stop permanently Mr Mayor, got something here in the back that might interest you and the good people of your town." Joey walked over and stood next to the mayor and the driver as they talked. "I'm a newspaperman, Mayor and this here's my press. Like to stop and set up here, what do you say?"

Jasper looked at the huge white topped wagon. "I'd say that we, and I know I can speak for the rest of the council and the townsfolk, will be delighted. I'm surprised that it's taken so long for one of you people to find us." Jasper had heard that sometimes the arrival of a newspaper press had pre-empted the settlement it would serve. Joey listened to the conversation with interest. He would share the news with the other children and Lourinda when he reached the schoolhouse. Jasper reminded Joey that he would be late if he didn't get on his way. He left, allowing the two men to introduce themselves and to come to an amicable decision regarding the newspaper enterprise. Jasper Hawke is a forward looking man and knows that a regular newspaper would be a great asset to Hickok.

"Benford, George Benford, Mr Hawke."

"Jasper, George." The two men shook hands. "Well now George, I'd say you were wanting some breakfast. I'll take you to some friends of mine that'll fix you up. You'll have to see Jakey about the rig, he's the ostler around town. I'll show you where to find him, then we'll go and see Renee. We can eat at the Plainsman."

"So where are you from, George?"

"Georgia, Atlanta, Georgia. I got my name from there and I learned my trade there."

Henry joins the conversation and introduces himself to the newspaperman."

"You don't sound like you come from anywhere I'd know about!"

"England, the home of Saint George actually, though we of Cornwall are Cornish not English. England and Wales have their own identity, we do too."

"Ahh, I know a little of it, the land of Merlin and Arthur, Cornish not English. The round table eh?"

"That's right. Only we already had some bleddy magicians here. This place was wrecked by a Tornado not so long ago, though you wouldn't know it now."

"Why all the flags and whatnot, Jasper?"

"July 4th, Independence day. There is to be a baseball game between the town and the railroad workers. You should write a piece for your paper, George."

"I surely will, I will write a report for the first edition."

"You arrived just in time then, perfect!"

Jasper knew George would want to see to the welfare of his livestock before seeing to his own needs. The two men climbed up on the seat of the wagon and Jasper gave George directions to Jakey's livery barn.

David, with Henry's help, is polishing the sections of cherry wood that were to be used to replace the stained, warped planks. Renee watched over the work with a keen eye. She knew the removal of the planks would mean the removal of one of the final memories of Jack. Renee watched impatient but quietly as David put the finishing touches to the new bartop. Although early customers were already taking their place in the Plainsman, Gladstone was still able to serve them. Jasper Hawke and Henry guided George Benford into the establishment. The mayor ordered breakfast for George and himself while introducing the newly arrived newspaperman to David and Renee. Renee shouted to Jefferson, the new chef appeared and she passed on the food orders. Neither Henry, David, Renee nor Jasper noticed the mild interest shown to the departing chef by George Benford.

The two 'carpenters' continued their task with the bar top, leaving Renee to talk to George Benford about his plans for the newspaper.

"What are you thinking of calling the paper, George?"

"I don't know yet Renee, any suggestions?"

"No, but if I think of one, I'll let you know."

"Seems to me that you have already taken the best name, for this place!"

"I'm not giving it up George, you'll have to find something different, sorry."

"Don't you worry yourself Renee, I'll come up with something. Got to find somewhere to set up yet, that's my first job. I'll worry about naming the paper later."

"I'm sure we have something that'll suit you, George. Let's have breakfast, then the two of us can have a look around the town, get you to feeling at home."

"Why sure Jasper, that sounds good to me." Renee left the two men to eat their meal and went back to watching the carpenters.

Jasper and George Benford walked the length of the one main street. "That was a damn good meal Jasper, the chef certainly knows his stuff. What did you say his name was?"

"Jefferson! Funny you should ask me that. You know I don't rightly know if that's his first, last or only name, I never heard anyone call him anything but Jeff or Jefferson. No wait, Davies I think, Jefferson Davies. Anyway, another thing that might interest you, he's our minister too. In fact, just last week he married David and Lourinda, smack bang in the middle of a Tornado, can you believe that? Almost midnight it was, there we were waiting for the Almighty himself to arrive in town and take his place in the congregation, the big man had thrown everything else at us it seemed like. Anyway, David asked Jeff if he could marry him and the girl and he held a ceremony there and then. A pity you weren't here with us, would have made a good headline, don't you think?"

"I'd have liked to have seen that, Jasper. Jefferson Davies? Are you sure?"

"Far as I know, why do you ask?"

"No reason, just interested is all."

The two men walked on towards Jakey's corral. Jasper had an idea. "Let's have a chat with Jakey, see if he can't come up with something. "Jakey, morning."

"Morning Jasper, what can I do for you."

"Not me, George here. Needs somewhere to set up his press, get his newspaper running, sooner the better. A newspaper is just what this town needs, to put us on the map. So Jakey, any ideas?"

"Jakey scratched at the short bristles covering his chin. "Maybe Jasper. George, you can have some of the yard, if it's any help. You can sleep upstairs in the loft there if you want, at least until you get something better, more permanent."

"It'll do me fine Jakey, you work out what you need in rent, I'll make a start at sorting my gear." George is happy with the arrangement. He would run the press from beneath the canvas of the Conestoga's* white top. It is waterproof and there is enough room to work inside. "Thank you Jakey, I owe you, you too, Jasper." George gratefully acknowledged the offer.

Jasper Hawke is already walking away, he waved a hand at George. Jasper knew the town had a great need for this new business. He didn't want George to move on and find something better somewhere else. He had done the man a favour, that might pay dividends at a later date, he hoped. George was in a hurry to get inside the wagon and eager to put the press to work. 'The Hickok Pegasus' named after the mythical 'Messenger' that only appears as a pure white, winged horse was available to readers the following Monday. George Benford did use the story of the wedding and the Tornado in his first editorial. He gave a special mention to the reverend Jefferson and after consulting with Renee, he put in a notice of the death of Tungsaw. A mention of the intended game of baseball with the railroad workers was there too. The paper's one page sheet was a sell out. After the first edition, the sheet very quickly became two-sided.

"What do you think, Renee? Better than those damned planks?" asked Henry. David looked at her and waited for her

* *The covered wagon was long the dominant form of transport in pre-industrial America. With roots in the heavy Conestoga wagon developed for the rough, undeveloped roads and paths of the colonial East, the covered wagon spread west with American migration. The Conestoga wagon was far too heavy for westward expansion. Typical farm wagons were merely covered for westward expansion. Heavily relied upon along such travel routes as the Great Wagon Road, the Mormon Trail and the Santa Fe and Oregon Trails, covered wagons carried settlers seeking land, gold, and new futures ever further west. Throughout the 20th century, the covered wagon grew to become an icon of the American West. A common nickname for this type of transport was the prairie schooner.*

words, as he rubbed a polishing cloth across some imaginary smear once again.

Renee looked at the completed bar. Just for a second or two her mind travelled back almost six months, to when she had had to stand behind the planks and offer herself to the hard faced roughnecks that had been Jack's friends. Hardly ever did she get any of the monetary reward, Jack would take good care of that side of the business. Most of his hanger's on have departed since his demise.

Now she could hardly believe the magical changes that had occurred in the last few months. "About time, now the damage to the roof is sorted you can get on with the restaurant." Renee smiled as she spoke. Henry and David knew when Renee smiled, it was her way of showing approval. They too could remember the way it had been for her. They had both had strong words with Jack, they had both had dealings with the rat and Henry, though totally naked, had shot and killed him without a moment's hesitation. The reddish brown stain on the floor inside the back room would forever remind them all that Jack is gone for good, not through any personal feelings for the 'poor' Renee, but for the sake of justice, raw frontier justice. The abuse of a woman was something they would not tolerate. The stain will stay as far as she is concerned.

Henry called David to the side table they normally used for business discussions. With so much going on recently the two had hardly had time to catch up. The two sat down and engaged in a long conversation. During the storm, Henry had a lengthy conversation with Wild Bill. The lawman had drawn Henry's attention to the arrival of Jefferson also. The Marshal had informed Henry that the man showed a likeness to a deserter from the Confederate army. Wild Bill's information was that the man had been employed as a cook in the grey uniform of the South. A wanted poster also gave details of the man's penchant for impersonating men of religion and more importantly, for bank robbery.

"I'm sorry Davy, it seems that you might still be a bachelor. Until we have certain proof, I think we should keep this to ourselves for now."

"Fair enough Henry, I wouldn't want to have to tell Lourinda just yet, unless we are certain. It would break her heart if your suspicions are correct." With the agreement, neither man made any further mention of their conversation. It might easily be a case of mistaken identity. Henry is worried, so too is David. They would wait for absolute proof one way or another, as agreed.

CHAPTER THIRTEEN

No winners

Henry could sense trouble was brewing between the two ranch hands, their conversation had been getting progressively louder. Fists are being used to pound on the recently completed bar. Cussing from the two becomes audible to everyone inside the Plainsman. Henry directed a concerned glance towards David. From where he stood he could see his friend is already alert to the ever-increasing acrimony. The argument it seems has been brought about by talk of horseflesh. Henry couldn't hear every word but he is sure it was their subject. David had taken to wearing a Colt sidearm most evenings to keep on the safe side. The increasing population might have the side effect of more similar confrontations and right now it would appear to be a wise move by the Town Marshal when on duty as he now is. His Peacemaker, as the small Colt is affectionately known, has a leather safety strap across its hammer and David's hand begins to move towards it.

Henry watches as his friend carefully lifts the tiny strap away. Although he is aware David had been spending time practising with the gun he is unsure as to the level of his expertise with the weapon. He remembers the conversation the big Welshman had with the now sleeping Joey. Joey had asked David if he was going to wear a gun regularly like Marshal Hickok. He had said that it would be most unlikely. Now it seems the Welshman has gone back on his statement.

Henry continues to watch as his friend prepares to intervene in the spiralling disagreement. It is David's first real official test as peacekeeper for the community and he is naturally nervous, Henry could sense it. David won't thank Henry if he was to attempt to intervene and Henry is aware of it. He shuffles a little in his seat.

The Marshal stays his ground, but is ever ready to act and enforce the recently agreed law-abiding statutes of Hickok. It is his task to uphold these statutes and he is determined he would. The strap is now off the gun, his palm just a quarter of an inch or so away from the gun butt. The Marshal is wary, prepared to do his duty. He is nervous and hopes there would not be a need to resort to the use of the firearm, but aware it might become the case. David is prepared.

"You're joking, damn ya'! That horse will never get past my Sally, no way, wake up and smell the coffee, Frank!"

"Iffen I was asked Clint, I'd say you ought to be in the backhouse, you're so full of shit you should move in permanently. You got diarrhoea of the mouth, Jesus, you're runnin' off! Who the hell's Sally anyway, your mother, or your wife?"

Clint's face turns a deep red, his temper being pushed to the limits. His hand drops downwards to the Navy Colt holstered at his hip. "Take that back you son of a bitch!" Clint growled the request.

"Whoa now boyyos, let's not get to that stuff, it's noisy, it's messy and it makes me a little nervous. Another thing, it makes stains on the floor." David's thoughts absent-mindedly drift back to the stain in the back room where Henry had shot and killed Jack. David knows it is time to intervene. The Colt is still in its holster but the Welshman speaks with authority. Frank spins around at David's words, the cowboy isn't about to let the matter drop.

"Oh, so now you're poking your goddamn nose in! Iffen I was you, I'd get off somewhere's else. Go play with the little kids, leave the real men to deal with their own business, butt out!"

Suddenly David is outwardly calm, inwardly he is seething. Mentally he counts to ten. He uses the short time to counter his rapid breathing. Everyone in the room swore later that they never saw it happen but David's Colt is in his hand and pointing at Frank's belly. "You boyyo are under arrest. Now if you're still up to arguing, I'll be happy to oblige." David tilts the short barrel slightly higher. "Otherwise, let's go where you can sleep it off." The Welshman keeps his gun pointed at Frank and motions to him to move out of the Plainsman. Frank is stunned, he'd seen many so-called 'gunslingers' during his forty years. He'd not seen one that could equal the withdrawal speed of the commanding Welshman with the silver badge of authority on his chest.

Henry watches the scene with a growing fascination. Totally surprised by the happenings of the last twenty seconds, he still hasn't allowed the moment's action to distract him from the fact his good friend might still be in some danger. He too had taken to carrying a gun regularly, though the pistol he had taken from the 'bad loser' was in a jacket pocket. He is ready to produce it in defence of David. There is no need, Frank obediently does as he is asked and starts for the door without further argument. David holsters the pistol and follows a short distance behind. He hears the click of a hammer being pulled back on Clint's revolver as he moves closer to the door. Henry hears it too but is too slow to take any counter measures on friend's behalf.

David turns, standing sideways he stoops low making himself much smaller. The tiny, killing intruder enters Clint's chest just left of middle; Clint is dead before his body makes its last sound, the sound of his skull cracking against the hard timber floor. Unaccountably, Clint has two bullets inside his body; another had penetrated his forehead just above the eyes. David stares at the corpse, his hand involuntarily shivering, his body trembling increasingly. He had not even heard the entrance door open, though he is almost standing next to it. Wild Bill stood just inside; he dropped the smoking revolver back into its holster, butt forward. The saloon is in total silence. Almost another thirty seconds pass before anyone speaks.

No one is sure which man had fired first but the aggressive cowboy is dead. Nobody is certain who Clint's target was but it didn't matter. A spreading pool of blood bore testament to the would-be badman's stupidity. Wild Bill stared at David, something akin to disbelief is on his mind but not mirrored in his face. The lawman never usually being short of words stays silent. No one moves a muscle in the Plainsman; fear is infectious at this moment, even though the main antagonist has departed. David looks at his own smoking revolver, fighting the nausea until it subsides. Frank stood unmoving at the scene. Renee, hearing the fracas, had moved into the room. She had been helping Jefferson in the kitchen. On hearing the commotion she had come out and witnessed Clint's clinical demise.

A muttering is born amongst the Plainsman's clientele now. Gladstone, who had watched the event unfold, pushed out his chest and spoke out. "Thank you Marshal, a good job you were here." One by one, the crowd begin to agree. Henry is unmoved and silent, still trying to take in what he had witnessed, his mind attempting to connect his friend with the almost unbelievable movement, without success. He is unable for now to accept that the affable Welshman is capable of taking such an action.

Henry spoke up and went to his friend's side. "Put the gun away Davy, it's all over my friend, you did what had to be done."

The Marshal does as he is advised. Henry can see his friend is regretful though he did not speak of the gunplay, his only thought was for the Welshman's suffering. Henry quickly tells Gladstone to pour a shot of whisky. The barman passes it to David, who drinks it in one gulp. Henry thinks it is the first time he has seen his friend take whisky apart from round the campfire one time. Lourinda, who had been sitting to one corner of the saloon, is mesmerised by her husbands' actions; she too came forward now and took a hold on his arm, determined to stand beside her man, as Wild Bill approaches the couple.

"You had no other choice Davy, it was him or you. He slapped leather first dammit, but I ain't never seen a draw like yours. Only one man I know can get close to that, son." Wild Bill cut off his words at that point. He of course, is the other man, he didn't want David to have that information. Frank spoke nervously "Am I under arrest, Marshal?"

Davy is jolted from his nightmarish trance. "Sorry Frank, routine is all."

"No problem, Marshal." Frank slowly eases his pistol from the holster, taking care not to give the lawman any excuse to think he was going to use it. He drops his weapon to the bloodstained floor, it lands next to Clint's cocked but unfired weapon.

"Let's go Frank, I'm afraid I must lock you up at least until a hearing has been conducted by the circuit judge. You could be here a week Frank, but I'll let you go tomorrow. Just behave, don't disappear and I won't lock you in."

"I get it Davy, law and order every time."

"That's it. You'll be back at the ranch soon enough, my friend. Just a misdemeanour."

"Sure, Davy!"

"Henry, you and Gladstone might get Clint to the undertakers for me." David unnecessarily points at the dead man's remains.

"Sure, Marshal." Henry and Gladstone are almost in awe of what they have witnessed and take the order from David without hesitation.

David ushers Frank outside without waiting for an answer. He freed Frank from his cell a day later as promised. The hapless man apologised for his behaviour, insisting he was provoked and David knew this. The travelling judge agreed he had not actually broken the law. David sent Frank on his way, warning him that he wouldn't allow the unruliness that had led directly to the unnecessary death of a man. The Town Marshal did not want anyone in the cells right now, he hoped to be alone for a while. He sat back in the office chair. He thought about the shooting and didn't like what he had done but formed the opinion someone was going to get hurt or worse if he had not taken control of the situation. After all, it was what the town paid him to do. The Marshal, despite everything, will continue to do his job while he is employed.

Preparing the bar in readiness for the day's business, Gladstone couldn't help making an observation. "Excuse me Marshal Hickok, I was wondering, about that shooting. I reckon you scored the head shot, is that right?"

"Reckon so Gladstone, why do you ask?"

"It seems to me that David fired first*. I seen it all, the feller was hit in the chest, he was falling forward when he took the head shot. Now that tells me that our Marshal had his gun out and pointing before you did."

"An honest man would have to say you're right, Gladstone."

"Jesus Bill, that means he's quicker than you, don't it?"

"Looks that way, Gladstone." Wild Bill isn't trying to take anything away from the Welshman's dexterity with a handgun. The veteran lawman knows news of the kind might quickly travel far and wide, leaving open the possibility of would-be fast men with a pistol wanting to try their own skills against Hickok's Town Marshal. Wild Bill knows the consequences of notorious fame, he had lived with it for almost ten years. He hoped the affable Welshman wouldn't have to carry

* *Wild Bill Hickok and other exponents of the fast draw would expect to draw and fire a revolver in less than a half of a second. As David managed to draw and fire his weapon before Hickok, he would be in an elite group of possibly one. In modern days the celebrated entertainer Sammy Davies Junior would rate alongside Hickok and David. (See: Alamo Fast Draw & Sammy Davis Jr. - Bing video.)*

a similar burden. Hickok himself would not last another year before cowardly Jack McCall would blast him from behind when the aging gunfighter was going blind. In a quiet moment Wild Bill Hickok asked Gladstone never to reveal the detail. Gladstone promised Hickok faithfully the secret would lie safe at the back of his memory.

"I think that's enough talk about shootings and suchlike Gladstone, don't you?"

"I guess you're right, Renee." Gladstone could see Renee had indeed heard enough. He stopped short and continued with his duties. Occasionally he could be heard mumbling to himself, nothing more. Renee had a question for Wild Bill.

"Why did you shoot that feller, Bill? Why are you here?"

"Well now Renee, I just wanted to see you sweetheart." Renee smiled at the comment, she waited for the lawman to continue. "To be honest, I thought that big Welshman had bitten off more than he could chew, especially after the injury to his arm. I couldn't for the life of me see him getting that smoke wagon out and shooting the son of a bitch that way, I just never thought he could take it on. Oh don't you go getting me wrong, I never would take him for a coward and he proved not to be. I just didn't think he could pull a trigger on a man that way. He's good Renee, fact is, he's maybe the best there is. The three of us should never speak of it and I have warned your barman it would be best to stay quiet."

"Or he may have been lucky!"

"No he weren't lucky girl, David's as good as it gets. Only one thing."

"What's that?"

"I doubt he knows it. It'd be best it stays that way."

"Maybe that's a blessing, Bill."

"Maybe it is, I couldn't say. I can say, if there is a gunman in these United States that can better him, I ain't never heard of him."

George Benford had the second edition of the Pegasus out and on sale the following morning. Working almost all night with the only light given from three oil lanterns hung about the Conestoga, he'd managed single handed to get the story of the shooting onto the front page. It was a masterpiece in editorial reporting. George had written his editorial beneath the headline:

To be, or not to be, Clint!

Somehow, he had composed a complete and comprehensive history of the shooting, the argument that had preceded it and the consequences of it, without being seen in the vicinity of the Plainsman at the time, nor immediately after. Yet the sudden death of Clint had been recorded, with just one piece of information missing; although George had stated that both 'lawmen' had shot Clint, he didn't state which man had fired first. What had happened that night would be best forgotten for all concerned.

The second edition carried a sketched reminder to the people of Hickok about the forthcoming baseball match with the Gandy Dancers. The work at the station had continued to keep to schedule; the building and the short section of spur rail where extra carriages could be laid up until needed, were almost finished. Thursday would see the completion, Friday was the designated day for the sporting confrontation. Lourinda had agreed to finish her classes at noon, thus allowing all the schoolchildren to be present at the afternoon's game and festivities. There was an air of excitement about Hickok on Thursday, not least from the children who were to benefit from the early finishing time. The baseball match, a horse race and several bring and buy stalls were to be presented by Mrs Hawke and some of her ladyfriends who had made too much jam and were soon about to make too many cakes.

The day arrived accompanied by beautiful sunshine and a gentle breeze that allowed the sweet smell of freshly baked pastry to waft about the field designated for the playing area for today. The match is to be two innings; each team had contrived to have more than the stipulated nine members a side. Nobody seemed to be bothered, the result was not of consequence, the players attending only for the fun of the day and the spectators for the entertainment. Henry, who had no previous experience of the game, had volunteered himself the umpire's position. Jasper, knowing something of the rules of the game, planned to stand at his side and make any of the more important decisions concerning play. Jakey, equipped with the most knowledge, quickly briefed the Hickok team as to what was expected of them. Play got under way amidst great amusement for the enthusiastic crowd. The railroaders, who practised regularly, had easily become the eventual winners. A certain amount of friendly contrivance meant that the final score would be a particularly close one. Henry and Jasper between them did manage to control the play, but as much by luck as by their unified judgements. The two men hardly had a clue and joined forces to deliberate.

After refreshments the horse race is announced to the spectators by Jasper. It is the Mayor's first serious public engagement and he is determined to get the most from it. Four horses stood at the starting line, their course is laid out. It will have to be circled three times before any of the competitors could be named the winner. Jasper Hawke fired his six-shooter into the air, the four combatants took off with a fury. The first circumference could only be described as an equine free-for-all, the inexperienced riders fighting for control of the startled beasts giving the impression of Cavalry officers leading a charge. In the second, many of the spectators stated 'a good job they aren't carrying sabres' as they jostled for leadership of the race.

One person who was not present at the carnival had worked himself into a sweat at the door to Jasper's shop which doubled as the only bank. Finally the door gave way. Quickly he barged through the customer area and soon found an insufficient safe. Producing a small explosive stick he proceeded to set it in position; quickly lighting the short fuse, he retired behind the fragile counter. A dull boom would not be enough to alert the fun starved crowd at the sports field. After emptying the opened safe, Jefferson made good his getaway. Knowing almost every member of the community would be at the game, the bogus minister had guessed rightly he would have an easy task. The sports day had worked perfectly for him.

More than an hour would pass before the returning throng would notice the renegade preacher's actions. Jasper and his depositor's savings were more than twenty miles apart after two hours. Wild Bill Hickok was not far behind him. Hickok had felt uneasy about the too good to be true reverend Jefferson. After their first meeting, the lawman had travelled back to Dodge City and with the help of Jack Bridges, had searched through numerous wanted posters and files. After a half day searching, the two men found what they were looking for; the dog-eared sheet of paper presented a poorly sketched profile of the bogus minister. A short history of the man did indeed suggest he had deserted from his duties as an army cook. A general description of his features and previous crimes were listed below the rugged face. The sheet promised a reward figure of five hundred dollars.

Hickok had no interest in the reward. His reasons for wanting to apprehend the deserter were simple; his new found friends were being deprived of their hard earned savings. Wild Bill is not about to let that happen. He could tell by the deep imprints made in the long soft, Kansas grass, his quarry is not very far in front. The lawman followed the prints, without hurrying. He did not want to try and stop Jefferson from the back of a moving horse. He would dog the thief's tracks until the rider felt the need to rest his horse. Jefferson would not know he was being followed. He had rightly surmised that all the townspeople would be preoccupied with the fun and festivities, he hadn't reckoned on the seasoned Kansas lawman's skills.

Sally had won the race. Ridden by Clint's younger brother Toke, the horse easily passed two of the beasts, running neck and neck with Frank's favourite. Sally passed it at the very last. Without waiting for the plaudits of coming second, Toke trotted the horse away from the makeshift course. He had proved Clint right and now wanted nothing more to do with the people of Hickok; another time might suit any thoughts of revenge. The prize stayed unclaimed and was eventually donated to the school fund.

With all cake stocks depleted and fresh lemonade drunk, the ladies had packed up their stalls. Apart from Toke's show of surliness, the otherwise social afternoon came to an end and the people of Hickok made their way back towards the town's precincts. Some stopped to look at the as yet unused station building before continuing, Henry and David nodding and giving their approval of its design. They stop suddenly at a shout. Jasper, almost running, was coming towards them.

"We have been robbed Davy, the bank has been broken into, every cent gone. Who could have done it?"

"I have an inkling Jasper, but we'll find out, boyyo. Let's get down to the bank, see what we can discover." The three men turned towards town and hastily made their way to the bank building. Others are already there staring at the broken door. They looked at their Marshal, almost as if he could solve the crime right there and then.

David did eventually have an answer. There was one person he had not seen that afternoon. "Where's Jeff, I don't remember seeing him at the sports?" He looked around the crowd. Jakey stepped forward.

"I saw Jeff leaving town. I came back early from the field to get my smoke makings. He must have crept in and took his horse from my place this morning, I thought it was odd at the time. I'm sorry folks."

"You couldn't have known, Jakey."

Jakey and the second deputy, Gladstone, joined David, Henry and Jasper. Gladstone spoke up. "We have to get after the son of a bitch Davy, he need's stringing up if you want my opinion."

"I know why you're feeling that way Gladstone, though we won't be following your suggestion, boyyo. There won't be any illegal hangings in Hickok while I'm Marshal."

A crowd of onlookers had gathered; some liked the sound of Gladstone's words, most agreed with David, not wanting their town to get an unenviable reputation of lawlessness.

David had heard about some of the Texas Cow towns, where residents thought nothing of distributing instant punishment to rustlers, robbers and general wrongdoers. Without a trial, no one could ever be certain that the right man had been punished. Hanging was something that could not be undone. He remembered some of the many stories told to him by Soul Broadbent about these towns and their instant retribution. Soul had recalled the horrific tale of Bad Bill Longley, a badman that would eventually have his neck squeezed by a noose twice; the first time by amateur executioners had not worked. Longley had been freed when the rope had failed. His future rope dance would not be altogether successful, Longley's feet would hit the ground so hard that the imprints would stay long after he was pronounced 'gone.'

David accepted there would have to be a search for the suspect who had stolen the townsfolk's savings. He refused offers of help from some of the depositors, stating that he would find the man and bring him back himself. Leaving Jakey and Gladstone to keep the peace, he rode out of Hickok astride the horse that had been purchased by Tungsaw when he, Henry and the now departed Chinaman had gone in search of the Englishman not so long ago.

David had somehow and not without a little luck, pulled clear of Wild Bill in the search and he would come upon Jefferson's transit camp first. He couldn't have known that the Plainsman was just a few minutes behind him. David walked into Jefferson's camp without the Peacemaker, he also did not alert the bank robber he was coming. Jefferson had not expected discovery. Certainly he knew there was a chance the Marshal would try and search him out, but knowing David is as yet quite inexperienced in his job, he did not forsee being discovered in the way he had. With this knowledge to hand, the thief had not taken precautions, he had discarded his sidearms just a few moments earlier.

"Jeff!"

The camper spun at the sound of his name. "Davy! I sure didn't expect to see you out here. Want some coffee? Fresh brewed! You got a posse with you, Mister Marshal?"

"No posse Jeff, just me alone, I didn't think I would need help on this occasion. I'll have to take you in unless you hand over the money Jeff, and some explanations wouldn't go amiss, boyyo. We'll talk about things a little, decide what's to be done here."

David had spoken quietly. He had not even made up his mind to arrest the bogus minister. Like most Hickokians, he'd taken a liking to Jefferson in the short time since he had arrived in Hickok. David is only interested in retrieving the money and had thoughts of perhaps letting Jefferson go once his task had been achieved. Jefferson, who had become adept at getting out of such scrapes as this, is unaware of the lawman's thinking. He squares up now and is ready to defend himself against an attack that might not even begin.

Mistaken in his assumption, Jefferson dropped the half full tin mug; still hot coffee spilled into the earth as he attempted to make a grab for the gun belt. Swiftly David's foot shot out, the guns and belt travel beyond the bogus minister's grasp. Jefferson swore at the kicker. "Let's get to it then, Welshman."

David squared up, lifting his fists towards his chin he accepted Jefferson's challenge with little thought now the weapon was out of reach.

Wild Bill, now caught up, watched the titanic struggle of the two men from a distance; fists pounded at skin and bones for almost half an hour. At times, each man seemed to the half hidden lawman to be in control of the extended fight. Wild Bill is glad he was never the kind of fighter that relied on his fists. The pugilistic punishment continued. Blood showed at each man's nose and mouth, eyes became swollen, their semi closure would soon follow. David swung at Jefferson's jaw; the punch was too low and caught the top of his chest, knocking the deserter towards the gun belt. Jefferson was aware of it's proximity; he grabbed at the handle of one of the pair, pulled it from its holster and cocked the hammer. "The Lord giveth, The Lord taketh away, Davy. Sorry youngster." Jefferson's forefinger pulled at the trigger. An explosion of sound filled the little clearing that had been Jefferson's stopping place. David stretched his pained eyelids towards his attacker. Jefferson's contorted features showed he had died in complete agony. He looked across at the lawman's smoking Navy Colt, the smoke almost enveloping him. David stumbled and fell unconscious.

Wild Bill rode into Hickok three hours after he had left. Two horses trailed behind him; one carried the inert lifeless body, a carpetbag tied to the saddle bumped against the lifeless remains, the other horse carried another form. In the fight with Jefferson, David had not received any serious or life-threatening injuries, but he is only semi-conscious as Wild Bill leads the mounts the last few yards to the Plainsman. The tall lawman dismounted and straightaway barked orders to the watching Joey. "Get the doctor boy and don't be taking your time. Davy's in need of him and quickly." Joey had been idling outside at the U.S. Marshal's arrival and he quickly complied with the instructions given. Soon both boy and physician were returning at a fast trot.

Wild Bill, with Henry's help, untied and lifted the groaning David from the saddle. They carried him through the Plainsman and in the same way that David had laid the 'lifeless' Lourinda on the bar, he too is rested there, although even in his damaged state he makes attempts to escape the fussing of Doc Ryder. Early evening drinkers watched with a ghoulish-like interest as Doc Ryder ripped Davy's shirt away to reveal severe bruising and small cuts and grazes received in the fist fight. With their curiosity satisfied, they moved back and away to their tables, their cards and their beverages. David had one nasty wound where Jefferson's bullet had creased and burned his side. With the remnants of the shirt now ripped away, the hard scabs of congealed blood shifted, the wound started to seep thick red liquid again. Doc Ryder, helped by Renee, tended and cleaned the area and soon managed to stop the crimson flow. Suspecting too that maybe at least some ribs are cracked, if not broken, Ryder strapped the complaining patient's chest with some torn sheeting Lourinda had brought at Renee's suggestion.

"The bullet that Jefferson had fired at David had carved a shallow gouge through the skin, but he had been lucky it had not been a more serious wound. Still the onlookers watched from a safe distance, with most of them relieved that the big Welshman had not been seriously hurt. They sipped at their beer and commented on the doctor's style of nursing care, as well as any other subject that cropped up during the long drawn out medical process.

Once Doc Ryder had finished the surgical necessities and cleaned all broken skin injuries, the Welshman is again lifted and moved to the room he and Lourinda now shared. A tearful but relieved Lourinda followed behind. Wild Bill had informed her that she and David are still unmarried; he'd told the girl that Jefferson was not only averse to robbing banks but that he was also an impostor regarding church matters. Lourinda isn't at all worried by the lawman's statement as she is already aware of the fact. She has only one concern right now, to see the big broken man repaired and healthy. She knew given time the cuts and bruises would disappear, but he had lost some small measure of blood from his various injuries and so would need good care and a healthy diet to make his recovery complete.

David Evan's first official tasks as a lawman had so far been one of action. He hoped the gunfight with Clint and the more physical fight with Jefferson would be the last of it for a while but he had at least come through both with flying colours.

CHAPTER FOURTEEN
Henry sees Red

George Benford once again had somehow described every tiny detail of something he hadn't even witnessed. The third edition of the Pegasus carried a complete and full description of the fete, a good long report of the baseball game, and some of it was even the truth though nobody is really certain which sections. It had been the kind of game played for fun mostly. A long detailed account of the robbery and apprehension and swift demise of the crime's perpetrator was described. There was also a tiny mention at the bottom of the second page of the dead bank robber's interment in the town's cemetery but no mention of how many, or how few of the local people had attended the burial service.

Jakey had at the undertaker's request, furnished a hastily made cross to mark the fresh grave. Jefferson's name was etched across the spar but no other information was given, unlike those of other cemetery's where peculiar epitaphs are portrayed regarding deaths.

George had stopped Henry in the street that morning and showed a personal, as well as a professional concern for 'our Marshal.' Henry informed George that David is taking a rest but an improvement seemed to be 'about him.' George asked to be remembered to the Welshman. Henry promised to pass on the newspaperman's good wishes. 'Just as soon as the girl Lourinda will let me anywhere near him.' Gladstone has stepped up and was taking his deputising duties quite seriously in David's absence.

The general buzz around Hickok had quieted. Wild Bill had returned to his own duties over in Ford County. Lourinda, with her almost round the clock nursing and nagging of the shattered Welshman, had managed to continue with her classes at the school. Renee and Gladstone, with Maria's help, saw to it that the Plainsman didn't suffer while David's recuperation continued. Joey kept on top of his chores but was regularly absent from the saloon for long periods of time now. Renee didn't ask her son for explanations as to his whereabouts at these times and the boy didn't offer any information.

Now the station buildings and the spur line are finished, Atchison Topeka and Santa Fe had seen fit to allow three regular stops each week. Mostly there were goods to be unloaded; other times a stranger might alight for a meal at the Plainsman and wash it down with a refreshing beer or two, or even just to stretch travel-stiffened legs and maybe a clean up. At times passengers arrived in town via the regular stagecoach and did so to link up with the train to further their journey in slightly better comfort and in a much quicker time, depending of course on where they might want to go.

George Benford spent a great deal of time around the newly completed and now busy station building when the smoke-billowing Locomotives were due. He stayed until they arrived and studied anyone and everyone that alighted from the locomotive. If for any reason George was unable to attend, then Joey stood in his place, discreetly making little notes on his paper tablet.

Joey enjoyed this task and would drop whatever chore he might be doing whenever George called on him to help out with some story, all the time he is able to improve his writing techniques. Each edition of the Pegasus would have a comprehensive list of Hickokians travelling away from their hometown or those who were returning from some sojourn away from town.

Most provincial newspapers of the day regularly followed this practice. Localised newspapers would also inform as to whom might have held a card evening or some other homely social gathering. Wild Bill's Hickok's name had shown up in the visitor's column more than once now. Regular subscribers would like to scan the pages, especially if they had been away for some reason and had just returned, allowing them to see the names appear in the list. It became a talking point among locals as to how George obtained his wealth of fresh information. Frequently asked, George would give his stock answer; 'a good newspaperman does not reveal his sources.' A wink and a smile would always accompany the often repeated statement. George knew by this fact that Joey had been very unobtrusive in his sentry duty.

"It's time I was about Lourinda, I don't aim to stay here any longer, I might as well be in the jail cell as here, it can't be any worse."

David's demeanour has improved a little each of the days he has lain in the bed. Now although his ribs did still cause some pain, he is impatient to get dressed and move about the building if nothing more. At least he is far better off than Jefferson.

"Let Doc' Ryder be the judge Davy, you need to build your strength before you go riding or fighting again, you lost some blood in the fight."

"Hardly enough to fill a whisky glass. I won't be fighting and such, I just want to be out of this damn bed. I have to go see Wild Bill, he saved my life you know. If not for him, I'd be lying next to Davis. He needs to be thanked. I just wish Jefferson hadn't gone for that pistol. I had it in mind to give him a lesson and then let him go on his way. After all, he hadn't caused any other trouble while he was here and we got the bank's money back. That man could fight, best scrap I've had in a mighty long time. Just a shame Jefferson had taken the wrong choice and paid dearly for his crime."

"Wild Bill would rather be thanked by a live man than a dead one, Davy. I liked Jeff, we all did, but it has to be said he might have killed you!" Lourinda exaggerated her statement a little in an effort to keep the 'big' man on his bed.

David made sense of what Lourinda is saying. He thought about it for a minute, but it would make no difference. He pulled the cover back. "Now you can watch me dress or you can turn your back girl, either way that's what I aim to do."

Lourinda could see the Welshman's scars had healed well, the facial bruises had almost disappeared, the bullet and surgical wounds had lost their fierce redness and were pinking. He pulled a shirt over his head with Lourinda's help, only stiffness preventing him doing it for himself. He stretched. "Now where's the bleddy Cornishman?"

The man he is seeking is seated at a table playing cards with two of the day's early customers. "Davy! Good to see you about my friend." Henry dropped his cards and stood up to get his friend a chair. "Sit yourself Davy, I'll get you a beer." David did as he was ordered.

"Don't worry yourself Lourinda, I'll make sure the big lad behaves."

Lourinda turned away to allow the two men to talk alone.

"And who'll be keeping an eye on you, Henry Tamryn?" The girl had asked with a smile as she walked towards the bar.

As the afternoon drew into evening, David received greetings from almost every one of the Plainsman's customers; each saying how they missed him being around, but how well Jakey and Gladstone had coped without him. What a marvellous job he had done to apprehend the wayward Jefferson. Almost all saying they hadn't been fooled by the confidence trickster. Others enquired 'why didn't you just shoot the son of a bitch in the balls?' David had nodded and smiled at each as they went through their friendly questioning and not so friendly suggestions. Jasper and Mrs Hawke came and went, George Benford scribbled as he too questioned the recovering semi-invalid at first hand. Jakey and Gladstone wandered into the Plainsman with a request.

"Hey Davy! How about you coming and doing the rounds with us?"

David had instantly vacated the chair at the surprise invitation, he didn't think twice. Even with some expected stiffness still, he wasn't intending to let a chance of getting outside in the fresh Kansas air to go begging. On finding out what David had done, Lourinda waited impatiently for the three men to return. They were absent for more than an hour. David had wanted the chance to speak to the men. After the recent robbery and what he saw as an unnecessary death, he had decided he no longer wanted the job of Town Marshal and he had decided that he no longer wanted the need to carry a gun. Although he tried to explain his reasons to the pair, the big blacksmith had already guessed. 'Save your breath Davy, I don't blame you a bit.' Slowly they retraced their steps back to the Plainsman where Lourinda was waiting. David stopped her words and repeated what he had told the deputies. His promise to resign the next day had the calming effect he was relying on. Lourinda was particularly relieved, she said nothing to make him change his mind.

Henry had been listening to his friend's conversation. He congratulated David on his decision, adding that the growth of the town would mean it would soon need a more experienced peace officer. Jasper Hawke had informed Henry that same day, a new saloon is to be started at the other end of the main street 'The Golden Horseshoe.' The owner had for some time operated a similar business on the notorious 'Front Street' in Dodge City. Now finding that town to be over blessed with such establishments he was looking for a new start, somewhere quieter. Dodge was being overrun now with Texan cowboys bringing vast herds of Longhorns to be shipped east. Thirty or forty trail worn Texan cowboys arriving in one place at the same time were apt to kick up a lot of trouble and they did. Large amounts of alcohol would be consumed, trouble would follow. Occasionally two herds might arrive at the same time, a recipe for disaster. Hickok would never become another Dodge or Ellesworth. Even though it had its own railroad station now, they are too close to that town to be of use to the cattle shippers.

Lourinda is overjoyed to see that David is nodding in agreement with his partner. For some while she had harboured the same thoughts but had not, because of his injuries, been able to voice her concerns. Now she would not have to. David had made up his own mind. No further discussion on the subject would be warranted.

Early evening time the following day saw the arrival of the next of Fe Tylden's wagon trains pulling onto the land that had been used for the baseball match, the wagons forming two lines. The horses and mules that had pulled the wagons were picketed close by and the travellers prepared themselves for a two day camp before recommencing the gruelling journey West. Waiting two days would allow for would be newcomers to join up from the stage or the next A.T.& S.F train that was due the next morning. Cooking fat watched with interest the camp preparations from his bell tower home. He watched Joey's familiar form approaching the lines of white topped wagons. Joey saunters first along one line of wagons then returning along the other. He stops occasionally, talking to an adult and then maybe some youngster from his own age group. Half an hour later Joey returned to town, going straight to Jakey's livery and horse corral that still houses George Benford and his printing press.

Fe Tylden sat with Henry and the fast improving David. Again it is time for reminiscences. The three men recall and laugh once again at the antics of Tungsaw and his whisky drinking. The laughter is considerably subdued as Henry and David also recall the killing of the bank robber. They became sympathetically quiet when joined by the discernibly thickening Lourinda. She hadn't heard the part of the conversation that had concerned her.

"So Mr Tylden, will you give me away?"

"Never, I'd want something for you, honey."

"That's not what I meant and you know it, damn you, be serious!"

"I do? I will!"

"You do. I want you to give me away to Davy, at my wedding, my right and proper wedding!"

"Be my pleasure honey, on one provision mind."

"What might that be Mister Tylden?"

"You gotta quit calling me Mister, it makes me sound old."

"I promise Fe. Wait, you are old! Lourinda is pleased Fe had agreed to her request. She had only known the wagon boss a short time but he had shown her a fatherly kindness since their first meeting in Independence. She is also keen that she and David should soon be legally married.

"Dammit, I'm fifty, not one hundred. Plenty of life in this old dawg yet, lady!"

The following day was another that would bring two old friends together. Rather this was a case of two siblings. The Wells Fargo and Co stage pulled in front of the newly enlarged way station. Two men and a young woman climb out of the cramped confines, they proceed to stretch stiffened legs. Both men ask directions to a saloon. They would re-embark later to go on to their respective destinations but are determined to rinse the Kansas trail dust from dry throats first. The auburn haired young lady stands looking around, not knowing what she should do, nor where she might go. She too was to go on to Dodge when the stage pulled out. She had spent many hours in the stage's cramped confines with the two salesmen. Other passengers had come and gone since departing her starting point. Although the two had been gentlemanly during the trip she is pleased to be away from their stale, sweat smelling presence. She decides to stroll. Neatly and sensibly dressed, the red haired girl walks towards the town's more built up area. She stops at Jasper Hawke's and absentmindedly looks at the displayed goods. Mrs Hawke smiles at her through the window. The redhead moves on after returning the friendly smile. She passes Jakey's corral without stopping. She looks at the schoolhouse tower, watching with interest as a black cat paces backwards and forwards around the narrow parapet rather like a guard patrolling a castle rampart.

Joey approached the newcomer. "Good morning Ma'am!"

"Good morning, young sir" she replies.

Joey knowingly asks the redhead if she is travelling on the stage "and are you joining the wagon train, Ma'am?"

"No, I am going on by stage, I have to find my brother."

Joey asks if the lady had enjoyed her journey so far, if she knew where her brother might be.

"No, I know he's here in Kansas somewhere, boy."

Joey thought that her answer was a little vague. "You have some idea where he might be" he repeated?

The girl looks at the thirteen year old with something approaching indignance now. "Of course I have some idea where he might be. Do you take me for a fool, boy?"

"No Ma'am, I don't, I ain't lost no one though."

"Run along boy, leave me be, you're becoming a nuisance."

"Yes ma'am!"

Joey did as he was told, but a rueful smile spread across his lower face. Leaving the newcomer to her own devices, he walks slowly back to the Plainsman. Joey continues his thought that there was something vaguely familiar about the newly arrived stage passenger. He'd been annoyed at her attitude, the way she had spoken to and dismissed him. Yet the funny accent wasn't unlike the way Henry spoke. Joey turned his eyes back to the street. He thinks he might know who the newcomer is. She's walking back in the direction from which she had come. He saw the stage driver offer a hand to help her back inside the coach. Joey takes off running along the middle of the street. He manages to reach the stage before the driver is able to cluck the six large horses into action. He stops at the door, panting, trying to catch his breath. At last Joey is able to speak. He pokes his head inside the glassless carriage.

The other passengers look at Joey as he searches for the girl. She sits at the far side, opposite the same two men that were travelling to Dodge City. Because of the way she had spoken to him last, Joey used mock courtesy. "Excuse me Ma'am, are you from Cornwall?"

"What if I am?" the redhead answers. "How would you know anyway?" she added.

The driver is getting restless. "Come on boy, move yourself."

"Henry is from Cornwall."

"Henry, Henry Tamryn?"

"The very one, he's a very good friend of mine. I'll tell him I saw you. Bye Ma'am, have a nice trip." Joey turned to walk away. He is now certain the girl is looking for Henry but he is determined to get his own back on her before helping further.

The redhead steps out of the carriage once more. The horses become restless at the delay and the exasperated driver is already trying to pull the woman's bags from the neatly stacked pile he had carefully and conscientiously roped down on the back of the stage. Finally he found the right ones as the girl stands shouting to Joey to come back. The teasing boy turns and meanders as slowly as he can, back to the rear of the stage. He squints up innocently at her questioning.

"Look lad, I'm sorry if I was rude before, I've had a long journey in that thing, forever it seems. Those smelly men didn't help matters. I'm tired and have to get to Dodge City. Why on earth is it called Dodge?"

"Named for Colonel Dodge Ma'am, he founded Fort Dodge." Now that the girl is being more civil to him, Joey is happy to chatter.

"Henry, is he here? Henry Tamryn? Oh please take me to my brother, lad."

"Come along with me, mind where you tread." Joey picked up the girl's heavy bags and led her towards the Plainsman. She followed obediently and without stepping in any of the fresh horse droppings that littered the street and had been provided mostly by the stage horses.

Soul Broadbent is adamant he wants to play poker. Henry reminds Soul he had never beaten him at poker, that he'd never beaten anyone of note at the game, that he should keep his money in his pocket. The ranch foreman could not be dissuaded, having slowly loaded up with whisky all that morning, he now thought he was able to best Henry and he wants revenge. The two men play. David sits quietly and eventually joins the game, thinking that his presence at the table might allow Soul to have more chance of winning a hand or two. Henry is careful not to rile Soul. He is aware the cowboy is a sore loser and that he had a short fuse when whisky soaked. Occasionally he would have to throw away a good winning hand in the interests of prolonging their friendship. Even so, Henry manages to take a large chunk of the foreman's hard earned wages. David too lost cash to Henry, he always had. The ex-Town Marshal, like Soul, always did lose but he rarely played for long. The game went on into the early afternoon, it would soon come to an abrupt and chair crunching halt.

"Jesus! Would you look at that! What I wouldn't do to take my branding iron to her hindquarters, by god." The now slurring cowboy pushed his chair back and is already on his unsteady feet and steering them crookedly towards the redhead who has entered with Joey. Soul had only managed a half dozen steps when the discarded chair collided with the back of his head, splintering with the impact. He roared a curse and turned about unsteadily. With the breaking chair having a sobering effect, Soul flies at his attacker, the cash strewn table collapsing on top of the still seated David.

The furniture had been no match for the combined weight of the two brawlers. Henry and Soul exchanged punches as the bemused loungers looked on with great amusement from amidst the broken remains. David thought it was just as well he had given up the Marshalship of Hickok. Firstly he didn't want to have to separate this fighting pair, secondly he could see a backlog of carpentry work is building up and will be soon needing his attention. He watches as Soul swings a chair at the Cornishman. Hearing the crashing and smashing of wood brings Renee from the kitchen that she and Lourinda were once again manning, owing to the loss of firstly Tungsaw and the more recently deceased Jefferson. Other drinkers try to move away from the battling pair and to let them continue. Renee notices Joey standing just inside the doorway with the girl.

"What happened Joey, what started it?"

"Don't know Ma, I just got here with this lady and all bleddy hell broke loose. Henry started it, I think I might know why."

Renee looked at her son's companion and back at the two tiring fighters. "Henry! Soul!" Henry tries to turn his head towards the voice as Soul tries his utmost to turn it back to its original position. Soul takes the opportunity, while squeezing Henry's throat, to ask Henry what had provoked the sudden attack.

Henry said something Soul couldn't understand. The squeezer eased his grip slightly.

"That's Patsy, she's my fucking sister, you fat bastard. Now get off me!"

"How the hell am I supposed to know that?"

"You do now so watch what you're saying in the bleddy future mister, if you don't you'll be searching for more missing teeth, be warned!"

"I surely will, Henry. Is this yours or mine?"

Henry swishes his tongue around the inside of his mouth. "It must be yours, I still have all mine I believe. You'll need to see Doc Ryder, he can fit you with a new wooden one*."

"A new tooth? Get outta here, that ain't possible!"

"Yes it bleddy is. Now don't start arguing with me again, Soul."

"I didn't start it, you did."

"Go to hell, it was you."

"Might have been me now I think about it!"

"What did I just say to you, Soul?"

"Far too much dammit!"

"I rest my case. Now where's my bleddy sister? And you watch your mouth mister! Iffen you don't you'll be needin' to talk out of your arse even more, get out of my bleddy way."

"Broadbent attempts one last half-hearted swipe at Henry who sidesteps, allowing the cowboy to begin toppling and fall over in a heap. He tries to snatch at a chair but only manages to grab the skirts of the redhead as he goes down, his sudden actions exposing her undergarments.

"I'm gonna kill you for that!" Henry shouts at Soul. Renee picks up a chair leg and is ready to use it."

"Enough you two! Stop now!" Renee pulled back the piece of wood threateningly.

---

* The Japanese are credited with using the first wooden dentures. This style of denture was used up until the 19th century. Contrary to the popular myth, George Washington did not wear wooden dentures. He actually wore ivory dentures made from hippopotamus tusks. Other types of ivory dentures were also popular during this period. They were made from walrus, hippo or elephant tusks. Many people wore ivory dentures, even though the material deteriorated quickly. These types of dentures, bone or wooden were still being worn well into the eighteen hundreds. The first pair of porcelain dentures were developed in 1774 by a British physician. Porcelain teeth looked unnaturally white, and they chipped very easily. In 1820, a silversmith mounted porcelain teeth onto gold plates with springs and swivels, which allowed the teeth to work more efficiently and naturally. In effect, this was the first modern set of dentures. Porcelain was very expensive, and most people could not afford to wear this type of denture. An alternative made from hardened rubber was created in the mid-1800s.

"Okay, okay, I'm done, put that down, you might hurt someone."

"No might about it, mister!"

CHAPTER FIFTEEN
Thicker than Water

Renee demanded Henry and Soul should pick up the scattered debris caused by their fighting, before she would allow her partner to talk with his obviously beloved sister, Patricia. The redhead fully agrees with her and waits patiently.

Henry is unable to resist shooting smiling glances at his sister as he and Soul Broadbent do as they have been ordered. Although he has no idea why his sister is here, he is overjoyed to see her. Patricia smiles back while explaining to Renee that her brother had been known as a 'scrapper' in and around Bodmin and Innis Town where they had both been raised and before Patsy's failed elopement to Ireland. That in fact, he had been more than well known for his fighting prowess. Renee recalled in detail for Patricia, how she, Henry and David had so suddenly become partners in the Plainsman. Patricia is horrified with Renee's description of how her brother had been forced to kill Jack. She did laugh nervously at the idea of his nakedness, while performing the deed. She unknowingly looked at the brownish patch of floor. Renee seeing her glance, explained it was not where Jack's blood had spilled. "That was poor Clint" she informed the redhead and told her simply how that episode had occurred.

Patricia listened as Renee explained to her that David had no choice but to shoot the belligerent Clint. Renee explained that this is the way of the Western frontier.

"Doesn't anyone do anything but fight and shoot each other around here?" she asked a touch sorrowfully.

"Well Patricia, I'm afraid it was you that caused this latest one."

"I suppose it must have been."

"Soul said something about you and your brother took offence. Henry was not best pleased, he let it show."

"It seems that I did but I can't think for the life of me why, although to be fair, my brother and I were very much the same when growing up! We scrapped for dear life at times, I'm sorry to say!"

Patricia had not heard Soul's remark and did not realise it was she who caused the fight between her brother and a man who had only recently become friends. Soul again walked towards the red headed newcomer. The fight had sobered the ranch foreman somewhat.

"I'm right sorry Ma'am, I didn't mean no offence, we was just skylarking you understand."

"Jesus Soul, you sure are a bleddy crawler." Henry had enjoyed the fight with Soul and he felt comfortable enough to joke with his recent antagonist. He took the opportunity to officially introduce Patricia to all of the company inside the saloon.

Patricia accepted Soul's apology for the fuss, though she still isn't completely sure of its origins. She looked at Renee "Can Henry and I go somewhere private Renee, I mean, have you somewhere we can talk?"

"Henry, why don't you and Patricia go in the restaurant, you won't be disturbed in there. Unless there's someone in there you haven't had a fight with yet! Joey, take Patricia's bags upstairs, put them in your room. You'll sleep in mine tonight until we sort out something better." Joey carried out the orders given to him by his mother. Henry and Patricia did as Renee had suggested.

Henry looked at Patricia's unusually stern face, he knew she must have something of a serious nature to impart to her brother. "What's the matter Patsy, let's have it."

"I'm sorry H' it's father, he's gone, Henry. I wouldn't put it in a letter, I couldn't, I had to tell you myself. Three months ago, they think it was his heart. He missed you when you left. Mother took his passing very hard but you know how it can be with her, she doesn't say much, she just carries on without complaint. Father was tired, he went quickly and painlessly."

Henry took the news quietly. He had been completely shocked at his sister's appearance in Hickok, but very happy to see her under any circumstances. Henry and Patricia had forever been close until she had decided to go to Ireland on a whim. Now his sudden joy had been snatched away at the news of his father. "She always copes, doesn't she."

Patricia nodded her answer. "Should I go home Patsy, does mother want to see me?"

"No, she doesn't want that. She told me to tell you." Patricia's reply to his question was as Henry had expected. His mother was a 'tough' woman and would ride her personal storm in her own way as she always had.

"I shall travel to Dodge. I have to at least send a telegram. Unfortunately there are no facilities here yet but now that the railroad has arrived, it won't be long in coming. In fact, I'll go to Dodge City by train." Henry recalled the last time he had travelled along the iron rails. He gave a smile when he thought about the 'right hander' that David had offered the guard the first day when they had walked towards the village. "How are the young ones, Patsy?"

"They're all good. Francis and Teresa-Anne miss you as much as mother, I believe. I could not tell you in a letter H' it didn't seem right." Patricia knew Henry was steering away from the subject of his father's death but she was feeling guilty about not getting the news to him earlier. She had not realised how long the journey to Kansas would take her and then, once there, the search to find her brother although she realised she had been extremely fortunate in this respect thanks to Joey stepping up to stop her leaving.

"I understand. It is good of you to come so far, Patsy."

"I'm staying here in Kansas H, I'm not going back. I'm here for good and don't you try and change my bleddy mind, it's made up." Patricia looked at her elder brother and waited for his reaction. Patricia's answer was one of certain finality. Henry knows there is no point in arguing with her. He had always chided her that she had their mother's sense of obstinacy.

Joey seated on the wooden stool outside the wagon, related all the details of the fight to George Benford. George asked what they were fighting about. He made quick notes from Joey's description of the scrap. Joey explained what had caused the fight, that Henry's sister had arrived suddenly from England. Soul had made a loose comment on account of his being drunk and Henry had smashed a chair across him.

"They were all friends again by the time I left." Not that the two men had been friends in the normal sense, up until now they had only been acquaintances at most.

"Well done Joey, you're doing a fine job, we'll make a newspaper man of you yet." George flipped two coins to the boy, Joey gratefully accepted the money. Both coins would be put with all the others. Good money earned by the boy who is fast becoming a trusty cub reporter.

"Does anyone know you're helping me, Joey?"

"I haven't told a soul George, not Ma nor anyone."

"Good boy Joey, good boy, keep it up."

"I sure will George, I'm learning more here than I would at the bleddy schoolhouse!"

Henry and Patricia had finished their private conversation when Joey arrived back at the Plainsman. Joey wanted the opportunity to speak to the redhead and he did so.

"Ma'am, I'm sorry about earlier."

"So am I, Joey. In fact, I should be apologising to you. It was my own fault, not yours. Will you call me Patsy, Joey? I'd like it if you would consider it."

"Shucks, sure I will Miss, I mean, Patsy."

Henry interrupted at hearing his sister's request. "You're honoured Joey, there's only half a dozen people in the world can call her that, two of them are in this room. My little sister can be a fuss arse any time, you're bleddy honoured, lad."

Renee listened to the exchange, wondering what had occurred between the two earlier to convince Patricia that she needed to apologise to her young son, but she wouldn't ask. Henry too was unsure as to the origins of the apology. David, who had been joined by Lourinda, sat quietly and without interruption. Henry explained to his partners the reason in detail, for the girl's arrival in Hickok. He told them she was intent on staying, that she wouldn't be returning to Cornwall as there were too many best forgotten memories there. She had discovered soon enough her beau was not what she thought he would be. Lourinda, who in fact is much younger than Patricia, vowed to take Patricia under her wing, to help her settle in. Henry confirmed to all present that he would be travelling to Dodge the next day. David offered to 'tag' along' with him.

"It'd be best, someone has to keep you out of trouble!" Henry had hoped that would be the case and told his friend that he'd be glad of his company, 'that they would travel by railroad.'

"Henry, I'll go with you, someone needs to keep both you boys out of trouble."

"Okay Soul, I appreciate that!" The two men shake hands and quickly allow bygones to be bygones.

David's injuries had repaired sufficiently for him to make the journey with Henry and Soul Broadbent. He promised Renee that as soon as they returned, he would complete the work on the eating area, now that Renee had decided what she wanted. David also had to make a promise to Lourinda, that he would keep out of trouble and not get into any fights while away.

"I'll be a saint!" he teased.

"That'll be the day" she had replied.

Maria had decided she wanted to stay in the same line of business that she had become used to. The newly completed Golden Horseshoe Saloon had not set its standards very high and was encouraging the 'soiled dove'* trade. The proprietor, knowing of the waitress's popularity among 'the ladies of the night' had asked Maria to go there and she had agreed with only small reluctance. Renee had told the girl she would prefer her to stay but that she wouldn't stand in her way if she wanted to go. She had added Maria could always come back 'if it doesn't work out.'

Renee had offered Patricia some of the work that Maria had been employed in if she felt so inclined. Henry had not asked the favour but he is pleased he could keep a close and watchful eye on his newly arrived sister on his return. It had all been something very new for Patricia, she had never before had a paying position. Her latter years had been spent in assisting her parents in bringing up a younger brother and sister. Patricia had never quite known what had caused the fight between Henry and Soul, neither man had mentioned it to her, neither man ever would. Soul had talked to Henry since their battle, he'd apologised for his words, admitting his drunkenness. Henry had easily accepted the apology and the friendship between the two moved on a pace. Soul had been nothing less than a perfect gentleman to Patricia the few times the two men had met since that first day. Soul being a single man, saw a possible opportunity to alter his bachelor status. He liked the look of the newcomer and vowed to change his ways a little to help his cause.

Henry thought back to the last evening when Renee had left her door open, She knew he would need to pass by it on the

---

* *Soiled Dove: A prostitute.*

way to the room he would normally share with David. Only this night he didn't pass by as he tapped gently and looked around the door without waiting for an answer. Nothing was said by either, David will sleep alone tonight.

Early morning and Henry, David and Soul had bought tickets for the journey. Settling back in the rail car the three men reminisced about their first meetings and in Henry and David's case, their short rail journey that brought them to Hickok in the first place, the two laughing loudly when recalling the unfortunate guard. They were still laughing when that very same uniformed man had entered the carriage and began to check tickets. Both Henry and David sniggered childishly as the guard closed in on their seating positions. The uniformed man looked across at the two now well-dressed saloon owners. He looked down at them over the rim of tiny round glasses. He almost seemed to lean forward over the dividing seat to look at Henry. A puzzled frown crossed his features, a discernible shake of his head preceded the echoing 'tickets please, gents.'

Henry knows the man is in a quandary, he decides to tease him. "Do I know you?"

"I was jest wondrin' the very same thing feller" the bespectacled man drawled. "You been on my train before?"

"This is your train?"

"No."

"I might or might not, mister conductor."

The guard asked for and checked their tickets. He stomped off to the accompaniment of more laughter. The guard stopped and looked over his shoulder at the three, again he shakes his head and unconsciously rubs his sparsely stubbled chin. While Henry, Soul and David had boarded the Dodge train, they had taken little notice of the passengers disembarking before they could board. If they had cared to look they might have seen one of interest.

A little while later a stranger appeared in the centre of Hickok. Cooking Fat immediately notices the new arrival, he steps slowly over the narrow parapet, jumping lightly onto the tiny sloping porch before jumping down to the dusty street. The cat trots in order to catch up and fall into step with the lone man.

The newcomer walked slowly away from the station building. Over his shoulder is suspended a bulging clothes sling, around his waist a heavy gun belt carried a large early model Colt. The raised sights at the barrel end were almost aligned with the wearer's knee. The pistol is counterbalanced by a huge clip pointed 'Bowie' knife that hung at the opposite side. Anybody seeing the man approaching the Plainsman would get the impression of a small boy with an old man's face. Cooking Fat, having entered first, jumped onto the highly polished Cherrywood bar and purred loudly. Gladstone stared goggle eyed as the door swung shut behind the tiny newcomer, his mouth opening and closing not unlike a recently landed fish struggling for breath. The small man steps towards the bar. Gladstone is stood rooted to the spot, unable to comprehend the appearance of this newcomer. The small man slips the shoulder bag off and puts it at his feet. Taking some coins from his trouser pocket, he speaks to the goggling barman. "You put lard in your hair, it dirty habit."

Gladstone unconsciously rubs a hand over his hair. Bringing the hand down over the apron to wipe away the sheen, he notices the cat brushing its acceptance against the man's arm.

"You look like you have seen a ghost, my friend." The small man speaks again.

"If you were standing where I am, you'd think you had" Gladstone managed, struggling to issue the statement.

"You are Gladstone?"

"I am."

"My father told me of you, you his very good friend!"

Gladstone quickly realises he has guessed correctly. From the way he spoke it is certain he somehow knows of the old man's death. Though Gladstone could not decide how the man could possibly have known his father had passed away.

"Old Tungsaw had some funny habits, but yes, we were friends. Have you come to see his grave? We gave him a good send off, even gave him his own little bit of the cemetery. It will be reserved for any of his compatriots who might come here, or he might rest alone. The whole town took a vote, it was agreed. He was a good man, a brave man too. I put his sword in with him, he saved our Marshal's life with that sword, right outside those doors." Gladstone pointed in the direction from which the newcomer had come.

"That is good Gladstone, you did the right thing by my family, my father, he will be happy. I will ask you to take me to the grave when I have spoken to Mr Hawke."

"You'll find him at the general store." Gladstone does not know the name of the newcomer.

The Chinaman gave a slight bow. "I am Kai-Saw, you can call me Kai or Kai-Saw but not Saw."

"Are you staying in Hickok, Kai? Are you a cook like your father had been while he was here?"

"I can cook, I won't cook. I have come to see Mr Hawke about another job." Gladstone waited for Kai to explain. "I have come here to be your new Marshal." Kai brushed Cooking fat with the palm of his hand before leaving to find Jasper. "You take me to grave later Gladstone, please?"

"Sure I will, Kai."

The carriage rattled its way northwards. A darkening sky threatened, flash lightning started the heavenly bombardment. As the storm brewed and inched closer, searing forks begin to dance to the crashing tune. The three watch as the storm gathers momentum. Suddenly they see the eerie 'blue' lightning that neither had ever known existed. They feel a tingling sensation as the carriage accepted the charge, hairs bristled. Henry nervously pulls away from the window. Sulphur assaults the traveller's nostrils. Luckily the storm is travelling south and the train is beginning to build up speed as it moves northwards. Although potentially lethal, the sudden storm is short lived.

Dodge City is bustling when Henry, Soul and David step a little shakily from the train a few hours later. Although Henry is in a hurry to get to the telegraph office, he, David and Soul decide to wash the trail dust and storm fuelled fear from their throats. The friends walk to Front Street and enter the Longhorn saloon. The Longhorn is thronging with dusty cowboys, drummers* and many of the gambling fraternity. Heavily painted girls are in abundance. Dodge's saloons in its early trail-end days operated seven days a week, even twenty-four hours a day sometimes. Dodge has been described in many ways; 'beautiful, bibulous Babylon of the trail' was how one diarist of the time described it. It is unlikely to be beautiful, bibulous maybe, Babylonic possibly. Beauty should always be in the eye of the beholder! Eighteen-Seventies Dodge City is a much bigger sprawl, but hardly different otherwise to Hickok. There are more saloons and cathouses and it seems to the friends, a lot more drunks. It is one of these that would disturb the friends' eagerly awaited thirst quenching. The disturbance would have serious short term consequences and would keep them in Dodge for longer than originally planned.

It had been accidental, but drunks being drunks are mostly unaware of accidents when in an intoxicated condition. David had not meant to spill the man's drink; someone from behind had bumped his shoulder, pushing his arm forward and into the belligerent cattleman. A fist comes around, catching Henry's shoulder. Henry had not seen David's involuntary movement. For the Cornishman, old habits don't suddenly die, just hidden under the surface of his geniality. Henry catches sight of his assailant; he lifts the half-full glass of whisky and drinks slowly while sizing up his intended opponent. Remembering his promise to Lourinda, David turned to

* *Drummer: A travelling salesman.*

apologise to the man at the same time as the fist was landing on Henry. Henry emptied the glass just as the cowboy is about to launch another punch. He ducks the outstretched arm. David decides it is a good time to test out his regained strength. This time the bunched fist hit his shoulder, the reaching arm leaving the cowboy's face unprotected. Henry saw his opportunity and dropped the empty glass, his punch would take the drunk backwards and into the group of cowboys who had shared the trail drive with the falling cowboy. The drunk's impetus would cause more spilled liquid and would signal a free-for-all. David and Henry have time to glance at each other before each would be sending clenched fists powering indiscriminately towards the threatening mob. The first cowboy is down as a result of Henry's punch, down but not out. Henry yelps as he feels teeth nibbling at his calf; shaking his leg to escape from the man's mouth causes him to lose his balance momentarily. Luckily for Henry, as a fist brushes the cloth hat from his head, Soul Broadbent decides it's a good time to intervene and does so.

David stretches a long arm out to grab at Henry's collar and pull him back to his feet. As the Cornishman reaches his full height another unknown puncher catches the Welshman's jaw, only lightly, but the punch inclined him to serious brawling. A young cowboy, no more than sixteen, who had climbed onto the bartop threw himself at Henry, his arms encircle his neck. David sees the kid and throws a right, the weight of the clinging boy causes Henry to bob up and down. David's fist hit Henry on the right eye, his left caught the kid's nose but the boy still clung on, clumps of Henry's hair between his fingers.

"Hit him again Davy, for Christ's sake, get him off me!" Henry manages to screech the order in the melee. David did as he was asked and caught the boy with a roundhouse; still he clung on, but now the kid is unconscious, his fingers are entwined and Henry has to continue to defend himself with the extra weight of the kid's inert body hanging from his back until Soul pulls him off and drops him. Henry did eventually manage to shake the biter from his leg.

David felt no ill effects from his recent injuries. He relished the workout and laughed at his friend's comical predicament, but was unable to help him further as he had to stave off an attack from the cowboy who had first bitten Henry. The grounded man now had his teeth in David's thigh. David used his other knee to force the biter off, the use of the knee caused the kneeling man to upend more cowboys that had entered the fray. Now at least three men are on the floor, trying desperately to claw themselves upwards. A newcomer to the fight catches David between the eyes. Blinded for some seconds as his eyes water, the Welshman stumbles, his boots treading on the hands of the floored man. At each attempt to lift his foot from one hand, it would automatically come down on another. Cries and shouts came up from the floor as he fought vainly to gain his balance. Henry's fists continue to pump at the faces that bob up and down in front of him. David catches another cowboy; instantly unconscious, the cowboy falls on top of Soul who goes down. With his newly won freedom the Welshman is able to release Henry from his unwanted load. As he pulls the boy's hands apart, the unfortunate opens his glassy eyes. David gives the kid a straight jab, which allow his body to slide down. Henry treads on the scrabbling man already at ground level.

It seems to Henry that all the occupants of the Longhorn are involved now. He doesn't mind, there had been scraps of this multitude many times in the crowded Inns of Redruth, Iluggan and Bodmin; he'd been in the middle of plenty of them. On one occasion Henry had joined in a brawl not far from Innis Town and was thrown into the stream at St Lawrence Fair after fighting in the Miners Arms. His being thrown into the creek meant he would be honorary Mayor of the village for one year as a reward. Henry is a veteran of the style of fighting, though Soul Broadbent had got the better of him at the Plainsman. David too is no newcomer to the kind of brawl that is now in full swing. Henry thinks about Soul and the cowboy magically appears; the big ranch hand moves next to him and begins throwing his own punches with complete thoughtlessness as to who they might be hitting.

David looks at Soul "Good to see you, boyyo" he shouted through the yelps of pain and the crashing of breaking glass and splintering wood. Soul winks mischievously at the Welshman while avoiding more flailing punches.

"Thought you might be in here somewhere David, we'll have us a..." Soul's words are cut short as a fist splits his earlobe. David spies the ranch hand's attacker and throws a one two which sends another cowboy down with the others. Two gunshots echo around the bar area and the fighting occupants become instantly immobile. A tall, heavily built man with a waxed moustache spoke "You fellows are all under arrest!" The speaker sports the badge of Town Marshal, four deputies stand a little behind, ready to support their boss. The fighters have spent themselves, some grab at the fallen and pull them onto wobbly feet. Henry plucks up the kid that had been strangling him earlier, throws him over his shoulder. All the fighters do as they are ordered, none attempt to escape their well-earned punishment. The play hard and fight hard Texan cowboys know Marshal Jack Bridges has the reputation of being an unusually fair lawman, they know he would let them all go the next morning, providing they dip into their pockets to make right the Longhorn proprietor's losses regarding damaged property. Henry grabs at an unspilled glass, drinking the contents quickly as he walks towards the door with the lad still on his shoulder. He sets the empty glass down as he carries the half conscious kid out. David and Soul follow, each has an arm about the other.

"I enjoyed that my friend, a pity it had to end so soon."

"Old Jack didn't stop it straight away Davy, he was already in the saloon when we got here. He's a good lawman but he likes a fight as much as the next man. I heard he was in the British Army, in India or some such place." Soul was incorrect,

Jack M Bridges had not served in India but nonetheless, Bridges has always been admired by his peers and more than once he would recover from gunshot wounds received in the line of duty.

Henry regrets now he hadn't sent the telegram. It would wait until tomorrow. He accepted the temporary confinement with good grace, as did David, Soul and the Texan cowboys. The Texas travellers mostly disliked Kansas lawmen, deservedly so in many cases, but Bridges is highly respected by one and all. The prisoners are given water to bathe their battle scars and coffee to quench their fight induced thirsts. Henry pours a jug of water over the youth; the dazed Texan boy throws a half punch, which Henry catches. "Whoa kid, we're all done with that now."

The feisty lad took in his surroundings. "Where am I?"

"The best house in town my lad." Jack Bridges twists the end of his neat whiskers as he speaks. "Jail house!"

"Ma won't be happy if she finds out I got jailed."

Jack Bridges laughs and the battered Texans join in as the kid colours up from embarrassment. "Then next time don't get caught lad!"

Kai-Saw returned to the Plainsman, the badge that David had worn for the short time now pinned to his waistcoat. It gives Gladstone the impression of a much bigger man now. Gladstone had told Renee and Joey about Kai's earlier visit, neither is surprised by the likeness between the recently departed and the newcomer. Renee immediately introduces herself, pointing out that Joey is her son. The Chinaman smiles "I heard of you too boy, my father tell me all about Hickok City, he had many friends here."

Joey excuses himself. Leaving his mother to talk with the newly installed Marshal he goes straight to George's wagon and informs him of the Chinaman's appointment.

Gladstone had been given permission from Renee to guide Kai to the gravesite. He watches as the new Marshal kneels solemnly over his father's last resting place. Joey can hear the man talking but is unable to understand the meaning of the words. He waits patiently. The small man stands up to give a respectful slight bow over the thinly grassed mound.

"My father is happy Gladstone, he will stay here, close to his friends."

Gladstone would not know, but the Chinese when away from home have a custom concerning their dead. They are obliged to make sure the bones of the dead are transported back to their homeland for burial alongside their ancestors. Tungsaw's body would be spared the disagreeable custom of flesh being cooked and stripped from his bones. The bones would then normally be wrapped in cloth or wax paper and put into a zinc-lined box before being transported home to China.

CHAPTER SIXTEEN

Attack!

Jack Bridges would keep his promise of the previous evening; he freed Henry, David and Soul and all of the now sober Texan cowhands were discharged early that following morning. Henry, David and Soul stayed a while longer than the trail drivers, talking with Bridges. The affable lawman wanted to know how quickly and how big Hickok is growing. The fledgeling town is just inside the Ford County boundary and Bridges, in his capacity of County Sheriff, would have to start thinking about paying regular official visits to that part of his 'Bailiwick.'*

Bridges was aware the town had a Town Marshal, as David had imparted the information. It brought more smiles from the higher ranking lawman who knew there would be occasions when he would be needed to preside over more serious cases of law-breaking, perhaps sometimes in Hickok itself. Certainly in any cases of out and out murder or violent robbery he would want to be informed. The Sheriff already knew about the accidental death of Ritchie Stark and the necessary demise of Jack, he knew the bank had been robbed by Davis and the perpetrator was also now deceased. He had reviewed the three cases and was satisfied with the way each had been dealt with locally. Henry had mentioned his friendship with Hickok; he had described how Wild Bill

---

* Bailiwick: one's sphere of operations.

had turned up the night of the town naming and how his appearance had been the reason for taking his name for the town. Henry informed Jack Bridges he needed to find the telegraph office; the Marshal gave directions and the three men, after saying their goodbyes, first promising to get together again soon, left his office.

"Henry, before you go my friend, any chance you might rename the place? Bridges Town has a certain ring to it I believe." Bridges joked.

"Now Jack, you damned well know I would be strung up like a horse thief if I even mentioned it, most likely by Wild Bill himself." Henry replied.

"Fair enough, thought it worth asking." The conversation continued onto the street.

"Don't make a habit of it, Jack, it'll make me a bag of nerves."

"I won't! There's still time to change your mind, boys!"

"Jack, if we did what you suggested, we'd need a change of under garments is my bet. Adios my friend."

Although Henry had actively participated in the saloon brawl, he hadn't forgotten the more serious reason for his visit to Dodge. The fight in some ways had allowed him to vent a little of the anger and the sadness he felt about the loss of the man he had respected more than any other, his father.

Not usually prone to showing his private emotions, the scrap with the Texans had helped to take away some the pain of his loss. Henry glanced at his friends. "I'm not going to send a telegram Davy, I have it in mind to take a passage home to Cornwall, I believe I should."

David nodded his agreement. "I understand my friend. You should do what you think is right boyyo. Renee will understand, I will explain the situation, unless you are coming back to Hickok first?"

"No need, I have enough money with me, all I need. I can always buy anything more I might require."

"We'll miss you Henry, I'll come with you if you want?" Soul made his offer knowing full well that Henry's closest friend would be unable to accompany him. David would be needed at the Plainsman, more so if Henry is to be away for any great length of time, which would almost certainly be the case.

"No Soul, don't you be worrying about me and anyway, I don't think Corish folk would be too pleased with me for bringing you there, what with all your common drunkenness and brawling and other such bad habits." Knowing Henry was being humorous, Soul didn't take offence at the remark. "Appreciate your offer though. Let's us go and get a drink and some breakfast."

"Sure, but my offer is still open. I wouldn't mind seeing England just once in my life."

"What do you think David, should I take this reprobate to England?"

"Take the bastard, that way I won't have to throw him out of the Plainsman most every damned night."

"Okay Soul, if you still want to, we'll both go."

"Sure Henry, I don't need much, got most of anything I'll need with me, I always travel light. I've had enough of chasing cows all around Kansas, damn their hides."

David, Soul and Henry had the promised breakfast; they ate at the Longhorn Saloon on notorious Front Street and after toasting each other more times than once with accompanying whisky, the three friends made their way to the railroad station. David took the train that would take him back to Hickok. Henry and Soul Broadbent would need to stay in Dodge overnight to catch the eastbound locomotive. Later that afternoon they found a comfortable hotel and settled their small amount of private belongings into a drawer. After an evening meal and a minimal amount of whisky, Henry and Soul satisfied themselves with an early night, making the most of their last chance of a comfortable bed for some time. Boarding a train the following morning, which would take them on the first leg of a journey that would cover almost five thousand miles, it could take a month but may only take three weeks or more to cross the ocean.

David had promised he would explain Henry's decision to Renee. He walked from the new station building towards the Plainsman. It is early evening when he opened the door. The saloon is busy and Renee is stood with Gladstone. Cooking Fat sleeps contentedly on the Cherrywood bartop. Renee is pouring drinks and making conversation with customers. David instantly sees the little oriental and immediately notices the gleaming Marshal's badge. He gives an involuntary shake of the head at a sight he could hardly believe.

Gladstone can't resist an impulse to joke. "Jesus Davy, did you know, Tungsaw's ghost is the new Marshal." David ignores Gladstone's joked comment. He can tell Renee is already concerned at Henry's non-appearance. David thinks it best he should explain immediately of the Cornishman's decision. Renee took the news calmly and with complete understanding for Henry's dilemma.

"We seem to have a new Marshal Renee, what's the story?"

"He is Kai, Kai-saw, he's Tungsaw's son."

"Well he looks younger anyway, not by much."

David saunters across to speak to the man he had been discussing with Renee. The Chinaman gives him a slight bow. David informs the Marshal his help is available at any time he might need it. "I was the first to wear that badge, Kai. I'm not cut out for law work, but if you need my help anytime, you just yell. Welcome to Hickok, mister."

"Gladstone has told me of your law work, Davy. You don't give yourself enough credit for good work you have done here while you wore badge. I will call on you if there is a need, you can be certain. Thank you!" Kai-saw gives David another slight bow of respect.

Joey is already inside George's wagon; not only did he have the information that concerned Henry's sudden decision to return to Cornwall, he had also spotted the arrival of the new

Marshal. George is once again pleased with the boy's work. More coins change hands. Joey eagerly pockets the reward. George Benford had increasingly allowed Joey to help with other work in the big wagon. Whenever he isn't attending school, he would help with the intricate job of typesetting, as well as topping up the ink supply and carrying heavy bundles of white paper that had arrived on the most recent train. Joey had done well with his schoolwork; there are even times now he is able to rectify spelling mistakes made by the Pegasus' editor and founder. George, like many others of his calling in these early settling days of the frontier, is not overly endowed with education. He had been lucky enough to be offered a job in Georgia, not unlike the one Joey is doing for him now, although he had been a little older when he finished his own meagre learning. News is in George's blood, one day he hoped it would be in Joey's. A little encouragement is what he had received and he in turn is giving it to the boy, along with the coins. There would soon be more news than this little provincial newspaper could comfortably handle. George knew Joey has little more than a year now to complete his best level of schooling. At least the boy will have a worthy trade where there are few opportunities other than farming in the State.

Scores of Buffalo hunters are moving onto the Kansas Plains. They brought their one half-inch calibre Sharp's rifles and began their systematic decimating of the heaving furred mass. Meat is needed to feed railroad builders, for the many army forts and it is needed for markets in the eastern cities. Most of all the hunters come for the fur; buffalo coats and robes, even shoes and boots made from the hides become highly prized items. Buffalo hunting became sport for many others. Railroad flatcars would be employed to transport sometimes a hundred sightseeing rifle-toting members of the Kansas population; ignorant people that didn't realise that the Cheyenne and especially the more war-like Kiowa tribes relied on the animal almost for their very existence. The Kiowa actually looked upon the sacred Buffalo as some sort of guardian to their people. They believed the animal to be almost a part of their ancestry, in a spiritual sense, a part of their being. In the beginning they were unable to comprehend why someone would feel the need to kill the animals for nothing else but sheer, sadistic enjoyment and profit. The Kiowa nation as a whole would weep at the sight of so many discarded carcasses still with meat, indiscriminately left to rot on the Plains in the dry Kansas Sunshine.

Once the hunters had realised there is a stack of money on the four giant pounding hooves, they came with a vengeance. More carcasses, now headless, furless and in many cases hoof less, littered the stinking 'red' plains. The Cheyenne and the Kiowa could take no more, it is time to fight for their very existence. These two, and still so in the early seventies, well populated and proud nations begin to mobilise their forces; even some small groups of the fierce Comanche tribe would throw in their lot together. The Comanche had evolved into the finest horsemen in North America, much better skilled even than the highly trained but mostly poorly mounted U.S Cavalry troops that manned the various forts on the vast Southern Plains. They will attack wagon trains and the cattle drives, at times the steaming locomotives and far too often, the lone hunter; maiming, killing, even carving open their victims and with bare hands scooping out still warm and throbbing innards. They are determined not to give up their right to hunt the animal; the meat is needed to feed, the hides are needed for Moccasins and Tepees. There is no comparison between the painted warriors and the white hunters. For the Kiowa, it is need. For the white, it is only greed. The tribes would do all in their power to stop the wanton, unnecessary slaughter. They would attempt to do it in the only way they know. It soon becomes obvious to them that if they drive away the whites, the Buffalo would be spared. The inability to succeed would mean certain oblivion for the herds and near extinction for the proud Native American Plains tribes. It is that important!

Two cowboys that had helped dunk Ritchie in the trough had been caught out in the open. Late one afternoon the two men had been setting in fence posts. As always they were armed. Unfortunately the horses they'd ridden out on were tethered too far away to reach at the time of the attack on their camp. They'd fought manfully with their pistols when the screaming Kiowa had come across them; fighting for their lives they managed to thin the number of the war party, but not by enough, they had been overpowered, unmercifully tortured and eventually their bodies had been mutilated. Another ranch hand had found the sickening, smoking remains and reported firstly to his ranch boss, then ridden hard and fast into Hickok. Kai-saw is first to be informed, Jasper Hawke second, who searched out Joey and gave the boy instructions to sound the school bell. Hickokians, on hearing the 'alarm' converged on the building from all parts. Impatiently they sit at the little wooden desks that had been fashioned from the long bar that had been replaced in the Plainsman and waited to find out the reason for the summons. Some had already guessed why the bell had been sounded; the congregation whispered nervously to each other about the looming threat. Kai-saw stood quietly, allowing Jasper to announce the news to the saddened group.

"It seems that we are not in any immediate danger, but we will all have to be vigilant." Jasper explained. He went on "If anyone sees anything at all suspicious, you must tell our Marshal or myself or ring the bell on the schoolhouse immediately. I see no harm in anyone wearing side arms, or carrying a rifle at this time. We don't want any unnecessary gunplay of course. If anyone sees any sign of the Kiowa, spread the word. This building will remain unlocked, first person in here is to pull that bell rope to warn us all."

David sits with Lourinda, Renee and Joey. Joey has a question "Mr Hawke! Can I carry my rifle with me?"

Renee attempted to voice her refusal, David stopped her in her tracks. "I think the lad should Renee. Joey can be trusted, don't you think Mr Mayor?"

"I think Davy's right Renee, we all have to be on our guard. Those that have weapons should keep them near whenever possible."

Renee nodded, she can see the sense in what is being said. Kai-saw also nodded his approval at Jasper's words. Even before he is finished speaking, Joey is on his way out of the building. Although George Benford was at the meeting, Joey knew that the newspaperman would already be planning his next front page; he should be there to help, but there was something else to do first. Joey went directly to the Plainsman and collected the Henry rifle. Ever since Henry had brought home the present from Wild Bill Hickok, Joey had wanted the opportunity to carry it openly. Now he had permission to do so and for the best of reasons. He carefully loaded the rifle and went to Jakey's corral. George is already moving about in the wagon. Joey, swinging the weapon in his hand shouted "George!"

No answer comes from the wagon. A face appears, reddish blue streaks adorn the cheeks of the young lone Kiowa warrior, a decorated war axe gripped in his right hand. Joey could see the wicked blade is dripping fresh blood. He pulls the lever on the rifle that would push a shell into the breach, not even waiting to sight the gun. Joey fired instinctively; the Kiowa grunted as the lead entered his upper chest. The brave who Joey thought was no older than he, showed no evidence of pain; he raised the war axe and squatted in readiness to leap at his prey. Again the youth pulled at the lever and another shell dropped into place. Once more Joey fired. Smoke hid the hideous mass of flesh and bone that instantly exploded from the painted face. Joey never saw the brave fall, he was already unconscious from the shock of the forced action and recoil of his rifle. George Benford, recovering from the attack, leapt out of the wagon, almost landing on the remains of the dead brave. He rushed to Joey, expecting the worst. The deep shoulder wound George had received numbed his arm, but he did manage to find a water dipper to soothe the wound a little until Doc' Ryder can treat it. Seeing that his saviour is only unconscious, George pours the remainder of the liquid over Joey's forehead and face which brings him out of his malaise. Joey unknowingly, had saved George Benford's life in stopping the Brave's singular attack on the newspaper editor.

The majority who had been in the schoolhouse had already dispersed and returned to their homes and businesses. Mrs Hawke had heard the shots, she is the first on the scene. Joey is coming round as she arrives. Mrs Hawke wetted a handkerchief, she dabbed more water over the boy. Realising that Joey is unhurt, she offers George the damp cloth to put over the shoulder wound. Doc Ryder, hearing the shooting, had knowingly made his way in the direction of the rifle's reports; he quickly tended to the wounded newspaperman while Mrs Hawke helped Joey to his feet. Joey's face reddened when he suddenly realises what has just happened to him. Once George starts to relate the boy's actions to the mayor's wife, the blushes turn to a mixture of pride in his bravery, but a sincere regret at having to kill another human; a human who was most likely not much older than himself, a boy that would have certainly killed both he and George without the slightest compunction.

Kai came on the scene next. He points out to the gathering group the expertise of the boy's targeting. The first shot had pierced somewhere near the heart, the second had entered the forehead slightly above, but central to the eyes. The brave had prepared to mount his second attack through reaction and will power alone. Word got to the Plainsman. Renee ran the full length of the main street. Joey is standing straight and tall when she reaches him. Tears course his cheeks as reality sets in. Renee embraces her regretful son while the story is again related, this time by Mrs Hawke.

Doc Ryder helped George Benford to his house, suggesting the wound could be tended and stitched better there. Mrs Hawke left the scene to find her husband and tell him of the fight. Renee put an arm around her son and coaxed the unnerved and still shivering boy home. Kai is left to find the undertaker and Jakey; he would need to borrow a flatbed to transport the remains of the Kiowa brave out of town where senior members of his tribe will find him.

Joey pulls away from his mother when he spies David. The Welshman had restarted work in the restaurant, so hadn't heard the gunfire and Renee had not had time to tell him before she had rushed off to the corral. "I feel sick Davy, he was just a kid like me!"

"Easy Joey! If you hadn't done what you did, you and George would most likely both be lying dead now, even scalped and maybe worse. It was you or him, you had little choice, lad." David went behind the bar, picking up the unopened bottle of cognac. After taking the cork out he poured the boy a small glass of the rich brown liquid. He passes the glass to Joey. "Drink this boy, it'll help the stomach. Don't sip it, throw it to the back of your throat all at once." Joey did as he was told, the liquid did its best to return, Joey gulped and swallowed it back.

Instead of calling another town meeting, Kai-saw, Jakey, David and Jasper agree between them to visit every house and place of business around town, even the tiny cribs of the soiled doves are visited, and their tenants warned of the danger. They would ensure that those people who had arms knew how to use them, to keep them loaded and that each person should be on constant alert to the danger of another surprise attack. The citizens are warned to make sure certain doors and windows are locked and bolted before retiring for the night. They are also advised to fill any useful containers with water from the creek, in case of fire arrows. The deputies also suggest that it would be safer, if going out, not to go alone. The four peacekeepers - Gladstone is included in the important discussion - would split into two pairs. Each pair would take a turn in patrolling the streets through the next few nights; one pair would sleep while the other pair did a three hour tour of duty and vice versa. The street guardians worked this way for seven consecutive nights, each retiring pair at the end of their stint were welcomed in the Plainsman or the Golden Horseshoe and allowed food and a free drink before they went in search of well-earned sleep.

It seemed to everyone that the attack by the one Kiowa brave must have been an isolated event, a young brave trying to impress the elders of his tribe. There was no sign of war parties over the week of nights. The deputies separated and patrolled one at a time for the following seven days, still there is no cause for alarm. Hickok, after the early scare, slowly returns to normal, though the four insist the nightly patrolling should continue a little longer. Jasper agrees the plan is good and gives his blessing.

Joey knows he is the talk of the town right now, due to his swift actions. He ventures away from the Plainsman only to attend school and to work with George, who would struggle for a while after his injury. He'd argued with the newspaperman that the front page story of his heroic deed should be forsaken. George could not agree.

"It's news Joey, whether you like it or not, it stays in." George rubbed at his sore shoulder and hopes it won't take too long to heal. "If it hadn't been for you, this business would be finished." George had cleaned the war axe the Kiowa had wielded; he handed it to the boy. Renee would hang the axe above the bar as a reminder to everyone to be vigilant.

Henry and Soul, with return tickets to New York safely in their pockets, board their ship; they had paid for a very small but private cabin. For Henry, a far cry from the outgoing voyage from his home town. Storing the spare clothing they had purchased in New York and secreting their Colt six-guns and holsters beneath the new clothes, Henry had gone on deck while Soul wanted to sleep. He stood and watched the

Hudson River harbour disappear from view. He had no idea of the happenings back home in Hickok. He thought about Renee mostly and how he would miss her. Henry smiled to himself as he mentally recalled the day of the roof lifting, the day that he felt the first tiny stirrings of affection for Renee. Henry thought about and felt not a little guilty about leaving the newly arrived Patricia. He is confident his friends would see no harm come to her in his absence, she will still be there on his return.

The ship slowly and almost silently edged away from the bustling port. As the tall vessel crept through the Long Island Sound, Henry realises it is the very same ship that had brought him to the United States all those months ago. He licked away the salt taste from his lips. In the chill wind, he wouldn't be sure that the salt wasn't his own. Henry stayed on deck until they had passed Nantucket Island and he could no longer see the land they had left. Two hours were to pass before he returned to the cell-like cabin, with its tiny hard cots.

Henry's family had outlived the vegetable famines of the previous decade. There had been little money to spare and less food to waste. The all important potato had served as the staple to most of the poorer Cornish Families; most times it would have been the only ingredient in a stew or a Pasty. When the great provider decided there would be few, the Cornish people became fewer in many ways. The luckier would migrate in the worst of conditions and bare even worse discomfort than Henry was about to. Henry remembers what it would be like to be Joey's age now. He is determined that his surviving parent, brother and sister would never have to rely on that single vegetable again, not while he had breath. A pocket inside the thick woollen coat held enough cash to bring all three back home to Kansas with him.

He would return with the hope of news he might even become a father. He had spent his last evening in the confines of Renee's room! He scribbled a reminder of the date for inserting the details in his journal on his return to Hickok. He stuffed the scrap of paper inside an empty tobacco pouch he had found on the deck.

CHAPTER SEVENTEEN
Homecomings and Goings

The Cleopatra's voyage lasted almost four, mostly uneventful weeks. It had been completed in very quick time due to the prevailing winds. The course had taken the ship first in an easterly direction, then north and then shifted to the east again. Henry attempted to keep a written account of the crossing, mostly successfully, except during the all too frequent squally seas with waves suddenly reaching a height of thirty feet, possibly higher. Boredom was Henry's biggest problem and he overcame it temporarily by playing cards with off duty crewmembers whenever possible. Soul was a sleeper like many cowboys, especially those who rode the line* at night. A lonely job and usually for single men who might be single for many reasons, most times when a sweetheart had been involved but may have changed her mind.

When no one was available, or willing to play cards, Henry amused himself with solitaire and his writings. He would gamble when an opportunity occurred, mostly in just a small way, losing occasionally but more regularly winning.

* A Line Rider - Cowboys who patrol the ranch boundary lines, pushing stray cattle back over the line back onto their respective ranches. Later, on fenced ranches, a line rider would watch for and repair damaged fencing during the daylight hours. Many of these cowboys liked only to do the night shift where they could sing or whistle to keep the beasts calm or they could sleep whilst on horseback and be quickly alert when trouble appeared. Many country and Western songs became popular in this way. Most cattle owners had line shacks every few miles and these could be used to sleep in when a duty was finished. Many 'lonesome' cowboys lived this way.

On reaching his destination, he had become richer by accruing a small amount of pounds and several dollars, most times from the sailors when they were stood down. It seemed to him that the last handful of days were the longest of all. He knew it wouldn't be long before he saw his birthplace and his beloved parent again. He is anxious to have his feet once again on firm, familiar ground. Henry had never known someone to sleep so often and for so long, though once land was sighted, Soul was fully awake and ready to step foot on it.

On a perfect high tide, the Cleopatra coasted slowly and was handled carefully into Bristol harbour. Deckhands tied the big ship alongside plank walkways stretching out from the granite harbour side. Henry waited patiently as a small queue formed at the head of the walkway. There had been few passengers and so his wait is a short one. Once on solid ground, he and Soul began their long trek south and west by any means available. They eventually bought horses from a farmer after leaving the town.

Once clear of Bristol the pair veered slightly south towards Taunton. Soon after they head in a Westerly direction along the already ancient roadway. The two intend to put as many miles behind them as they can on their first day. They stop and sleep twenty miles North of Taunton. Soul is almost asleep before Henry has even dismounted. It is a warm evening and a fire isn't needed. Henry smoked a half cigar he found in his pocket. While smoking, he had two directions of thought uppermost in his mind: Hickok, a growing settlement and Innis Town, town it is not, much like Hickok is not a city. Innis consists of a handful of cottages with few occupants. There will be much less if Henry has his way and takes the family back to Kansas with him.

Henry could see the grey towers of the castle at Taunton, a jumble of a building having been altered many times over eight or nine centuries. It will soon disappear from view as they head towards Tiverton where they will rest again, after that they will leave the turnpike and cut across country via Crediton towards Okehampton, which they hope to be clear of by the third day. The fifth or sixth day might with luck, find them on the outskirts of Bodmin, another resting place and a chance to prepare for returning home after almost a year away.

The two have talked on and off on the last leg of their journey. For Henry the countryside is well known, for Soul, he had no idea how green and hilly it is in the West Country. Soul was born in Kansas and had hardly ever crossed the state line unless working on a cattle drive and it was necessary to do so. The only time the cowboy ever travelled at all was when cows needed to be moved to the railheads at Ellsworth, Abilene, Wichita and Dodge City among others.

They stop over at Okehampton's White Hart, it's oldest known Inn. They ate and slept in the stables at the rear of the building without asking permission for the latter. They were away before light and riding on towards Launceston, which will take most of the fourth day on the road.

"Tomorrow we'll rest up at Bodmin for the night before going onto Innis, Soul" Henry informed his dozing partner.

"Do they have a saloon at Bodmin like that other place, Henry? I liked it there apart from sleeping in the stable."

"Okehampton? It wasn't so bleddy bad as stables go."

"Rats or mice everywhere, I heard them."

"Wait until we hit Bodmin, they have the biggest rats you ever seen. Better load your pistol Soul, or they'll get you!"

"I surely hope they make a try, Henry."

"You'll get your chance my friend. We'll stop off at the Barley Sheaf in the town, I know them and they know me, we'll have a bed there."

"A bed you say, well don't that beat all. I didn't think you English had beds, I ain't hardly seen one yet dammit."

"Do you ever stop complaining, Soul? And I'm bleddy Cornish, man."

"When I'm asleep is all Henry, anything you say. Cornish, English, there ain't no damn difference."

"Nope, that idn't true let me tell you."

"What was I saying, Cornishman?"

"No idea, just mumbling mostly like you do when you're awake."

"Well, maybe I was dammit."

"Maybe, if so, who's the lady you kept calling?"

"I don't like to talk about it."

"Well you don't have to in the daylight, you talk about her in the bleddy night."

"Are you sure it was me?"

"I didn't see anyone else in the bleddy stable. It must have been you, Soul."

"What's that you said, bleddy? What the hell is bleddy when it's at home?"

"It's a cuss word, Soul. We use it around these parts when we're pissed off with somebody."

"Really, who are you pissed off with Henry, there's only me here."

"That's right Soul, you got n."

"I won't damn talk to you at all, not when I'm awake, not when I'm asleep. How do you like that, Englishman?"

"I'll tell you when it's over! I don't want to hog the conversation."

The two friends sleep in a barn just outside Launceston. They make another early start with their shortest ride since they left Bristol. They reach Bodmin at midday, put the horses in the stables at the back of the Barley Sheaf in the main street and walk inside for a drink.

"Soul, don't you ever take that bleddy hat off?"

"Only when I'm asleep."

"I just knew you would say that. How can you take your bleddy hat off when you're asleep for Christ's sake?"

"Well Mister Tamryn, you'll just have to sit up and be awake to find out, won't you!"

"I'll give that a wide berth."

"Just get me another of them warm beers for Christ sakes!"

"I'm glad you came with me, Soul."

"Why's that, Henry?"

"Fact is, I don't remember."

"You English have a lot to answer for, did you know that?"

"I might have if I was English, I'm Cornish and you're really starting to bleddy annoy me now. I should have left you asleep on the bleddy boat! Where's my bleddy gun?"

"Are all you Cornish folks ornery?"

"Shut up, I'm trying to think."

"Let me know when you make a start at it."

"Like hell I will!"

"I'm for that bed, Henry."

"Don't remind me. I've never known the Barley Sheaf so full. I was planning on having a bed of my own."

"So was I."

"Drink up and don't bleddy talk all night."

"The cows like it."

"Then why don't you go sleep with some bleddy cows then?"

"You're one miserable son of a bitch, ain't ya."

"Sure, do you blame me?"

"Why don't you ....?"

The next morning they pass through the toll-gate at St Lawrence and drop down into a steep, narrow valley. Just where the ground rises and then levels out, a cottage, a Long House, comes into view, wood-smoke drifts along the thatch and drops down into the yard. No sound comes from the two riders.

Francis saw them first. Henry could tell that the younger Tamryn could not make up his mind whether to run straight to his newly arrived big brother or run inside to inform his mother, he is in a two and eight. The boy attempts a combination of both, he runs towards Henry and his unknown companion whilst shouting at the top of his voice "Ma! Ma! It's Henry, he's home!" Henry chuckles at the young siblings' comical antics. He looks across toward the small barn at the far end of the house, he knew if Teresa Ann was at home it would be where he would find her, she would be somewhere near the animals. He saw her head appear from behind the barn door, the boy's yelling having alerted her. The barn in which the animals sleep is an integral part of the cottage. The Tamryn family and all of the animals share the same lengthy roof.

"H! Is that you, H?"

Henry smiles in answer to Teresa Ann's ridiculous question; her brother has only been away for a year, he hasn't changed that much. Or maybe he has. Francis is almost on him now. Francis, who is a little smaller and younger than Joey, jumps at his elder brother and wraps his arms around him like a ten-year-old greeting a parent. Teresa Ann would have loved to do the same, but Francis had already beaten her to it.

Mary Tamryn stands outside the door and watches her children frolic. Mary is particularly proud of her brood, she takes so much pride from the way they had always cared for and looked out for each other. She watches her son's approach to the little homemade gate. Francis has to let go of Henry's shoulders to allow him to pass through. Teresa Ann tries playfully to push Francis away, but he is having none of it. He did back away to allow Henry to hug their mother. This done Henry turns back and embraces his younger sister. Mary beckons all to come inside. She is already lifting pans preparing a welcome home meal. She knows there is a complete stranger standing aside with a hat in his hand, it doesn't matter, he's in the house and that's that.

Francis asks half a dozen questions before Henry has any chance to answer the first. Teresa Ann is just as impatient to discover everything her brother has been doing in 'America.' Mary makes tea to go with the pastries. Later they will eat the Cornish Pasties that are already beginning to bake in the blackened cloam oven!* Henry is hungry, any food aboard the Cleopatra had been sparse and bland and he had missed the home cooking provided by the now departed Tungsaw. He and Soul ate quickly, taking mouthfuls between answering the young children's constant questions as best they can and doing their best to include everyone in the conversation. Henry bit on a Cornish scone, smothered with homemade fruit jam and freshly made clotted cream atop, which as always, seemed to melt when making contact with the inside of the mouth. He washed the food down with hot, sweet tea. Henry is glad to be home, even if the stay is only to be a short one, though he has what might be a controversial plan to put to his remaining family members.

Mary asks "Did Patricia find you, have you seen her? She gave you the news of your Da'?"

"Patsy was good when I left town, she told me." Henry, having had his fill, sat comfortably, stretching out his legs, before starting at the beginning. He told them everything that had happened to him since his departure, deciding it would be best to leave nothing out. Mary and Teresa Ann each gave a gasp as Henry told them of his killing of Jack. He explained how there he had no other choice, a man was about to cut a woman's throat. Francis listens excitedly at the recalling of the shooting. Henry describes his meeting with David, he told how Wild Bill had 'blown' through the door just as they were voting on a name for the town. He talked of the Plainsman and of Renee and Joey, Tungsaw and the cat.

"So you are David, I'm sorry my son has not introduced you. You're welcome in my house!"

"No ma'am, I'm not David, I'm Soul, Soul Broadbent and thank you for your hospitality ma'am, this is sure good grub, ma'am."

* A cloam oven is a type of masonry oven. It has a removable door made of clay or alternatively a cast-iron door, and was a standard fitting for most kitchen fireplaces in Cornwall and Devon. The oven would be built into the side of the chimney breast, often appearing on the outside as a round bulge in the chimney.

"Oh, I'm sorry, Soul. Thank you."

"No need, ma'am."

Francis wants to know more about the boy, Joey.

"You'll get to know more about Joey, Francis, don't be worrying about that!" Henry isn't ready yet to tell his mother that he plans to take the remainder of his family back with him; he knew that to convince Mary to return with him would be a difficult, maybe almost impossible task. He is careful not to disclose his plan until the right time. First he would work on Teresa Ann and Francis, although Henry is certain Francis would not put up much of a fight, once he knows more about Hickok and Kansas. Henry tells them of the night of the Tornado and how the whole town had sheltered in the new schoolhouse. Henry told his listeners of the fight with Soul, that it had been caused by Patricia's arrival. Remembering the fight made both Henry and Soul chuckle along with the family. He told Francis about Tungsaw's black cat, how it had taken up residence in the tower and only came down for food.

Francis is fascinated by his elder brother's storytelling and begs to know more. He wants to know everything but at his age, Henry decides enough is enough for now. Certain things should not be retold!

There has been no further attack on Hickok. Cowboys came in from time to time with news of atrocities from other parts of the plains country. Buffalo hunters were still being attacked and killed, stagedrivers had needed to be at their best to outrun war parties and isolated farms that had been attacked, burned and looted. The Hickok town Marshal and his deputies' still patrol late into the night and one would always be on duty, though there were no further sightings reported.

David had kept the promise to complete the restaurant and its little eating booths. Since returning from Dodge, he'd put all his energies into the work. Renee was forever coming in and watching, making suggestions, which David almost always ignored. She bought new Gingham tablecloths and curtains that just matched. She made up her mind to improve the free food counter in the bar area, for those customers that didn't want to eat in the restaurant. She knew it was the practice in many Kansas City saloons, it was good enough for her drinking customers. Being the only other partner present, David had been consulted and had agreed with Renee's proposals.

Fe Tylden brought another wagon train in to town. Once the wagons had been encamped he made straightaway for the Plainsman. Pleased to see the wagon boss, Gladstone set about getting him fresh coffee. Fe was a man of habit, always he would order coffee on his arrival, later partaking of stronger alcoholic beverages. "How are you doing, Gladstone? Seems quiet in here, where is everyone."

"Poor Tungsaw is dead, Henry is in England, Soul went to England with him, I hope he behaves! Renee is around somewhere and David's making all that noise next door. The two farm hands that drowned poor old Richie are dead, god rest their souls, they didn't mean no harm when they dropped him in the horse trough. We have a newspaper here now. The owner was attacked by a lone Kiowa, Joey killed the brave with the rifle he was given by Mister Hickok."

"Don't leave nothing out now Gladstone, tell me everything man!" Fe said humorously. He looked at the war axe that hung in front of him. "That's Kiowa, I reckon."

"Belongs to Joey now. I told you, he killed the feller that was carrying it. Put one bullet through the brave's heart, put another between his eyes. Some smart rifle shooting for a young kid like that if you ask me. I can't figure out how anyone could be quick enough to shoot a man between the eyes when he was already most likely dead from a heart shot and already falling, the boy has a good eye." Gladstone went on to describe how Joey had come across the Kiowa. "Saved the newspaper-man's life he did, then upped and fainted on the spot. Joey and that Kiowa couldn't have been more than six feet apart when the kid fired."

"I'm impressed."

On hearing Fe's voice, David appears from the restaurant. "Hey Fe, good to see you. Gladstone telling you about the boy?"

"Sure is, not sure I believe it all mind. The kid must have been real lucky, or he must be a damn good shot with that Henry rifle!"

"I couldn't say, one thing's for sure though."

"What's that?"

"The Kiowa's dead and he's got two holes in him, both dead centre you might say."

"Gladstone tells me Henry has gone home to England?"

"That's right and he'd better come back, I don't know how long he'll be away. He had news that his father had died. We were in Dodge with Soul Broadbent. Henry decided to go and took Soul with him, just like that. Henry's sister Patricia brought the news here. She's here, not going back by all accounts. Patricia's a real nice girl too. I guess there has to be one decent member of a family!" David winked at Fe Tylden.

"I'm a married man Davy, not interested."

"I didn't know you had a wife, Fe. Anyone I know? Give the poor girl my condolences when you see her next." The Welshman joked easily with Tylden.

"Remember the young woman on the wagon train, the English woman, she was with that son of a bitch that Tungsaw ran his blade through. She was alone with the new born, so I got to thinking, decided it was time I settled down. I asked her. She said, 'why not?' I said 'Shucks, why not.' I'm a real daddy now anyway."

"You must have twisted her arm some, boyyo."

"Didn't have to, seems like that Englishman had given her a pretty bad time, same as Lourinda. In any case, she grabbed at the chance, was worried that some heathen Welshman would come along and drag her away to his cave or some other terrible place.

David ignored Tylden's gentle chiding. "Well good luck to you both. I'll be praying for the poor girl!"

"Thanks my friend. Now, I'm damn near to starving, my belly thinks my throat's bust. Ain't you finished that eating place yet?"

"No, I might have if you hadn't come in to interrupt me." David suggested.

With his stomach eventually satisfied, Fe Tylden intimated to David he wanted to talk.

"What's on your mind, Fe?"

"I've a mind to retire from the wagon train business Davy. You know old man Ross?"

"The stage line owner?"

"The very one. It seems he needs a partner. Says he needs to expand, he's looking for an investor!"

"You?"

"Made me an offer I can't take up!"

"Why not?"

"I don't have that kind of money, Davy."

"How much is that kind of money?"

"A whole five hundred dollars. Exactly the price of a new Stage, give or take a cent!"

Davy looked thoughtfully for a moment at his friend. "Let me speak to Renee, Fe, we might come up with something, no promises!" Fe Tylden hadn't even considered asking his friends for a loan. He was surprised at the Welshman's willingness to even discuss the possibility, especially as they had not been acquainted for more than just a few months. He left to complete the settling of his charges. There was just a little more spring in his step as he returned to the campground.

Although the coming of the railroad would take at least some business away from the stage lines, the ever increasing population of Kansas would still need to be able to move shorter distances not yet covered by the steel tracks.

Mary is sleeping. It is her habit to rest in the afternoons. The arrival of Henry had tired her a little more than usual.

Henry now grasps the opportunity to talk with Teresa Ann and Francis about his plans to take all the family back to Kansas, especially now that Patricia had arrived in Hickok. Brother and sister listen intently to Henry's pictorial-like descriptions of Kansas Plains life. He tells Francis how they had built the school and how there weren't enough pupils to fill it. He told them all about the hotel, going into more detail than he had when arriving. He tried not to pressure Teresa Ann and the boy. He told them that if they were in agreement, all three would then have to convince their mother that it was for the best they return with him to Kansas.

Mary had dozed for only a short while and unknown to the three secretive siblings, she had soon awoken and was able to listen to a large amount of their conversation. She smiled quietly to herself but never spoke aloud. Mary had no intention of going to Kansas, she did want Teresa Ann and Francis to have the opportunity of a better life, she wouldn't stand in their way knowing that Henry and Patricia would see to it that the younger children would continue to have a decent upbringing and just as importantly, a good education. Mary closed her eyes again.

Henry is tired. Soul is already dozing noisily in a chair. Sleeping aboard the Cleopatra for Henry and Soul had been at best spasmodic most nights. Henry had wondered how the crew were able to sleep with all the constant movement of the ship. He'd been warm enough and their tiny cabin had been mostly dry. He'd been better off than the first voyage where the sleeping quarters had been meagre and overcrowded. Henry had also given one of the grubby blankets to a child that had caught a bad chill and had become chesty. The child's cough had worsened during the voyage. Henry remembered the morning he heard the woman's painful, tortured screams. He had given over the blanket, but it had been too little too late. Pneumonia had taken hold of the infant, it had only let go with her death. The ship's doctor had shown a remarkable lack of competence and eventual disinterest, caused by alcoholism.

The heartbroken young parents had not allowed the body to be lowered traditionally beneath the waves, they had begged the ship's captain to allow them to bring the little girl to America and bury her there. Henry recalled the sad scene as the infant's father had carried the little stiffened body, still wrapped in the donated blanket, from the ship, at the end of their voyage. He had offered his help, it had been refused in a friendly manner, Henry understood the father wanting to carry his small daughter ashore. He understood too why they would want to keep their child where they will be, where the child was promised she would be at the end of the voyage.

Henry and Soul slept while younger brother and sister whispered to each other of what life for them might be like in Kansas, each deciding they would go!

Mary never stood a chance. "The youngster will need you ma, if you don't come, he can't!"

Henry had slept long and well, Soul continued to do so. He wrote a message for Soul. Fully recovered from his journey the Cornishman left the long house. As his first task, he had set himself to try and sell their livestock. The smallholding is rented and could easily be handed back to its landlord. He called on the nearest neighbours. After a small amount of haggling on the price, Henry disposed of two milk-producing goats and their Billy, throwing in a handful of good mature laying hens to clinch the deal. He was pleased with the outcome. He called on various other acquaintances to dispose of the stock. Lastly he would have to call on the landlord of the smallholding. Henry expected to get some resistance from the owner, his suspicions would prove entirely correct. Henry knocked on the door of the ramshackle cottage. The door was opened with a swine-like grunt. A hugely obese middle-aged man looked at the caller through drink-reddened eyes. Henry could hardly breathe for the man's odour, saliva dribbled a little from the 'pig's mouth.

"What the hell do you want, Tamryn?"

"That's a good question Connell, one that deserves an honest answer. The fact is I don't want anything from you. Moreover, I have come to give you something!"

"You have nothing I want Tamryn, unless you're here to pay the land rent you owe. You can do that and piss off back from where you came. Leave me alone!"

"I beg to differ, you fat robbing bastard!" Connell, belying his size and almost permanent inebriation, jumped at Henry at the words. Both men immediately tumble, Henry rolls away from the fat man. "I owe you nothing, Connell!" Henry was remembering that Connell had had him beaten just months before he embarked on his new life. Henry had beaten the man at cards and taken a small amount of cash from him. Connell and friends had jumped Henry while on his way home from the Tavern at St Lawrence, beaten him senseless and had taken the loss back. They had also taken Henry's own money while he had lain unconscious in the darkened street. Henry had not seen fit afterwards to rescue the cash. He had already decided his future was in the United States, the cash had been of little amount and little consequence. The historic attack had helped Henry to make up his mind.

Now that Connell had opened the ball, Henry showed a keenness to dance, he is determined to make amends for the beating he'd received. He climbed to his feet a second before Connell; he waited, timing the withdrawal of his right fist. Connell heightened, turning his head up and round. Henry powered the fist forward. Luckily for Connell, Henry didn't connect fully, though the punch unsteadied him he was still able to mount a swift counter attack. Henry took a return blow on the upper cheek under his left eye, swelling is already taking place. Both men were now balanced, exchanging blows equally. At times they move in close, wrestling for control, neither achieving the aim. Separating again and swinging powerful arms, Connell would try and use his extra weight and bulk to bring the scrap to an end.

When the two had fought previously, their efforts had always been influenced by alcohol. This time Henry is stone cold sober. Connell is as before and it would begin to show soon. Henry could smell the fat bastard's rancid breath as they closed, he could hear Connell breathing shallowly now. Henry guesses correctly Connell is struggling; he throws a left and right in quick succession, catching his opponent fully this time. Connell rocks backwards. Realising Henry has the beating of him, Connell snatches a knife from a boot side hiding place; he slashes at Henry, swearing, grunting swine-like, waving the blade in sideways motions. Henry pulls the Peacemaker from its holster that had been hidden by the length of his woollen jacket. He'd surmised there could be a problem of this sort and had taken the precaution of carrying the weapon. Connell is labouring but still he has the intention of opening Henry up. Henry pulls back the hammer: even with the swollen eye, just as it had been with Jack, his aim is true. The knife spins backwards as Connell's hand partly disintegrates under the impact of the heavy forty-five-calibre bullet. Connell screams and howling, falls to the floor. He has never had to face a pistol before. The gun's report and the sight of a finger separating from his pudgy hand causes his last meal to reappear. The fat man, now on the ground, howls and whimpers alternatively.

"We're even, Connell." Henry looks at the newly disfigured bully in disgust, he spits and the phlegm hits Connell's boot. The stricken man recoils like as if another leaden messenger has struck him. "Another thing, if I ever see you again, I'll kill you!" Connell held up the shattered bleeding hand, his mouth working, there is no sound but a child-like whimpering now. Henry turned away from Connell, he is hurt but content in the knowledge of having repaid his opponent for earlier beatings. He staggered back toward the House.

As Soul continues to sleep, Teresa Ann pours cold water into the basin. She dampens the clean cloth and puts it to Henry's face; he winces with the water's coldness. Ignoring her elder brother's complaining, Teresa Ann works on. It isn't the first time she has had to bathe her brother's wounds. Mary has guessed what has happened.

"You know I hadn't planned on going with you Henry, though I imagine you put this pair up to trying to convince me that it will be for the best. I suppose I have little choice now in the matter!"

"I'm sorry mother, but it is for the best. I'll look after you, we'll look after you, all of us. I'll get us a wagon to take our stuff to Falmouth harbour, tomorrow we will sail."

Henry added "We can't take father with us and I'm sorry for that."

Francis and Teresa Ann both speak in agreement with their elder brother. "We want to go ma, we want all of us to go."

"As you say, it will be for the best, now stop mollycoddling your bleddy brother."

Henry smiles at Mary. It had been easier than he had thought it would be. He pushed Teresa Ann's nursing hands away. "You heard, stop your damn fussing girl and get to packing your bits and pieces, you too boy, we're heading for Hickok, all of us!"

Soul awoke and looked up at his friend. "What the hell happened to you?"

"It's a long story, it ended well enough."

That evening Henry disposed of the only cow, some ducks and the remainder of the hens, the aged Cockerel followed the purchaser, dancing and leaping up with a worried annoyance at the swinging, bulging sackful of cackling hens.

It is a little before dawn the next morning. Henry has the wagon almost fully loaded. Mary flits back and forth, picking up the remains of her belongings. Francis and Teresa Ann stand by the wagon, waiting patiently. On hearing some slight noise from the thick privet hedge behind him, Henry pulls the colt, firing twice high into the bushes at the side of the lane. Nothing nor nobody emerged. "Come out Connell, you sneaking coward."

Henry waits, still nothing. Mary emerges from the cottage with the last of her belongings. It is at this moment Connell emerges from his hiding place, an aged single barrelled shotgun pointing at the group. Connell aims the gun and attempts to pull the trigger; in his drunken stupor and boiling temper the bully has forgotten the recent loss of the finger, nothing happens. Realising Connell's predicament, Henry strides towards the shotgun wielding bully, he reaches out and snatches at the cold barrel, jerking the gun away from the drunken would-be ambusher, then the Cornishman coolly smashes the long gun on the ground. Connell stares at his tormentor. Henry reaches into his pocket and takes out a handful of coins, Connell winced as they him in the face. Henry gave a satisfied shrug. Connell's words would not come out. Henry helped Mary onto the wagon. Francis and Teresa Ann climbed aboard without help. Henry looked back at the oil lamp, he changes his mind and clucks the ponies' into action. The travellers could just see the outline of Connell's face as he sinks to his knees retching and crying as if a baby.

"Can we go home to bleddy Kansas please, Henry?"

"Kansas might not want you back, Soul!"

CHAPTER EIGHTEEN
A flame goes out

"Joey, Quick! Another circus!" David laughingly shouts through the half open door of the Plainsman. The Welshman hears the boy approaching behind him. Joey shoves past to see why the Welshman has called him. He watches with interest as the heavily laden flatbed comes to a grinding halt at a hitching rail outside the saloon's door.

"Ma, ma, it's Henry and Soul, they're back, they're here ma, they got others with them, a girl and a kid, some other lady." Joey squints into the sunlight at the newcomers.

Henry Tamryn looks across at his welcoming friend. Smiling he climbs down from the hard seat, his outstretched hand waiting for David's welcoming response. The two greet each other with a hug. David is relieved to see the travellers. Renee came out into the afternoon sunshine, Kai-saw followed just a few steps back, not knowing what has caused the sudden excitement.

Henry smiles warmly at Renee and straightaway notices the tiny man with the shining badge and the long barrelled pistol that hangs almost to his kneecap. "Who the hell is that?" He points at the little man, Henry asks the question and guesses the answer.

The Oriental stares knowingly. "I am Kai-saw, son of Tungsaw. Now you take gun off, or I throw you in jail, Henry Tamryn."

"You can go to hell hombre, in a bleddy handcart!"

"You will know where it is to find, so you come with me or I might shoot you dead, Tamryn!"

"That's all we need, another bleddy knackered Marshal!" Henry held out his right hand to the Oriental, Kai-saw laughed wickedly, knowing the returnees are now having a little fun at his expense. He is aware Henry is in no way being rude to him. From the others Kai-saw had learned plenty of Henry Tamryn and his humorous ways, he accepted the banter without offence. He bowed respectfully before taking hold of and shaking the offered hand vigorously. Soul Broadbent followed suit.

"Welcome home, Henry Tamryn. You are Soul?"

"You could say that, I wish you didn't." Soul Broadbent couldn't help smiling at the question and his reply.

"You are welcome here Kai-Saw, as was your father, a great man and sorely missed."

"Thank you, Henry Tamryn."

Renee just resists a temptation to put her arms around the Cornishman's neck and kiss him; instead she shows a willingness to hold back her feelings, apart from a relieved smile, pleased at his safe return. Anyone noticing might easily have read her mind, coming to the correct conclusion she isn't just greeting a good friend or a business partner. Renee looks towards the older lady, instantly knowing who she must be, but not realising that at least here was one person who had seen through her. She watched as Henry and Soul helped Mary from the makeshift seat, gently lowering her to the ground. Francis and Teresa Ann alight unaided and take her hand to steady her. Once everybody is on solid ground, Renee ushers the travellers into the Plainsman, offering each of the group refreshment and beckoning them to sit at the biggest table.

Gladstone brought enough full glasses of beer for all, even the younger members of the party were allowed to partake of the thirst quenching drink. The children and their mother had endured a long and arduous journey.

"Good to see you back Henry, glad you made it." Gladstone gave a friendly nod to each the rest of the family group.

"Thank you Gladstone, so am I. It's good to be here!" Although Henry didn't formally introduce the barman to his family, each one acknowledged him. Renee excused herself from the table. She had to make the sleeping arrangements for each of these newcomers. There is little time for organising, knowing correctly the travellers would be weary and ready to sleep.

"Don't you keep Guinness, lad?" Mary asked of her beaming son, while looking around the inside of the Plainsman Hotel.

"Not yet mother, but I'll see what I can do." Henry liked the black Irish Stout himself and made a mental note to seek a supply.

Renee, with Lourinda's and Maria's help, is doing her utmost to make adequate sleeping arrangements for the newcomers, only succeeding in doing so by annexing part of the back room that she and Joey had shared in Jack's time almost a year ago.

Now that the undertaker had moved to his own premises in another part of town, there would be enough space for all at the Plainsman. Mary and Patricia would sleep in one room, David would again share with Henry and Lourinda would share with Teresa Ann in the small room that David had recently shared with Lourinda. Francis and Joey would have the back room to themselves, Cooking Fat had made his own decision, he had already moved in with Kai-Saw at the Marshal's office with the recent appearance of the little Oriental. The feline had easily settled in. The little Marshal now shares his bunk with the cat. Later, Soul Broadbent would need to return to the bunkhouse at the ranch.

Once her task was complete, Renee informed each person where he or she would be sleeping. Questioning eyes were directed at David, to see his reaction regarding Renee's statement. Ever since he and Lourinda had been 'married' by the bogus Jefferson the night of the Tornado, the two had spent their nights together. David didn't flinch on learning the arrangements. Henry winked at the Welshman, there was no discernible reaction to the gentle unspoken taunting by the Cornishman. Henry also realised that Renee hadn't made provision for anyone to share her room, it seemed to him that Renee might have been deliberate in her omission. He watched her from out of the corner of his eye, wondering if this night he and Renee would again share something other than the Plainsman. Henry knew something had changed between them, and his return from Cornwall had brought the change to the surface, still unsaid, but the thoughts are there, nonetheless.

"Tomorrow we'll try and organise things a little differently." It had been Renee's intention to do as she was stating. She was teasing the affable Welshman.

Renee's words remind Mary that she hadn't yet seen Patricia. As she was about to enquire, the girl who had been at Jasper's hardware store at the time of her family's arrival, walked through the entrance door. Patricia's face is the perfect picture of astonishment and not a little bewilderment at the scene that met her eyes. She had never dared hope that Henry would bring the remainder of her family back with him. With tears starting down her cheeks she went to the table and gave each newly arrived member of her family a welcoming embrace. Henry is the last to receive the treatment from his sister.

"Thank you brother, I never would have believed you would get mother to come here, even if you had told me it was your intention. We're all here now, it's as it should be. Father would have wanted it this way." Henry stayed silent, but felt not a little pride in himself for completing the task he had set before he left.

After her long trip, the reunion would take it out of Mary. She tired easily not being used to such long journeys such as that which she had recently undergone. Noticing, Renee took her hand and led her to the room she would be sharing with her two daughters. Thinking that Francis might be feeling awkward, Joey sauntered across and steered him away from the table. It isn't yet late and Joey thought it a good idea to show Francis the town's sights as the boy is far too excited to sleep.

David decides it is time to bring Henry up to date with the happenings since his departure and while he was absent. The Cornishman and Soul took the news of the two ranch hands deaths with sadness. Henry and David have built an enduring friendship since they first met in the stinking rail carriage, neither could explain it but they are as close as family now and each fears for the other in times of trouble.

David went on to tell of Joey's exploits with the rifle. He pointed out the war axe and told how the Kiowa had sunk it deep into George Benford's shoulder. Henry and David had listened with almost fatherly respect to the retelling of the shooting; not that he didn't regret the killing of the native but pride was with the boy for not turning tail to run away as most children might have under the same circumstances. Henry had never shirked a fight, as Connell would remember for the rest of his squalid and disfigured life. He tried to picture the scene that Joey had endured. David brought up the subject of Fe Tylden's visit, he informed Henry of all the details of Ross's offer and told him of Fe's predicament. Henry had thought for a moment or two about the proposition. He thought of Fe as a good friend and at this moment, as a friend in need, he knew the stage lines gave an alternative to saddle sores. "Well Davy, what do you and Renee have to say about it?"

"We are agreed, just wanted you to have your say before we made Fe any promises, H."

"Then methinks there is nothing else to do than get the money from Jasper's bank! Let's wish Fe luck, it'll be good to have him here in town. He is a straight guy, we all of us know that."

"It will boyyo and yes, they don't come much straighter than Tylden!"

The lights at the Plainsman did go out early the night of Henry and Soul's return. David had by this time relieved Gladstone at the bar so that he might have some time off. Henry had taken the opportunity to enter an account of the day's happenings that would fill another page in his ever thickening journal. He looked at the scrap of paper and made a note of the date before placing it back inside the tobacco pouch.

Gladstone decided a visit to the Golden Horseshoe would be in order. Since being given the extra responsibility at the Plainsman, none of the partners had seen him the worse for wear. He decided it is time to have some relaxation. The affable barman hadn't purposefully got quickly intoxicated. Gladstone didn't even know that alcohol was absorbed into his bloodstream, he had never considered it. Gladstone could never have comprehended the biological process.

With no late customers that night, David and Lourinda doused the lamps, leaving just the one Henry is employing to scribble the memories of how he had brought the remining members of his family back together. With David's departure, Henry dropped the pencil and allowed his thoughts to drift to Renee. He emptied his glass and with the oil lamp still burning, strolled to the stairway. On tiptoe, he went up and without hesitation he approached the door, which he knew he would pass through. Although words had not been spoken by either, he is certain Renee is waiting for him inside. He pushed open the door halfway and knew his instincts were incorrect. A solitary candle flame burned at the side of the bed. Renee is sleeping soundly. It had been a long day. Henry returned downstairs to his diary. Once completed, he stayed in the chair and thought through everything that had happened since he left Cornwall the first time. He had known the transition wouldn't be easy and at times it had been particularly tough but now he thought of nothing other than the love between them that had built almost as quickly as the town itself. It is after one as the Cornishman poured himself another glass of beer and lit a cigar, content in the knowledge he and Renee would surely become husband and wife in the nearest future and that he would join her in the bedroom when he is finished with the diary, which is now full. Another waits to be started in a draw.

While journeying to England and back, Henry had much time to consider the possibilities of some kind of future with Renee. Many plans had passed through his head whilst attempting to sleep on the ship. Now is the time to put them all into action he vowed to himself. Henry is satisfied now he has every member of his family all in the place. His thoughts return to Renee who he hopes thinks the same way. Henry is impatient to tell everyone of his plan.

Gladstone had paid the house Madam for a full night with Maria. Since being in employment, he had hidden away most of the wages earned at the Plainsman. He has quite a sum now. This was the very opportunity for him to pursue and realise a dream, one that meant he could spend a night with Maria. He could afford the five dollars, it is little enough he thought. He had more than fifty dollars in his inside pocket. With two glasses and a bottle of expensive French wine, he followed the girl upstairs to her room. It is late, very late, more than two o'clock when the girl discards most of her clothes for her impatient customer and her friend. She drank with him. They had both drank at the table. Normally Maria would drink very little while on duty. As Gladstone was a friend and she'd seen very little of him since leaving the Plainsman, the girl had made an exception, Maria did like the barman. She perched on the bed dressed in only her scant underwear. Through the flickering glow of light, Gladstone could see the outlining curves of Maria's body, the lantern that sat on the occasional table at the foot of the bed accentuated her shape. Gladstone could feel his need rising for the girl, he'd felt it before, though as far as he knew, Maria had certainly been unaware. He satisfied himself within her. She too had unusually enjoyed the experience. Maria normally only gave pleasure in return for money, she didn't have to enjoy her work, just the wages.

Gladstone discarded the lambskin condom, he wanted more of the French wine. He pulled his clothes on and went downstairs where the Golden Horseshoe's barman is washing down his bar. He looked up at the sound of Gladstone's bare feet on the board floor.

"Could do with another bottle, Frederick!"

"Sorry Gladstone, no can do, we shut early, quiet night. I'm to my bed, you know how it is my friend!"

Gladstone swore quietly to only himself, but he understood Frederick's reluctance. He still needed more wine, Maria needed more wine. He stumbled back upstairs to Maria's room. "I'll get us some wine from the Plainsman, don't you go to sleep now Maria, I'll be back before you know it." Gladstone stepped gingerly down the stairs at the side of the building. He walked the length of the street. The door to the Plainsman is unlocked; he steps inside quietly, on high toes he moves almost silently towards the bar where he feels a nail head dig into his toe, he stops to rub the injured part.

With the pencil still in his hand, Henry is sitting in the semi-dark. He had completed the sums that meant the partners of the Plainsman could help Fe Tylden buy a share in the stage line owned by Ross. He had also brought the diary fully up to date. He and David will keep their promise to see what could be done to help. Renee had easily agreed to the proposal, providing all three partners were happy. Hearing someone outside, Henry dropped the pencil and looked across to the door, waiting for it to open. "Gladstone, you've been drinking!" Henry's voice came across the room in a whisper from the slightly darkened corner table. He slid the diary away in the draw next to the new one.

"Henry, I er ...."

"It's alright my friend, what is it you want?"

Gladstone, somewhat rightfully now, felt guilty whilst creeping deftly, apart from the nail, around the Plainsman.

He was about to take a bottle of wine for him and his night lady. "I need a bottle Henry, I have paid for a night with Maria but the Horseshoe has closed its bar."

"Take one Gladstone, on me, go ahead." After the arrival in Hickok of all his family and his recent exertions, Henry is wholly content with his lot. He is perhaps for the first time in his life, certain of his future. A still smoking cigar nestled between his fingers, a beer glass stood within reach. The half-empty bottle stands close by, the pencil safely in the draw with the full diary and the new one waiting to be started, possibly tomorrow. Henry had been about to take to the already warm bed he expected to share with Renee. At the completion of the conversation between the two men, Henry picked up the half-full glass. "Cheers my friend, get on with you, don't you know you shouldn't keep a lady waiting!"

Gladstone did as he was told. Walking behind the bar he picked up the required bottle. "Thank you Mister Tamryn, can I go?"

"You go Gladstone, you have yourself a good night, see you tomorrow. Tell Maria I said hello!"

"Why sure Mister Tamryn, goodnight." Gladstone opened the door to leave and is stopped by a question.

"Say, Gladstone!"

"Sir?"

"I'm puzzled, why did you call me Mister, you never did before that, I'd remember."

"I don't know, it's just that you and David and Renee, Joey, all of you have treated me so good. I don't deserve it. I was about to steal the bottle you know!" Gladstone hung his head slightly as he confessed to the uncommitted crime.

"I don't think so my friend, you're not a thief, you would have paid for it tomorrow."

"Reckon maybe you're right at that Henry, goodnight."

"Goodnight Gladstone, sweet dreams."

Henry re-lit the cigar that with inaction on the smoker's part, had extinguished itself. He thought about Joey's bravery against the young Kiowa warrior. He could not know that his own bravery would soon be put to the test in a somewhat different way. He would have to delve into his own conscience and act upon the result. He picked up the pencil again and opened the new diary to record the exchange between him and Gladstone and his nocturnal quest. Henry stopped and took out the empty tobacco pouch and altered the date on the scrap of paper before tearing it out and placing it in the pouch.

Maria did fall asleep, not for any other reason than the lateness and the deeply red alcohol that had taken its effect. She turned, rolled and turned back again, something slipped from the bed, it clattered. The glass from the empty bottle and that from the lamp smashed together. Maria didn't hear, feel nor smell anything. She didn't even remember Gladstone's leaving. The joyous barman skipped back towards the Golden Horseshoe. He was thinking of the genial Cornishman, the man who had known he was about to steal a bottle of wine.

Gladstone walked on to the end of the main street and turned down the short side street towards the outside stairway, he stepped up. Suddenly it hit him, something isn't right. Smoke is coming through the gaps between the doorframe. On reaching the top step, Gladstone sobered instantly as he touched the door handle.

"Maria! Maria!" Gladstone squawked frantically at the door, afraid to open it. He could smell the wood varnish smouldering on the inside. Again the barman tries the door, more burning. Gladstone almost throws himself down the stairway. Hitting the ground he runs back towards the Plainsman shouting again and again, only this time he is calling Henry's name!

Henry hears the yelling, he knows who it is that is shouting his name aloud. He stands up, dropping the pencil back onto the still unused page, he let the now cold cigar butt fall into the brass spittoon that stands close to the desk. The door crashes open, a hinge gives way and it drops crookedly. Gladstone tries to get his words in order. "Henry, the

Horseshoe, she's burning, Maria she is in there, in her room, you have to help her, oh god she'll die, please, please Henry, help me!"

Henry barged the chair away and looked at the already despondent Gladstone. "Come on man, let's go."

As Henry follows the panicking Gladstone, vivid Crawler lightning floods across the heavenly dome, spreading like an incoming ocean tide it slides across the high Cumulonimbus clouds that cover the angry, purple Kansas sky, almost turning night into day for just milliseconds. Henry could hear Gladstone's whimpering plea. "Hurry Henry, please hurry."

Henry chases after the distraught barman, he can see the glowing Horseshoe now. At the nearest sidewall the flames are licking skyward, mingling with the lightning. Henry is sweating already, he fleetingly remembers the one time before he had experienced and felt the airborne heat, the night of the Tornado! He quickly dismisses the memories and chases after Gladstone.

Joey wakes, sweat streaming from every pore. He looks around at Francis, he can see the other boy is also awake. Nervously, Francis asks what is happening.

"Why is it so hot Joey, what's happening outside? I'm scared."

Joey thinks for a few seconds, he listens. In the distance he can hear the distant low growl he had heard only once before. A peel of overhead thunder brings instant recognition. "Tornado! We have to get to the schoolhouse, get dressed boy, hurry now."

The two youngsters pull on trousers, not bothering with shirts as it is too hot anyway. Joey leads Francis through the deserted saloon. He glances quickly at the broken door and steps through it. Francis runs hard to keep up with the older boy, they tear across the still dry, wide main street, the sight of the lightning somehow speeding them on. Neither boy notices the flaming building at the far end of the parched road, nor the small stream of people that are coming from the direction of the Horseshoe. The two youths reach the porch of the schoolhouse. The door is locked! Now that the threat of Indian attack had subsided, the building had been left locked again regularly.

"We'll have to smash the door Francis, we'll run at it together, okay."

Francis nods "I'm ready when you are Joey, let's do it!"

Two small bodies crash against the wood, nothing gives; they step back, again they throw their light, youthful bodies at the unforgiving door a second time, stepping back once more they try for a third time. This time the door gives way under the shouldered onslaught. Both boys step over the splintered wood.

"What now, Joey?"

"We have to ring the bell, it's the Tornado warning!"

"What's a Tornado, Joey?"

"Never mind, follow me."

Joey leads Francis to the far side of the room where the unmoving pull-rope hangs limply, he catches hold and motions Francis to do the same. They tug and the rope stretches down and then rises, nothing; they pull again, down, up, the bell clangs its warning. Lightning streaks through the schoolroom. Joey and Francis stick to their task pulling with all their might, ignoring any danger of a lightning strike on the bell tower.

Some townsfolk are attempting to put out flames with water fetched from the roadside creek. It soon becomes apparent they are wasting their time as new spurts of flame appear, they cannot keep up. They retreat and join the others in the so far undamaged schoolhouse.

Henry stares at the flames. His mind going back to the long house where he thought to set it afire, meant to consume the family home, at the last he had changed his mind. He felt retribution is being thrown at him for the having the thought. Henry is afraid! He knows Gladstone could never go inside the now flaming hulk. Gladstone, like Henry, isn't brave enough to risk his life but Henry knows he has no other choice, there's no one else. He looks up the side stairs to the already enflamed door, where Gladstone had first felt the heat. There is no chance of going through. Henry makes up his mind and retraces his steps down to the front of the building, striding towards the double saloon doors. He hesitates, looks back at the fear panicked face of his trusting barman, then turns, kicking the swing doors aside, Henry disappears into the glowing wreck. Gladstone is shouting, not to anyone in particular, there is no one else outside the Golden Horseshoe now. He can hear the school bell clanging its message of sanctuary and he has no idea why the bell is challenging his own shouts.

The heat of the night is soon draining the boys of their energy. Sweat seeps from them both. The bell has awakened David who races across the broad street and glances up at the boiling sky, immediately knowing the reason for the tolling. He went inside. Seeing the dilemma, David immediately takes hold of the rope. "You boys stand down now!" Joey and Francis are already moving away before David had finished his order. The Welshman begins to pull hard at the rope as more people enter the schoolhouse. Jasper will help David now, after settling Mrs Hawke at a desk. Jakey waits to take a turn at the rope when one of the men tire. The schoolhouse becomes an oven. As each group enter, the remains of the door would be propped up again against the jamb, in case the dancing, growling monster might suddenly enter.

Henry has seen the sky, he realises he had been right, a Tornado must be approaching as he hears the tolling call. He crosses the hot smouldering boards and looks up the stairway as flames and smoke appear alternately and the sounds of fire strengthen. Henry thinks an open window and the strength of the gusting wind must be the culprit. At the top of the stairway, he looks left, that side of the building seems to be untouched so far. Only the intermittent Crawler lightning lights the corridor now. Henry tries each door, he yells inside to any possible occupants. "Get out, fire! fire!" He sees the doors ajar and is sure most rooms are already empty. On reaching the end room, the Cornishman retraces his steps until reaching the top of the stairs again. He looks forward. Flames form a fiery wall to the opposite corridor. Henry breathes deeply, for a second, he thought his lungs would burst; he breathes again, stepping through the wall of fire, his foot catches something on the floor, he looks down, Frederick! Henry decides the barman must have tried to get to the bedroom where Maria must be sleeping. He pulls the man away from the flames. Only one door is closed in this corridor. Henry inches towards the wooden shield, leaving Frederick where he lay, seemingly unconscious. He stabs a foot out at the offending door, it collapses instantly under the kick. Henry's feet crunch the wood. The room is burning on three sides, he can see the unconscious girl lying on the floor. Scooping her up he returns towards the wall of flame. Breathing heavily with the extra load he steps across the still unmoving Frederick. The bedroom at his left is completely caught alight now. Henry's shirt is sticking to his back in the intense heat, his breathing becomes laboured. Maria isn't heavy but the lack of air inside the building makes the sweating man struggle. He turns at the top of the stairs. Flames have found their way through the upstairs floor, the tops of the walls in the saloon area glow yellow and orange with rage, red now. Henry stumbling, not being able to see where he is going, is almost forced to drop the now groaning form.

Gladstone has conjured up courage of his own to take himself inside. He looks at the rescuer, lifting the girl from Henry's arms, he turns to carry her away.

"Frederick's in here Gladstone, I've got to get him, find David! Find Davy." Henry is oblivious now to the imminent storm's threat, sounds of the increasing wind and fire have mingled into one with the noise of the burning wood. It seems to the Cornishman the bell is sounding slower now, the way it had at Tungsaw's funeral. He turns again towards the bottom of the angry, flaming stairway.

Gladstone looks up at the stairs, the rails at each side have ignited, paint bubbles and bursts into flame.

"No, don't try again! You can't go back inside there Henry, please don't, it's too dangerous now."

"I have to, Frederick might still be alive." Henry steps up, taking care not to touch the glowing side rails. The flaming wall has grown, flames lick at the ceiling. The Cornishman mouths a prayer and steps forward.

Sitting together, the two boys, now resting, hear the ripping timber as the tiny tower above them is torn from its supports. Conversation is at a premium. The congregation wait in fear-filled silence. Renee attends the frightened Mary. Lourinda, Joey and Francis sit expectantly with the calm Kai-saw, the lawman cradling and gently smoothing Cooking Fat, who had just strolled inside as if nothing out of the ordinary is happening. Lourinda and Teresa Ann watch in awe as David pulls the rope for the last time as he gives in to Jasper at the bell rope. Sweat has slicked the Welshman's shirt to his body. Mrs Hawke helps a young mother with her screaming child. Patricia sits alone at a desk, her head sunken while quietly she prays, wondering where her brother can be. Once again the schoolhouse comes under bombardment from flying debris. It seems to the occupants that the roof is heaving, trying to wrench itself loose. The twisting monster has entered the broad main street tearing at everything, the horse trough rises and spins crazily, David's sign is sucked into the bubbling atmosphere. The Plainsman's roof lifts, drops and lifts again, turning a little before settling back. Tungsaw's marker flies skyward in the graveyard, now it lies in the street. Eardrums reach bursting point in the schoolhouse.

Gladstone carries Maria away from the doomed building, defying the maelstrom. He reaches the schoolhouse, careful not to allow the girl's head to hit the splintered doorframe as he enters. All eyes are on the last Hickokians to seek sanctuary this night.

Henry can smell his own singeing hair now. He turns Frederick, grips an arm as he bends his knees and lifts the big man to his right shoulder. Slowly he straightens, pain searing like the lightning through his arm into his chest and into his brain. Henry saves his last thought for the woman he loves. The Cornishman slumps, his weakened lungs uselessly trying to refill themselves, he cries out "Renee!"

Gladstone catches his breath. He lowers his burden onto a bench. "Davy! It's Henry, he needs you, the Horseshoe, it's burning. Maria, she was in there, Henry got her out. I tried to stop him, he went back inside again, Frederick was in there, he said he wouldn't leave him. He went back in Davy, I don't think he can get out."

The Welshman roars animal-like, kicking aside the remnants of the schoolhouse door, he disappears outside. Turning, he looks towards the far end of the wide, rubble-strewn main street. The Twister sends biting grit into the Welshman's eyes as he strides purposefully forward. An eyewitness might have sworn that the already huge body is expanding, drawing large lungful's of breath before moving forward into the screaming, spinning, living creature that seems intent on devouring the building, not unlike Ahab's Whale swallowing a whale-boat. With just one thought on his mind, David defies the blast and strides forward, he can see the Horseshoe's glow. It seems nothing would stop him from reaching his goal. In seconds he is at the door, there is no break in his stride. Shouting as he searches the disintegrating building, David looks up at the burning stairway and steps forward. A second more tentative step shows the Welshman it might be too late. The stairway begins to stretch apart before him, he backs away slowly, deliberately, before racing forward. The stairway sways now as he climbs doggedly forward. David discovers Frederick's already smouldering body. He sees Henry collapsed close-by and lifts like he never lifted before.

Tripping backwards onto the road with his load, he catches his balance and kneels and stares at the now completely engulfed hotel. oblivious to the raging storm above and around him, The Welshman remains motionless, he watches, staring, until the Golden Horseshoe becomes a mass of glowing ash. Doc Ryder is already massaging Henry's chest.

At the storm's subsidence, Kai-saw, had been first to leave the schoolhouse. The still glowing pyre lights the way for him as he stumbles forwards. He approaches the kneeling man and steps away so not to get in Ryder's way. Kai-saw stepped up to the broken, crooked porch, a wooden bench untouched and undamaged allows the Marshal to keep vigil over the already grieving Welshman. David is aware he was too late to save his friend.

In the Plainsman, Renee, Lourinda and Patricia nurse and comfort Maria. She is unhurt, though groggy, her eyes burn as she coughs the last of the smoke from her lungs. Once she regains full consciousness, she wants to know what had happened, she had little recollection of the recent happenings. She knows nothing of the tornado and nothing of the rescue! She, like all the other occupants of the schoolhouse at that time, knows nothing of her rescuer!

Doc Ryder and Soul Broadbent carry Henry into Doc Ryder's house. After carrying out the given orders the two men sit and wait as Ryder continues his work even when he is sure it is already too late. He looks at Renee and in the now silent Plainsman, she knows, they all know!

CHAPTER NINETEEN
Giving Thanks

As dawn arrived, the tornado's natural violence had passed almost as suddenly as it had arrived. David Evans had knelt sentinel-like in the street throughout the longest night of Hickok's short life. Kai-saw and Gladstone sat silently watching from their unbroken bench on the sidewalk. Soul Broadbent leaned against the wall behind them, he says nothing as he rolls another cigarette and lights it from a still burning night torch. The two men on the bench speak in whispers. There is no need, David is oblivious to every word, he doesn't hear a thing. The three had waited patiently as the Welshman had continued his vigil into the silvery light. The Marshal and the barman talked in quiet tones to each other now. Kai-saw tells Gladstone he should not blame himself for the death of Henry or Frederick. Soul has nothing to say.

"It has been a terrible accident, nothing else, my friend."

The bartender believes Henry and Frederick would still be alive if it wasn't for his wanting more wine. The barman could have already left for home before the fire had even caught. He or Maria would have blown out the solitary candle if he had not left her alone to get more wine, the barman unknowingly spoke aloud.

"You can't know that." Tungsaw said, trying to ease his friend's guilty feelings and very much failing to do so.

"Poor Henry, poor Frederick, he was just a bartender like me!"

"A fine man and a damn fine bartender too! Gladstone you have to move on, my friend. We must all move on, it is what Henry would have wanted."

"Easy for you to say, Kai."

"I did not say it is an easy thing, it is the right thing, Mister Gladstone, the right thing!"

A fledgling town, Hickok has been in existence for just a year in its present form. As long as it survives it is difficult to think it could endure a worse night. Henry Tamryn had done his utmost to bring the man out of the Golden Horseshoe and had lost his life in attempting to do so. The big man could not have known Frederick had already expired when he lifted him to carry him outside. The scenario could not have been worse, two good people, two sad deaths. Maria may never comprehend what Henry had attempted to do.

The town's remaining buildings suffered to varying degrees, most of the damage is superficial apart from roofs. The roof of the Plainsman might need to be restructured. Under normal circumstances, David would just say 'Don't worry, we'll do that first job.' The Welshman had been aware that he isn't alone in the street but had spoken not a word to either of the two sitting on the bench or Soul Broadbent, nor anyone else who wandered quietly past. All three had watched until the Golden Horseshoe disintegrated too barely nothing.

The mounds of ash started to turn to dust as the early sun rose. David Evans stood up and walked forward into the smokey remains, he wanders through the building's crumbs as if in a useless search for anyone else who might have been inside. The Golden Horseshoe is no more. David crouches and with his huge hands scoops up an amount of the still warm powder and takes it to the undertakers where he orders some be placed in two full sized coffins for the two men who had been in the wrong place at the wrong time. Outside, Soul is still silent, he has nothing worth saying as he rolls another cigarette. Soul and Henry had become friends late in the day but the ranch hand feels no less sad than any other.

David will surely regret he had arrived too late to be of any real use apart from pulling the bell rope. Although the two boys had worked hard, it needed someone like David to continue. Like Henry, David didn't know Frederick well, he did know he was a pleasant man and popular with everyone so he had heard, unusually so for a bartender. The two had passed away in the Golden Horseshoe. The lack of breathable air and Frederick's weight had proved too much of a strain for Henry. Hickok will be in mourning for arguably its most popular citizen. There could easily have been more fatalities, but so far as anyone knows, it is only the two.

David felt he had been the fortunate one the day he met Henry on the smelly train. Neither man knew the other previously, everything happened so quickly from the day of their arrival in a town with, at the time, no permanent name. Henry and David had been instrumental in the expansion of the former canvas village. Henry's bravery had more than once been put to the test but never in such a way as this. Henry had walked through the swing doors to look into the face of death. When he shot Jack, he had no time to think. David too had shown bravery or even stupidity with his devotion to duty.

Since their arrival, each man had shown a strength of character that would endear them to their fellow citizens. Now those friends and business associates gradually appear and gather in the street to mourn Henry Tamryn. Jasper Hawke stands close to Ford County Sheriff Jack Bridges, who had been summoned to attempt to find out what had caused the ferocious fire. He quickly announced his task was useless. There is just not enough left of the building to tell a tale and of course, however it began, it was still just a fire and fires in Kansas mostly burn until nothing is left. 'One of those things' he had said uselessly shrugging his shoulders. Bridges and Henry had met briefly and the two had instantly gained a mutual respect for each other.

The day seemed to drift along in slow motion. In the same way the village came to life, slowly and surely the villagers just got on with whatever needed to be done to get their own lives back to normal, whatever it may be. They will all come together and begin the task of resurrection as Henry would surely have wanted. Today they have all come to the cemetery to pay their respects and shed their tears.

The open graves lay adjacent to that of two other friends of Frederick, two ranch hands who had been murdered by an Indian war party. Renee and David had agreed that this would be the most suitable resting place for their friend. David stands with an arm around the weary and red eyed Renee and the other around the slowly blossoming Lourinda. Jakey, Jasper, George and Joey stand close by, George, Joey, Francis and Teresa Anne stand a little apart. Maria is just a little way behind these three. Maria, being a prostitute, knows her place isn't to be in the limelight and brings up the rear. Soul Broadbent stands directly behind the red-headed Patricia, a calloused palm rests lightly on her shoulder. Behind the group stand every member of the village's population.

The visiting minister, having completed his part in the graveside service, had turned to Jasper Hawke. With a swish of his hand he invites Hickok's Mayor to speak for the gathered citizens. Jasper first looks around the whole group which consists of almost every other member of Hickok's population. Mary and Henry's siblings are here of course, every one of the family is sobbing at their loss. Jakey, the town's one Blacksmith, had dug the fresh graves. Gladstone and Kai-saw stand a little closer to the open graves. Hats are being crushed by hard, calloused hands. The mourners form a huge circle. A tear on every face except for one, David doesn't have the energy to cry. George Benford is scribbling, not just about Henry and Frederick but also about the people of the town who have faced adversity and survived against terrible odds.

Mary and Patricia have arms around the youngsters now. Mary wonders why she had agreed with her son to bring them to this place of sadness and remembers she had suffered other tragedies back in Innis Town.

Hawke continued. "Everyone here knew the Cornishman, what Henry Tamryn meant to this town, what he meant to all of us who lived here and shared it with him. Henry had shown his strength and his courage in many ways since his arrival here just a year ago! He showed it when he put an end to Jack, and when he fearlessly rescued Maria and when he tried to save Frederick, a virtual stranger to him!" Jasper waited for some moments before going on with his vocal report. His words are strong, although there is little need, he waits for them to sink into the gathered congregation's psyche. "Almost all of us here have been helped in one way or another by Henry, most us here have been victims of his wicked sense of humour, some of us have sat at the poker table with him and left the worse off, I might add. I can personally vouch for that. Some of us have fought with him and most of us have laughed with him!" Jasper Hawke stops, he looks at David. The two men exchange wan but knowing smiles. Hawke continues. "It was a poker game which had prevented Henry and David leaving us prematurely. Their acquisition of the Plainsman has kept these two friends in Hickok."

Still scribbling frantically on his tablet, George Benford was the first to hear the slowly approaching horses. He turned towards the echoing sound and stopped his scribbling, looking at the hangdog faces of the two riders, instantly recognising Wild Bill Hickok and Fe Tylden. The two riders halt and dismount to stand just inside the entrance to the graveyard, neither speak as they climb down from their heavily lathered mounts. Hickok's locks fall loosely onto his buckskin clad shoulders as he sweeps off the low crowned, wide-brimmed hat. Tylden had ridden through the dawn to fetch Hickok once he had received the awful news. Hickok had donned the twin pistols and is ready but changes his mind until Jasper has finished his tribute. Hickok looked across at the huddle of the Tamryn family and nods as he takes off the hat.

Everyone present listens intently to Jasper as he continues on, no one attempts to interrupt the vocal flow of the mayor. When it does become apparent the eulogy is complete, Mary and her children step forward to bend down and each pick a handful of the dark, Kansas earth. As they throw the grains onto both coffins, the silence is suddenly and willfully broken with a fusillade of a dozen gunshots. Hickok fires until both his Navy Colts are empty, returning the pistols to their holsters, he spoke aloud.

"If the Mayor will allow, I have something I would like to say!" Wild Bill looked across at Jasper. Seeing the short affirmative nod and taking this as permission, he continues. "I believe that there is one important thing to do here, Mister Mayor, it is time to name the main street of this town. I believe you good people should name it for Henry Tamryn. Seems to me Tamryn Street has a perfect ring to it!"

A murmur of agreement emits from all the occupants of the graveyard and it seems to have the effect of lifting the spirits of the congregation. A lot of hard work will still be needed to complete the repairs to the damage caused to the town by the freak wind and the hail, every man will have to do his bit to make it happen.

Jasper Hawke waits a moment for quiet. "It would seem that we have a new and fitting name for our street. I don't believe there is a reason to take a vote! Tamryn, Tamryn Street. Long may she live and long may the tornados keep their evil away from it."

Renee crosses her arms and hands over her lower abdomen, she already knows there is something more that will carry the name of Tamryn forward and into the town's future even though they were never married she thinks of herself and Joey as such. Unconsciously she is already protecting the Cornishman's last offering to the continued future of the town he has helped to nurture since the demise of Jack the Rat. She allows her eyes to stray across the small patch of ground, they rest on the face of the Welshman who had one day walked into the unnamed village alongside the jovial, roguish Cornishman; one a stranger to the other though she was unaware at the time, but very quickly both becoming a friend to everyone who lived in Hickok and those who will now walk up or down and chatter on 'Tamryn Street.'

"What's done is done, goodbye Henry." It is all Renee can muster.

They had all nodded their agreement to Wild Bill's suggestion. The man Tamryn had become a huge part of Hickok's folklore already, the little town named Hickok has turned its back on the day it almost disappeared and has arrived with renewed strength to call on its unknown future!

"Come now Joey, you and I have a lot of work to do, we must get the paper out, it won't print itself." George Benford looks at the tear-stained face of the youngster and smiles softly as he speaks. "Wipe your face, boy." George dabbed at his own eyes as he spoke.

"You're bleddy right George, there's plenty to be done." Joey summoned strength of his own to accompany George to the press. He and Francis and David had done their bit when sounding the alarm and maybe saving more lives " Can I write the editorial, George?"

"It's your right boy, there will be no argument from me. I will put what I have written in the ground with Henry."

Joey took up his pencil and began to add to his own notes. Not far away inside the Plainsman, Henry's diary still rests on the table.

"People like you, young Joey, will see this town grow. One day this will all be yours my lad. You might be taking a youngster under your wing in this very spot in years to come." George Benford chattered on while Joey tried to concentrate on his given task.

★★★★

They stand idly and quietly. In front of them lie two graves so close together they are almost touching. The partial remains of a wooden cross states the single burned on initial 'H' followed by a date: 1876. A score or more of other little mounds are dotted around the cemetery. The small group step closer. Maccy Tamryn stares hard, he does not yet realise the significance of what he is seeing. A slight noise makes the friends look across the small cemetery, they are unspeaking. In the distance stand a group of leather-clad bikers. They are silent.

"They couldn't have known his last name Rio, bleddy shame isn't it, I wonder who he was?"

"I've never been in here Maccy, hardly knew it was here until now. I lived my whole life a mile or two away and never even thought to look in here, darn it."

Maccy points at the distant group. "It's tidy enough, now those guys will need to continue on and keep it this way, they just won't know their names, they're all gone. I wonder why these two are so close together? It it's a pity about the H."

"Some guy who was more important, special I guess. He ain't surrounded either. Just the one other grave close to it." Maccy J pointed out.

"Funny how the 'H' is so clear, it must have been burned on. Time to go Lenny, ready Lyndsey?"

"I went before we came out, Maccy!"

"Not now, Lenny! Wait, it's bleddy obvious, it's Henry, my great grandfather! Renee didn't say. Why didn't she tell us when we came twenty years ago? Why didn't Dusty and I bleddy realise?"

"I can't wait until we read about the rest of this stuff. She must have had her reasons, Maccy."

"Me too Rio, haven't hardly read half of it. You're right but it's a shame we didn't know. It's time we were getting back, it's a couple of hours drive to the bleddy airport."

"Hey, Brit."

They hadn't noticed the Angel's approach the cemetery entrance. There is no mistaking them. "Hey Rio, Maccy,

Lenny, how're ya doing, we sure didn't expect to see you guys back here."

"Still here then, Chuck!" Maccy nods and smiles to every member of the group, there are one or two new faces he had not seen almost ten years ago on their last visit to Kansas.

"Hell yes, we never did leave. No one wanted to. There are others now, they'll get back soon. Have you changed your mind and come to run us off, Brit? You did give us the lease and we kept our promise, Brit."

"I can see that, it's all good. This will most likely be our last visit. We came to see the old cemetery and the town, most likely for the last time. I see you got the bridge finished, Chuck. Where are you guys living?"

"We all got us R.V.'s backed on to the old schoolhouse over there, we tidied up the old building as best we could. Even the old bell works good now. There are one or two little kids learning here, more actually. The guy who bought the place from Rio told us we can use the place, it being the only one of any use, most all have gone now."

"That's great."

"Yeah but the old newspaper office did more or less fall down to a while ago. You wouldn't believe it but there were still a few old papers in there, couple of books, journals I guess. Some in the old hotel too. I'll get them for ya, bro.' They ain't much, jest names and suchlike, but they're yours sure 'nough, Maccy. A little ol' baby tornado came through here a while ago and scattered some to hell and back, we picked up almost all I'd say. It didn't do much damage apart from the office, there's hardly anything left to break now. Even the old gas station is no more, shut down. Reckon we found most of your papers anyways."

"The Bridge of Tears is still standing Chuck, that's good."

"It sure is and your coins are cemented in and will be forever, Maccy. Yep, the Bridge of Tears still stands Brit and long may she!"

"Amen to that Yanks, good work, thank you guys and by the way, we might be back, it would be wrong not to return now, though it might be the turn of our kids next time."

"That'd be great, Brit. Here Rio, y'all best take these, keep 'em safe now."

Rio flips through the small bundle. "Maccy, you should see these books, they are all handwritten, honey!"

"When we get back my luvver, when we get home. Adios Yanks and thank you!"

"Naw, thank you Brit, everyone! Vaya Con Dios, compadres!"

"Maccy, shall I hit him this time?"

"Naw Lenny, not this time. Adios Yanks."

★★★★

"Read it to me, Maccy, all of it."

"Get on with it, dad!"

"How old are you, MJ?"

"Old enough."

"Best you keep an eye on yourself in case you bleddy idn't."

"So, my great grandfather Henry, might never have had a proper restaurant, going by this, I think we have a tad more to show for it at the Doom Bar. It's just my own opinion, ma."

"Just bleddy read dammit!"

"I'm trying, maid."

"You got that right husband, tryin' my damn patience mister!"

"I'm not good at reading!"

"You ain't good at much!"

"That's what I keep telling him, 'ma."

"Shut it Michael, don't you have some praying to be doing, mister bleddy vicar?"

"Maybe I do but you're way past saving Tamryn and it's Minister, mister!"

"Mister Minister, why don't you go fourth and ....."

"I tried that but my maths wadn't up to much."

"Shut your face, reverend. Anyway, it says....."

'I emigrated to Kansas in eighteen seventy-four, I arrived as safely as the ocean allowed. Our ship, The Cleopatra set sail for Falmouth first to pick up more passengers, from there onward we came to America, New York, The United States, it took bleddy weeks.'

'I disembarked and met David Evans who told me had been travelling on the same vessel. We two did not meet straight away but drekly when we had clambered aboard a bad smelling train.'

'I decided to steal a free ride on the cattle car. I had no idea where it was going. There was not much point in my standing around and doing nothing. I found David already inside by luck. A big man, not much bigger than me, we rubbed along fine soon enough. Another Celt, a Welshman, he was already inside the carriage and we two decided to travel together for a while and see what might occur. After jumping off without paying for our rides, we didn't have to walk far before reaching a rail side village with no name.'

'Our money was short. I and the Welshman decided to try to fill our pockets by playing poker and by enormous luck we won the saloon from its owner. We won it by default when our final opponent had lost all of his stake money to me and some hours after had become very deceased. A bad loser.'

'I had to shoot the gambler who owned the saloon. He had returned angry enough to attempt to kill both me and even his own common law wife, the 'cook' Renee. I use the term loosely while writing this. The woman was at least cohabiting with him, she did not cook well.'

'I had to defend myself, my friend David and the woman and her boy. I had no choice but to shoot to death the poor card sharp who was waving a knife around at Renee in the

early hours of the morning. So we got and kept the saloon. We did share it with Renee who already owned a part of the Inn at the time. I had paid a sum of money over to the now dead saloonkeeper. He did not live long enough to make use of the gift. David and I even paid for the funeral of the skunk the following day. We paid with his own money.'

"You have a go, Lyndsey."

"I will, ma." Lyndsey Evans is in the habit these days of calling Maccy's mother 'ma,' most of us do.

Lyndsey continues:

'I and David Evans became popular in this small town now called Hickok City which was named after the famous Marshal and our good friend, Wild Bill Hickok. He sure could be wild!'

"So then he says" *'Renee was forced to be a prostitute until we arrived. Now I live with the wife of the man I had no choice but to murder.'*

'Renee had a boy child called Joey, he is twelve or thirteen I think. David became a Marshal, a policeman of this small town. A chap called George Benford, a good man, started a newspaper in the back of a wagon.'

'Joey killed an Indian warrior in town. I was away in England at the time. We met Wild Bill Hickok again. We bought a piano.'

'David has almost completed the school after a Tornado visited.'

'Joey killed a native to save George's life and his own.'

'Wild Bill killed the fake minister.'

"He killed a preacher! That's a bit bleddy strong."

"That's what it says. I could be more like him than you think! Give it a rest Michael, I'm his kin don't forget."

"But I was trying to be helpful."

"Fair enough, I'm not used to it. Carry on, Lyndsey."

'I took Soul Broadbent to Innis Town, Cornwall. He complained about the rain. When he isn't sleeping, Soul is complaining. We brought all of my family back here to Hickok. I do not think I will ever return to Innis Town.'

'I think Renee wants us to marry. I thought her to be smart, never mind. Joey will have two parents very soon. He won't be a lone boy.'

'Renee is carrying my child, she thinks I don't know it! A son I hope for.'

'Another bleddy tornado is here right now, dammit .....'

"Where did Chuck and his bunch say they found this stuff, maid?"

"The newspaper office most of it, except for the diaries, they were in the Plainsman. There is nothing more, Henry must have stopped writing for some reason. That's all there is in this one. Shall I open the next one?"

"There's no point, it's empty."

"It's not quite empty."

"H must have been your great grandfather! What a shame, but it does make sense."

"Don't look at me, maid. If H was my great grandfather he obviously wadn't too clever. He had a bleddy pub, poor sod. So Henry is mine and Dusty's great grandfather! Who was my other one, that's what I would like to know?"

"Maybe it's best left as it is, Maccy. Padraig might tell you some day, boy."

"Is he talking again now? I thought he gave it up."

"So what does all this malarkey make you, Maccy?"

"Bleddy confused, Lenny!"

"Nothing new there brother."

"Thanks Dusty, if you have any more pearls of wisdom, please feel free to shove them where the sun don't bleddy shine."

"You want me to take them to Camelford or Delabole, brother?"

"Might as well. Another thing bro, don't forget whoever was my great grandfather was yours too. Never mind, can't be bleddy 'elped, Kid. Show me that one again Lyndsey, please."

"Turn the page over, Maccy."

She passes the diary. Maccy opens it at the first page, it is blank. He turns to the second. 'The Plainsman Hotel' on Tamryn Street is to reopen after the funeral!' That's all there is."

"Well I'll be damned!"

"What, Maccy?"

Maccy passes the partly rotten book to his brother. "There might be more, we finally agree on one thing, Maccy. I'll be bleddy damned too!"

"Only one person could have written this Lyndsey, David Evans! Another thing, Henry and Renee must have married and had the child."

"What makes you think that? She might just have taken his name."

"The Renee Dusty and I met when Dusty and I went to Kansas the first time, she was a Tamryn, she could have been the child, another Renee. She must have been, Dusty. Bleddy 'ell, mother you could be bleddy right!"

"Yes I knew Maccy, I didn't want to go with you boys. I thought she must have died years ago. I never thought she would still be with us back then. She must have been well over a hundred when you boys went."

"What are you saying, ma?" Dusty and Maccy are unusually in unison with their question.

"Not now boys, we'll talk about it another day, maybe."

"So what else does that diary say Maccy, what did David write?"

"It says"

'My good friend, Henry Tamryn, 'H' died a bleddy hero, eighteen-seventy six! Goodbye boyyo R.I.P. Cornishman.'

David Evans.

"Oh my god, David Evans, my great grandfather!"

"H, so that proves it, it's Henry's bleddy grave, Maccy."

"So brother, there's been two cowboys in our family, who would have thought it?"

"Who was the second one, Maccy?"

"I'll let you to think about it, Dusty. Another thing, you know what all this bleddy means?" Maccy looked at each puzzled face in turn. They wait in silence.

"We will all have to go back again, mob handed next time!"

"What for?" Ma and Rio ask the same question.

"You'll find out when I'm good and bleddy ready!"

EPILOGUE
History today

More than one hundred and thirty years later, two teenagers arrived in Hickok, almost on the same spot where Henry and his good friend, David had walked as twenty year-olds. They stood at the very same spot Town Mayor Jasper Hawke had stood when he made a speech about the bravery of their great grandfather. The main street had no sign to tell them they were standing on Tamryn Street. If there had been one, it might have been ripped away by a passing tornado or it might just have turned to dust, who knows?

Did Maccy and Dusty Tamryn see or even feel Henry Tamryn standing on the sidewalk taking in and accepting the honour bestowed on him for his heroic deeds in eighteen seventy five? Maybe they did, maybe they didn't. It doesn't matter, but in some way their decision to come here adds another honour to Henry Tamryn. What had made the boys decide to come all this way? Nobody can answer the question and that doesn't really matter, they did stay a short while on the beautiful green plains of Kansas. What on earth made them do it, what drove two devil may care kids to travel six or seven thousands miles to see an ancient village where most of the buildings had already fallen down or were just about to? No one can answer the question, not even them. Something drew them like a magnet that's for sure. Did Henry call them, did he draw them towards his last place on earth? I'm not suggesting anything supernatural here, I might be suggesting we all carry a smidgen of memory of our forefathers.

The teenagers were almost unfortunate to meet a wizened old lady who hefted a rifle to her shoulder and attempted to write them both off, or maybe she just meant to scare them, she did that. The old lady was so ancient she could have hardly seen what she was aiming at anyway. Again, no one will ever know her reasons for so doing. She must have been a tough lady who had led a tough life, possibly spanning a complete century.

Nothing could have been easy out in Kansas, especially if one was possibly one hundred years or more old and was shooting in the direction of two members of her modern family she didn't know existed. Renee, the ancestor, could not have known, could she? Surely not! If she had realised who they were, would she still have fired at them? Your guess is as good as mine.

Was Renee continuing to emulate Henry, her father and keep the streets of Hickok safe? I believe she was. He may not realise it but Maccy Tamryn in a way does the same in Little Petrock in this twentieth century. He may not be carrying a firearm across his shoulder but Maccy does try to keep his family, his friends and himself safe in his own way. How much of Henry is in Macdonald Tamryn? Enough I guess. Maccy and Henry may have had a similar sense of humour – they both liked to laugh, though their practical jokes may have a different grounding.

Now Maccy has his own youngsters. Will his children carry some of the genes of Henry Tamryn? Surely they do? I would be very surprised if they didn't! Time will tell for the twenty-first century Tamryns.

A footnote might be useful here: Maccy eventually went back to Kansas after his beautiful wife Jennifer, had suddenly passed away, leaving him with Maccy Junior. This time he went alone. One day he saw a young girl at the side of the stream that borders Hickok, she saw him too. They didn't speak, just a slight stare and a hint of a smile, nothing more was shared on that day. On arriving home and going about his business for the next year or so, Maccy thought about the girl again. He did return to Hickok and stayed a week or so and they finally caught up with each other. They shared food and a sleeping bag but through the night she had gone, after leaving Maccy a scrap of paper with an email address scribbled on it. Maccy went home, taking the scrap of paper with him. Home, where he would continue as before until once again he has the urge to go back. This time the two did not meet. She was there, he just did not see her. The young American girl did see the Cornishman!

An aged Kansas petrol pump attendant, a Native American, told him she would come to him. Maccy didn't understand but the girl did eventually arrive at Little Petrock and waited for the Cornishman to appear. He did of course and the rest is todays history apart from one last piece of the jigsaw. What drove these two people to do what they did. It had seemed early on the odds were stacked against such a thing happening. None of us know why these things happen but they do. It's what we call fate, do we have a choice, we might think we do but we can't be sure and never will be so. Maccy didn't even believe in fate and neither did the girl, or did she? I would bet they both do now and when the Tamryn's tell their kids one day in the future whilst sheltering from the constant Cornish rain, inside the Maltsters Arms how it all came about, those kids will marvel and allow their brains to accept the fact that although fate may play a part in their lives, it isn't always just fate, or is it?

As for walking in someone else's footsteps?

CORRECTION

According to the elders of the Benford family Hickok was originally named McCarthy by its first settler. When the erstwhile, early 'Irish' pioneer decided to leave for pastures new he took the sobriquet with him and it was forgotten. This information may or may not be true but for the benefit of thi story I will assume it is.

CHRONOLOGY

Five new novels set in North Cornwall and the USA by Martyn Benford. Martyn settled in Cornwall in 1970, both living and working in Padstow for many years and eventually marrying a local girl. Martyn currently resides in Lanivet – the geographical Centre of Cornwall!

The Mermaid and Bow by Martyn Benford. Published 2019. First in a series of stories of the Tamryns, a slightly dysfunctional, perhaps multi-functional North Cornish family.

Little Petrock by Martyn Benford Published July 2020. Second in the series featuring Maccy Tamryn, his family and his friends.

Doom Bar Days & Nights by Martyn Benford. Published 2021. Third in the series featuring Maccy Tamryn, his family, old friends and new.

Kernow to Kansas by Martyn Benford. A saga of the 'Old West' set in Kansas 1875, featuring Henry Tamryn and David Evans.

The Black Prince (working title, in preparation) Fourth in the series featuring Maccy Tamryn, his family and his friends.

All titles are available locally at 'dydh da', Padstow and Wadebridge bookshop, as well as various other retail outlets throughout Cornwall. A full list of local retailers is available by request, direct from Martyn Benford, either by telephone, email or Facebook. They can also be purchased direct from Martyn Benford. Martyn will sign and even write a personal message on request. Orders by phone or email and can be contacted on social media, see below.

Facebook Martyn Benford

Email: Pablo18812000@yahoo.com

Martyn Benford Mob: 07434803382

Alternatively, order from any major bookshops.